...Paradox" © 2018 by Cynthia C. Scott
..." © 2018 by Leslie Burton-López
...s and Oats" © 2018 by B.T. Lowry
...r" © 2018 by Alison McBain
...es Past Teatime" © 2018 by Elizabeth Chatsworth
...ce Call" and "A Winter's Day" © 2018 by Edward
...

...ion" © 2018 by Gabi Coatsworth
...2018 by P.M. Ray
...© 2018 by Abhishek Sengupta
..." © 2018 by Robert Tomaino
...egacy" © 2018 by Barbara Russell
...'s Time Travel Agency" © 2018 by M.K. Beutymhill
...unt in Time" © 2018 by P.C. Keeler
...2018 by Nikki Trionfo
...018 by Jacqueline Masumian
...© 2018 by Teresa Richards
...© 2018 by Eddie Cantrell

...949122-06-0 (Paperback)
...949122-07-7 (eBook)

...by Gerd Altmann.
...design by Alison McBain.

...erica

...2018.

WHEN TO NOW

WH
TO

A

ISBN-13: 978-1-
ISBN-13: 978-1-

Front cover image
Cover and interior

Fairfield Scribes
Fairfield, CT
United States of Am

First printing Octobe
www.fairfieldscribes

This book is dedicated to the writers
who are just starting out.

Never give up!
Your voice is worth hearing.

Contents

FOREWORD

THIS ANTHOLOGY STARTED OUT LIKE most things in the Fairfield Scribes—with someone posing the question: "Who wants to be the editor for our time travel anthology?" and everyone else putting their fingers on their noses and saying, "Not it!" Being a bit slow on the uptake, I was the last one to realize it was an actual, official Scribes' vote and was therefore nominated by the group to be the lead editor.

Well, that's how it goes in the Fairfield Scribes. We tend not to take too much seriously, most especially ourselves. The one thing that we all agree on, though, is that writing is no joke. It's hard work to produce a good story, harder work to edit it, and hardest of all to then give it to others to read. It's easy enough to write for yourself, but it can be a very difficult thing to realize that eyeballs will be scanning your lovely (or not-so-lovely) words and pronouncing judgement on them.

At one point, all of us in the Fairfield Scribes were first-time writers ourselves. We've been in the hot seat more than once. And the purpose of producing an anthology like *When to Now* is twofold—one, to give voice to new and up-and-coming writers who otherwise might not be playing in the big leagues yet. This anthology is a place to showcase a group of very talented writers who are still near the beginning of their careers, but most definitely have a lot to say.

Two, this anthology is a place to welcome writers from all different creative backgrounds, to gather together around a central theme but approach it from our many diverse perspectives. In these pages, there are science fiction and fantasy writers, surrealists and literary writers, novelists and poets, horror and humor writers, and everything in between. We wanted to have a something for every reader, and I think we accomplished that splendidly.

I want to thank you for taking the time (sorry, couldn't resist) to pick up this anthology, and I hope you enjoy reading this collection of truly amazing authors.

—Alison McBain

Ruby's Paradox

Cynthia C. Scott

"Ruby's Paradox" was the winner of the 2018 Fairfield Scribes' Feature Story Contest.

August 18, 1958

WE WERE IN CENTRAL PARK, enjoying the warm weather during a trip to New York, when I saw The Man in the White Suit. He was with a small crowd of youth enjoying a bongo performance near the Bethesda Fountain. He looked younger than he did the last time I saw him fifteen years ago, when I sent him away for good. He looked like a hipster in a black leather coat, turtleneck, and beret. He fit in with this crowd, far more so than he did when he came to me as a child on the sharecropping farm I grew up on. His hair was still parted in the same fashion he wore then and he still had that large mustache, only this time it had a goatee for a companion. Others might very well mistake him for a Beatnik—I can see him now sitting in coffee houses in the Village, sipping espressos in little cups, and listening to folk music—but I knew who and what he was.

I smiled and clutched Hector's fat, little hand. It made perfect sense that he would come here now. In recent years, there had been a huge folk revival. Our radios still played jazz and rock and roll, but the young, college-age crowd had discovered the spirituals and folk songs Mama used to sing on the weather-beaten porch of our run-down shack. This would be the perfect era for a man in search of things that were lost. He didn't appear to have any recording devices. Both hands were in his pockets. Perhaps he had more advanced technology—a device as small as a button and less conspicuous.

"I know that man," I said and pointed him out to Reginald.

The Man in the White Suit was enthralled with the music. He nodded his head to its steady, propulsive beat. But, as if someone had suddenly snapped his fingers in his face, he became distracted and looked in my direction.

I smiled and started walking toward him, leaving my husband and son behind. My heartbeat quickened as I approached. He stared at me. The crowd writhed to the syncopated beats of the bongos. A woman nearby tossed her blonde hair wildly in the air. A cheer rose up, nearly drowning my voice as I reintroduced myself.

He grimaced.

"It's me," I said, my voice cracking. "Ruby."

He wrinkled his brow and said in his familiar accent, "I'm sorry, but do I know you?"

I blinked in the harsh sunlight, then shook my head and slowly backed away. "No, I'm sorry," I said. "I thought you were someone else."

April 28, 1933

We are picking cotton in the fields when a Man in a White Suit comes up the road. Junie notices him first and hollers out to Papa. We all look up and cover our eyes with our hands. He just a dark speck through the heat waves that rise up from the dusty clay, but as he comes closer we can tell that he don't look like nobody we'd ever seen around these parts. Just something in the way he carries hisself, cool as can be under that hot, sticky sun. He stops for a second, like he's taking a breather, then puts his hands over his eyes. He sees us out in the field and waves.

Papa looks at Mama. They both got that look in their eyes like they expecting trouble but can't do nothing about it but shrug. Papa sighs heavy, then starts walking toward the man.

I start to chase after him, but Mama says, "Girl, stay put," and I stay put. I'm like a puppy, always got to be sniffing at something new. And The Man in the White Suit be something new all right.

We get strangers that come this way sometimes. Mostly union organizers what come to organize the colored field hands. They hand out flyers and tell folks to come to their nightly meetings, but don't none of them ever go. Not when Boss O'Hara got the run of things. He the one what owns the land my family lives and works on. He owns half the land in

3

the county. Boss O'Hara got everything run up tight and he'd just as soon as cut off his right pinkie than let a bunch of niggas get out of hand.

"Betcha he a union man," I say to Junie.

Junie ain't so convinced. "He ain't union." Junie only fourteen, but he acts like his britches are bigger than Papa's.

Papa and The Man in the White Suit head back to the cabin and Mama mutters something before she goes back to picking cotton. A few minutes go by and Papa and The Man in the White Suit head straight toward us.

"They comin'," I say. Mama says, "I see," though she don't look up from the cotton bolls she picks off the stalk.

When they come closer, I get a better look at The Man in the White Suit. He real young and real skinny, too. He's got a tight little hairdo with a part in the side and a thick mustache. His suit look neat, if a bit dusty, and he's got a white hat in his hand. A satchel hangs down his side with a strap that go across his chest and shoulder. He tugs on the strap as Papa introduces us. Mama straightens up and nods her head. Papa introduces Junie and me to him. He looks straight at me and smiles. I look up into his face. It's haloed by the sun. I can barely see it, but I see his smile. A big ole smile with a row a white teeth.

"Hello, Ruby," he says, and I know straightaway he ain't from around here. His voice is like a song. I give Junie a look and a quick wink. I was right all along about him being a union organizer. Junie spits a wad of saliva in the dirt and stares beady-eyed at the stranger.

Papa explained that The Man in the White Suit works for the government and is recording old spirituals and field hollers along the country backroads. Papa done told him that Mama is the best singer in the county. Bar none. She sings on the church choir and everybody what hears her sing find the spirit, they say. So The Man in the White Suit looks at Mama all soft-like and asks if he can hear her sing one of her favorites.

This whole time, Mama is still picking cotton, moving forward up the row while Papa and The Man in the White Suit follow behind her. Junie still workin' hisself and I'm following behind Papa and The Man in the White Suit, staring up at him like he a angel dropped from the sky. That's how he look like to me with the sun haloed all around him. I nearly trip over my feet staring up at him and following behind. I knock into him and he turns and holds me up by my elbow. He smiles at me real soft and says, "Are you all right, Ruby?"

My tongue gets stuck in my mouth.

Mama yells at me to get back to work. "That cotton ain't gonna get picked by itself," she says. She yells at Papa too. But to The Man in the White Suit, she says she'd surely love to sing 'cause every time's a good time for singing for Jesus. So she sings "O, Mary Don't You Weep." I know right off she was gonna pick that one 'cause she sings it all the time and it is her favorite. She starts off nice and slow, finding the right key and harmony to sing in. But when she gets rolling, her voice soars clear over the cotton fields, shakes and trembles in the stiff hot air till it seems the whole world done stopped turning just to hear her sing.

The Man in the White Suit pulls something out of his satchel, a strange-looking wand that's silver all 'round and thick as a thumb. He holds it in the air. It lights up like a junebug on one end and makes a strange humming noise, real faint-like. It seem like I be the only one what hears it 'cause everybody else is busy listening to Mama sing. When Mama finishes the song, The Man in the White Suit puts the wand back in his bag.

Mama is still singing, but now mostly to herself. She moves up the row, picking cotton. She stops only to warn us we got to get back to work or else we won't pick enough bales before the sun sets. Mama is fast and so is Papa and Junie, but I can lag behind when my mind gets going. I wave good-bye to The Man in the White Suit as he turns and starts walking back up the road. He starts whistling the song Mama sang to him. I hear his whistling and it's a nice, comforting sound, something that fills me up inside in a way I can't explain, and as it gets fainter, I feel my fingers moving faster as I pick that cotton.

Then the whistling stops. I look up to see if he's reached the road, but he ain't nowhere in sight. The Man in the White Suit has disappeared.

September 10, 1933

The Man in the White Suit comes again. We are at Sunday services. The choir is singing now, and their voices raise the roof off our tiny church. Folks are clapping and swaying back and forth on the wooden pews. Me, Junie, and Papa sit together, rocking and swaying as Mama's voice rises and soars like a eagle. I get to my feet and do a little jig, like Mrs. Wilcox do. Mrs. Wilcox is the oldest member of our congregation, with skin like paper and eyes like the sunset, and yet when she get the holy spirit in her, she a young girl again. I smile as she dances in the aisle, till my eyes catch The Man in the White Suit. He standing by the church door,

6

holding his silver wand in the air. Nobody but me notice him, even though the silver wand is flashing and humming.

I point him out to Junie and we both smile. The Man in the White Suit been up and down the county, taking the hi-ways and byways to record songs, but he always comes back to us 'cause there ain't nobody in this county who got a voice like Mama's.

When services end, me and Junie run out the church and look for him. The elders cut us with their eyes, and we remember to mind our manners. But soon as our feet touch dirt, we're yelping and running again. We notice him right off standing by a grove of oak trees across the dusty field. He's looking through his satchel. When we run up to him, he is still looking, barely noticing we right there in front of him, until a few seconds pass and he looks up and smiles his magic smile. And not a bead of sweat on his face.

"Did you bring us books?" I say.

"You brung us new books like you promised, didn't you, mister?" Junie says.

He smiles and pulls out two books and hands them to us. He tells me my book is called *Self-Teaching Arithmetic* and Junie's is called *The Interesting Narrative of the Life of Olaudah Equiano*. I stare at my book and frown at the words. I don't understand none of it.

Mama and Papa come out the church and walk toward us and greet The Man in the White Suit. He agrees to walk home with us. We walk down the dusty road, me and Junie following behind with our books. I read the front page of my book real slow to get the fill of the big words in my mouth. "*Self-Teaching Arithmetic*. Published in 1962," I say, stumbling over the big words. I stare up into the bone-white sky. 1962, I mouth.

The Man in the White Suit talks about the services and how interesting it was and how grateful he was for hearing the choir sing. He talks like he ain't never been inside a church before. Papa asks him what he gonna do with all them songs he records, and he says with a smile, "Preserve them."

"You don't need to record no songs to preserve 'em," Mama says with a laugh. "Just pass 'em down, like my Mama did with me and like my grammy did with my Mama."

"Where I'm from," he says, "we've lost everything worth passing down."

"Where is you from?" Papa asks.

The Man in the White Suit flashes a mysterious smile and says: a long, long way from here. I whisper to Junie that The Man in the White Suit must really be a angel 'cause nobody can smile like he know all the mysteries of the world, like he do.

March 20, 1974

I was thinking of The Man in the White Suit again. In the office I shared with two other professors, I stared at the equations written in white chalk on the blackboard. The equations were the coordinates for the interior and exterior regions of a wormhole, the location for its event horizon, and my own mathematic equations to complete the expressions I believed, hypothetically at least, would crack the code to time travel. It was just one simple step, a very small step, but—to paraphrase Neil Armstrong—all small steps in science lead to giant ones. I rose up from my desk, putting my hands in my skirt pockets, and approached the board with a smile.

Fifteen years I'd been an adjunct professor in the science department at Morgan State University. I'd watched the faces of one class evolve into the next, noted with mild interest the changing of fashion from poodle skirts to bell-bottoms, from short hair to Afros, and absorbed my students' unchanging, youthful passion for truth and knowledge. And all the while, I read the latest papers in scientific journals, calculated, theorized, imagined, wrote. And now, after all those years of hard work, my greatest discovery was finally cracked. I smiled again, this time more broadly and more proudly of myself. In my moment of glory, who should come back to me now, in thought if not in physical form, but my muse—my strange and enigmatic Man in the White Suit.

I had not seen him in so long, but he was the one who set me down this path and turned me into this lovely paradox.

I closed my eyes and mapped out that path in my mind.

The dirt had barely settled over Junie's grave when I fled Lowndes County for good. I had a teacher, once, who thought I had promise. She came down from D.C. to teach at our little schoolhouse for a year. Before she left, she gave me her address and told me to contact her if I needed any help. I wrote her a letter. By winter, I was living with her and her family. She helped me get into a local school and receive my diploma. It was also through her help that I got into Morgan State, her alma mater. I was twenty-three then. By my late twenties, I graduated with a degree in science. I was in my mid-thirties when I earned my masters in theoretical physics at NYU. In my forties when I earned a PhD. Whether he intended to or not, The Man in the White Suit sent me on this journey and there was no turning back.

There was a knock at the door. I said, "Enter," and returned to my desk. I was already sitting when I glanced back at my visitor, Professor Emeritus Stanley Braithwaite. I rose again and greeted him warmly. Professor Braithwaite was my advisor during my undergraduate studies at the university and my mentor when I was working toward my PhD. He was, by far, one of the most brilliant men I had ever known, and yet he was a giant stuck in a land of very small and petty-minded people.

I helped him over to the chair in front of my desk. At seventy-eight, he was a small, slender, and fragile man. Three years ago, he had had a nasty fall in his home and tore a cartilage in his knee. Now, he walked with the assistance of a cane. The cane itself was a beautiful specimen he bought on a trip to Kenya, hand-carved from ebony wood with the head of a lion on its tip.

Once we were seated, he smiled at me and glanced at the calculations on the board. He pointed his cane at it. "So, I take it, this is the discovery I've been hearing so much about lately." I beamed as he continued to examine the expressions laid out in chalk, adjusting his glasses on the bridge of his thin nose. "Interesting," he added with a nod. "A very interesting conclusion, I'd say."

"It opens up a whole field of questions," I said. "Like whether it's possible for organic matter to pass through a wormhole long enough to exit a white hole without collapsing, or whether paradoxes are inconsistent with the laws of physics within closed, timelike curves—you know, I've been reading some very interesting theories on that recently—"

"I see," he said cautiously. "Yes, quite interesting."

I knew what he was thinking and said so. Professor Braithwaite had been more than a mentor and advisor, but a dear friend. He tolerated my wild flights of fancy and never judged me for it, though he cautioned me to stay on the path of true scientific inquiry. I told him not to worry, that I wasn't expecting to unlock the keys to time travel in my lifetime or my grandchildren's, for that matter. "One small step," I said.

"I take it, then, you'll be publishing your findings."

"Of course."

He nodded and offered some advice. "Your calculations will be valuable to the research community. But please, for your sake, don't mention what you hope these conclusions might lead to."

"That's the most important part of these conclusions," I said. "I realize that we're far from realizing my hypothesis, but that's no reason not to include it in my paper. This has been my life's work, Stanley."

"Yes, I know. Much to the detriment of your career."

I threw myself back in my chair, feeling suddenly like a rebuked child. I had heard this argument before, just as I'd heard it from Reginald, who likewise thought I was foolish to limit myself.

"Ruby," he said, "you have one of the most gifted minds I've ever encountered. I've seen you fight against those who doubted your intellect, but you've always soldiered on and stood up for your principles."

"You were one of the few who went to bat for me," I said. "I've always appreciated that."

"Then listen to me now when I tell you: don't waste such valuable research on a pipe dream."

"But, my dear Stanley," I said, "it's not a pipe dream. I know it isn't."

"How can you be so certain?"

I leaned forward in my chair and smiled. "Because I met a man from the future once, and he told me so."

July 1, 1934

The Man in the White Suit brings me more books. Lots and lots of books. He has brought me plays by William Shakespeare, a book of poetry by Langston Hughes, and a book about a man named Einstein and his theory of relativity. He brings them to me in secret. I read each book by the lantern till my eyes hurt and my belly starts to grumble and I can't read no more. I feel myself getting smarter and smarter from his books. I can feel them changing me, too.

At the little one-room school for colored kids, I sit at the front in my desk and raise my hand to all Miss Hester's questions. And I can answer them now. I quote Shakespeare and DuBois and parts of the Constitution. I tell her about the theory of relativity. I don't understand it entirely, but when The Man in the White Suit comes, we talk about the books I read. We sit down on the rock beside the creek near the cabin and he explains things to me. So I explain them to Miss Hester. But Miss Hester doesn't like having things explained to her. She slaps her ruler down on my desk and asks me how a black gal like me knows so much. I try to tell her, but she doesn't want answers. She gets the other kids to make fun of me and tell me I ought to know my place.

"You's just a nigga," they say. "You ain't any better than all the other niggas here."

"Why do folks got to be so cruel?" I ask The Man in the White Suit one day. We sit by the rock, our secret place by the creek, tossing pebbles into the water and discussing the book on quantum mechanics that he give to me. Where we sit is nice and cool in summertime, 'cause the oak trees are tall and thick and heavy with Spanish moss, and the water is fresh and green from their reflection. Cicadas ring in the high grass and nuthatches and treecreepers send up a choir of song. This is our favorite spot. When we come here, the whole world seems to stop and listen. We are happy here. But my question has put a sour mood over everything. The sun doesn't shine so bright no more. The birds in the trees sound like they're screaming. And I can smell the rot of a dead animal in the brush.

The Man in the White Suit sighs and says he don't know why folks are so cruel. "I thought by coming here I'd have an answer."

"I thought you came here to record songs."

"I did. At least, that's why I'm supposed to be here. Now, I'm not so certain anymore. Sometimes I feel like I'm here for another purpose altogether."

I wrinkle my nose 'cause I don't know what The Man in the White Suit means half the time. He looks at me and sighs. In the future, he says, some things will get better and some things will stay the same.

I ask him what he means and he sighs again, like he's arguing with himself over something, then he says: "One day, a black man will become president of the United States."

I look at him with my eyes bugged out. I try to look in his face to see if he's joshing me, but he looks as serious as fire. He tells me it will happen in the twenty-first century and his name will be Barack Obama. He tosses a pebble into the water and it splashes loudly over the crying treecreepers and the droning cicadas. The water parts for it, then smooths over like glass.

November 3, 1935

It is a Sunday—Mama and me are snapping peas for supper, Papa and Junie sit on crates on the front porch, and I am thinking of The Man in the White Suit. My fingers snap at the peas and my eyes go dreamily across the fields and toward the road near the line of oaks when I notice two figures on horses riding toward us. I don't need to see them up close to know who they are. I point them out and we all stare in that direction.

Boss O'Hara and his son come riding on dark brown horses toward our cabin. They cradle shotguns on the front of their saddles.

Boss O'Hara tips the brim of his hat and says, "Rachel. Ezekiel."

I notice how Papa's shoulders sink in and how his head hangs low. I look to Junie, expecting him to do the same, but his back is straight as Georgia pine and his eyes stare straight at Boss O'Hara and his son. His skin's growing hard over the veins and muscles in his face. His hands are on his knees. He's got his fingers in one hand squeezed around a rock. Too small to knock a man out cold with, but big enough to spook a horse. I put my hand on his and squeeze tight.

Boss O'Hara chews his jaw around like he's chewing tobacco and glances across the fields of white. His skin is red and splotchy and his hair looks orange under the hot sun. He starts asking if we'd seen a uppity English nigger who's been coming 'round recording songs. We all look at each other and shake our heads. We don't know nobody like that, we say. He looks at us like he ain't convinced and starts telling how somebody fitting that description came to his store the other day and started asking his son Jimmy a bunch of questions. Jimmy sent him away with the barrel of his shotgun but when he went out the store to follow him, the man was gone. He and Boss O'Hara have been looking for him since. All the while he telling us this, his son stares right at us, eyes cold as death.

"You sure you ain't seen nobody fitting that description 'round here?" Boss O'Hara says.

"No, suh," Papa says slowly, rubbing his hands on his knees. "Don't know nobody like that, suh."

Boss O'Hara shifts in his saddle and looks at Mama. "How 'bout you, Rachel? I know you sing in the church choir. You might've heard something about 'im."

Mama looks briefly up at Boss O'Hara, her face hard as clay. "I ain't heard nothing about it, Boss."

Boss O'Hara's horse hoofs at the ground, snorts, and dips his head like he anxious to get going. "I thought it was all just a bunch of malarky," he seems to be saying to hisself. "Oh, well, we'll find 'im. If he comes 'round here again, we'll be ready for 'im."

He glares at Papa, more like a command and a warning, clutching his shotgun at the trigger. He's letting us all know he's laying down the law. In this county, Boss O'Hara is the law.

My heart turns cold.

Boss O'Hara tips his straw hat at Mama and turns his horse and rides back in the direction he came. His son follows right behind him.

15

For a long time we don't say nothing. Junie throws the rock hard in the clay dirt and hops off the porch. He starts walking up the road, hands stuck in his overalls, his body hard as that rock in the sunshine.

December 16, 1981

"What did you say?" I screamed over the phone in the lobby, trying to listen over the hubbub of the conference attendees filing toward the main auditorium for the next panel and trying to peer among the crowd of interchangeable faces for the one face I thought bore a strange resemblance to The Man in the White Suit. Reginald was on the other end of the line, giving me the run-down on holiday festivities, family get-togethers, and the trip to the airport to pick up Hector and his fiancée, but my thoughts were racing in a million different directions.

"Can you hear me?" I heard Reginald say in the faintest of connections. I pressed my finger against one ear canal, as if that will help. I stood on my toes and tried to gaze above the heads of a group of men in similar white shirts and chinos. *Where did he go?* "Ruby, you there?"

"I'm here," I said. "It's insane, Reg. I can't hear a damn thing. I'll call you back. At the hotel."

He asked me to repeat what I said. I promised to call again, gave him, Hector, and Lisa my love, then hung up. I ran toward the center of the lobby and searched for the face I thought I saw among the crowd. When I couldn't find him again, I headed toward the front entrance.

Outside in the thin, cold Coloradan air, as a flurry of snow fell from the night sky, my gaze darted toward a dark figure across the street walking in the opposite direction. I shouted his name and waved my arms, but he didn't respond. I ran in the same direction, waving and shouting. He stopped, looked absently in my direction, then turned to greet a crowd of young people turning round the corner. In the traffic light, he looked nothing like The Man in the White Suit.

I let my arm fall slowly to my side. Snow soft as feathers fell on my face and melted from the warmth of my skin. And yet the cold bit under my clothes and nipped at my troubled thoughts.

I bit my lower lip and re-entered the building. I followed the crowd toward the main auditorium. Near the entrance was a board announcing the schedule for the panels. My name was listed among the other speakers joining me, famous assassination conspiracists and UFO experts. Under my name was listed my credits and the phrase: "Well-known time travel theorist."

My mind sank like a body in quicksand.

January 15, 1936

It is winter again and I wait for The Man in the White Suit to come. He has promised me more books. Mama done took the books he gave to me and used the pages to line the walls. I cried when she ripped out those pages. She slapped my face and told me to stop my foolishness. "God provides," she praised.

The Depression has hit us hard, like a cold, cold winter. The chopping season has ended. The entire field has lost its white. But the money Boss O'Hara owes us went to pay for rent and the goods and equipment Papa buys on credit from his store. We got only so much flour and beans left, and if we

17

buy more on credit, we sink further in debt. The government's been handing out provisions like wool and flour and milk, but they only give 'em to the white folks. So we slaughtered the hog for meat and we wear the hand-me-downs Mrs. O'Hara gave us for Christmas. When the heavy rain leaked through the cabin walls last December and ruined the newspapers Mama lined them with, she replaced them with pages from my books.

"Don't worry," The Man in the White Suit promised. "I'll bring more."

He comes to me alone now. After the business with Boss O'Hara last year, Papa said The Man in the White Suit can't come 'round here no more. When he puts his foot down, there is no means of moving it. I was in the shack when Papa turned him away, watching from the window with tears streaking down my cheeks. He looked at me and I could tell there was as much a world of hurt and confusion in his eyes as there were in mine.

A few days later, I was coming in out the field, when I saw him hiding behind the trees. I went to him, prepared to say good-bye, but he gave me a little gadget with buttons and numbers and symbols on it. "Press this button with the asterisk," he said, "and I will come." We promised to meet in our secret place by the rock.

Since then, The Man in the White Suit comes to me, bringing books and lessons and a world I never thought could ever exist.

CYNTHIA C. SCOTT

October 15, 1939

The Man in the White Suit tells me scary stories. Apocalyptic stories about the sea rising and drowning millions of folks and about wars breaking out among the survivors as they fight over what's left. He tells me stories about regeneration and rebirth, about progress and new hope. So much was lost, he says, but now folks can go back in time to rediscover the past, to learn and grow from it, and preserve it. He returns to the past to preserve old folk songs, spirituals, and field hollers. He wants future generations to know their ancestors created beauty and joy, and not just death and destruction. He tells more stories, some scary, some hopeful, some just downright crazy: the Japanese bombing Pearl Harbor, the war, the Holocaust, the atomic bomb, the civil rights movement, men walking on the moon, assassinations, planes crashing into buildings.

He tells me things he knows he ain't supposed to tell me, but I got too many questions he can't ignore anymore.

I ask him about me. "What's gonna happen to me?" I say. He looks at me and his eyes cloud over of a sudden. I want to slap him to make him stop looking at me that way.

He stares across the creek and sighs heavily. "This world is so beautiful," he says softly. "It hurts to remember why."

For all the world, the treecreepers and nuthatches are singing, but I don't hear nothing much anymore.

August 4, 1996

When I was a little girl, a man in a white suit once told me I was going to grow up to be a very important person. Fifty-five years ago to this day, I sent him away and told him never to come back.

Augusts were never good. Three days earlier, I recognized another anniversary, a more tragic one, with a return to Lowndes County and to the tiny segregated graveyard where my brother was buried. When my name was called and I rose uneasily from the chair and took my side by the president, my thoughts wound back to that past few days in August when everything changed for me.

I stared across the rows of people seated in the East Room, my eyes landing on Reginald's, on Hector's, on his wife's, and on my grandchildren's, and smiled softly, but my thoughts were not in that room or on the president's words praising my contributions to science and to ending nuclear armaments. Even as I bowed my head slightly so the president could place the Medal of Freedom around my neck, I was not there. I had disappeared down a vortex in my own time machine.

August 4, 1940

I tear into the woods, my mouth holding screams that don't never come out, running, running to The Man in the White Suit. He waits for me by the creek, standing next to the rock. How many years did he come to me, never growing old while I got older and older? I know what secrets this man holds and now I run screaming to him, begging him to throw a bit of his secret magic on me.

I hurl myself into his arms. The look in his eyes change so many degrees that it look like day turning to night. I look up into his face and all I see are shadows. I miss his kind eyes and his kind smile and I weep some more for the loss of it. I weep for the loss of everything. He asks what's wrong but all I can do is weep.

He sits me down on the ledge of the rock and speaks gently to me. He is such a gentle man. I wish he could take me with him wherever he goes. I wish he could make this whole damn world disappear and take me to the world he knows. But he can't and I know I can't ask him nohow. I choke on my sobs as he wipes away tears with his thumb.

"What's wrong, Ruby?" he says. There's a hint of fear now in his voice. He knows how bad it is.

"They killt him!" I scream. Katydids chirp all around us. It seems like they could bore holes straight into my brain. My head gets heavy and I hold it up for fear it will roll off and land in The Man in the White Suit's lap.

"Killed who, Ruby?" His voice is as firm and sturdy as the rock I sit on. There is no shock or surprise or nothing in it. He speaks his words like he reading it out of a book.

"Junie," I say.

I close my eyes and see Junie. Young, strapping, handsome, and wild with a fire growing inside him. A fire Papa tried so hard to blow out. Mama and Papa said it was The Man in the White Suit what helped light it with his strange ideas and even stranger ways.

"What happened, Ruby?" he says. His voice is gentle now, and sad.

I open my eyes and tell him. I tell him how Junie and his friends were in town a few days ago when they ran into Jimmy O'Hara, the Boss's son. O'Hara thought Junie was showing airs and tried to knock him down some, but Junie wouldn't stand for it this time. Junie, who once had it in his mind to spook Boss O'Hara's horse with a rock when he came by with his shotgun and made Papa sink in like a body in mud. He cold-cocked O'Hara and knocked him out flat to the ground.

Junie and his friends managed to leave town and go into hiding. But the posse Boss O'Hara put together was swift. They found Junie and two of his friends later that night.

They tortured him. There was no other way to put it. My Papa, who wasn't the sort of man to show his emotions openly, collapsed and wept when he saw what they did to Junie.

After I heard what happened, I pressed the button The Man in the White Suit gave to me and ran to the creek, my head filled with screams.

I beg him to fix this. "Go back in time and help him."

He shakes his head again, but I continue to beg.

"You come here to record all those old songs. You said they were lost and you were trying to save them. That's what I'm asking you now: save Junie."

"Ruby—"

"Just go back a few days a piece and help him get out the county. Please, I know you can fix this."

"I'm sorry, Ruby," he says.

The katydids are screaming.

"You sorry?" My breath come out of me like steam. "How you say you sorry? You come here and put ideas in our heads like we can do anything, even travel through time. Before I met you, I never knew nothing like that existed. You come here from the future and tell me things that's gonna happen and…"

My words run out as the worst thoughts fill my head. He looks at me with eyes clear as night.

"You knew," I say. "This whole time you knew and you didn't say nothing."

He looks at me with tears of pity. He starts to say something, but I slap him. When he looks at me with that same pitiful look, I slap him again.

"Go to hell," I say. I run away as katydids scream in my ears.

November 4, 2008

"Grammy, Grammy, wake up. It's starting."

I opened my eyes and sighed deeply. I didn't know I had fallen asleep. I was sitting on the couch in the living room with a quilt draped over me. I stretched and smiled at my granddaughter. For a second, I thought I was staring into a mirror. She favored me more and more each day. She smiled back at me with wide, glistening eyes, her fingers oily with butter in a bowl of freshly popped popcorn. She nodded to the flat screen. Wolf Blitzer was talking about election returns to other reporters and pundits.

"The polls in California close in a few minutes," she said.

Her boyfriend emerged from the kitchen with more popcorn. Its salty, buttery odor filled the air. He smiled and set the bowl on the coffee table, tucked a lock of his long, brown hair behind his ear, then dropped in the leather armchair. He grabbed the remote and turned up the volume. Wolf Blitzer's voice was unapologetically excited tonight.

My granddaughter and her boyfriend had decided to spend the night watching the election results with me. Earlier that day we all went out to the local poll and waited in line for close to half an hour. I'd never seen so many folks at the polls in all my years.

"Never thought you'd see this happen, did you, Grammy?" her boyfriend said. His blue eyes flashed warmly in the light of the TV screen.

I thought of The Man in the White Suit. He had told me this would happen one day and I had believed him.

"Oh, she could imagine it," my granddaughter piped in. "Remember, she's got a time machine."

Yes, my time machine, I said with a smile.

I had spent forty years theorizing the possibilities of using wormholes as time manipulators. Forty years of ideas that were mostly ridiculed in the scientific community. I became a pariah after I published my paper on wormholes. My mathematical calculations on the supposition that the Einstein-Rosen bridge could exist comfortably with quantum mechanics was not the problem. In fact, it survived the peer review process and was greeted with excitement. What sunk me was the conversation I had had with a science journalist for the Christian Science Monitor in a hotel bar in Washington D.C. He asked me why I chose this field of research. I had one drink more than I should have and all my defenses were down. I told him the truth—I met a time traveler, and when he refused to change my past, I decided to change it myself. I had enough presence of mind to insist that my remarks remain confidential. I was a fool.

But time had a way of softening old wounds. Others read my research and expanded on and validated my theories. That was the will of science, constantly pushing forward, building on successes and failures alike, no matter how idiosyncratic.

I let others finish the work I had begun and concentrated on other battles—ending nuclear armaments, sounding the alarm on climate change. Instead of changing the past, I concentrated on changing the future.

"Here we go," my granddaughter said, her voice trilling with excitement.

The countdown began. It felt like New Year's Eve. In a way, it was. It was a new year, a new era, with the worst yet to come.

But that night I did not think of the future; I thought of the past—Junie, always, and my Man in the White Suit.

June 19, 1933

The Man in the White Suit comes again. He sits with us on the porch of our shack, recording Mama singing her songs. Papa be on his crate, smoking his pipe and nodding along. I be on the porch steps with my reader from school in my lap. It is old and tore up with a few pages missing. The Man in the White Suit notices my book.

"May I see it?" he says.

I give it to him. He holds it like it is the strangest and most precious thing in the world.

"I've never seen anything like it before. My people can learn a lot from this."

"It's just a reader, mister," I say, wrinkling my nose. The Man in the White Suit says the strangest things sometimes.

He asks me if he can keep it. But it's my only book.

"If you let me keep this book, Ruby," he says, "I'll be more than happy to bring you more."

"For sure?" I say and he nods in that quiet, funny way of his.

Junie dashes back into the cabin and brings out his own tore-up, dusty books. "Can I trade these for some better books too, mister?"

He nods and takes the books from Junie. His eyes go sad of a sudden when he looks at him. Mama scolds us for bothering The Man in the White Suit, but he says it's all right. "I don't mind," he says and looks at me. He thanks me for the book and says, "One day, Ruby, you're going to grow up to be a very important person."

"Really?" I say, and he smiles at me. It's a sad little smile, but it warms me up like a thousand suns.

Baggage

Leslie Burton-López

FIVE

AT 4:00 P.M., A MONTH AFTER Mom died, Aunt Peggy first came to my doorstep with her black bag. She held her hand out to me and said, "Hello Maggie, I'm your Aunt Peggy." I was five.

"What's in the bag, Aunt Peggy?" I reached out a hand to touch it. She looked so like my mom. Her dark brown hair was longer, though, and her eyes were different somehow . . . but still!

She turned sideways, the bag swooping away from me with her movement.

"*Nada, nada, limonada,*" she sang. "Nothing in here for you." She smiled. "Yet."

That was Aunt Peggy's only rule. I would scamper to grab the black mystery bag, but it was always within her reach, preventing me from seeing inside its mysterious depths. It became a little game for us. "Margaret Elizabeth Yu." Her mouth would be stern as she used my full name. "You know better."

She continued to arrive at exactly four every fourth Friday, neatly coinciding with Dad's monthly bowling night. With punctuality like Admiral Boom in Mary Poppins—only without the cannon—she would appear at the front door, just as the second hand ticked to the twelve. I always knew it was time to change the batteries in the clock when the timing of her arrival didn't match that thin line of red plastic. If they didn't sync, it was time that was wrong, never her. And like the magic in my favorite movie, I somehow knew that adults would not believe in her. So her visits remained our little secret.

SIX

Aunt Peggy called it "playing $kittles." "So," Aunt Peggy began, "you borrow ten purple $kittles from me because you want to buy a lifetime supply of burritos, but you'll owe me one extra purple every week until you pay me back. That's called interest. If it takes you a month to pay me back, how many purples will you give me at the end of one month?"

We had a $kittle Bank building that we had made from cardboard on my sixth birthday, with little doors and columns drawn in black crayon. We even made a sign for the front that showed the name of the bank. It had a little M&M piggy bank inside it that we pretended was a rare brown $kittle.

I sat cross-legged on the floor with Aunt Peggy in front of me. She very seriously acted as bank teller, counting out my $kittle loan, interrupting her important task with huge, gulpy pulls of grape soda.

I had trouble with geography, but $kittles I could handle. I imagined all of those delicious microwave burritos, and concentrated hard on how I would pay for them. I counted, then re-counted, and felt the candy run through my fingers as I made the deposit in front of our cardboard bank. "There! All paid off. I'm going to eat them all at once!" I giggled at the thought of climbing a mountain of burritos and nibbling my way down to the ground.

Aunt Peggy tucked her long brown hair behind the big ears that I also suffered from, to get a better look at my little candy payment and said, "Yes! Well done, magpie!" I beamed at her, then stuck my purple-stained tongue out. She continued, "So what happens if you pay off your burrito loan sooner than one month?"

At six years old, I already had great credit at the First National $kittle Bank.

SEVEN

"I once knew someone who moved all of their stuff into an apartment in the City," she began one night just after my seventh birthday.

"Who was it?" I jumped in.

"Just a friend I know."

"What was her name?" I interrupted again.

"Let's call her Marnie, okay?" This time, she continued without a pause to keep me on track. "So Marnie moved all of her stuff to the City. I'm talking all of the cool posters in her room, her favorite hat, her $kittle Bank, *everything*." Aunt Peggy leaned closer to me as she spoke, her long brown hair brushing my arm, and her dark eyes reflected my own.

The emphasis on the word "everything" gave me the feeling that I was going to end up very sorry for Marnie at the end of this story. The "everything" made me think of my prized possession, a battered and dirty canvas safari hat that went with me everywhere, even when Dad said I couldn't wear it. I would ball it up and stick it in my back pocket.

"So Marnie set everything up in her new place, put up all her posters, hung her favorite hat in the closet, and found a hiding spot behind her bed for her bank. After doing all that, she got super hungry, so she left to go buy some grape soda and corn chips at the store downstairs."

"Ooooooh, grape soda. She liked our soda, Aunt Peggy!" Sometimes she would bring some and we would sit and look out the kitchen window, sighing happily over our fizzy, purple-y drinks.

"That's right, she did!" She smiled at me, but then her mouth got serious again, the corners tilting down.

"So she went downstairs to get her snacks, but when she came back up, everything was gone! I'm talking *everything*."

I gasped. "Someone stole all her stuff?"

"Yeah, it was awful. The only things she had left were her black bag and her snacks." There was an odd pause as Peggy's eyes unfocused for a second. Her voice sounded like it was coming through a tin-can phone when she continued, "I was so sad."

I tilted my head to peer at her through her curtain of hair. My movement snapped her out of her reverie.

"I mean, I was so sad *for her*. Doesn't that sound awful?" She straightened back up, tucked my own long hair behind my ear, and smiled. "You know what, though? Marnie was sad, but she learned that if she had changed the locks on her door right when she moved in, the robbers wouldn't have been able to use the old key."

"Really?" I said. "So Marnie could have saved everything?"

"Yup! *Everything*." Aunt Peggy hopped off the couch and pulled me up with her to grab two grape sodas from the fridge.

EIGHT

When I heard the front door open at 4:00 p.m. on a sunny fourth Friday, I grabbed my geography test and ran to the door waving it. I squealed, "Look what I did!" as I jumped to hug her. Aunt Peggy's chin peeked out from under the hood of her rain jacket, and I could see the roof of her mouth as she smiled when she saw the big "A+" at the top of the page.

"Holy moly, Maggie, you did it! I've never been good at geography." She set her bag down next to the door, then dug her toes into the heels of her heavy boots to pry them off her feet, even as I continued to cling to her. "I'm so proud of you, little magpie." She was gentle as she unpeeled me from the hug. She smelled like gardenias and cigarette smoke.

As we parted, I frowned at my damp shirt.

"Why are you all wet, Auntie?"

"What? Oh . . . I got hit with some sprinklers down the street. Yeah, one of them was turned the wrong way." She smiled at me, flashing her dimples, as she pulled off her coat. "Bummer, huh?"

31

"Good thing you were wearing a raincoat, then." I flashed her my own dimples.

"Totally a good thing." She stooped to pick up her bag by the handle, carefully cradling it to herself. "So what else is new, besides that you're the smartest third-grader ever?"

"*Nada, nada, limonada,*" I sang over my shoulder as I skipped back to the kitchen table. The sun poured in through the windows as Aunt Peggy followed. She sat next to me, carefully setting her bag on the bench seat next to her. She pulled out a set of keys from her bag, deftly diverting my attention. "Okay, now check this out."

Whenever the bag produced something, I was all in.

"Hold them like this." She took my hand and put a key between each of my fingers. The keys sticking out looked like claws.

I giggled. "I'm Wolverine!"

"Yes, you are!" she giggled the same giggle back at me. "Now sit down and show me how Wolverine uses his claws."

I wondered why Wolverine had to sit, but I plunked into a kitchen chair and slashed at the air.

"Very good!" Aunt Peggy encouraged. "Now aim higher."

NINE

We were curled up reading "*Are You There God? It's Me, Margaret.*" to each other. When we got to the part where Gretchen gets her period, Aunt Peggy stopped reading and looked at me. "You'll get your period soon. I brought you some pads so you're ready."

I squirmed on my couch cushion and rolled my eyes. "Um, okay, thanks?" I twirled a chunk of dark hair with my fingers and stared at it. "But I'm only nine!"

"It never hurts to be ready, Mags. Keep one in your backpack, okay?" She looked at me with her serious mouth on. "When I was little, there was a girl who got her period for the first time at school. She was the first one in her class that it happened to, and she was ten, too. She didn't come out of the bathroom for two hours, and by then everyone knew what had happened." Aunt Peggy had her sad mouth on now. "They called her Bloody Mary for years."

After Aunt Peggy left that night, I looked at the box of pads she had pulled out of her black bag and put on the bathroom counter for me. I looked at myself in the mirror and bit my lip. My stomach cramped with nervousness.

Ugh, fine. I ripped open the top flap of the box, pulled out a pink-wrapped plasticky pad, unzipped the outer pocket of my backpack, and slid it into the hidden pocket inside. I double-checked the Velcro security. It looked totally hidden among my keychains and pogs, but knowing it was there made me feel kind of grown up.

TEN

Aunt Peggy glanced at her watch. It said 7:53 p.m. "Okay, girly. I have to be heading out." Her voice sounded funny, like she was choking. I tried to twist around to look at her face, but she held me in an iron-grip hug. She held me for a long time, smoothing my hair and whispering something under her breath. ". . . better every time . . . you can do this . . ."

"What, Aunt Peggy? I can't hear what you're saying." The kitchen clock was ticking so loudly that it echoed in the small room.

She finally released me and turned away, eyes shining.

"Nothing. I just love you, okay?" Despite the bright sun outside, she shrugged her way into a pillowy black jacket, put up its fur-lined hood, and closed the door behind her without another word.

I stood there for a long moment, dazed. The second hand on the clock lurched to hit the twelve. I turned my head toward the sharp sound and saw Aunt Peggy's black bag sitting on the bench seat at the table.

I lunged to pick up the heavy bag and ran to open the door. "Aunt Peggy? You forgot your . . ."

But there was no one there to hear the end of my sentence. I stuck my head out farther to see if maybe she had walked around the corner of the house.

Huh, that's weird. Bummer.

I shrugged, pulled my head back in, and stared at the bag. I could hear the red plastic second hand on the kitchen clock tick noisily.

"I'm not supposed to open this," I said aloud, hoping that my ears would give it more weight. I walked to the bathroom instead to brush my teeth.

Another glance at the bag when my teeth were clean. "I am never supposed to look in Aunt Peggy's bag." I moved to my room to change into jammies.

"Aunt Peggy will be *very* disappointed if I even peek," I told myself again as I walked past it to get a glass of water.

So . . . I didn't look. Instead, I put the heavy black bag gently next to the $kittles bank on the floor in the living room.

After waiting until 5:00 p.m. for Aunt Peggy to arrive on the next fourth Friday, I pulled the bag out and stared at it, willing it to open.

After waiting until 6:00 p.m. on the fourth Friday after that, I dared touch the clasp with trembling fingers, but pulled back before it could fall open.

After waiting until 7:00 p.m. on the fourth Friday after that, I was brave enough to yank on the clasp, ending up frustrated by 7:05 because I couldn't get it to open.

After waiting until 8:00 p.m. on the fourth Friday after that, I had had enough of the temptation and climbed the ladder to the attic with black bag in tow, teetering on each rung as I grappled with the bulky mystery, and placed it between the old lawn sundial and Mom's dusty books.

Aunt Peggy never came back, though strangely, at seemingly random moments, I would think of her.

TWENTY

"What the hell?" screamed my neighbor. She stood in the doorway to her apartment. I ran down the hallway, clumsy with my awkward grocery bag, to see what made her scream. I stopped dead at the sight of her wrecked home. Couch innards were strewn about like oversized dust bunnies, the kitchen table was on its side next to the splintered, matching chairs, the fridge stood wide open. The intruders had even ripped down sheets of wallpaper behind her bed, presumably seeking some hidden stash of money.

I took in the aftermath. The beautiful silver candlesticks were gone. The paintings, the microwave, the TV, the speakers, missing. *Everything.*

My poor neighbor slid down the doorframe and put her head in her hands, choking on sobs. "They took everything!" she wailed at me.

I moved to comfort her, shifting my heavy grocery bag to the floor. I had no idea what to say, so I pulled a soda free from its ringed plastic and handed it to her. She took the purple can as tears slipped down her face like hourglass sand. I silently thanked the universe that I had changed the locks on my door when I moved in last month, and took a swig of my own soda.

TWENTY-ONE

I curled my hand around the keys in my jacket pocket. Weird things happened on subways all the time, but this guy was getting loud. Clearly drunk, he stumbled down the aisle, tripping on nothing, singing a slurred version of "Downtown." He supplied his own words when he couldn't remember the lyrics.

"Grab yer jimmies and yer johnnies and meet me at the . . . hotel!"

I was sitting quietly, trying to distract myself by looking out through the dingy glass. An adult held a child carefully by her plastic claw on the platform as she karate-chopped invisible villains with her free hand. A little superhero.

My hand rearranged the keys in my jacket pocket, evenly spacing three of them in the bases between my fingers.

"Have a gran' ol' tiiiiiiime in the motelll!" drunk-guy screeched, as he approached my seat with a lecherous up-down-up look.

Concealed behind the seat back in front of me, I eased my hand out from my pocket. I clenched my fist and felt the ridged keys dig into my flesh as I looked up into his face.

TWENTY-TWO

I skipped down the street toward my brand-spanking-new car. I probably looked silly doing the skipping, but it felt right. I owned the shiny little darling parked a block away.

"With your credit, you'll qualify for a great price, don't worry about anything," the sales-dude had smarmed. "Hell, you could have any car on the lot if you wanted."

I had smirked at that one. I knew I couldn't afford the fully loaded version of this one, though my good credit had tempted me to go for it. Not this time, sales-dude.

What a rush! *I own a car. I am a car owner. This car is mine. My car is this one.*

TWENTY-THREE

Damn. I looked down at the crimson smear in my underwear as I sat on the toilet. *Why does this always happen to me at work?* Luckily, I had just arrived and decided to pee before I got to my desk. My purse dangled from the metal hook overhead. I fished around and found what I was looking for.

Fourteen years of monthly visits. You'd think I'd have a handle on it by now.

TWENTY-FOUR

The back of my throat was raw and sore as I pushed my finger in deeper. Nothing was working this time. I couldn't throw up. My gag reflex was just gone.

The tears came, hot and salty. I sat next to the toilet, letting all the awful things of the last year wash over me. I thought about my father's last breath as he lay in that hospital bed in March. I thought about all the food that made its way in, and quickly out, of me since April. I thought about my DUI in May.

My sobs echoed in the small bathroom, as I ugly-cried to the hideous beige-and-turquoise tiles. And lucky me: the air conditioner had chosen to break on the hottest day of the year right when I had to clean Dad's stuff out of the house. "I hate you, heat!" I yelled stupidly to no one.

After a few minutes, I finished crying. *This place isn't going to clear itself.* I sighed and pulled myself up, using the back of the toilet for leverage, and stumbled over to the attic ladder. The old sundial gleamed dull gold in the shaft of half-light from the single, yellowed attic window. I shifted it to reach for something more manageable to take downstairs. The dust puffed in patterns as I strained. The sunlight, freed from the dial, now lit on something else.

There it was. Not a speck of dust on it.

Aunt Peggy's bag.

My mouth hung open a bit, but then I grinned.

"Aunt Peggy will be very disappointed if I even peek," I said aloud. I grabbed at the bag and pulled it out of its resting place. My tattered life lay on my shoulders like the moth-eaten stole, but this memory was whole.

"I'm not supposed to open Aunt Peggy's bag." From two rooms and a ladder away, I could hear the clock tick noisily. I sat down on the dirty floor, the dust sticking to my sweaty legs. I cradled the bag in my lap and hugged. The smell of gardenias and cigarette smoke stung me, or at least that is what I blamed for my again-wet eyes.

This time, the clasp opened easily, as if it had been recently oiled. The handwritten note nestled above the bulk in the bag said simply: "Make us better."

Signed, M.E. Yu.

TWENTY-FIVE

I took a deep breath and knocked on the familiar door when it appeared, a little disoriented from seeing sunny skies after drenching rain. I turned the heavy clasp on the black bag to close it, then folded up the dripping umbrella. It had been a year since I had been here for the estate sale. The paint on the door then had been faded, and the spiders had created clutches of cottony brown wisps on the siding. A quick glance at my watch showed exactly 4:00 p.m.

Jesus, what am I doing? I could hear scrambling, as the deadbolt turned in the bright door. Suddenly, my gag reflex returned, along with a hopeful feeling that maybe I could keep it this time. *Oh, please, please let this work.*

The door was answered by a small, bright-eyed girl whose dimples showed as she smiled at me. I reached out my hand.

"Hello, Maggie. I'm your Aunt Peggy."

Dinosaurs and Oats

B.T. Lowry

CYNTHIA WAS REARRANGING HER MOM'S yesterday when someone aware came in.

He looked about seven, a little younger than her, and had a stuffed brontosaurus under his arm. He seemed normal enough, and that was what was so strange about him. Besides a few babies crawling around, everyone else in the coffee shop appeared foggy. Cynthia's mom, her teacher, and even her daytime-self all looked like trees do when they're outside a window on a rainy day.

The boy was like now-Cynthia: colorful and solid and right there. "What are you going to do?" he asked in a voice just as clear as him.

She didn't reply. Whatever *he* was doing here, Cynthia had a mission. She looked up at her mom, waiting by the counter for coffee, and took a deep breath to yell "succulent."

But before Cynthia had even gotten "su" from her mouth, something knocked the wind out of her. The boy had tackled her to the floor.

"What are you doing?" she demanded.

He got to his knees and picked up his dinosaur. "You're not gonna take my dad away from my mom!"

Twelve hours earlier

In the coffee shop they always came to, Cynthia and her mom reached the front of the line. Her mom ordered something with a really long name, full of words that made it sound exciting but also relaxing, creamy and sweet but healthy, and she got Cynthia an oatmeal chocolate cookie. Everyone smart knew that oatmeal was the best kind of food, and oatmeal cookies were even better because you could carry them around without making a mess. The chocolate just made them better.

While they waited for the coffee, Cynthia munched and looked around. As usual there were a lot of new mothers and their babies. But today someone new had come. Her English teacher, Mr. Ferguson, was sitting at a round table near the counter, holding a notebook in one hand and pressing a pen to his lips with the other. A boy sat opposite him, about Cynthia's age with a bowl haircut, drawing on a napkin.

Cynthia smiled and started to go over to Mr. Ferguson—he was her favorite teacher—but Mom held her shoulder. "Don't wander around, we're in a rush."

"But that's . . ." Cynthia began, but Mom was speaking quickly to the aproned guy behind the counter. She got her cup of stuff that sounded delicious, but which Cynthia had tried once when Mom went to pee and so knew it actually tasted bitter and horrible, and they left the counter.

One of the ladies in line touched Mom's shoulder, smiling. "Oh! I was thinking of trying that. How is it?"

Mom had seemed flustered since checking her phone an hour ago. Now she looked like she was staring into a bright light. "It's . . . um . . . tasty."

As they passed behind Mr. Ferguson, his head suddenly jolted up. He pulled his pen from his mouth, then bent to write furiously in his notebook. The boy was doodling a brontosaurus. He looked up, too, and waved as though at a friend, but Cynthia didn't follow his gaze. She wanted to see what her teacher was writing. She didn't catch many words because his hand was in the way, but she saw something about oats, and the phrase, "As though from highest heaven sent."

When Mr. Ferguson moved his hand, she saw the last word he had written: "succulent." She had no idea what it meant, but she liked the sound of it. It sounded like Mom's coffee smelled, what it *should* taste like but definitely didn't. Mr. Ferguson said to the boy with the bowl cut, "I've got it!"

"What?" asked the boy, looking up from his drawing.

Mr. Ferguson acted as though he'd seen something where the wall met the ceiling. "Just a minute. Got another idea." He bent back to his notebook.

Cynthia liked Mr. Ferguson, more so now that she knew he liked oats enough to make a poem about them. He often read funny poems in English class to teach the kids new words.

As soon as Mom sat down, she checked the texts on her phone. She looked really pretty today, with her long blonde hair tied in a pink ribbon and a dress like a flowery meadow.

But whatever she was reading on the phone made her face shrivel up like a slice of apple in her food dehydrator.

Cynthia kept looking over at Mr. Ferguson, trying to catch his eye so he might come over and read his new poem to her and Mom, but he was too absorbed. She bet it was a good one.

Before she went to bed, Cynthia looked up "succulent" in the pocket dictionary Dad had given her before he'd left for good. She smiled; it was the *perfect* word to describe an oatmeal cookie: tender, juicy, buttery, and tasty. The word *itself* tasted good . . . *succulent*. And when Mr. Ferguson taught it to the class, she would already know the meaning. He'd call her learned; that was another word he'd taught her.

Mom made a weird sound in the living room, like a short bird call, then blew her nose loudly. Cynthia tiptoed out to see her mom curled in a ball on the couch, crying, her phone glowing in her hand.

"You wouldn't even talk to me," Mom said to the phone, but she wasn't on a call. Cynthia knew who she meant. It was that stupid boyfriend, the one with the smile pasted on his stupid face like he'd drawn it on paper and stuck it there. Cynthia had seen that smile fall, and he was like a skull underneath, all frightening and mean and only thinking of himself. From the kitchen, Cynthia had heard him yelling at Mom in the car, swearing and saying all kinds of things that Mom said Cynthia should never say. Mom was better off without him, and she'd have more time for Cynthia now, so that was good, too.

Cynthia sat on the couch and placed her hand on Mom's knee.

"Your mommy's getting too old to be liked."

"I think you're really pretty and nice. You don't need him."

Mom sniffed, watching her. "You're a smart girl, you know? Only let people into your heart if they really love you, okay?"

Cynthia nodded. "Why do you need a stupid boyfriend anyway?"

Mom nearly laughed, but she seemed too tired. "I don't need a *stupid* one. I do need a partner, though."

"Why? They just take you away from me."

"Oh, baby." Mom sat up, tears in her green eyes, and stroked Cynthia's cheek. "A good man wouldn't. He'd help me be a better mother to you."

"Really?"

Later, while lying in bed trying to sleep, Cynthia thought of the nicest man she knew. She got an idea. That night, she dreamed of what had happened during the day. At first she dreamed of bits and pieces, eating an ice cream or petting a funny little dog on the sidewalk. It was always weird to see herself, gray and foggy daytime-Cynthia, going about her day. One day when she was awake, she'd have to remember to wave at her night-self. That would be fun.

Once she'd seen a movie about a man who had become a ghost, and when she got old enough to think about it properly, she had worried that maybe she was becoming a ghost every night. But the man in the movie couldn't go back to make himself not die or anything like that. He couldn't go back at all. He had to try really hard even just to push a bottle cap around. Cynthia couldn't push anything, but that didn't mean she couldn't change things. Maybe if she yelled loud enough, she could be heard.

Before long she found her way to the coffee shop. There was her daytime-self, washed out and wispy like everyone else, chewing on an oatmeal cookie next to Mom. Geez that had been a good cookie.

A few dreaming babies crawled around, clear and present. One gurgled and laughed at Cynthia. For some reason new mothers really liked this place, maybe because there were so many of them already here. They drank coffee and talked about baby stuff like pooping and eating while the babies gurgled and kind of wrestled with each other.

The wispy boy doodled, and Mr. Ferguson had his wispy pen to his wispy lips, looking at the ceiling as though trying to catch something there with his eyes and pull it down into his head.

Cynthia walked over to her mom and took a deep breath to yell "succulent!" but before she could even get out "su," something bright and colorful caught her eye. It was a boy, about Cynthia's age, with a bowl cut and angry eyes and a plush dinosaur stuffed under his armpit.

"What are you going to do?" the boy demanded, his voice just as clear as him: solid and vivid.

Cynthia couldn't get distracted. Mom's coffee would come any second, then Mom would leave the counter and Mr. Ferguson would think of his great word and the chance for him and Mom to meet nicely would be gone. Cynthia pulled in her breath again, but before she could yell, something bowled her to the floor.

"What are you doing?" Cynthia yelled up at the boy.

"You're not gonna take my dad away from my mom!" He rolled back onto his knees, clutching a stuffed dinosaur.

"Who's your dad?" she demanded, getting to her feet.

"Him." He pulled her by the hand over to Mr. Ferguson, all streaky and thoughtful-looking, then to the doodling boy. "And that's me." The streaky boy looked up from his drawing and waved.

Cynthia gawked. "He can *see* you?" But no, the streaky boy wasn't looking at the real one, just somewhere nearby. "You knew you'd be here, so you waved to yourself? That's really cool. What's your name?" She had to win him over so he'd let her yell at Mom, and she only had a few moments. He did seem cool though.

"I'm Billy and I'm seven."

"I'm eight and I'm Cynthia," she said proudly, but she was confused. "How can you do this when you're so old?" She pointed at one of the babies, crawling around a table next to their twelve-hour-ago selves. "Usually only babies can."

"They think they're dreaming," said Billy. "They don't know how to change anything."

"Yeah, but how did you remember?"

"How did you? You're even older."

Cynthia said, "My cousin forgot when she went to middle school, and I didn't want to be like her, so I tried real hard."

Mom was already talking to the guy behind the counter.

Cynthia turned to Billy. "Listen, I *need* to yell something at my mom."

Billy balled his hands into fists. "You just want her to take Dad away from Mom!"

"How would you know what I'm going to do?"

"Because it worked," he said.

Cynthia stared at him, mouth open. "You're not just coming from half a day away. You're from—"

"About two weeks from now," he said. "Yeah, my dad and your mom get together, all fuzzy and pink and stupid like in the movies, makes me want to barf. Then Dad leaves Mom for good."

Cynthia looked toward the counter. Her mom was already coming toward them, cup in one hand, phone clutched in the other. She looked pretty, even all ghostly, but sad, and she was about to pass Mr. Ferguson. Cynthia had to do this now.

"How do you like the coffee?" a woman in line asked Cynthia's mother, sounding like she was underwater.

Cynthia pushed Billy aside and ran up to her mom. She tried to grab Mom by the leg but her hands went through, of course. Billy grabbed Cynthia from behind as she yelled, "Succulent!" As the boy pulled her to the ground, she managed, "Succulent, succulent, succulent!!!"

Mom's head jerked, and she nearly dropped her coffee. "Succulent!" she cried out. "The coffee's succulent!" The other lady nodded politely, but her smile seemed too fixed in place.

Cynthia bit her lip and grinned like crazy. Mom had heard!

Mr. Ferguson turned and looked up at Cynthia's mom, a mystified smile on his face. "That's *it*! That's the word I was looking for. How did you even *know* that?"

Mom touched her hand to her mouth in a most charming way. "I... It just came to my mind."

Cynthia felt Billy let go of her back.

"That's incredible," Mr. Ferguson said, then looked down at daytime-Cynthia. "You!"

"Hi, Mr. Ferguson."

Her teacher looked up again, smiling. "Mrs. Davis, I presume."

She showed her hand. "Oh, I'm not married."

He nodded. "You know, Cynthia's a very smart girl."

Mom and Mr. Ferguson started talking like two rivers mixing together. He said that Cynthia appreciated his poems more than any other student. Even *he* didn't like them as much as her. Mom laughed more in a few minutes than she had in the last few months, and her eyes kept asking Mr. Ferguson questions. Cynthia couldn't understand them, but his eyes seemed to answer "yes."

Heart full and happy, Cynthia heard a sound behind her, like a clogged sink trying to drain. She turned to see Billy sitting on the floor, grabbing his knees with his arms, sobbing.

"I'm sorry," said Cynthia.

"No, you're not! It keeps happening this way no matter what I do. If you were sorry, you wouldn't do it!"

The next day, Cynthia's mom smiled every time she checked her phone. She hadn't even cried last night when her stupid boyfriend had broken up with her, and she'd given Cynthia as much honey and butter as she wanted with her toast.

But Cynthia felt sad. She had to talk to Billy, though she didn't know what she'd say. He seemed like a nice boy, and she'd for sure play with him if they were in the same class. But even if she knew what to say, where could she find him? She looked for him at the coffee shop, but Mr. Ferguson was never there. He never usually went there. Billy wasn't in any of the nearby parks either, or in the library.

Then one day she saw Billy in school, wearing too-big overalls and walking the main hallway between classes. She called his name and he turned, eyes wide and with half a hopeful smile. But when he recognized her, he scrunched up his face and shoved his hands in his pockets and marched away as fast as he could.

That night, Cynthia went back to the hallway where they'd met. Wispy students strode around, opening and closing lockers, laughing or arguing with each other, going in and out of classes. She waited a long time, hoping Billy would come back. Of course he wouldn't. He was angry at her and Mom. If he did come, he'd just yell at her. The school day wore on, and Cynthia knew she'd have to leave. She couldn't remain here after her day-self had left.

After the last dismissal bell, a small figure passed through the double front doors without opening them. Billy's hands were in his overall pockets, his shoulders raised. He hardly glanced at her, but stopped nearby and mumbled, "Just don't say you're sorry."

"Okay."

"You didn't—" His face was pinched up like he was trying to keep tears from leaking out. "But they weren't *really* together anymore, you know."

"I kinda thought so."

He showed his teeth like an angry monkey and pointed at her. "But you still shouldn't!" He let out a sigh like a balloon emptying. With the last of it gone, he sat cross-legged on the floor, hands back in his overall pockets.

"Do you wish your parents were still together?" she asked.

"Of course, don't you?"

She sat too on the shiny linoleum floor. The voices of students leaving for the day rushed around them like an outgoing tide sealed behind glass. "My dad was kinda mean, not like yours." She knew they didn't have much time, that they'd soon wake up or go to some other place from their daytimes. "What was your dad writing in that coffee shop?"

"Oats." Billy smiled, showing two missing front teeth. "It's a really good poem."

"I wish I could hear it. I mean, I guess he'll read it in class."

"Nope. He wrote it down for me." Billy foraged in his many pockets and eventually came up with a crumpled piece of paper. In another pocket he found a little plastic dinosaur, one of the swimming ones. He put it on his lap and turned it toward him as though making sure it could see and hear him. He cleared his throat and straightened his back, then read, "With butter they give a rapturous scent / As though from highest heaven sent / Even if I can't pay the rent / I'll eat oats, for they're succulent!" He put the paper back. "What's 'succulent' mean?"

"Really tasty. Usually it's more for fruit and stuff than cookies, but your dad's such a good poet he can do what he wants."

"Mph. I don't even like oats."

"Really?" Cynthia found that hard to believe. "Do your dinosaurs like them?"

He looked at the one on his lap. "They'll eat anything, as long as it's a lot."

"I've got more than anyone!" said Cynthia, but as her own voice faded, she didn't know what else to say. She really wanted this to work. "Are our parents still together two weeks from now?"

He put the dinosaur back in his pocket. "Yeah."

"Are you still angry at me, then?"

"Not as much as now."

She sighed, felt like crying. "Do you think maybe you could stop being angry with me? I just want my mom to be happy."

He traced a shape on the hallway's floor.

Cynthia bit her lip. She couldn't think of anything to say except what was on her mind. "Can we maybe be brother and sister?" Her voice went too high at the end.

Billy stood up and shoved his hands in his pockets. He wobbled from side to side. "They probably won't get back together again."

"I'm sorry."

He narrowed his eyes. "I told you—"

"I mean I'm sorry your parents aren't together."

"It's not your fault."

"I know, but it's too bad."

"Yeah." Billy hugged his sides through his pockets. He shifted from one foot to another and stared into space as though she weren't there. "I've got like fifty dinosaurs, you know."

"Wow, that's a lot."

"You think you got enough oats for all of them?"

Cynthia stood, too. "I'll have enough left over to make cookies."

"That's good. They like them more than just a pile of oats."

"I was thinking for us, and for your mom and my dad."

"Careful the dinosaurs don't eat them, though. They might bite you while they're doing it."

"Okay. I'll be careful."

"Okay." He looked up and smiled and looked at her straight in the eyes for the first time. He had nice brown eyes, the color of Mom's coffee. He said, "So you and your mom should come over this week with a bunch of cookies."

"Yeah?"

"Yeah."

Disjointed

Alison McBain

"The crisis of today is the joke of tomorrow."—H.G. Wells

BUSIGO, FIRST BASEMAN OF THE Red Sox, hit a homer off the rookie Yankees pitcher.

"That's it!" Carson took a drag from the joint and handed it over to David. "That's a sign this idea I had is going to be excellent, dude."

David inhaled deeply and blew out a cloud of smoke. "What's going to be excellent?"

"This—this! I've wanted to do this since I was a kid." Carson stuck the roach in an ashtray filled with cigarette stubs and cellophane candy wrappers, then picked up the device that has been sitting, unnoticed, on the coffee table. It looked like a cardboard paper towel roll, except with buttons and an LED display on one end that glowed faintly. It was even the same light brown.

"What is it?" David asked, his eyes glued to the tube. Not the one in Carson's hand, but the one that was showing the Yankees losing. Badly, as usual.

"It's a TM."

"ATM?" David didn't look up. "Where's the money come out?"

"Dude." Carson shook his head. "It's a TM, not ATM."

"That's what I said!"

"No, like, *T-M*. TM kind of TM!"

"Ohhhhh. A TM? You're kidding." David dragged his attention away from the TV, but then again, the game had just gone to commercial. He took the device out of Carson's hands and shook it next to his ear. Why people thought shaking a piece of electrical equipment would reveal something otherwise unnoticed, Carson had no idea. "If that's a TM, then I'm a gorilla's uncle. That doesn't look like it'd transport you five feet from your chair, let alone five years into the past. Although it would probably make a really great bong . . ."

Carson snatched the device away from David before his friend started drilling a hole in the side. "Don't you dare."

David laughed, lighting a cigarette. "Those things are illegal. Like, really illegal."

"Illegal is a state of mind, man. Time machines aren't illegal. Time travel is. But if no one knows . . ."

David mouthed the word, *Okay*, then said out loud, "Where'd you get it anyway?

"I picked it up real cheap in a junk shop. Nine ninety-nine, ninety-nine. Even came in the original packaging."

"Holy crap, how much did you pay for that?"

"Nine ninety-nine, ninety-nine."

"Nine ninety-nine . . . a thousand bucks? You got had." David opened up the ratty pizza box on the wobbly table and grimaced at the green and fuzzy slices. He closed the box and settled back on the sofa.

"Nah, dude—there's a thirty-day return policy. A quick zip back in time to see a few things, meet a few people, and I can bring it back to the shop. No harm, no foul." Carson propped his boots up on the coffee table, which groaned under the weight. "I kept the receipt and peeled the tape back real slowly. See? You can't even tell it's been opened. Didn't tear the cardboard."

"Clever."

"Genius, I tell ya. So you wanna come with me?"

David rolled his eyes. "That's dope bravado, but doobie stupidity. Thanks, but no thanks, genius. I'll pass."

"You're missing an opportunity of a lifetime. Several lifetimes, in fact." Carson grinned.

"I bet. But, no, I have to get going. I've got to go take care of my cat."

Carson smirked. "You need to wax it?"

"Wax my cat? What the heck are you talking about?"

Carson snorted with laughter while David rolled his eyes.

"Ooookay." Carson picked up the controller. "Here goes nothing." He double-checked the display. *August 15, 1969, Bethel, NY.* Perfect. He pressed the red button.

David's eyes were fixed on Carson, who was still sitting in his beanbag chair. The room hadn't dematerialized around Carson and reappeared as the soggy hills of Woodstock. Women wearing nothing but mud in pivotal places at the most pivotal moment in music history hadn't snapped into place around him.

"Are you sure you know how to work that thing? Or have you already been and come back?" David grinned.

"Shut up." Carson waited for one more second. Pressed the button again. Jabbed his finger up and down. "Okay, it's not working."

"Well, what did you expect?" David rose to his feet, stretched, and ambled to the door of Carson's studio apartment. "I'll be back in a bit. Better go find that receipt."

"Yeah," said Carson glumly as the door shut behind his friend.

Carson fiddled with the dial, spinning it up and down to its preset dates and locations. He actually recognized most of them. In theory, at least, he was still a world history major. In practice, he would have to stop sponging off his parents and actually attend class once in a while to qualify. Two things that seemed more unlikely to him than the possibility of the government giving out free weed with every tax return. Not that he'd ever paid taxes, but he understood the theory . . .

November 22, 1963, Dallas, Texas. July 14, 1789, Paris, France. 1725, Dublin, Ireland.

As the last date spun into place, all of a sudden there was a horrendous shriek. The controller writhed in his hand. He tried to drop it, but it was as if the device had fused to his skin—no matter how much he shook his fingers, he couldn't let go.

The ground dropped out from under him, and his screams echoed the machine's. How long it lasted, he couldn't say afterwards. His lungs were frozen and he burned with the need to breathe, to inhale.

The ground spanked his ass hard. The controller dropped from his hand and rolled away, stopping in a pile of dung just in time to avoid getting crushed under a horse's hooves.

"Hey, eejit, get owt o' tee road!" bawled a voice from overhead. Football-sized hooves thudded around him. Carson spun through the dirt and muck until he bumped up against the solid wall of a building. But then that he realized he'd left the time machine sitting in a pile of horse crap.

Of course, he was also now liberally covered in the stuff himself. With a grimace, he darted into the road, grabbed the controller, and headed back to the general safety of the building before he got run over.

Across the street were two-story grey stone houses built into one another like jigsaw pieces. He glanced up from where he was standing and realized he had taken shelter against a cathedral. The building rose several stories up into the air, with a towering clock tower crowned with crenellations and rocket-shaped windows. On the very top of the pointed roof was a cross.

"Great. A cathedral. I wonder if they have a shower," he muttered, edging away from the road. He quickly climbed the steps and went through the carved wooden doors.

Inside was as splendid as the outside—vaulted ceilings, mosaic floors in complex geometric designs, and velvet-cushioned seats. "What's this place?" he asked a man who was standing just inside the doors. The man was wearing a green, patterned robe with tassels.

Wow, had clothing styles changed. Carson didn't think he had the figure to pull off that look, so it was a good thing that fashion had progressed.

The man raised eyebrows. "Saint Patrick's Cathedral, sir."

"Saint Patrick's Cathedral? Where?"

"In Dublin, sir."

"Dublin? Hey, this is where Jonathan Swift is! I love him. Eating babies, man."

The man's eyebrows were nearly to his hairline. "Eating babies, sir?"

Carson waved a hand. "Never mind. Where is he?"

Without a word, the man led him past rows of pews and into a darkened corridor near the back. Down the corridor, then into a small room where a man sat at a desk, dipping a quill into ink. When they entered, the man glanced up.

"I towt I sait not to be disturbed. And who is tis?"

"Begging your pardon, sir," said the robed man.

"I'm Carson," Carson said. "I love your writing."

It was Swift's turn for raised eyebrows. He waved a hand in dismissal, and the other man left the room. As Carson approached the desk, Swift brought a white cloth to his nose—a handkerchief. Carson looked down at himself, remembering his incident with the horses.

"How can I help you, sir?"

"I just came to thank you. I'm from the future." Boy, would David get a kick out of this.

"The future? And what, pray tell, are you tanking me for?"

"Well, the idea about babies. Brilliant. Our main food source."

After an awkward silence, Swift merely repeated, "Babies?"

Carson grinned. "Yeah, your essay 'A Modest Proposal,' where you suggest that people eat the babies of the poor, because they aren't really contributing to society anyways. Some people thought you were just being satirical, but most of us thought the idea was genius. Babies are great eating, especially with barbecue sauce. Without you, we never would have thought of it."

Laughing at Swift's expression, Carson walked back outside. In the doorway, he nearly tripped over a young girl covered in rags. "Sorry!" he mumbled automatically, then *really* looked at her. She said nothing, merely held out a well-worn wooden bowl.

Carson patted his pockets. Empty. He glanced down at his wrist and saw his Homer Simpson watch. "Here," he said, unfastening it and dropping the watch into her bowl. "I expect that back in the year 2055. Just have one of your descendants bring it to Boston—that's in America—and look up Carson O'Connell. It's magic and will bring you great fortune." Whistling, he went down the rest of the steps.

At the bottom, he turned the dial of the time machine. "The past blows. Okay, now for a look into the future . . ."

Scream, falling, choking, then the ground punching his ass again.

Wheezing, he sat up. Looked around.

Grass. As far as the eye could see. And trees in the distance.

"What the heck?" He shook the time machine, but the date and place remained fixed. *2500, New York City.*

Suddenly, he heard a terrible hooting behind him. Out of the trees streamed a bunch of people . . . naked.

From their apparent ages and love handles, not a pleasant sight. When they spotted him, they made a terrible outcry, but Carson couldn't understand a word they were saying. But before he had a chance to ask, they ran off.

"That was weird," he said.

The ground rumbled. A group of gorillas sprang out of the forest and came running towards him. They seemed to be wearing clothes. No—monkey suits. Of the black tie variety. And they didn't look happy.

"Uh-oh." Carson tried to move the dial on the time machine, but it was stuck. He knelt down and pounded the machine on the ground. He glanced up. The gorillas were close enough he could see the whites of their teeth as they roared.

Carson flicked at the dial with his thumb. "Come on, come on," he said, sweating. Without warning, the dial shifted, and dates flew by in an unending stream of numbers and letters. He closed his eyes without looking and pressed the button . . .

. . . and the ground smacked him again. He lay there for a moment, groaning, staring up at skyscrapers reaching for the night sky. Their lights twinkled peacefully, and he couldn't tell if he were back to his present time or years ahead or behind. Either way, it seemed gorilla-free. "Must remember pillows next time," he muttered before sitting up.

"There won't be a next time," he heard in bad, Austrian-accented English. He looked up. And up. And sideways a bit, too.

The voice came from a man so stacked he looked like a bodybuilder who snorted steroids the way normal people breathed air. His square face was distorted with a muscly emotion. "I am daking you in for breaking da law," the man said.

Carson held up his hands. "Okay, okay. I get it. You're just doing your job. You a cop?"

"A dime cop," the man said.

"A dime cop? What does . . . oh, a *time* cop. Okay. What's the punishment?"

"Depends. You have a permid?"

"A permit. Yes, I do. Wait just a second." Cautiously, Carson lowered his hands and patted his pockets. "It's here somewhere. Just wait a second, I'll get it . . ." Quickly, he spun the dial on the time machine and pressed the button. "Hasta la vista, bab . . ." he managed to say before the traveling space stole his breath again.

His apartment materialized around him. He glanced around for a moment, but it seemed the badly-accented time cop hadn't followed him.

"Whew," he said, glancing at his clothes. The incinerator would be too kind for them. Too bad, it was his favorite shirt. He put down the controller and went off to take a shower.

Just as he stepped out, the doorbell rang. Carson wrapped a towel around his waist, but spent a moment dithering by the front door. It could be David, come back to laugh at him. It could be the time cop.

Finally, he pulled open the door.

An old woman stood outside. If she appeared surprised by his wet, undressed state, she did well to hide it. "Are you Carson O'Connell?"

"Yes?" he said.

She smiled and tears came to her eyes. "Finally! This has been handed down in my family for generations. Without its magic, my ancestors would've starved. But it brought us prosperity and happiness, just as you promised." She reached into her purse and pulled out an item, now scarred and marked by time. "I was told to bring it to this place and this time, or the magic would fail us."

Homer Simpson peered out from beneath the grime and scratches of the beat-up watch face.

He took the timepiece from her trembling hand. "Uh . . . thanks," he said. She nodded and bobbed her head at him, and he slammed the door before she started tugging on her forelock, too.

The watch had stopped long ago, and he shook it in that futile attempt that all people make when faced with a broken watch. "Cheap piece of trash," he said. He turned and tossed it towards the waste bin. "Score!" He threw his arms up in the air.

Just then, there was another knock on the door, this one quite loud. He turned back around and opened it. "What do you want now—"

"I want to kill you," said the gorilla standing outside. "You have traveled across the Homo-Gorilla temporal border, which is punishable by death." The beast grabbed his arm.

"Take your stinking paws off me, you damn dirty ape!"

Carson hadn't really thought sounding mean would work, but the gorilla let go of him.

Then it leveled a gun at his chest. *By comparison*, Carson thought, *the paw wasn't so terrible.*

The gorilla snarled, "By the power vested in me through the berengei-sapiens time alliance, you are hereby sentenced to have a *really* bad day—"

Suddenly, the gorilla's hand was empty and the Austrian time cop was there, judo-chopping all over the place. Despite its size, the gorilla was no match for the fury of a thwarted time cop, and it was flat on the ground with the cop cuffing it at lightning speed.

"I'll be back!" the cop yelled over his shoulder as he led the gorilla away.

Carson reached for the time machine. "Not if I have anything to say about it!"

Wham, bam, thank you, ground smacking his ass again. But at least he wasn't alone this time.

Carson blinked at him. "Whooooah—what are you doing here?"

"Don't do it, man!" Carson yelled at the earlier version of himself. "It's a world of trouble! Just say NO to time travel!"

"But I've always wanted to, ever since I was a kid," Carson argued. "And I got such a deal on this time machine! Only—"

"Nine ninety-nine, ninety-nine," Carson said in unison with his double. "I know. But aside from a few laughs, it's just a big pain in the ass." He got up, adjusted his towel, and rubbed his sore butt. "Literally."

"How do *you* know?" asked Carson.

"Because I'm *you*, you idiot!" Carson yelled.

"So what should we do?"

"Do what I do. Hold tight and pretend it's a plan!"

"Just so we're clear . . ."

The Carson in a towel rolled his eyes, then reached out to smack the time machine from the original Carson's hands. It fell to the floor with a thud. He stomped down on it, hard, and the cheap plastic casing shattered instantly.

"There! Now you can't do it!" he said triumphantly.

"Except what about this one?" said the other Carson, picking up future Carson's controller. Then, "Ew! Is that poop?"

Exasperated, Carson grabbed the other controller and stomped on it, too.

"Dammit," he said, looking at the bottom of his foot. "I just took a shower, too."

"Aren't you supposed to disappear, man?" asked the original him.

Carson felt himself up and down, a process that sounded dirtier than it really was. Well, except for his crap-covered foot. "I have no idea," he said.

Just then, the door crashed open. The Austrian time cop stood in the doorframe.

"You're under arrest!" he yelled.

"Me?" said original Carson. "I didn't do anything. I've just been sitting on this couch watching the baseball game."

"Then *you're* under arrest!"

"You can't prove I did anything, either. Look. Two time machines—destroyed. No harm done."

The time cop looked from one of them to the other, then scratched his head. "Vait, vhich vun of you broke da law?"

"Not me," the two of them said in stereo.

After a second, the Austrian shrugged. "Ah, screw it. I don't get paid enough for this." The cop turned around and left. On his way out, he passed a guy coming in.

Carson's friend, David.

David stopped in the doorway when he saw the two Carsons standing next to each other. "Dude, what's going on?"

Towel Carson slumped down on the sofa and grabbed the remote. "Whatever you do, don't say 'I told you so.' "

"I told you so," David said automatically, then, "Dude!"

"Now what?" asked original Carson, settling on the other side of the couch from towel Carson.

Towel Carson shrugged and flicked the Yankees-Red Sox game back on. After a second, David sighed and sat down between the two Carsons on the couch. It sounded as if he muttered under his breath something that sounded suspiciously like, "*One* of them was bad enough." But a bit louder, David suggested, "I could go for a pizza."

"Hey! Me, too! Baby and barbecue sauce? With anchovies?" said original Carson.

Towel Carson raised his eyebrows. "Are you kidding me?"

Original Carson shrugged. "Sure, why not?"

"That's gross," said towel Carson.

"What? It's good." Original Carson tapped his fingers on his thighs.

"*Really?*"

Original Carson laughed. "Just messing around with you. No anchovies."

Towel Carson thought for a moment, then laughed. "Dude, you got me!" At a sudden cheer, he looked up at the TV. The Yanks had struck out. "At least one thing hasn't changed. The Yankees suck, no matter what time period I'm in."

David rolled his eyes as original Carson grinned and high-fived his double.

"Amen to that."

Ten Minutes Past Teatime

Elizabeth Chatsworth

June 12th, AD 1896, 4:10 p.m.
The Irish Sea

MISS MINERVA MINETT WAS RAPIDLY losing faith that her hired sailors were of the highest caliber. Or sober. Or able to obey the simplest commands without discussion, pontification, and an inordinate amount of cheek. She huffed as the unfittingly-named Captain Smart kicked tentatively at her vessel, a twenty-foot-long copper-and-glass goldfish. The submersible swung mere inches above the steamship's deck, caught fast in a net of chains by the *Saucy Sal's* cargo crane.

From his deepening frown, it appeared Smart had not expected to awake from a drunken stupor to find a giant goldfish on his ship. Nor had he anticipated that his first mate would charter the *Sal* to a forty-three-year-old Englishwoman with a fascination for temporal experimentation. He kicked the bug-eyed goldfish once more, then turned to study Minerva's unconventional attire: tweed trousers, a white blouse, a leather over-corset, and a pith helmet strapped with brass goggles. If he had comments to make upon her bizarre dress, he wisely chose to keep them to himself. Perhaps because of the blunderbuss shotgun Minerva held with an unusual familiarity for a lady scientist. "So, what you're saying, Miss Minett, is that you're going to climb into that metal fish alone—"

"Yes."

"And we're going to toss you over the side of the ship—"

"Launch my vessel, yes."

"And on the way down to the waves, you're going to fiddle with them controls—"

"Set the exact time and destination of my journey through the vortex of time and space."

"And you're going to end up—"

"In this area, but a thousand years ago. I will then propel the *Tempus Pisces* toward land, where I shall seek an audience with the monks at the Cell-Ruaid Monastery."

Smart scratched his beak-like nose. "That monastery's been abandoned for eons."

"Hence my need for time travel. The Royal Society for Paranormal Peculiarities has offered membership to any layman who can persuade the monks to create a scroll with specific words. Once completed, the parchment must be buried in the monastery's graveyard. Tomorrow, in a grand ceremony, the Society elders will dig up graves undisturbed for centuries to find the scrolls."

The Captain's jaw dropped faster than any anchor. "Are you telling me there's a club for time traveling grave-robbers?"

"No. There's a club for gentlemen who spend their afternoons drinking brandy and discussing time travel, parallel universes, and the occult. I intend to be the first member to actually achieve temporal fluidity. And the first female member to boot."

"Why would you want to—?"

"To demonstrate to the members, to my condescending older brother, Mortimer, to *all* who insist that women have no place in the scientific ranks, that the female mind is just as capable of ingenious invention as the male mind. Probably more so, given that we consume less brandy per capita and have to work five times as hard to gain access to the same education and opportunities that men take for granted. Why, I had to—"

The Captain groaned. "Oh, my God, a suffragette." He glared at his first mate. "You let a bloody suffragette on board. Didn't I tell you *not* to go trawling for charters down by the library?"

The brawny first mate shrugged. "She seemed normal enough at the time. I thought she wanted to go fishin'. By the time I realized she wanted us to put her *fish in* . . ."

Smart held up his hand. "Spare me. Well, Miss Minett, pardon my manners, but male or female or something else entirely, you're as nutty as a fruitcake to believe you can swim through time in a metal fish. You can't seriously believe—"

"It will work. In theory."

"Aye. A lot works in theory. But flinging a madwoman into the ocean sounds like a good way for me to end up in jail. You'll drown."

"My life, my choice. However, there is a fourteen point eight percent probability that I will revolutionize our scientific understanding of the universe. The proof will be in the pudding. Well, in the grave, at least."

He shook his head. "I don't like it."

"I'm not paying for you to like it. Shall we begin? Or shall I show you how much damage this blunderbuss can do to the things you love?"

The Captain glanced furtively at his first mate, who blushed beetroot red.

Minerva swung her blunderbuss to point at the barrel of rum that stood beside an oak table littered with tankards. The crew had taken advantage of the Captain's incapacitation the night before to borrow his personal keg.

Smart blinked at the keg. "That's not supposed to be up here."

"Do we launch, or do I shoot?"

The Captain tut-tutted. "No need for violence. I barely know you, Miss Minett, but I've identified why you're a spinster miss, not a married missus."

She snorted. "I highly doubt it. Launch or shoot?"

He sighed. "Go on then, you daft mare. We'll try and haul you up before you drown."

"Excellent." She strode across the deck toward the *Tempus* as the ship's crane operator climbed into his cab. The crane's steam engine rumbled into life. Minerva ascended a staircase of packing crates next to her vessel. She stood on the top step, preparing to leap across to the *Tempus*'s open hatch. Nothing traveled through time as reliably as a giant copper goldfish.

In theory.

Minerva eyed the hatch, calculating the kinetic energy required to leap aboard in a single bound. She had no desire to land face-first on the deck before an ever-growing band of onlookers. A dozen sailors now stood around the goldfish, showing various stages of amusement and concern.

Smart said, "You know, miss, you'd be a lot safer throwing your vessel around on dry land—"

She sighed. "Hardly. Dry land means earth, stone, animals. If I stand on the ground as I dematerialize through time, I could rematerialize inside a rock, a tree, or even a surprised cow." She nodded at the *Tempus*. "As you drop my goldfish into the sea, I'll activate my chronetic engine, transporting my vessel back in time and space so I'll fall safely onto the waves, no matter their height. A short paddle east, and I shall encounter the good monks of Cell-Ruaid. Then back to my goldfish, a temporal leap to ten minutes from now, and you should find me bobbing in the sea approximately five hundred feet starboard. Naturally, I will avoid re-materializing directly in the hull of this vessel."

"Well, that's considerate of you, miss."

"Indeed. Are you ready, Captain Smart?"

"No, not really—"

She leapt across to the *Tempus*, squirmed inside to the oohs and ahs of the crew, and slammed the hatch closed.

The Captain shrugged and gestured to his crane operator to proceed. Through the bulging eyes of the goldfish, Minerva watched the sailors back away to safe distance. The fish slowly rose and swung out over gray waves that melted into an overcast sky. Not ideal weather for time travel, but anything short of a squall should not impede her journey.

Her fingers danced across the controls, checking and double-checking her instruments. She set the chronometer to June 12th, AD 996, 4:10 p.m. as her vessel swayed on its chains. A flick of the switch, and the chronetic engine beneath the floor hummed. Anticipating the coming drop, Minerva placed her left hand on the steering wheel, her right on the time lever, bracing herself on the pilot's chair.

Perhaps some sort of safety strap might have been a good idea? One that attached to the chair and fastened over the lap, similar in style to a gentleman's trouser belt. Maybe she could call her new invention the *seatbelt* . . .

The sailors leaned over the side of the ship, keen not to miss a moment of her possible demise. Smart shouted, and the fish dropped.

Her stomach lurched, then . . . BANG!

A nightmare swirl of spectral light. The universe set upon her, tore her apart, built her anew, slurped down her atoms, and spat her out like a bad oyster into the year 996.

The electric light within the *Tempus* flickered between life and death as monstrous black waves seized the vessel, shaking it as a terrier shakes a mouse. Darkness clawed at the windows, winds howled, and pain shot through Minerva's fingers as the steering wheel wrenched from her grasp. She flung herself at the wheel, wrestling for control as her goldfish writhed and tossed in the tidal maelstrom. She locked her body against the wheel's force, leaning back, praying to a god she didn't believe in as the fish almost bellied up, almost sank like a stone, almost . . .

The cabin shuddered and groaned, torn between the outside forces and Minerva's will. She swore as her favorite teapot smashed onto the riveted floor behind her, and dozens of leather-bound history tomes tumbled off the bookshelves. Her library-inspired décor had been designed to provide a pleasant research setting should she find herself adrift in time.

But perhaps interior padding would have been a more suitable complement to the *seatbelt* she didn't have?

A dive to the depths was an option, but her experiments in the River Thames had been fraught with fear that the fish would fail to rise on command. For now, staying atop the waves seemed her best chance of survival. If her dashboard compass was correct, the shore lay a mere two miles ahead.

The fish groaned, and a couple of rivets popped like champagne corks from the interior seams. Sea water sprayed across Minerva's cheek as she engaged the main propulsive drive. The floor rumbled beneath her boots as gas turbines ignited. Had she finally run out of the luck that had kept her alive through laboratory fires, exploding submersibles, and one very public crash in Hyde Park on her prototype flying bicycle? Decades of solitary study, public mockery, and the occasional flash of genius cut short by a watery grave. Would she never walk into the Royal Society with her head held high, accepted as an equal at last?

The *Tempus* lurched from wave to wave like a drunken sailor. She kept her course as best she could, glancing between the compass and the fish's bug-eyed portholes. A black wall of water swelled before her. And then . . .

A golden dragon's head crested the giant wave, eyes staring, jaws gaping, teeth glinting.

Minerva blinked. Her chest clenched, squeezing her heart into a thudding tattoo.

The dragon's long, slender neck broadened into a wide body . . . no, a hull? Good heavens, was that a . . . ?

The longship's bow swept toward her, sail down and oars drawn in. Minerva yanked her wheel hard left, the engine screaming as nature's might tossed her fish at the oncoming beast. Two toy boats, powerless to resist the wrath of the sea.

Mouth dry, Minerva braced for impact. Her teeth shook as the longship's wooden planks smashed against the *Tempus'* reinforced glass portholes. The longship's boards splintered, revealing a single-masted boat with its sail furled, shattered rowing benches, and sailors clad in furs and leather scrambling to escape her goldfish's attack.

Minerva slammed her engine into reverse. The *Tempus* wrenched itself away from the dragon, allowing the sea to rush in through the broken boards to claim its prize. As waves battered her vessel, Minerva watched, horrified, as the longship began to sink.

Alfhild held tight her sister's son as titanic waves smashed over the side of the foundering longship. Dreng's skin was almost blue from the cold, his left arm bloodied and limp against her leather breastplate. The thirteen-year-old's blond hair hung in rattails as Alfhild barked orders at the warriors struggling to plug the gaping hole in the ship's hull with sacks of plundered grain. A far cry from the riches she'd promised them.

She bit her tongue to stop herself from cursing the gods. What had she done to anger them? Did she not follow the sacrificial rites correctly? Were her gifts not pleasing? Had she not lived her life, putting her clan first, her honor next, and her happiness last of all? Two dead husbands, one dead wife, and a string of stillborn babes had left her dried and ready to die.

But not like this.

Lightning flashed, once more revealing the giant copper beast that circled their ship, impervious to the axes and spears thrown at its metal skin. Alfhild narrowed her eyes at the shining horror. Was it sent by the sea goddess *Rán* to drag them to her sunken lair? For Alfhild's warriors—twelve men, three women, one boy—there could be no worse fate. Their deaths should come on a battlefield, stained with their enemy's blood, the sound of axes clashing upon shields in their ears, the smell of victory close at hand. The *Valkyries* would lead them to Odin's hall, *Valhalla*, or Freya's great warship, the *Fólkvangr*. In hall and ship, the warriors would feast until *Ragnarök*, when the gods died and man would be reborn.

But not if *Rán* the sea-witch claimed them first.

Dreng strained to turn and watch the copper fish. Alfhild clutched him tighter with her left arm, releasing her right to draw her throwing axe from her belt. Maybe her axe would be the one that took down the creature. Maybe if she hit one of its glowing eyes . . .

Dreng gazed up at her, his blue eyes shadowed with pain. "That's a good way to lose your best axe, Auntie."

She snorted. "I've taken the head off a snake at fifty paces with this axe."

"That's no snake."

He wasn't wrong. Too clever for his own good, Dreng had been nicknamed *Loki's son* by the clan elders. Nicknames meant glory or an early death. Usually both.

Alfhild sighed. She tucked the axe back into her belt a split second before a colossal wave smashed against the starboard hull. Water exploded through the hull breach, sending her men and the sacks of grain flying. The deck lurched, swamped beneath the influx of seawater. Rowing benches disappeared beneath the waves, and the deck tilted toward its doom.

Dreng half-laughed, half-sobbed. "We're dead, aren't we?"

She nodded. "Aye, so it seems. But be cheered. I've heard *Rán* provides the finest feast for those who drown bravely."

He scrunched his nose. "Seafood?"

"The finest haddock you'll ever taste."

The boy groaned. Alfhild buried her face in his matted hair and prayed to Freya.

Lightning flashed, and a boom of thunder shook the world. *Rán*'s waves reached for the Norsemen, hungry to devour their souls. Beyond the broken hull, the copper sea-beast approached, light glowing from its orb eyes. The warriors cried out prayers and curses in equal measure as the creature shot out a missile. A metal claw attached to a chain soared across the space between them. The claw grasped the dragon's head that decorated the ship's stern. The copper fish turned into the waves, tightening the chain and dragging the wreck in its wake.

Alfhild squinted. Beyond the beast, a distant light flickered in the darkness. Could it be a shore beacon, lit to guide home fishermen caught in the storm?

The copper beast swam on through the crashing waves, drawing the ship toward the light.

Was the monster foe or friend?

Minerva steered the *Tempus* for the shore, choosing a landing point a half-mile west of the coastal beacon. There was no need to frighten the local Irishmen with her anachronistic vessel. She suspected that many tales of sea monsters could be traced to incursions by delinquent temporal tourists. She shuddered to think that the Nordic sailors she towed might, at this very moment, be composing a tawdry sea shanty starring her giant copper goldfish.

Minerva hummed tunelessly as she engaged the secondary thrusters. What would they rhyme with goldfish? Swish? Dish? Ugh. So much for remaining inconspicuous as she traveled into the past. Hopefully, her collision with the longship would have no impact upon her own timeline. In theory, if she so much as stepped on a butterfly, its death might alter her future reality in a million different ways.

She made a mental note to avoid all butterflies.

The waves lessened in ferocity as she drew closer to the shore. The rain ceased, and the barest sliver of sunlight pierced the dark clouds above. According to her chronometer, it was now six p.m. on a Dark-Age Sunday. A rocky beach, shadowed by steep granite cliffs, reared ahead. The depth counter ticked down . . . ninety feet, fifty, thirty, twenty. Minerva released the grappling hook from the ship behind her. Hopefully, the Nordic sailors could swim the final few feet to shore without her assistance.

She had her own landing to deal with.

She stood, knowing full well that the top of her pith helmet would stop short of the curved copper roof by exactly six inches. A squirt of liquid rubber from her trusty Mosborough Multipurpose Gum Gun sealed the leaking rivets. She tucked the gum gun into the custom holster on her utility belt, swung on her expedition backpack, and poured additional buckshot into the flared barrel of her blunderbuss shotgun.

Now, she was ready for anything the century outside could throw at her.

In theory.

Minerva clasped the submersible's recall transmitter bracelet around her wrist and opened the ceiling hatch.

A bedraggled, flaxen-haired woman with piercing blue eyes glowered down at her. She raised her axe in what could surely not be a polite greeting.

Minerva smiled sweetly and said in her best Icelandic, "*Góður dagur!*"

The blonde frowned and lowered her axe. "*Wes hāl,*" she replied in Anglo-Saxon.

Aha! That was *hello*, spoken in the common trading tongue of the Western Isles.

Excellent. Minerva's long winter nights spent listening to the British Museum's wax cylinder recordings of ancient languages was about to pay off. How lucky this disheveled woman was a seafarer. Those who traveled the world, whether by sea or time, knew the benefits of being able to converse with fellow travelers.

Minerva switched to Anglo-Saxon. "I apologize for the damage to your vessel. It was an accident. May I introduce myself?"

Curiosity seemed to overcome the woman's desire for violence. She sat back on her haunches, laid the axe across her knees, and nodded.

"I'm Miss Minerva Minett, of the Hyde Park Minetts. And you are?"

Head tilted, the sailor studied Minerva from head to toe, as scholars study exotic beasts at the London Zoo. Yet it was she who would surely prove to be a greater draw than any lion or tiger. Her tooled leather breastplate, cinched over a sea-green tunic and deerskin trousers, would thrill Victorian spectators. As would her dragon-engraved axe, and the wolfskin cloak that draped from her broad shoulders. A silver *torc* encircled her neck, perhaps an indicator of high rank?

If so, the rank may have been hard-won. Blue knotwork tattoos adorned the woman's calloused hands and sinewy forearms. Faded silver scars traced across her tanned cheeks. Her left earlobe appeared to have been gnawed off in some long-ago brawl, and thick blonde braids framed her chiseled cheekbones and a strong jaw. Not a conventional beauty perhaps, but striking.

The woman scratched her chin. "Minerva the wise, from the sagas of the Romans? Your magic fish has taken you a long way from home, goddess." She thumped her leather breastplate. "Know that I am bound to Freya. I owe you no sacrifice."

Minerva's eyebrows raised. "Umm, I . . . that is, well, good. I'm not really in the mood for sacrifices at the moment. One gets so tired of them, Miss . . .?"

"Alfhild Hrafnkelsdóttir," the sailor said, "Commander of the *Gulldreki*."

"*Gold dragon*? What a fitting name for what was surely a fine ship. Well, it's a pleasure to meet you, Captain Hrafnkelsdóttir." Minerva dropped into a curtsey, made somewhat awkward by the tweed trousers and the loaded blunderbuss.

A ghost of a smile played across the sailor's full lips. "Alfhild."

Minerva smiled. "Thank you, that's a little easier to pronounce. I'm so sorry that we didn't meet in more pleasant circumstances. Our unfortunate collision has surely rendered your vessel—"

Alfhild poked her head down into the *Tempus* and surveyed the book-strewn interior. She appeared spectacularly unimpressed by the cutting-edge technology within.

Minerva continued, "—far beyond all hope of repair. May I offer my deepest—"

The woman snorted, pulled back from view, and disappeared overboard with a loud splash.

Well! What appalling manners! Clearly Alfhild had never attended finishing school.

There again, neither had she.

Minerva pushed aside the books littering the floor to reveal a three-foot-wide levitation disc. She twiddled the controls on her recall bracelet and stepped to the center of the copper circle. Bolts released, and the disc ascended. Minerva soared up through the hatch, swooped along the goldfish's spine, and dropped to hover a foot above the gray, choppy waves. Before her, a rocky beach was strewn with lounging Norsemen, recovering from their shipwreck. The remains of the *Gulldreki* stuck up from the seabed like rotten teeth fifty yards east.

Guilt racked Minerva's insides. If she hadn't run into the longship . . .

Recompense was clearly in order.

She floated the disc toward the beach, drawing the Norsemen and women to a slack-jawed stand. Captain Alfhild helped a bloodied boy to his feet, his arm strapped to his chest with leather bindings. A victim of the collision?

Minerva swallowed hard and stepped off the disc onto the pebbles. A flick of a switch on her bracelet, and the disc shot back toward the *Tempus* and entered through the hatch. The hatch slammed closed, and the copper fish's engine hummed. It reversed straight back, as no normal fish ever could, sinking slowly beneath the waves until it could be seen no more.

The Norsemen drew their axes.

If there was one thing that Minerva had learned from reading the travel tales of English explorers, it was that they never let foreigners see them sweat. She strode confidently toward Alfhild and her bloodied charge, keeping her chin high and her spine ramrod straight within her leather corset. The sailors watched her, their eyes darting between Minerva and Alfhild, waiting for a sign of threat or weakness.

Minerva gave neither. She reached into her utility belt and drew out a squishy magenta gel pack. Except for a second pack she'd left in her steamship cabin in 1896, this was the sole prototype of her universal cure-all, the Pink Poultice of Panacea.

Alfhild's eyes narrowed, and her hand moved toward her axe.

"Captain, I cannot repair your ship. But I can repair your shipmate. Allow me to administer this medicine, and your colleague shall be returned to full health within hours. I guarantee his full—"

Before she could blink, Alfhild had shot behind her, grabbing her throat with a calloused hand, hot breath warming her right ear. The blade of the axe pressed against her neck, cold, sharp, unforgiving.

"—recovery." Minerva froze, staring directly into the blue eyes of the swaying boy. Blood darkened his makeshift bandage, and his jaw was firmly set against the pain. He stared at Minerva, at the pink pack in her hand, and a wry smile lit up his filthy face. In Icelandic, he said, "So, Auntie, this is the goddess who saved us from *Rán*?"

Alfhild grunted. "She says she's Minerva, a Roman deity."

"Not a local goddess, then? Shame. I hear the Irish had mighty powerful goddesses before the Christians drove them away with their hymns and liturgies."

Minerva held her breath. One false move, and the axe would sever her carotid artery. She suppressed her fear, staring at the boy with what she hoped was defiance. Hadn't she and Alfhild shared a moment of connection on the submersible? A hint of a smile, the exchange of names, it had all been so civilized. How could the sailor suddenly turn so . . . feral?

The boy held out his good arm. "Let her go, Auntie. I'll take a wandering goddess' magic over this pain."

Auntie. The wild woman was defending her sister's child. A laudable action, though terrifying in its execution.

The axe blade lifted from her neck. Alfhild whispered, "Can you really save him, goddess? His wound has grown sick, and his days grow short."

"I'll do everything in my power. I promise."

Alfhild released her. Minerva felt her back chill without the sailor's embrace. She turned to face Alfhild, whose eyes were clouded with hope and despair. She must surely love this boy like her own son.

Minerva's heart ached for her pain.

The boy cleared his throat. "Ummm, goddess Minerva, if you're not too busy . . . this wound isn't healing itself."

Minerva flushed, and she turned away from Alfhild. "My apologies, master. . . ?"

He tilted up his chin. "Dreng *Lokisson*."

This proud declaration raised a ripple of laughter from the sailors. Minerva nodded.

"Right, young fellow-me-lad. I'll need you to take off your shirt and lie on the sand. This will only take a minute. Ten, if it works correctly."

He gaped. "What do you mean, *if*?"

An hour later, Alfhild stroked the hair from Dreng's forehead. The pulsing, pink blob on his shoulder had eaten his pain and grown new skin over his ragged wound.

"It took longer than ten minutes," grumbled Dreng.

Alfhild snorted. "It was faster than a slow death from evil spirits. They were inside your wound, Dreng, gnawing away at your strength." She kept her eyes on Minerva, who sat alone on a rock beneath the cliff face, drawing pictures in a leather-bound book.

Dreng followed her gaze. "She's an odd bird, your goddess."

"Immortals aren't like you and me. They live by their own rules."

"That fish of hers, anything inside?"

"Nothing useful. No weapons, no food. Just bound pages like those she draws in."

"Books?" Dreng's eyes lit up. Ever since a captured English monk had taught him to read and write, he'd been obsessed with all things written and carved.

"Not for you, *Lokisson*. You get in enough mischief without adding more learning to the mix. Your mother should never have let you read the philosophers. Aristotle can only lead to heartbreak. I told her so at the time."

"I could teach you to read."

"I read the weather and what's in men's hearts. I don't need anything more."

Dreng nodded toward Minerva. "And what do you think is in her heart, Auntie? Or rather, *who*?"

Alfhild's chest tightened. "How should I know?"

"I think you know. She keeps glancing over at you."

"She does not."

"She does too."

Alfhild studied Minerva, who caught her stare, and blushed.

Dreng snickered. "Hah. Why don't you talk to her? See if she'd like to work her magic on you? That heart of yours could use a healing touch."

Alfhild pursed her lips. "If you're well enough to spout nonsense, you're well enough to walk. Come on, we need to find shelter before the night rolls in."

"Will you carry me?"

Alfhild snorted and rose to her feet. She shouted, "Everybody up. Time to greet the locals."

The crew laughed, each tapping their axe blades and drawing the symbol of Odin or Freya in the air.

As the warriors stood and stretched, Alfhild noted Minerva kept her head down, oblivious to the movement before her. She approached the goddess stealthily, curious to see her artwork. The deity had stuffed her pages into her backpack whenever Alfhild's crew members had approached. It seemed a more cunning approach was needed.

Alfhild swung wide and slipped along the cliff face as silent as a ghost. She crept up behind Minerva and peered over her shoulder. There, sketched in charcoal, she saw her own portrait, smiling. Her hair tumbled as wild and free as a sea nymph's, cascading over bare shoulders and breasts.

Minerva squealed and clutched the sketchbook to her ample bosom. "Don't look."

"Let me see."

Minerva shook her head. "It's not finished."

"I see I'm not wearing anything."

"It's art. You don't need to be."

Alfhild ran her hand along her thick, unkempt braids. When had she last combed out her hair? Six months ago? A year? "You draw everyone you meet?"

"I draw people and things that interest me. My sketchbook is a record of everything unusual I encounter. It's my personal history, laid bare. It's not something I readily share."

"Not ever?"

"Not for a very long time."

Alfhild tugged at her remaining earlobe. "Seems a crime not to share such a wondrous talent."

Their eyes met. This time, it was Alfhild who looked away.

Minerva smiled. "Perhaps later tonight. I assume you're heading for the monastery?"

Alfhild blinked.

"You know, Cell-Ruaid Monastery? According to my travel compass, it should be no more than fifteen minutes' walk along the beach, just around the headland. Records indicate there was—is—a small fishing village there that supplies the monks with fresh fish. I assume it was their beacon that guided us to shore."

"A monastery, with monks? Robes, crosses, incense, that kind of thing?"

"And a superb group of calligraphers who produce the finest scrolls south of Dublin. I intend to purchase one."

Alfhild looked at Minerva's backpack with new interest. "With gold?"

"With a trade. An assortment of religious artifacts in exchange for a simple scroll. One would imagine monks have no interest in earthly treasures such as gold."

Alfhild chuckled. "You haven't met many monks, have you?"

"Well, no. Not one, to be honest."

Alfhild straightened her posture. "Goddess, you saved Dreng's life, and I am indebted. I swear now before Freya, Lady of the Vanir, that I'll help you get your scroll or die trying."

Minerva's eyes widened. "Oh, I'm sure dying won't be necessary."

Alfhild drew the symbol of Freya in the air. "We'll see."

Minerva, compass in hand, led the way toward Cell-Ruaid. Burdened by her backpack, she slipped and slid on the slick rocks. Alfhild followed on her heels, as close and silent as a shadow. It was still light, but within the hour, night would shroud the land and make the journey far more treacherous.

Minerva rounded the headland, spying the flaming beacon that had guided them when the sky was dark with storm clouds. Four men in tattered gray cloaks sat cross-legged beside the fire, passing around a wineskin and laughing. A double-masted ocean *curach*, a hybrid of the skin-covered and plank-built boats favored by the Irish, was moored besides six smaller cousins in a wide, pebbled bay. Thatched, mud-walled cottages, a dozen or so, dotted the steep cliffside. A winding track led up to the top of the cliff, where the square bell tower of Cell-Ruaid protruded from a gray stone barn-turned-monastery. It was hardly the most impressive place of worship on the Irish coast, but had achieved fame for both its calligraphers and the rosy dawns and sunsets that painted the tower red against the sullen sky.

"We don't want to alarm them," said Minerva over her shoulder. "Perhaps I should go and greet them alone, to inform them that we are here to purchase a scroll, not to—"

Alfhild sprinted by her, axe raised, her crew drawn behind her like a cloak.

Minerva gasped. "Wait, what are you—"

The Norse raced along the beach, bearing down on the oblivious Irishmen.

Dreng appeared at her side. "Don't worry. They'll be fine."

"What are they—?"

"Our main goal is to secure the ship. Most likely still got its last catch aboard. Plenty of fish to see us home." His eyes were fixed on the compass in her hand. "May I see your pretty bauble?"

Aghast by the sailors' charge, Minerva absently handed him the compass. "But . . . I mean, they're not, you're not—"

The Norsemen reached the beacon. Before the Irishmen could call out for help, Alfhild and her crew expertly thumped them unconscious.

"—you're not *Vikings*, are you?"

Dreng turned the compass over in his hand. "No. What are Vikings?"

"Well, for want of a better word, pirates."

"Oh. Well then, yes, we're pirates. What did you think the axes were for, chopping fish?"

Minerva bit her lip. "I thought maybe for cutting ropes. I'm not well-versed in nautical ways. Oh, dear. I never intended—"

Dreng sniffed. "We won't kill 'em unless they fight. There's no honor in slaying cowards. Let their own Gods punish them for their weakness."

"Kill? Heavens. This is *so* much worse than stepping on a butterfly."

The Norse ran into the cottages, driving out the inhabitants to join their comatose comrades. Alfhild and two men raced up the track toward the monastery, as quick as greyhounds set upon a hare.

Minerva temples throbbed. "Should I try and stop them?"

"With magic?"

Minerva glanced down at the boy. "I'm not an actual goddess, you know. I'm something even better. A scientist."

His eyes lit up. "Like Pythagoras?"

"I suppose, minus the beard."

He grinned. "I read the tale of Agnodice, the ancient Greek physician. She was the reason the Greeks changed their laws to allow female doctors."

"Then it seems the Athenians were more civilized than my own countrymen. In my world, women are merely chattel in the eyes of the law, forced to depend on male relatives for allowances and small freedoms. It's just not fair!"

An Irishman burst out of a cottage holding a sea bass he'd apparently been skinning. Minerva winced as a Norse woman snatched the fish from him and slapped him across the face with it.

"He should have brought the skinning knife," Dreng noted sagely. "Though it wouldn't have done him any good. These folks aren't warriors."

A dozen Irish men, women, and children had now been herded to the beacon. They cringed upon the pebbles, crossing their chests and clutching one another.

Minerva murmured, "This is terrible."

A sly grin crept over Dreng's face. "Maybe your copper beast could help you cast a friendship spell? Make all the Irish happy to see us, thrilled to share their winter stores with the Norse?"

Minerva glanced down at her recall bracelet. "I don't think so. It's merely a transport. A scientific wonder, perhaps, but not magic."

Dreng eyed the bracelet curiously. Minerva frowned and tugged down her lace sleeve, hiding the copper band from view. "Speaking of friendship spells, you're being awfully sociable, Dreng, for a pirate."

The boy pointed to his healed shoulder. "You helped me, I help you. You're one of us now. An auntie, like Alfhild, without the blood tie. My auntie, the goddess-scientist."

Two Norse women climbed onto the *curach* and tested the rigging as their clanmates cast booty from the cottages into the ship. To Minerva's relief, the Vikings showed no interest in further harming the villagers.

Dreng said in a serious tone, "If it makes you feel any better, we're doing these people a favor. From now on, they'll keep watch for attacks from the sea. Not all Norse are so kind to their prisoners."

"You should tell them so. I'm sure they'll be overflowing with gratitude." With that, Minerva tightened the straps on her backpack and set off on the long walk up to the monastery.

Dreng and the crew followed her, cheerfully herding their prisoners while composing a jaunty shanty.

Minerva cocked her head. Surely, she didn't hear the word *goldfish* in the chorus?

" . . . *Minerva's Magic Goldfish. Answers every sailor's wish . . . "*

Oh, dear.

Three hours later, Alfhild checked the rope binding a monk's wrists and gave him a gentle shove back to his fellow prisoners huddled in the monastery's great hall. The former barn was lit with tallow reed lamps made with pig fat, and the smoky scent of roasting pork made her belly rumble.

Dreng brought her over a hunk of bread and spit-cooked cod. "You're always the last to eat, Auntie."

"I'm stronger than the rest."

"Aye, that you are." He flopped beside her as she sat upon a wooden bench. She chomped down on the buttered bread, counting the prisoners. The village had sheltered ten women, five children, and sixteen men. The monks added eight men more, one blind, one deaf. An easy target for her crew. Not one of the villagers had put up a fight, which both pleased and disappointed her. She hadn't lost any warriors, whose strong arms she'd need to guide the stolen *curach* home, but then again, her axe had not sung a song of blood to Freya. Their good fortune at finding this settlement could surely not last without some sort of sacrifice.

"Thirsty?" Dreng pulled a swollen wineskin from his belt. "The monks say it's blessed, not for us 'heathens.' Want some?"

She took the wineskin and drank the blackberry-and-grape blend. "I've had better." The monks muttered to their neighbors, but none dared look her in the eye.

"Dull lot, aren't they?" said Dreng, playing with a metal bauble in his hand. "You know, Minerva might appreciate a little wine. She's stretched tighter than a drumskin. If we're to set sail at dawn, you've got plenty of time to share a drink and a laugh. Might help you both relax."

"You tryin' to play matchmaker?"

"What if I am? You deserve a few hours of pleasure. I've barely seen you smile the last three winters."

"Maybe your constant troublemaking took away my smile."

He grinned. "Hah. I just add a little excitement to everyone's day. Imagine how boring life would be without me?"

"Spoken like a true *Loki's son*."

"I wear the name as a badge of honor. Why are you still sitting here? Don't you have a goddess to charm?"

Alfhild swigged down the full-bodied wine, ignoring the monks' glares.

Now, what exactly could she say to charm a goddess?

Minerva sat on an oak desk in the scriptorium, a former hayshed, as Brother Fergal put the finishing touches on her scroll.

". . . And I really am most dreadfully sorry about the, well, hostage situation. I'm assured that the Norse will be setting off at first light, and no one will be harmed."

The stout, red-haired monk glowered at her. "Your heathen friends are taking all our stores."

"Not all. They're leaving you a month's worth of dried fish. There's plenty of time for you to restock before winter."

"They're also taking our biggest ship."

"But you have smaller ones that will surely suffice until you raise the funds to build another. As I said, these relics I brought you— Saint Crispin's finger, four shards of the holy cross blessed by the pope in Rome, an illumination of the Virgin Mary—"

"Which seems to be a copy of my original design."

"Well, it's a very popular likeness where I come from."

"Which is where?"

"Umm . . . never mind. Are we done?"

The monk held up the parchment scroll, blowing gently on the inked letters. "There's your message."

"Good." Minerva rummaged inside her backpack, and drew out a lead-lined tin. "Please place it in here. I need you to bury this box in the third grave from the southern corner of your graveyard. Don't worry, you only need to dig down for a foot or so."

Fergal blinked at her. "And why should I desecrate our dead?"

A woman's voice growled from the doorway, "Because I'll hang you from the rafters by your guts if you don't."

"Alfhild!" Minerva beamed at the tall Viking. "How goes your . . . salvage expedition?"

"They don't have much to take. But it's enough to keep my crew happy." She walked over to Fergal, who leaned back on his stool, wide-eyed and pale. "And you want to keep my crew happy, don't you, monk?"

He nodded.

"So, take the nice lady's box and put it where she says."

The monk held his hand over his heart. "I swear by Almighty God it shall be done."

Minerva breathed a sigh of relief. "Thank you, Brother Fergal. That's most kind of you. Once the tin is buried, please hurry back. I have further questions about your calligraphy technique."

Alfhild said, "Yes, hurry back here, Fergal, or your robe-clad brothers will be making the long voyage back to *Sogn Fyord* as our slaves."

Fergal gasped and sprinted out the door, scroll and tin in hand.

"But, Alfhild, you wouldn't really—"

"Nah. Too much trouble. I don't need surly monks bringing down the crew's spirits. They've soared since Dreng found the Abbot's stash of valuables. Crosses, goblets, you name it!"

"Oh dear, surely you're not taking . . ."

"Red wine?" Alfhild held out a bulging wineskin.

"Umm, well, I don't normally imbibe alcohol."

"Then maybe it's time for a change."

Maybe it was.

Minerva took the wineskin, removed the cork, and pressed the horn mouth to her open lips. Fruity warmth raced down her throat and burned across her chest. "My, that's quite strong, isn't it?"

"It gets better the more you drink."

Minerva tipped back her head and gulped. "Is this a Beaujolais?"

Alfhild shrugged. "You want to go see the Abbot's cell? Seems he doesn't care to sleep on a simple reed mat like his fellow monks. He's got a feather-stuffed mattress and a wolfskin blanket."

"Ummm, well, I've never seen a wolfskin blanket. It sounds—"

Alfhild leant in and planted a soft kiss on Minerva's lips.

"—intriguing," said Minerva, with a smile.

Minerva awoke to the sound of distant horns, trumpeting an off-tune melody. She lifted her head from Alfhild's shoulder. The Viking's blonde hair flowed over her gently rising chest, coaxed from its braids and combed to silk by Minerva. She'd sung songs as she worked, silly vaudeville tunes, a half-forgotten aria.

She'd never felt so free.

Alfhild told her tales of the fjords, of cruel gods, and long-lost loves.

And they'd kissed.

It was delicious. Dangerous. Divine. Alfhild was the true goddess, not she.

Or maybe they both were?

It was a thesis she would have to explore in more detail. For the sake of science.

The horns grew closer. A bell tolled once, twice.

Alfhild flicked open her eyes and leapt to her feet in one feline movement. She dragged on her tunic and breastplate, trousers and boots, as Minerva blinked and reached for her bloomers. "Stay here," the Viking commanded.

"Not likely," said Minerva, buttoning her lace blouse. She stopped, staring at her bare wrist where the submersible's recall bracelet should be.

But . . . she'd had it on last night, even throughout her passionate embrace with . . .

Alfhild was gone, racing out into the night with her axe in her hand.

Two leather wineskins lay empty on the floor.

Two? She thought they'd shared only one. How had the second arrive?

Someone appeared in the doorway. There stood Dreng, panting, a bulging burlap sack slung over his shoulder. "We've got to get down to the ship. Some shifty monk took off in the night and raised the militia from a nearby town. There must be sixty of them, armed to the teeth, and hungry for blood. Our best warriors are holding them off so the rest of us can scarper. At least one of us has to get home to tell our tales."

"I can't recall Brother Fergal returning from the graveyard. He must have . . . oh, that devil! And he swore he would bury my . . ."

The room spun like a kaleidoscope. She half-sat, half-collapsed onto the bed. The scroll didn't matter now that her bracelet was gone.

She was never getting home.

Heaven help her.

The next few moments were a blur. She rose, numbly pulling on her remaining clothes. Dreng was hardly a traditional lady's maid, but he did a good job lacing up her leather corset.

"Nice armor," he said, testing the leather with the point of his knife. "Should come in handy as we head for the ship."

"I'm not going to the ship." Minerva picked up her blunderbuss. "Show me to the battle."

Alfhild swept through the militia's ranks like a whirlwind, hacking, punching, and kicking. Her axe sang its song to Freya, glinting in the dawn light as *Dellingr*'s fiery chariot burned away the stars. A trance-like serenity wrapped her in a silken shroud. She danced, laughing, with the dead of decades past. Her children, never grown, clutched at her tunic, striking out with tiny fists as her enemies closed in. The sky dripped with blood, the earth claimed the dead, and a chorus of *Valkyries* sang her name. "*Alfhild, Alfhild . . .*"

It was a good death.

And yet . . .

Amidst the blood and the gore and the shrieks of the fallen . . .

A vision of Minerva. Dark hair tumbling. Brown eyes shining. Smooth, perfect skin unmarred by blade or sun. Her laugh, tinkling like a spring set free from glacial ice.

Their time was over.

Goodbye, my goddess.

The *Valkyries'* song swelled. "*Alfhild, Alfhild . . .*"

"Auntie!" Dreng screamed.

A thunderous boom. A sea of soldiers rippled before her. Warriors fell, howling with pain.

There stood Minerva, black smoke curling from her long metal stick.

"I'm out of buckshot," she shouted, waving the stick. "A retreat might be in order."

A deep cut above Alfhild's left eye poured hot blood down her cheek. She wiped it away with swollen knuckles, bones grating in broken fingers. Dreng picked his way over the wounded men, whacking several with his laden sack as they clawed at his legs. The remaining combatants backed away, muttering of witchcraft and drawing the sign of the cross.

Four Norse lay dead amongst twenty or more foes. Grim smiles twisted their faces.

The *Valkyries* had sung their names.

Freya was kind.

Minerva tucked her metal stick under her arm and drew a strange device from her belt. She shook it at the militia. "Gentlemen, don't make me use my Mosborough

Multipurpose Gum Gun for violence and mayhem. I warn you, its burns can be quite horrific."

Dreng grasped Alfhild's bloodied arm. "To the ship, Auntie."

The *Valkyries* sang a new song. "*To the ship, to the ship, to the ship . . .*"

The *Fólkvangr* awaited her.

The ship of the dead.

Drops of seawater from the *curach's* oars splashed across Minerva's cheeks, adding to the tears that dripped off her chin onto Alfhild's broken body. The Viking's blue eyes were shuttered, her head cradled in Minerva's lap. She rested on a blanket in the bottom of the ship, surrounded by dried fish, sacks of grain, gold goblets, and silver chalices.

Only the faint rise and fall of her breastplate confirmed that Alfhild yet lived.

Minerva wiped her lover's face with a lace handkerchief and sobbed until her tears ran dry.

Eight Norsemen rowed on, with no jaunty song to lift their hearts. Their ragged breaths were lost in the wind as Dreng and three Norse women unfurled the skin sails.

The sails caught the breeze, and the ship surged out to sea.

Dreng crouched beside Minerva, staring at his fallen aunt. "She's leaving us?"

Minerva nodded, stroking Alfhild's golden hair. "Her blood is on my hands. I sank the *Gulldreki*. I led you to the monastery. I distracted her as the monk escaped. I may as well have struck her down myself."

Dreng placed his hand on her shoulder. She shrugged it off. "Don't. She was everything I didn't deserve. Brave, selfless . . ."

Kind. Beneath her warrior exterior, she'd been extremely kind. Gentle, even.

And funny.

Minerva's heart ached for what might have been. The places they wouldn't see, the moments they wouldn't share. She wiped her eyes on her sleeve. "Damn my arrogance. She'll die because I had to prove myself to a world that couldn't care less. I'm a monster."

"No auntie of mine is a monster. A goddess, maybe. Perhaps a goddess with a healing touch?"

She shook her head. "I don't have another Pink Poultice of Panacea with me. Your shoulder took my only supply."

"With you? You have more?"

"Back in my cabin, a thousand years from now. Without my vessel, I'm shipwrecked here. Cast adrift in time and—"

"Might this help?" Dreng pushed up his tunic sleeve. Her copper transmitter bracelet encircled his grubby forearm.

"How on earth did you—?"

"I found it. In the Abbot's cell."

"No, you didn't. The floor was bare."

"Then I found it outside, in the mud."

"You took it off my arm while I slept!"

He shrugged. "We'll never know for sure."

"You know!"

"Do you want it? Or not?"

"Well, yes. But . . ."

He clasped the bracelet onto her wrist. "Freya can wait. I put my faith in the goddess of science."

She blinked. "You don't understand who I am."

"Of course I do." He grinned. "You're my second favorite auntie in the whole wide world."

Alfhild drifted from a dream of battle into the soft embrace of a feather bed. Her body tingled, but didn't ache as it usually did upon stirring. She flexed her fingers. No broken bones. She opened her eyes to darkness and gingerly lifted her head. No pain shot down her spine.

Being dead felt better than she'd expected.

She reached out her left hand, brushing her fingers against a cold metal wall. Waves crashed outside, the air tasted of salt, and her bed gently swayed. She was on a ship.

Of course she was.

The *Fólkvangr*.

High up in the wall, a round portal was open to the night sky. Dark clouds obscured the moon until *Mani's* silver chariot burst through, and the moon god cast light onto the world. His divine luminescence revealed the full glory of her afterlife.

She was in a metal room strewn with books and clothes.

And a goddess dozed in a chair beside her.

Minerva.

Alfhild grinned and stretched to stroke her lover's cheek. Minerva awoke, her eyes bright in the moonlight. "Alfhild! You're awake! Oh, my goodness, it worked! I didn't know if it would. I had to dilute the Pink Poultice to cover all your wounds. There were so many, Alfhild. I thought I would lose you forever. I deserved no less. I'm so sorry for everything. It's all my fault—"

Alfhild swung her legs to sit on the edge of the bed. She leaned over to Minerva and kissed her with a passion that left them both breathless.

"Wait." Minerva pulled away, her cheeks pinker than any poultice. "Later. You need to recuperate, gather your strength."

Alfhild flexed her biceps. "I feel like I'm twenty years old."

Minerva laughed. "You look it! The Poultice healed your old scars. And your tattoos. Sorry about that. It's unfortunate about your earlobe. Perhaps if a body part is removed, it can't be replaced."

"It's all right. I wasn't using it." She reached for Minerva's breasts.

The goddess wriggled away, batting at her hands playfully. "Behave. You don't understand what I've done."

"I'm sure I've done far worse."

A shadow crossed Minerva's face. "Have you ever upset the natural order of the universe?"

"I've had my moments."

"Seriously, listen. This may not make sense to you right now, but I'll do my best to explain. I'm a time traveler."

"All right."

She blinked. "What? That doesn't shock you?"

Alfhild shrugged. "Nothing shocks me anymore. The world is full of gods and magic. Anything is possible. So, if you say you can travel in time, so be it."

"That's . . . well, right now, that's quite a helpful worldview. In brief, my giant goldfish is my time ship. Dreng stole my 'magic' bracelet and boarded her. He stole every one of my science and history books. That sack he was carrying around was stuffed with the collective knowledge of a thousand years."

"Did he now? He's a light-fingered devil. Always has been." Alfhild's belly grumbled for attention. She rubbed her stomach. "Doesn't the afterlife hold massive feasts with unlimited mead?"

"I have a few slices of fruitcake in my trunk. Hold on." Minerva stood and went to a large leather trunk at the rear of the room. She lit a candle and searched within. "I'm sorry my cabin's such a mess. I've been trying to figure out all the changes before returning to dry land. It seems when Dreng Lokisson became the first Emperor of Europe—"

"He what now?" Alfhild shook her head. "Oh, that boy, nothing but mischief. Him and his books."

"Him and *my* books, to be exact. He used the knowledge in my library to build a vast Nordic Empire that rules the world to this day. The Norman invasion? Never happened. The War of the Roses? Didn't occur." She brought over a slice of cake. "Here, you'll love this."

She did. "Beer to wash it down?"

"I can put on a pot of tea. Or maybe we should open a bottle of champagne? We either have to celebrate or drown our sorrows. I'm not sure which."

"Let's drink while we decide."

Minerva went and drew a green bottle out of the trunk. "I brought this on board to make a toast in case my temporal experiment proved successful. I'll pop the . . ."

A projectile exploded into the ceiling. Alfhild's hand flew to her axe.

It wasn't on her hip.

"Oops. Sorry," said Minerva. "Your axe is in the trunk, with your clothes, cleaned of all the . . . well, cleaned."

The skirmish. It was time for the difficult question. "Am I dead?"

"What? No. Not even slightly, despite your best efforts."

Huh. Freya must have an even greater battle planned for her.

Alfhild chuckled.

Minerva handed her the bottle. "Bottoms up. I don't have any glasses."

Alfhild took a hearty gulp. It tasted almost as good as mead.

She passed the bottle to Minerva, who swigged like a pirate. "So, we're celebrating the fact that yesterday, the Royal Society for Paranormal Peculiarities dug up my scroll from the abandoned graveyard at Cell-Ruaid Monastery. It seems that wretched monk *did* bury my tin before running off to fetch the militia. I'm now officially a member of the Society."

No matter what nonsense words Minerva used, just hearing the joy in her voice made Alfhild's heart swell. "That's good."

"But here's the thing. I'm not the first woman member. There have been women in science for centuries. Women and men are seen as equals, Alfhild. Equals!"

"Why wouldn't they be?"

"Ah, yes. Your clan had ideas ahead of its time as regards equal rights for the sexes. Dreng passed on the teachings of your people. Women can vote and stand for office in the Danelaw Assembly. We can be teachers, doctors, and astronomers. No one raises an eyebrow to a woman speaking her mind."

"I should damn well hope not."

Minerva handled back the bottle. "Many things have stayed the same. But the place names are different, there are dragons carved into every form of architecture, and Queen Victoria has been replaced by Emperor Sven Lokisson the Thirteenth. Your great-great-great—"

"Nephew?" Alfhild groaned. "Not another one. Is that the sorrow part?"

"No. The sorrow part is that I've created an entirely new reality. Where does that leave me, morally? The world seems prosperous and peaceful. No one is starving. The arts and science are revered. But am I morally obligated to try and put things back the way they were?"

"And ruin Dreng's fun? He'd never forgive you."

"Then I can live this life? Here, with you?"

Alfhild leaned in kissed her champagne lips. "Can you think of a better way to spend your time?"

"I honestly can't."

"Then let's toast." Alfhild raised the bottle. "To time. Goddess of second chances."

"May she always show us what truly matters. To time."

And in a realm between now, then, and forever, a forgotten deity smiled.

The Service Call

Edward Ahern

"WELCOME TO DO OVER. *WE reset you.*"

"I just killed my wife."

"That's what we're here for, sir. My name is Pradeep. But first, your name, member number, and password please."

Bryce had already taken the card out of his wallet. "Bryce Keeler, 47A23C2N, putupon."

"Thank you. Yes, sir, I have your informations here. I notice that you currently have our basic membership. I'd like to tell you about the benefits of our advanced 'No Regrets' level—"

Bryce felt himself shaking. "No, stop! I got a real problem here. And speak more clearly, please. I'm having a hard time understanding you."

"No problem, sir, I am trained to clearly speak. But, please, to tell me of your problem."

Bryce keyed the video on his phone and pointed it at Dora, who lay belly-down across a coffee table. The slug had torn a large hole in her back, and blood dripped down from the table top, staining a white carpet.

"I couldn't take it anymore. It was her screaming at me again, ripping me up. But I only meant to scare her. The gun just fired. It's been almost five minutes now. I only have ten minutes more to reset things on my Orange watch and bring her back."

"Yes, that appears exceedingly messy. And you are so correct, sir. The Orange can only reverse your prior fifteen minutes. But you still have plenty of time. Just please to be pushing the reset button."

"No! No! I already did that. Nothing happened. Help!"

"Ah, sir, please to turn off the watch, wait five seconds, and turn it back on."

Bryce's voice got shriller. "I already did that, twice! It didn't work."

The cell phone went silent for several seconds. "Mr. Keeler. Would it be permissible to call you Bryce?"

"Yes, yes, damn it, what can I do?"

"Ah, Mr. Bryce, I am not receiving a signal from your watch. It would appear to not be functional. I have attempted to restart it from here, but without success. It would appear that you do not have recourse."

"But it's an Orange watch, it's guaranteed!"

"Let me please recheck. But Mr. Bryce, sir, have you perhaps poked or prodded her to ensure that she is not still living?"

"God help me! She's got a hole right through her, and her stomach is all over the wall. Don't ask foolish questions. Oh, hell, sorry."

"Not to be sorry. Mr. Bryce, we understand these little moments of life stress."

Bryce paced back and forth, skirting the parts of the floor splattered with blood. "You have to help me!"

"Ah, Mr. Bryce. Sir. You should perhaps have taken the 'No Regrets' option when you subscribed. I see that the limited warranty on your basic membership expired as of last month. Unfortunately, we at Do Over are no longer responsible for watch replacement, nor for indemnifying your acts of carnage. You may wish to dial 9-1-1 when we are finished.

"Or, should you go into hiding, we can offer you a reduced rate on a new and much improved watch."

"Jesus, you can't leave me like this! There must be something, some way to get my wife back. Please, you have to help me."

There was another several seconds of silence on the phone. "I have just turned off my recorder. There is a remedy I have seen on YouTube. But it is highly irregular."

"What? I'll do anything."

"Do Over does not approve of this procedure, and I will deny that it was ever suggested."

"Please!"

"To remove your watch and place it in your microwave."

"What?"

"Remove the watch, Mr. Bryce, place it in your microwave and set the timer for fifteen seconds on high."

"What?"

"The watch may explode, in which case we are not responsible for damage to your microwave. If it does not explode, you have thirty seconds to remove the watch, place it again on your wrist, and to touch the reset button. There is a slight chance you will be electrocuted, but then that may be your outcome in any case."

"And that will bring me back in time?"

"Nothing is certain in this life, Mr. Bryce, but I certainly hope so, for your sake. Oh, and if you are able to reset, please remove immediately the watch. It is known to violently explode fifteen minutes later, causing accidental death. Good luck. I have erased your call, there is no record of it."

The phone went dead. Bryce held it to his ear for another two seconds, then ran to the microwave and tossed his watch in. He set time and power, begged for mercy, and pushed start. Sparks crackled, but the watch held together.

Bryce pulled the Orange out, strapped it on, and screamed when the back seared his skin. Ignoring the pain, he ran back into the living room and punched reset . . .

And he was reaching into an end table drawer to take out his gun, while Dora was screaming at him, "You worthless turd, why don't you die, so I can move on! And what are you going to do with that gun, you ball-less coward?"

He shut the drawer without touching the gun and turned to her. Dora kept screaming. Bryce knew he had to do something, but he didn't want to go to jail. When Dora paused for breath, he said, "You're right, Dora, I'm sorry."

The words choked him, but he continued. "We were so good together, let's try and start over. Look, I'll make a peace offering."

He unstrapped the Orange. "Take my watch, please. You've always wanted to try it. I promise you'll have a unique experience."

107

Misconception

Gabi Coatsworth

MARCIA LAY ON A LOUNGER along the shady side of the pool with the latest copy of *People* magazine. She'd almost finished the gin and tonic she'd carried out with her. Through half-closed lids, she could see the sparkle of sun on water as a light breeze caressed her skin and then the pool itself. She was reading an article about a film star who'd given up hope of having a baby of her own, and so had recently adopted a baby boy. Minutes later, the magazine slid off Marcia's lap onto the hot concrete paving.

Her mind drifted as she thought about the life the celebrity child would have. It was so much easier these days. No one cared if a single woman raised a child by herself. Marcia was never sure she'd been right to give up her own newborn son, but her father had made it clear that, if she didn't, her life would be ruined. So would the child's. She wondered sometimes about the people who'd given him a home, though she didn't try to find out. Knowing might have been too painful, and her feelings for her baby had been tamped down for so many years that now only fear of exposure survived.

She'd been a few days past her seventeenth birthday when she and Frank became engaged in 1977, twenty-two years earlier. Before he went abroad on a one-year assignment, he'd given her a ring—the diamond solitaire catching the sunlight on her left hand now. She'd agreed they would marry when he returned, though she hadn't been quite sure he was the one.

That party. She'd regretted going almost immediately. She'd had too much to drink, and flirted with Peter Schultz, the handsome quarterback she'd had a crush on at school. He'd seemed so charming, though some girls had warned her he was trouble. She should have listened.

She wound up in a bedroom, with nothing but hazy memories of protesting, being slapped, then held down, then . . . her mind went blank. Just that one time. That one, fateful, time.

All she knew was that after, she felt broken, and too weak to fight either him or what came later.

She missed a couple of periods and realized, with a sense of nausea that might not have been due to her condition, that she was pregnant. Her father, a rigid pro-lifer, wouldn't countenance an abortion, and sent her away to her aunt, insisting the baby be put up for adoption. When her fiancé came home, she played the happy bride people expected. After all, if anyone found out, no one would ever marry her. That's how it used to be back then.

The only way to put her son's birth behind her had been to let him go. She believed her parents when they said the son of a single mother would never stand a chance. She'd be shunned, and so would he. So what she did was best for the baby, too. She had to keep his existence safely in the past, where her husband wouldn't find out. Frank might forgive a lot, but never a lie of that magnitude.

They never had children. Frank blamed her; she had no way to explain why that couldn't be her fault, so she remained silent. He wouldn't even discuss adoption, and she felt the universe was punishing her for having let her own baby go to someone else. She wondered, occasionally, what her child looked like now. Was he blond, like her? Did he manage to do what she'd never done—stand up for himself? Was he happy?

Was that the doorbell? Sliding her feet into the sandals she'd kicked off outside, she walked through the cool house to answer it. She opened the door and took a step back, a feeling of nausea washing over her as she recognized the man standing there.

What the hell was Peter doing on her doorstep? Had she conjured him up? How had he found her after so long?

She shook her head to clear it. There must be some mistake. Of course this couldn't be him. He'd be her age now, and this guy was much too young. Surely it wasn't . . .

Marcia brought the visitor into focus again. He was a carbon copy of Peter, with his father's dark good looks—so there could be no mistake. She swayed slightly on her feet, still unwilling to believe it.

"I'm your son, Troy," he said, and waited for her response. He even had his father's colorless voice, and she shivered involuntarily.

His handsome face was pale and his cold eyes seemed somewhat unfocused. Was he sober? She couldn't read his expression, though she imagined, if he were to smile, he might be as hard to resist as his feckless dad. She hoped he was less callous. They stood, silently staring at each other for a moment, as succeeding emotions surged through her. Curiosity. Anxiety. Fear.

She was struggling to feel something maternal for this familiar-looking stranger. She wished she could, but confused questions buzzed in her head, along with a sense of dismay, because she felt nothing for him. Only as if a rock had settled in her stomach.

What if Frank found out? He was away on a business trip, thank God, but he'd be back tomorrow. He would never accept this. It might even be grounds for divorce.

He must not find out.

"Come in," she said, grasping Troy's arm and almost pulling him into the hallway. This wasn't the kind of neighborhood where strangers walked up to people's houses. If her neighbors saw him, they'd wonder—and gossip. Maybe she could talk to him for a minute and he'd leave.

The social graces her mother had instilled in her took over. Taking a deep breath to steady herself, she indicated a chair and began to behave like any hostess.

"Won't you take a seat?"

He raised an eyebrow but didn't resist.

"So—your name is Troy?" Marcia tried to smile.

"It's what my parents called me."

Parents. Of course. She ought to ask about them. Something was preventing her from forming clear thoughts. She must concentrate.

"They've been kind to you?"

"Kinder than some."

Marcia sensed an accusation hanging in the air. He was right, of course. *They* hadn't given him away.

"Have you had a decent life?" Her voice sounded stilted even to her.

"Not as decent as this one," he said, studying the room as if appraising the expensive antiques and Oriental rugs. He stared at the swimming pool through the glass that formed one complete wall.

"Well, yes . . ." She didn't know what to say. Materially, she'd done well, as her parents often reminded her. The fact that she felt trapped in her marriage was her own fault. She'd always been too weak.

She needed to steer the conversation elsewhere.

"So why have you come?" This was the crux of it. What did he want from her? What could she give him?

"To see you. Get to know you a little. Ask you . . ."

She could guess what he wanted to know.

"Why I gave you up?" Her heart stopped beating for a moment, and she sank farther into the white leather sofa, unmarked by any childish fingerprints. He said nothing.

"I . . ." She hesitated. She owed him an explanation, at least. "I was too young, and promised to someone else. I made a mistake . . ."

He interrupted her, his face hard.

"And he married you anyway?"

112

"He never knew." Why had she said that? It was one thing to tell the truth at last, and another to expose herself to being judged.

"He still your husband?"

She nodded, biting her lower lip.

"I can see why you'd want to hang onto him. This setup must be worth a pretty penny. Looks like he keeps you in style."

Marcia thought she'd recovered from the shame, but now it was seeping back. She lifted her head to look at him. This wasn't how she'd visualized such an encounter. His voice had a distinct edge to it. Was that just his manner? Or was he trying to frighten her? She shivered.

"I'm guessing it'd be worth something to keep your dirty little secret quiet." He jerked a thumb toward his chest. "What do you reckon it would take, huh?"

She could understand he might be angry. She'd heard adopted kids sometimes were. But he wasn't trying to blackmail her, was he? She rejected the thought.

Though she tried to sound casual, her voice came out as a croak. "You're not my dirty . . ."

He interrupted again, impatient.

"Oh, I think you might be glad to keep me out of the picture. I don't think hubby would be too thrilled to be financing me, do you?"

What did he mean? He wasn't Frank's responsibility.

"Financing you? Like through college?"

He laughed. It was an unpleasant sound.

"Nah. I'm thinking a little something to make my life easier right now." He stood and picked up a crystal decanter from the end table, holding it up to the light.

"Nice vase," he said. Then he dropped it.

Marcia flinched as she saw it shatter. The shards winked at her as a sunbeam danced across them. This was all so wrong. She had to do something.

"Say, a thousand bucks?"

A thousand. Could she manage that? If he told Frank, that upright church-going citizen, her marriage would be over. And then what?

"Each month."

"No!" The word escaped her mouth before she had time to think.

"Really? I thought, being my real mother and all, you'd agree. After all, what have you ever given me? Don't you think you owe me?"

Did she? She'd only done what her father wanted her to do. Troy had said his parents had given him a good life. Yet his voice made her shiver, and the rock under her heart turned to ice.

"Don't you? Owe me?" His tone reminded her of Peter's that night.

A drop of sweat rolled down her back.

"Well, yes, I suppose so, but I can't . . ."

In a matter of seconds, he was standing in front of her, and his hand was twisting her hair into a knot, jerking her head back. She felt herself falling before she passed out.

She was fighting for air when she came to in an unfamiliar room. As her breath slowed down, she could hear a murmur of voices nearby, punctuated by the occasional shriek of laughter.

Where was she? Who were these people? She couldn't make anyone out in the dim light.

The smoke cleared a little and there stood Peter, twenty years old, laying siege to a blonde girl in a scarlet dress, leaning into her. Marcia felt a little nauseous. How had she ended up back here again? She stared at her hand, which was gripping a glass of something. She sniffed and wrinkled her nose as the unmistakable tang of vodka and orange juice brought back memories; it had been her favorite tipple until that night.

Peter glanced in her direction and smiled.

Whatever happened, she mustn't respond. She turned her head away, hoping he wouldn't recognize her. The blonde was laughing at something he'd said. If she stayed out of their way, maybe he'd end up with that girl. And maybe that girl would find him easier to resist. All Marcia had to do was keep very still—blend into the background. She thought about leaving right now. But she had to be sure Red Dress had distracted him. She'd wait a few more minutes.

Peter was grabbing the girl's hand and making his way up the stairs. Marcia allowed herself a sigh of relief. She began to relax; she'd be all right now. That girl looked like she could take care of herself. Marcia scanned her surroundings for someone to talk to, but couldn't catch anyone's eye. She sipped at her cocktail, determined not to let it go to her head this time. It didn't taste so bad, after all. Although she *was* feeling a little lightheaded. Not drunk, precisely, just somewhat detached from her surroundings.

Then all her senses were on alert. She sat up straight and checked her watch. Ten minutes had gone by, and there, coming downstairs ahead of the blonde, was Peter. The girl, with the look of a rabbit who'd barely survived an encounter with a hawk, followed several steps behind. Unmistakably a teenager, face flushed, hair tousled. Her eye makeup had run, leaving her looking like a raccoon. She wasn't laughing now, poor thing. And her fire-red dress was torn.

Exactly like the one Marcia had thrown away the day after the party.

But no. It couldn't be. Marcia gasped and stared, horrified, at her seventeen-year-old self. An acid taste rose in her throat. She shook her head. This wasn't right. If the girl was Marcia, then who was she?

"Hi, honey."

She started. Who was this? Against the sun, now lower in the sky, the face of the man in front of her was hard to make out. He leaned down and kissed her forehead.

Frank. She could smell his familiar aftershave. Her eyes fell on the broken glass which had contained her drink. She must have let it drop when she fell asleep.

Had she been dreaming? Was she safe?

"I came back early to surprise you," said her husband.

So everything was okay. Thank God.

"Just as well I did," he went on. "I found a young man on the doorstep, asking for you. He's waiting inside."

Shifting

P.M. Ray

ONCE UPON A TIME, THERE was a young prince named Baqir. He lived in a land called Al-Andalus and its ruler was his older brother, Rashid.

One spring morning, Hussam came to visit him. Baqir was sitting in a garden smoking a pipe and reading a book under an orange tree. "Baqir," Hussam called, his voice loud and clear as a Nafir signaling the charge, "it's too fine a day to waste. Come, call for your horse, lance, and bow, and let's go boar hunting."

Baqir set down his pipe and greeted his friend with a kiss on each cheek. "I am weary today, Hussam, and should rest." He turned to his slave-physician and said, "Is that not so, Fulke?"

Fulke stepped away from the two and bowed, keeping his head down as he spoke. "My apologies, prince. I thought the

117

sunlight and the orange blossoms would cure your melancholy. Vigorous exercise should get your spleen to rid itself of excess black bile and bring balance to your humors."

Baqir cuffed him. "Nonsense, my weariness is not some vulgar organ malfunction. It is of the spirit and far beyond your ken. Stop prattling and go." Fulke masked his rage with a tight smile, bowed, and left.

Baqir turned back to Hussam and, with a languid yawn, said, "I have come to the realization that there is nothing great left to accomplish in this land. The notion vexes me."

"You have your health and can look forward to a long life."

"Anybody can say that."

"Brothers of an Amir can't. They only look forward to a red silk cord from the executioner. Allah has blessed you with a gift that you should appreciate."

Baqir set his pipe down on the bench of yellow marble and said with a wave of his hand, "Yes, yes, praise be to Allah, blessed be his name, blessings on my brother, and so forth."

Hussam's mouth quirked. He picked up the pipe, sniffed, then sat down, setting the pipe out of reach from Baqir. "All right, what is it?"

Baqir heaved a sigh. "We live in a dull land at a dull time, doing dull things for dull people."

Hussam nodded. "Next time get rid of all those repetitions of 'dull.' It's a bit much."

Baqir snorted, nodded at his book. "Now, that was a heroic time."

Hussam leaned in. "It's some foreign script."

"Latin. It's a Christian history of Al-Andalus."

"Now you need to read Christian books? You read too much. I prefer talking. When a man says something stupid, I tell him he's an idiot. When I read something stupid, I can't tell the author he's an idiot, so it annoys me, and I think too much."

Baqir flipped to a well-worn page, where there was an illustration of a woman standing proudly, her long, wavy, dark hair draped like a chador over her nude figure. She was menaced by sword-carrying men with crosses on their surcoats.

Hussam nodded. "I have never seen a book with pictures. It's forbidden."

"Christians. Those blasphemers show feeble images of mankind, when the only true artist of a man is Allah."

"Still, I admire their feeble efforts," Hussam said as he stared at the illustration of the nude woman.

"It is a picture of the death of Wallada Al-Tulayfulah."

"Who?"

"She was a princess and the most beautiful woman in the land. In my poetry, I describe her as flowering toadflax blooming in rocky soil, while . . ."

"Toadflax?" Hussam interrupted.

"It needs tweaking, but it's a good metaphor. Like the flower, she bloomed during harsh times, right before the coming of peace to this land."

Hussam pursed his lips at that, but Baqir continued, too busy to notice.

"Long ago, before we had finished conquering Al-Andalus, there was only a small Christian kingdom left in the mountains in the Northwest, ruled by a lord named Pelagius. When invaded, he refused to give combat. Instead he hid in the mountains and harried the invaders until, exhausted and out of food, they had to leave."

119

Hussam grunted, "I have hunted there. It would be nigh impossible to corner him and force battle."

"Eventually the Amirs squabbled amongst themselves and gave up. For a while, it seemed like the Christians would keep that one small part of Al-Andalus. Then Pelagius' soldiers killed Wallada. When word of her death spread, angry Mullahs preached in every Mosque throughout the land. Shamed, the Amirs rallied and defeated Pelagius, although it took a decade to do so. And that is just one example of how much more exciting and glorious the past was."

"Well, I was going to wait until we were hunting to bring this up, but if you are bored, I have a cure far better than hashish and books. Your brother is sending an army north to fight the Franks under General Shakr. I am sure if you ask, your brother will let us join them."

"Shakr? I want glory. All he ever talks about is logistics, drilling men, and needing enough money to support the army on campaign."

"But you can still win glory. If anything, it would be more obvious."

"I will consider your idea more, but not today."

Hussam left, and Baqir spent the rest of the day in the garden.

The following morning, Baqir woke up with a headache and an idea. He sent for Fulke and demanded, "That Jewish adept who we heard last month. Where is he?"

"Which adept, my prince? There were several learned men here last month and I didn't notice you listening to any of them."

Baqir slapped Fulke. "Imbecile. The one the Jews censured and expelled from their temple."

Fulke sent men out, and after three days, they found the adept.

Baqir asked him, "You said that everything is one picture: past, present, future, North, South, East, and West. They are all one?"

"Yes, prince."

"So if I can go North, could I not also travel to the past?"

"Anything is possible, certainly, but it is not practical."

"But you said it is so. Did you lie?"

The adept shifted from foot to foot.

"Well?"

"Prince, it is said that if you turn something so that it becomes the opposite of what it is, it would travel back in time. Adepts have spent years trying to understand this mystery. The problem is too complex for a single man to solve in a lifetime. To apply . . ."

Baqir interrupted, "Then many men will do it in less than a lifetime." Baqir turned to Fulke. "Let my brother Rashid know I wish to speak with him."

Rashid agreed that in one week he would meet with Baqir. During that week, Fulke and the adept worked out a plan for how to study time travel. On the seventh day, Fulke summarized the plan in a scroll, along with a list for the Amir of what would be needed for the plan. Baqir carefully read the scroll three times to be sure he understood it.

Afterwards, Baqir went and spoke to his brother. After Baqir left, the chief advisor, who had also listened to Baqir, said, "You should have had him strangled with a silken cord."

"I promised our mother," said Rashid.

The advisor started to speak, but Rashid raised a finger. "No, I gave her my word. Besides, he is . . ." Rashid shrugged, "harmless."

"He's a fool. Somebody is using him."

"Nevertheless, 'Paradise lies at the feet of our mothers,' and I will not kill him unless there is no other choice."

The advisor picked up the list, started to read it, and snorted. "Ridiculous. Castrate him and send him to Egypt. The Sultan would keep him as a favor."

"Not yet. If you get me proof he is more than a foolish dreamer, I will reconsider."

The advisor said, "There is a way. He has a friend named Hussam. Hussam seems to be one of those big and stupid types. We can order him to talk with Baqir about this and try to get him to betray himself while you secretly listen. If Hussam warns him, or doesn't try to get Baqir to admit to treason, we will kill them both. If Baqir betrays himself, then we reward Hussam and kill Baqir."

"What if he really wants to study time travel?"

The advisor chuckled. "Then I advise you to let him do it in some remote place far away from here."

Rashid summoned Hussam and ordered him to trick Baqir. For a moment, Hussam did not speak. He took a deep breath. "His heart is true. But he often says things that are," he breathed out, "impolitic." Hussam looked at Rashid, "If he says something careless, as one might say while drunk to a friend, you will not hold that against him?"

"Of course not."

"If you see he is loyal, will you will let us go North to fight against the Franks? It would give him something to do and get him away from here."

Rashid studied Hussam. "If he is loyal, he may ride with General Shakr and have you as his aide. He could learn the ways of war and become a valuable servant for me. It will not happen, though. He will say he wants to go, but will have excuses for why he can't. When that comes to pass, you may serve General Shakr instead."

So Baqir and Hussam met again in the garden, while Rashid hid nearby to listen. They talked for a while and finally Hussam made himself say, "Your brother is a good man, but I think you're smarter than him."

Baqir shrugged. "Yes, but his animal-like cunning serves him well."

Hussam twitched. "There are some who whisper that you would be a better ruler. Idle gossip, surely. But I can see why some might say that."

"Bah, morons. Who would want to rule? He starts his day with trade routes, treaties, and tariffs. He listens to bloviating ministers trying to undermine each other so they can get ahead. I would sooner throw myself from the tallest tower of the palace than be Amir."

Hussam beamed at those words.

Baqir smiled back. "Enough of that, my friend. We should talk about our adventure!"

Hussam looked around, then leaned forward and said, "You will talk with Rashid about going to fight the Franks?"

"Of course not."

Hussam sat back.

"We will find our adventure in the past."

"What are you talking about?"

"It is possible to go back and rescue Wallada. And marry her. With her by my side, I would unify Al-Andalus a century before it happened the first time."

"Somebody has been feeding you dreams to flatter you."

"No, I will gather the best adepts to do this, and it will happen. It might take a few years, but it will happen."

Hussam thought for a while, then said, "I don't understand. If you change the past, how can we be here now, knowing the past as it was, but will no longer be?"

Baqir laughed. "Sophistry. Don't worry about such things. Just help me figure out how to persuade Rashid to let us do this."

Hussam said sadly, "I will help you. But, afterwards, well, we'll see."

Later that day, a messenger from the chief advisor informed Baqir he was being given a manor house in the countryside and a stipend to support the project. Delighted, he sent his own messenger to Hussam, but Hussam had already gone north with General Shakr.

Baqir built a place of learning and gathered together many adepts of strange and mystic arts. But he could not get the adepts to work together. They argued about trivial matters. Frustrated, Baqir angrily berated them, to no avail. Baqir then had one of the most argumentative adepts whipped. But instead of making the adept more docile, he left. Baqir then put Fulke in charge of the adepts. After all, Fulke was a clever man, even if he didn't have a poetic soul like Baqir. And while Baqir couldn't risk losing more adepts by beating them, he could now have their leader beaten, which was surely even better.

Working together, the adepts discovered a way to turn something inside out. Much to their dismay, they discovered that turning a living creature inside out killed it. They tried to solve this problem in many different ways, but all they had to show for it were piles of fragmented insects and rodents.

Meanwhile, Hussam served General Shakr, fighting against the Franks. He did so well that he was promoted to lead a tulb of twenty Ghazi warriors. The campaign ended after three years and Hussam returned home to see Baqir.

Baqir said, "I am glad you did well. Though I wish you could have stayed with me. It is dull with nothing but those bickering scholars and servants to keep me company."

Hussam replied, "Then join me. Fulke is overseeing the project now. There are tales of a strange land over the ocean far to the west with men who do not look like us and riches beyond measure. Your brother has made me an admiral and is giving me a fleet to go find this land. Think of it, a new land to discover. Surely that is an adventure worthy enough for you."

Baqir shook his head. "Fulke needs me. He is just a cheap trickster. Like a showman controlling a bunch of drunken dancing bears. Listening to them prattle on and on about mystic energy flows and other nonsense about how the cosmos works, to keep them happy." Hussam shook his head in regret and left soon after.

During the next three years, Baqir and his adepts succeeded in finding a way to keep a creature alive by using a cage to protect its essence. Excited, they turned a mouse inside out and watched it go back in time. But there was no way to know if the creature actually lived afterwards. So once again, the adepts all argued and debated fine points of academic detail while Fulke patiently listened.

Meanwhile, Hussam's fleet found land in the west. They discovered exotic plants and animals, people with customs so unbelievable that many at home thought Hussam was jesting. Best of all, Hussam had negotiated a trade alliance with one of the rich kingdoms, which would bring more prosperity to Al-Andalus.

Hussam returned to visit Baqir, "You should join me. Your brother wants me to fight the Christian corsairs from Italy who attack our merchants. Surely that has enough glory and adventure for you."

But Baqir refused because he knew the time traveling cage worked, even if nobody could prove it.

Fulke argued that the adepts should try to build a way for the machine to return back to them in time and test it again with an animal, just to be sure it worked. Baqir thought Fulke was a fool. However, all the adepts who had never agreed on anything before all agreed with Fulke on this. Angry, Baqir relented, though he had Fulke beaten for his impudence. It took a year to add a second set of controls to the cage. They tested the new cage with a rat, which to their horror came back dead. Fulke examined the rat and opined that the rat had frozen. Baqir had Fulke beaten for this latest failure.

The adepts sought to discover what had gone wrong, and after two more years, discovered that sending something back in time also made it move to somewhere very cold. The adepts had many debates on this. One even speculated that maybe it wasn't the object that moved, but the very earth itself. Baqir had this adept whipped for such an outlandish notion. After many more experiments that created a mound of dead rats, they discovered how to compensate so the cage stayed in place.

Meanwhile, Hussam won many great battles at sea and on land. He was so successful that the forces of Al-Andalus conquered the island of Sicily. When Hussam returned home, he went to visit Baqir again.

He said to Baqir, "Come with me. Your brother has made me the Satrap of Sicily, answerable only to him. There are many wise men in Italy. I will build you a place of learning that will house one hundred times the number of scholars you have here."

But Baqir refused, because he was finally going to be able to do something exciting and save Wallada. So Hussam once again left without his friend.

Baqir and his adepts spent the next month preparing the device for the journey and moving north to the village in the middle of an oak-covered mountain where Wallada had been murdered. Baqir decided that Fulke should accompany him back in time and tend to any minor things that needed to be done. When Fulke suggested that maybe a younger man, more suited to the hard life that might be ahead would be a better choice, Baqir slapped him and told him shut up and be ready. In addition to having Fulke study maps and pack enough food and water, Baqir made ready by arming himself with a fine bow, a scimitar, a shield, a simple helmet, and quilted armor. While they packed, a team of adepts set the cage up by a large boulder.

With all their preparations made, he and Fulke entered the cage and engaged the controls to go over 750 years back to the day when the attack happened. During testing, all Baqir had seen from the outside was the cage fade out and disappear. From the inside, while he was experiencing it, it was dark. It was also cold, so cold it felt like his skin was starting to swell. The cage was moving impossibly fast. While, objectively, it was probably only a second or two of cold darkness and vertigo, it felt much longer.

Once Baqir recovered his balance, he looked around. It

was hard to see much because of all the oak trees. They were still on the mountain and the large boulder was still there. But there was no path and no village. He looked at Fulke, who shrugged.

"The village must be from after this time."

"Idiot, why didn't you know this?" Baqir got ready to take a swing at Fulke when he heard a woman screaming. He ran toward the sound. Fulke, weighed down with all their supplies, ran after him, trying to keep up.

Coming over a ridgeline, he looked down on a path. There was a woman running down that path, a dirty, bedraggled peasant in an embroidered tunic. Three grubby-looking spearmen chased her. Baqir decided that the woman might be able to help him and was far less dangerous than the men, so he strung his bow. He quickly planted arrows point-first into the ground, so he could grab them easily, and waited for a clear shot.

Neither the woman nor her pursuers looked up the slope where Baqir stood. As the woman ran past, Baqir smoothly drew an arrow. Inhaled as he pulled the string. Started his exhale and released. He shot the second and third arrows the same way. As he reached for the fourth, the first arrow had already struck the first man in the chest. The second arrow hit while the other two men looked around, bewildered, and the third man looked up to see Baqir just as the third arrow struck him.

The woman that had been running down the path stopped when she realized she was no longer being chased. She saw him just as Fulke, carrying all their food and supplies, finally caught up,

Baqir ran toward her, taking off his helmet to call out for

her to speak with him. When he was close enough, he noticed that a couple of her front teeth were missing. For an instant she watched him run toward her, then she turned and fled down the mountain.

Baqir careened after her, leaving Fulke behind once again.

After five minutes, Baqir saw the woman was standing in a circle created by a cluster of hovels, excitedly talking to a group of people. Seeing Baqir, she pointed at him. A mob of men, many carrying clubs, axes, or slings, ran up the path toward him. He stopped, waved, and called out to them. They were yelling angrily in a language he didn't recognize. They were not slowing down or looking any friendlier while he waved at them. There were a lot of them.

Baqir turned and ran back up the mountain. Looking ahead, he saw that Fulke had dropped the supplies and was also running away. As Baqir ran, he felt a rock bounce off of his back. He ran faster and saw the traveling cage just ahead. Fulke had already entered the cage and started to set the controls.

Baqir ran into the cage. "Stop! We must find Wallada!"

A stone hit him in the head—bare still from when he had removed his helmet to talk to the peasant girl. The world spun. The last thing he saw, losing consciousness, was Fulke working at the controls.

When Baqir came to, he was chained to a wall, lying on some moldy straw that was the only thing between him and a cold stone floor.

"Fulke!"

Fulke did not come, only a burly man who opened a door a few feet above his head and poked at him with a stick. Baqir tried to speak to the man in Arabic. "Where am I?" The man just poked at him again and shut the door.

A short time later, the burly man came back, accompanied by a Christian priest.

The priest spoke in Latin. "Good afternoon."

Baqir replied, "Do you know who I am? My brother will have you whipped to death for treating me like this!"

The father nodded to the burly man, who opened the door and started hitting Baqir with his stick. Baqir tried to shield himself from the blows.

The burly man stepped back and the father said, "Better. Where are you from?"

"Al-Andalus."

"I will have him beat you again."

"I am telling the truth."

The priest shrugged. "Who is the man that was with you?"

"Fulke, my slave."

"And what religion is he?"

"Christian."

"Good, and where are you from?"

"I told you, I am from Al-Andalus."

The father nodded to the burly man, who started to hit Baqir across the shoulders.

Baqir protected his shoulders with his arms, so the burly man switched to his legs until the priest held up his hand.

"Are you ready to make sense now?"

"I don't understand."

This time the burly man beat Baqir unconscious.

When Baqir came to, it was dark except for some light coming through the open door above him. There were rats eating food from a bowl nearby. He rattled his chain to scare the rats off. The bowl had a meager serving of cooked cabbage that was brown and wilted, and the remains of rat-nibbled brown bread. Revolted, he set the food aside. Eventually, despite the ache from his bruises, he fell back asleep.

Baqir lost track of time. His beard and hair had grown scraggily, and he had been fed at least five times. The priest returned to ask him again where he was from and why he was in this kingdom. Baqir answered truthfully, and the priest had him beaten again for lying

At least ten more feedings went by. Exhausted, Baqir lay in his cell, drifting in and out of consciousness, unable to tell when he had been asleep and dreaming of food or awake and thinking about food. The priest came again and started asking questions. Instead of trying to answer, Baqir just begged the priest to tell him what to say. The priest did not bother to have him beaten again and just left him there without answering.

When Baqir woke up again, there was food. He ate it, any scruples about the taste and smell long past.

After he finished, he heard, "Ah, you are awake." For a moment he assumed he was dreaming because it was in the language of home. "Fulke?"

"Yes, prince."

"Why are you out there?"

"I came to visit you."

"I see that, you donkey turd. Why are you not shackled and a prisoner?"

"I must thank you for that. You told them I was your slave and a Christian. They are Christians, too, so after interrogating me, I was found innocent of any crimes and freed."

"But what about me?"

"I am sorry, my prince. You are accused of being a spy

131

and a sorcerer. The priest who questioned you is investigating these charges."

Shocked, Baqir leaned against the wall for support. "We should be in Al-Andalus. What happened?"

"I engaged the control right before a sling stone smashed it. The cage brought us forward in time, I think." Fulke moved a candle toward the doorway so they could see each other in the dim light. "We had shifted in time and the boulder was still there, but there was no village."

"Then what year is this?"

"We are in the right time. It is year 850 of the Hijra. But we are in a country called Castile and its ruler is Christian and called King Juan II."

"This makes no sense. I am dreaming."

"It does make sense. Once, the Moors ruled this land, except for a small Christian kingdom in the northwest ruled by Pelagius. In their history, his kingdom, known as Asturias, was never conquered. Like the nose of the camel in the tent, it was from there the Christians reconquered most of the land—now there is only a small area in the south ruled by Muslims."

Baqir could think of nothing to say. He lay there, wishing that the ache of his bruises would stop hurting.

"Nobody has ever heard of Wallada Al-Tulayfulah here."

Baqir's head throbbed. "I am tired. Be silent, slave."

Fulke reached down and slapped him, hard. "I am not a slave here, prince." Fulke paused. "For that matter, you are not a prince here."

Angry, Baqir tried to hit Fulke, but the chains stopped him. He shouted and pulled against his restraints.

Fulke started to walk away. He hesitated, stopped, and turned back to face Baqir.

"That woman's tunic had nice embroidery work. I didn't think about it, but none of the men had clothing as fine as hers. Her father might have been the head of a village or even a minor noble. From there . . ." He shrugged. "I have seen a story get exaggerated when it goes from one end of a caravan to another. Who knows what could happen in hundreds of years? Your people never completely won here. I think I know why.

"Congratulations, Baqir. You rescued Wallada."

The Swing

Abhishek Sengupta

PROLOGUE

THE QUIET GIRL IS BREATHING.

He sits beside her on the shore watching her breathe, while she stares away—into the sea and the setting sun. He worships the perfection of her features, wonders if perfection is an anomaly of this universe—a design manufactured on a faltering machine and meant to gainsay the designated order. He's still wondering if her beauty is an exception when she stops.

She stops breathing and turns to him. "In this breath, I hold a thought," she says. "I'll set it free once you can guess what it is."

She smiles at him but doesn't breathe as she approaches the 18th of her deaths with equal calmness.

ACT I

In the crowd that gathers on the shore after her 18th death to watch her perfectly beautiful corpse, there are children. They realize it's a forbidden pleasure, and thus cherish every moment they spend in the warmth of her death. But for her, it's embarrassing. The disgrace of being watched dead. The shame of it. She wants to crumble into herself. But death, among other things, prohibits movement.

And if he were there, The Quiet Girl thinks, he certainly would have cloaked her naked demise with himself.

But where is he, she wonders. He is still supposed to guess the thought stuck in her last breath.

Therefore, she chooses to disobey the tenets set forth by death. She gets up from the sand, shrugs, sweeps the particles off her dress, and addresses the crowd with a straightforward and sincere—"Would you please excuse me?"—asking for passage.

They oblige, although they don't seem comfortable doing so.

She doesn't care. She takes any one of the random streets—each of which leads to his home. She walks gracefully, the children from the shore following her as if she were one of their playthings, as if death had transferred her ownership to them.

She pushes the gate open, marches in, climbs the steps, feeling as if she's more buoyant than the air above. By the time she reaches upstairs, a dizziness encapsulates her—a déjà vu, as if she were revisiting one of her own deaths.

The door to his apartment, as always, is unlocked. The Quiet Girl steps in and spots him sleeping peacefully in the green halo of the nightlight. The hue hurts her eyes.

ACT II

So that he is not disoriented when he awakens, she places one of her reflections inside the mirror—positions her mirror image at the precise angle for the soft haze of the blue streetlight to illuminate it, and then leaves for him to wake in its presence. She silently closes the apartment door behind her so as not to disturb his sleep.

As The Quiet Girl proceeds down the stairs, a familiar feeling returns—of becoming more buoyant than the air above. Then, the fear of soaring through the block of air and reaching the floor she commenced from—of finding the door ajar that she had closed before she left—of finding him sleeping in the green halo of the nightlight. The memory of that hue still stings her eyes.

When she slips off the stairs, it's not an accident, but a deliberate act intended to set her free. The stairs take her down to her 19th death, which is just as casual and unmindful as many that preceded it. Her death down the stairs ensures the disappearance of her discomfort but not of her bloodstains.

Her blood goes nowhere. It lingers in the thin air a few feet away from the steps—steps on which no one shall step for a few more hours. No one shall see her blood metamorphose into the strangest of hues. Perhaps it's the green light in her last thought. A green thought in the last light fills up her eyes—fills up her heart—her belly—her breasts—and fingers, staining her perfection forever.

INTERLUDE

He dreams of waking up.

The valley is dew and nothing else—dew that rests nowhere in particular but is everywhere.

Each dewdrop confines her. He strives to seize one of them to set her free, but it gently slides down his palm. As it does, it slowly metamorphoses into a waterfall of dewdrops, transforming into a green stream gushing in full force. The flow propels her away as The Quiet Girl keeps drowning. Attempting to save her, he jumps into the creek and discovers the water is salty.

Once in the creek, he locates not one but a multitude of Quiet Girls, each as perfect as the other, and discerns she isn't drowning in the stream at all, but into herself, repeatedly—into her own deaths.

He finds it disconcerting. Although he recognises her immediate death, he cannot remember a number with which he would staple that death. He cannot enumerate.

With a start, he wakes in his room illumined with a green nightlight. The first thing he notices is one of her images stuck in the mirror, its arms stretched toward the blue streetlight that pours in through the glass window, trying to hide.

When he directs his electric torch at it, the image attempts to crumble further into itself. The poor thing always finds it tricky to stare at the man behind the source of the yellow torchlight. It wants to escape from this playful invasion by an alien light, but has nowhere to go. A reflected world ranges only as far as the mirror-eyes wander.

Slowly, the torchlight blends with the blue streetlight, creating the green hue, and an old, rusty air of discomfort returns. He wonders if, somehow, she prefers that feeling of discomfort. Perhaps it is acquaintance. Maybe death again. Or perhaps it is a swing between the two, as it has always been.

ACT III

They meet on the swing for the first time in a grey, cloudy dusk that invades their childhood.

After other children run away as the clouds unroll their dark blanket, all that persists in the park is the promise of a storm and the two of them staring at two transparent swings. A zephyr around them orchestrates a music of fright and foreboding; the trees in the park nod in affirmation. He senses the same fear in her eyes that exists in his own.

When fear captures one's heartbeat, it becomes their heartbeat. Suddenly they are not frightened of their fears anymore. They breathe them in. Strange forces. Strong. Unlike the other children, the two of them wait until the storm takes them in.

Two lone swings in the storm. No one sits; only a frenzied wind plays with them. At once, the swings are libertines. Swings that dance in the storm's lap and invent all possible directions they had never known. Those routes that don't exist start calling the two children. They run to the swings; they run through the storm.

While climbing on the swings, they look at each other and smile. It's their first conversation, and it stretches over an hour without a single word spoken, two differing notes of incessant giggling, mingling with each other. The storm transforms into rain, and the rain into a dense fog of droplets through which they can no longer see each other. The tune of two swings going back and forth creates a symphony in the rain. A relentless rain, until their giggling drowns in it, too.

After the storm disappears, the park shrouds itself in darkness and silence. The streetlights churn a shadowy hue into the dark. He gets down from the swing and, through those shadows, reaches out to her on the swing next to him. The Quiet Girl rests in there, in an undisturbed stasis. Disturbing.

She has fallen asleep on the swing, a perfect serenity radiating across her face. He doesn't desire to break her out of her slumber but knows he must. It's night already. He nudges her, but she doesn't answer. She doesn't wake. Nor does she breathe.

The first of her deaths that evening coincides with their first meeting.

ACT IV

The trapeze is a moment of trespass. An extreme form of the swing. The only thing it covers in the dazzling lights is time. It also brings them closer to her 21st death—the most important of them all.

Graduating from the swing and her many deaths in between, he arrives yet again in The Quiet Girl's life inside a circus of multicolored lights. On the trapeze, which is also the only place in the circus they ever meet, he grasps her hands in his and swings. Her tiny hands are cold most of the times—just as impassive as her eyes and her lips. Silent. When he holds her hands while swinging on the perpetual trapeze, it seems her arms are detached from her body. Indifferent. She doesn't stay in her body—is never there inside. A perfect disappearing act. Irreversible.

The name of the process is decay. Bacteria, fungus, and him.

Most of the evenings, he's afraid. He fears the audience will fail to notice her on the trapeze. Lately, the multicolored lights seem to pass through her body. She's becoming transparent, like an empty swing on a stormy dusk.

Most of the evenings, he's afraid. He fears the audience will fail to notice him holding her hand. They would find him clinging onto a piece of nothingness and start laughing.

And most of the evenings while he's afraid, he discovers her independent feet, her cold hands, her impassive lips—all staring at him. She has eyes all over her body. On the swinging trapeze, she stares at him with her entire being.

Her tiny hands are cold most of the time, except for the evening she speaks on the trapeze for the first time, with actual words, while still holding his hands.

"A swing is a staircase of unending. It has no bottom, no crux," she says.

He doesn't bother to decipher the meaning. Now that she's speaking, he wants to ask her something else.

"Who are you?"

The Quiet Girl stares at him, vacuous for a long time, and a time that stretches longer than a long time. Only after watching her unchanging expression with a painful sustenance of eyes not permitted to blink, does he realize the answer she's about to give.

"That's the smallest possible query to the longest answer."

He doesn't know what he's expected to say in return, so stays silent as The Quiet Girl continues.

"I haven't been able to reach the conclusion of that answer myself, but I've always had the beginning. As a child, I used to believe its inception would lead me to the conclusion. But beginnings never lead to an end; they only give birth to newer beginnings.

"As I grew up, I learned to surrender to the beginning itself; there was no escaping from it. Unlike my girlish thoughts of inception as a bridge to the other side of the river, to the conclusion, I soon recognised the beginning as a dark room that I was meant to build around, above and over me to trap myself in, eternally. Though never announced, it was always wanted of me. The day that realisation was complete, I moved on to a greater awareness—that I was no longer a girl but had transformed into a woman."

Woman. Cold hands on the trapeze. Silent sleep on the swing. First smile in a stormy dusk. Last words on the shore. Beginning. Bridge. Swing. Libertine. Blue streetlights. Mirror. Green room. Green creek. Dewdrops. Rain. Quiet girl. Shadows. Children. Her corpse. Thoughts in a breath. His lone brain. Forgetting. Jumbling thoughts. Gobbling words. Too much. Jesus. Alzheimer's. Bacteria. Fungus. Him. Woman.

And words keep lingering, irrespective of who uttered them.

"I know that all of us are immortals. Life and death are as beauty is: in the eye of the beholder. Relative. We don't live forever, neither do we die. The line that divides life and death is threadlike. Delicate. We must overstep it repeatedly as we keep living our death and dying into our lives. Swing."

Her tiny hands are cold most of the times, except for that evening.

That evening, her cold hands grow warm. Burning. And all her eyes catch fire too.

"Independence is a leap of faith," she says before he leaves her hand and lets the freefall take her in its unending arms.

And swing.

EPILOGUE

He dreams of waking up in a dream.

They are sitting on the shore when she points her finger at something inching toward her in the sand. A beautiful insect. The Quiet Woman picks it up, places it in her palm.

He puts his glasses on, then notices there are more insects, and they are crawling all over her body, walking along the contours of her wrinkled skin.

She whispers in his ear, "They're eating through me."

That's when he discerns pieces of her are missing. Bleeding. Like the second-to-last finger of her left hand, the section of her forehead where a sweet wrinkle appears when she's in doubt, her right foot, bits and parts of her lips, a strand of her greying hair, the left corner of her last thoughts.

Thoughts The Quiet Woman wanted him to guess, and he knows why—for she cannot. Alzheimer's won't let her. Alzheimer's won't let him. Their ailment is no different from the years they spent together: sliced and shared. Those years were now more imaginary than they were real. He wonders how many share that gift in common—how many get to rewrite their fading memories—how many see their loved ones die a thousand deaths, and yet return every time.

He looks at her; worships the perfection of her features. Neither age nor forgetting knows to harm those, for she never yields to either of them. She doesn't yield to the pain.

And while the insects keep eating through her, she goes on playing with them, swinging between memory and forgetting.

She goes on.

A Mother's Legacy

Robert Tomaino

ANNA REACHED TOWARD HER MOTHER'S abandoned research, but paused. A thin layer of dust obscured the covers of the notebooks and the folders atop the antique bookcase. Her eyes shifted, scanning the spines of the books on the shelves below—Jules Verne, Madeleine L'Engle, and Octavia Butler. Along with an interest in temporal displacement, she'd inherited her mother's favorite science fiction writers— ironically, her mom had never liked H.G. Wells. She claimed his stories lacked scientific theory.

Anna remembered tearing into the forgotten research after she graduated from Stanford. The work was innovative and daring, but incomplete. Despite her best efforts she couldn't finish what her mom had started. Over time, her zeal ebbed, and the notebooks lay undisturbed on the bookcase.

And then, a few days ago, her mom's former fiancé, Adam Walker, called.

Their brief conversation stirred only vague memories, hazy recollections that were peppered with starkly lucid moments, like the infrequent trips to Ferris Creamery for turtle ice cream, or when she crashed her bicycle and Walker carried her, legs covered in blood, into the emergency room. She remembered his kindness and generosity, but his face drifted on the perimeter of her memory, shifting and indistinct.

She walked over to the grandfather clock in the corner. Her pale face reflected off the glass door. She fidgeted, undoing and redoing her ponytail. She had her mother's auburn hair and wore it long, unlike her mother who always tied it up in a tight bun.

The doorbell cut through the room, shrill and echoing.

She glanced at her phone. *He's early.*

"Hello, Anna," he said when she opened the door. Adam wore a rumpled gray suit that seemed to suggest he had something to sell. Faded brown eyes stared intently at her. He was markedly smaller to grownup Anna than to her six-year-old self, and she met his gaze straight on. He had kept most of his hair, but the thick, curly bush atop his head now sat flat and gray, as if the curls no longer had the strength to roll up into spirals.

"Come in, Mr. Walker." Anna smiled uncomfortably, lacking both the practice and sincerity for the expression.

He shuffled into the room and glanced around. Books lay scattered about, piled haphazardly on chairs, end tables, and the scuffed, hardwood floor. An old dining room table, buried under mounds of paper and bindings, dominated the center of the room. The table's thick oaken legs bore the weight without a problem.

"Thank you for meeting me," Walker said. "I know it's out of the blue." He stood in front of the table next to two mismatched desk chairs, his body sagging as if supporting his own weight was a struggle.

"Please sit down, Mr. Walker." Anna winced as he teetered in front of the chairs.

He remained standing. "I wonder how well you remember me?" he asked softly. Walker looked at her with such familiarity and sadness that Anna hesitated. He noted her expression and withdrew into himself.

She shrugged. "A bit. It was a long time ago."

"Twenty-five years." He walked to the desk chairs and stopped, placing his hand on a backrest.

Anna waited till he looked back at her. "Yes. The year my mom died."

Walker's grip tightened on the backrest. "I'm sorry, Anna."

"Like you said, it was a long time ago."

"Yes, I left. I should have stayed. I should have helped."

Anna was surprised at the apology. Walker didn't owe her anything—then or now. "Why? I wasn't your responsibility."

"Yes, I suppose that's true. It's just that I like to think that if your mother . . . hadn't passed away that you would have, I mean, we could have been like a family."

Anna's back stiffened. Twenty-five years later, and it still affected her. "My mom didn't pass away, Mr. Walker. She was murdered."

He clasped his hands together. "I stand corrected. You're definitely your mother's daughter."

"Am I? If you say so, but I didn't really know my mother."

Walker's face sagged, matching his crumpled suit. "I'm sorry. Of course. You never got the chance."

Anna hesitated.

Walker turned his head, his gaze steady on the corner of the room. "Is that your mother's?" He walked over to the grandfather clock. Tucked into the corner, the clock looked like a steampunk version of an antique with an array of gears and chains in place of the pendulum. The chimes hung interspersed within the little space left.

"Yes, it is." Anna smiled. "I love how it looks, but it doesn't work. I wish I had the money to get it fixed."

Walker smiled for the first time. "You don't remember the trick?" He opened the glass door and reached inside the clock.

"What are you doing?"

"Don't worry. We always had problems with this clock. Your mom and I rigged a solution. There's a suspension spring that would pop off." He fiddled with something inside the clock.

"That should do it," he said as he shut the door. "It won't chime, but at least it'll tell time." His broad smile crumbled when he saw her quiet reaction. "Is something wrong?"

"No," Anna said. "Thank you. It's just I'd always put off fixing that clock. My boyfriend said it'd be too expensive, but it took you just a minute."

"Well, I fixed it as best I could. There's a piece missing."

Anna walked to the clock and Walker pointed out a small, empty, crescent-shaped molding connecting two of the gears.

"Is that why it won't chime?" Anna asked.

"Yes," Walker gave her a sheepish grin. "You snap in the piece, set the time, and turn this small dial here." He pointed next to the empty molding. The copper dial looked insignificant amid all of the larger gears and machinery.

"That's it?"

"Well, yes and no." he said. "Unfortunately, your mother had this clock custom-made. But we also altered it on our own. You'd need someone to design that piece."

"That sounds expensive."

"You never found a crescent-shaped circuit that would connect to the flywheel?"

"Not that I remember, but I wouldn't have known that's what it was for, or what a flywheel was."

He stepped back, assessing the clock again. "Your mother taught you all about this clock," he said. "You really don't remember?"

"I can barely remember *her*." Anna couldn't keep the frustration out of her voice. "I sometimes struggle to remember what she even looks like."

"That's normal, Anna. You were so young."

"I guess it's normal." She stared at the clock. "You know, I had this old, stuffed bunny. My favorite toy. I lost him the night she was killed. I can still remember that bunny right down to his torn ear. But I have trouble remembering my mom's face."

"Reginald." Walker's smile returned.

"Yes. My God, how'd you remember that?"

Walker stammered. "Well. Ah . . . you carried him everywhere. You two were inseparable."

Anna smiled at the memory. "I haven't thought about him in a long time. I looked everywhere for him. I can't believe you remember him."

He shrugged. "Like you said. It's funny what stays in our heads and what doesn't."

The two of them stood silent for a moment. Anna waited, but he appeared reluctant to talk. "I know reminiscing about a stuffed rabbit is not why you're here."

"No, it isn't." He hesitated, as if looking for the right words.

"You said on the phone that you wanted to talk about my mom's research," Anna said. She glanced over to the bookshelf. "Actually, I've been thinking about it a lot lately."

"What do you know of your mom's work?"

"Just that she had a promising career and threw it away chasing a fantasy."

"That's harsh. Your mother was brilliant."

"I realize that. To become a tenured professor in astrophysics, she had to be twice as good and twice as smart as the men. She could have made a real difference."

"Is that why you went into astrophysics? To continue her work?"

Anna frowned. "How do you know what I studied?"

"I Googled you."

"Oh. Well. Maybe at first, but I think my mom's work was a wasted effort. I can't believe she didn't lose her tenure."

Walker smiled awkwardly and hesitated before speaking. "Princeton almost pulled her tenure, actually." He shook his head. "But your mother's work was funded by the government, and Princeton didn't want to lose the money."

"The government funded her work?"

"Absolutely. It wasn't disclosed publicly, but the government had scientists working in your mother's lab. They were very interested in her research."

"I didn't know that," Anna said. She reached back to tug on her ponytail forgetting she had unbraided it. She ran her fingers through her hair instead. "When I went to Stanford, I was given all of her research after . . . afterward. I know Dr. Livet read through it. He told me her ideas were ingenious, but that something was missing. Like a key concept had been removed, leaving a donut hole."

"Did Dr. Livet ever speculate as to what was missing?"

"No. He only said it was like she had figured something out, but never wrote it down. He was frustrated. He tried to get other opinions, but most other scientists concluded that the theory was fundamentally flawed."

Walker snorted. "They were fools."

"Really? I spent years digging through her research. I thought if I could dig deep enough, I'd find the answers. I think my mom was wrong."

"You mother wasn't wrong," Walker said. He paused and looked directly at her. "The reason I'm here is because your mom was right."

"What do you mean?"

"Your mother . . . she . . . she discovered how to travel through time."

Anna blinked. "What?"

"Your mother figured out time travel."

Anna wondered just how crazy Walker was and whether meeting at her home was a mistake. But, as he had spoken, his shoulders had rolled back and he stood taller. He reminded her of the younger version of himself; the hazy memories grew more recognizable. She remembered him standing alongside her mother, always with a smile for her. "That's not possible."

"I know this sounds absurd. But she succeeded."

"I don't . . . What are you talking about?" Anna stepped back slowly, trying to appear unconcerned.

Walker's newfound confidence faltered. He shrank back a little before taking a deep breath. "Please listen to me, Anna. Your mother succeeded. She traveled through time and that is why she was killed."

"That's ridiculous." Anna placed a hand on the wall to steady herself. Walker's words were a stark contrast to his reserved behavior.

He shook his head. He gestured to the desk chairs. "Will you sit down, Anna?"

"No." She tried to keep her voice steady. "I . . . I think you should leave."

"I know what I am saying is upsetting, but please let me finish. I'll go, but I've come a long way."

Anna nodded, but she moved toward the corner of the room, where her golf bag leaned against the china cabinet.

"Your mother revolutionized the world. Her success was one of the most celebrated achievements in history. But we didn't understand the implications. Her discovery led to chaos and ruin."

Anna opened her mouth, but Walker held up his hand.

"You're an astrophysicist. You understand time paradoxes. The ability to go back in time has consequences. We were unprepared for everything that came with your mom's discovery." His breathing became ragged.

Anna tried to maintain her composure. "Mr. Walker, I told you to leave. I don't need to hear this."

"No!" he snapped.

Anna started and stepped back, jostling the golf bag.

"I'm sorry." He held up his hand again. "Please, just let me finish."

Anna's fingers tightened on one of the irons.

"I know what you're thinking. Time travel isn't real, so I must be off my rocker. But time travel was real. It was real before . . ." He paused and took a deep breath. "They went back in time, Anna. They went back in time and killed your mother before she could finish her work."

Anna's legs shook so much she needed to lean against the dark oak cabinet for support.

Walker dropped his gaze. "And the reason I know this is because . . ." He stopped again, his breathing labored. He looked up. "Because I'm responsible. I brought back the man who killed your mother."

Anna pulled the golf bag in front of her. She yanked one of the irons from the bag. "Get out!"

Walker hesitated. "I didn't know what they were planning, Anna. I swear. Please, believe me."

"Get out!" She stepped toward him, brandishing the five iron.

The look of dismay on Walker's face almost made Anna regret her words. Despite the momentary hesitation, her hands remained clutched around the five iron.

"Please, Anna. I've been a coward."

"Out!"

"I can't fix it, Anna, but you can." He walked to the front door, pausing after opening it. "I'm sorry. I'm sorry for everything." He left without looking back.

Anna didn't look up when David entered the apartment. She stood in front of the dining room table. She'd spread her mother's notebooks and papers across the tabletop, but hadn't opened them. Speckles of dust remained dotted along the covers.

He dropped his luggage at the door. "Are you all right?"

"I told you on the phone that I'm fine."

"He didn't come back or call?"

"No. I haven't heard anything more from him."

"You shouldn't have let him in in the first place."

"I don't know. He . . . he just looked so sad. So harmless. I couldn't turn him away." Anna hesitated. She glanced at her mother's research.

David stepped toward the table. He picked up one of the notebooks. "You took her research down. I don't get it."

Anna didn't say anything.

"I've been telling you to pursue your mom's work for years and now this guy shows up rambling about murdering your mom and you take her notes down?"

"It's different." She fiddled with the ring on her index finger. One of the few things she had from her mother. The titanium ring had gold and black dials decorated with Roman numerals. She spun the numbers when deep in thought.

David watched her play with the ring before he spoke. "How's it different?"

Anna ran her finger across one of the folders, leaving a small trail in the dust. "I know he's probably crazy, but what if . . . ?"

"What if . . . ?" His voice dropped.

She looked at David. He was six months younger than her, but his thick black beard and broad frame made him seem older. He had pushed her for years not to give up on her mother's work. But, since he was a geologist, that belief was based on wishful thinking and endless *Dr. Who* marathons, not hard science. She found his ardency endearing, despite his lack of scientific rigor. That, and those bright green eyes, which offered her warmth and comfort despite the vicissitudes of life.

"What if he's right? What if my mom found the key to time travel?"

David tilted his head. "What? And he just remembered this now? C'mon, Anna."

"He was so earnest, so pained."

"Did he have proof? Time travel should be easy to prove."

"No, I threw him out."

"I don't get it." David shook his head. "He said time travel led to disaster. Why show up now and dump this on you?"

"I don't know. Maybe he wants to see my mom's work finished."

"Wait, you're really going to start up her work again? You believe him?"

"I don't know," she said. "Of course not, who would?" She picked up one of the notebooks. "It's just . . . My mother died unrecognized. And the scientists, who did know her, derided her work. Maybe this is a chance at . . ." She stopped. She flipped open the notebook, but snapped it shut almost as quickly. A puff of dust sprouted into the air.

"At what? Redemption?"

"Vindication."

David stepped forward. He tugged on the hem of Anna's shirt, pulling her close. He hugged her. "Your mother deserved better, Anna. Absolutely. She was a trailblazer. But don't continue her work because of what this nutjob said."

"Look at us." Anna laughed, her head jostling against David's shoulder. "You've always pushed me to continue my mother's work, and I stopped. And now, when I wonder if digging back in is the right thing to do, you have doubts."

"I have doubts about him, not you," David said. "I want you to continue your mom's work because I think it's important for you. Not because of the ramblings of a crazy old man."

"I know," Anna said with more force than she intended.

"Did he say if he was coming back or how to get a hold of him?"

"No, why?"

"I'm thinking that maybe I should go talk to him and tell him to leave you alone."

She stepped back, frowning. "How chivalrous. I can take care of myself." She sauntered to her golf bag and yanked out the five iron. She swung it like a samurai sword. "I'm ready if he comes back."

David laughed. "Okay, okay. I need to get some sleep, but we'll talk about this more once I'm past my jetlag. Okay?"

Anna took one last swing with the club. "Sure."

"Who was it?" Anna asked as David returned from the front door the next morning. He wore an old green sweatshirt that highlighted the green flecks in his eyes.

155

"UPS. You've got a package."

"Really? I wasn't expecting anything." Anna took the box from David.

"No return address," she whispered. She walked to the desk and took out a pair of scissors. She cut open the package and folded back the newspapers inside. "Oh, my God!"

"What is it?" David tried to look over her shoulder.

"*Reginald.*" The name barely escaped her lips.

"What did you say?"

Anna reached into the box and pulled out a small, gray, stuffed bunny. His left ear, torn in half, sagged and gave him a woebegone look. Paperclipped to the other ear was a small card. The card read: *The past does not have to stay lost. A.W.*

"Who sent you a stuffed animal?" David asked.

"It's not a stuffed animal. It's Reginald. I lost him the night my mother was killed."

"I don't understand," David said.

"It's my bunny. I lost him when I was six."

David picked up the card. He looked at her. "Then how did Walker get it?"

Anna held the bunny as gently as a new parent holds their first child. "I don't know. It's not possible." Anna's gaze was firmly affixed to the stuffed animal, but when David didn't respond, she finally looked away. "Do you think it's possible?"

"Anna. Slow down."

"What if Walker is telling the truth?" The words rushed out of Anna like a stream after a heavy rainfall. "What if . . ." She looked at David, almost pleading. "What if he went back somehow and got Reginald, or had him all along?"

David's face remained impassive. "Anna, what are you talking about? He just bought a bunny off eBay. You realize that, right?"

Anna shifted uneasily. "The ear is torn in half, just like my Reginald."

"And he couldn't just buy one and cut the ear himself?"

"Are these bunnies even on eBay, David?" Anna asked. "Do you think he'd remember a toy of mine from twenty-five years ago, to cut the ear just right? It's exactly the same."

David's whole face hardened. "Anna, please."

"Is it impossible, David?" She held the rabbit against her chest. "I mean truly impossible?"

"It's highly, highly improbable," David said.

Anna held the rabbit in front of David's face. "And yet here he is."

"Fine. It's Reginald. But so what? It's not proof that he's not crazy." David looked over at the box. "Maybe if he knew something about your mother's work, had some of her papers or something? I mean, we're supposed to take a childhood toy as what? Proof of time travel?

"I don't know. I pretty much threw him out after what he said."

"Maybe we should call him back?"

"Why?"

"This obviously bothers you. I don't want you dwelling on it. We're meeting him again. I'll get him to apologize."

"It's not necessary."

David frowned momentarily, then his expression softened. "Okay. Let's forget about this for a while. I'll jump in the shower and then we'll go to Spumanti's for dinner. Sound good?"

"Sure. We haven't been out in a while."

She settled against his chest. He stroked her hair and said, "Don't worry about him. He's just a crazy old man." He kissed her softly on her forehead and disappeared into the bedroom.

Anna sighed and walked over to the UPS box. She pulled out the tattered newspapers. A plain manila folder sat on the bottom. She opened the folder and almost dropped the contents in shock. She immediately recognized her mother's handwriting. She pulled the folders out and flipped through them. Page after page of calculations and computations—the missing work from her mother's research. She couldn't be sure until she studied them in detail, but she knew.

She glanced back down and saw a *Time* magazine still in the box. Dated nearly twenty years ago, the headline screamed "PRINCETON SCIENTIST CONFIRMS TIME TRAVEL." A group of people stood on a stage and she recognized her mother waving to the crowd, a young Dr. Livet by her side.

Anna put her hand on the table to steady herself.

Two men in dark suits stood behind her mother. Dour-faced and emotionless, they looked like extras out of *The X-Files*. The man on the right looked familiar.

She sucked in a sharp breath, picked up a pen, and drew a dark, scraggly beard on the man's face. The flecked green eyes intensified when contrasted against the black ink. She glanced at the bedroom door before picking up the magazine. Despite their brightness, the eyes bore right through her, possessing neither the warmth nor comfort that she had grown accustomed to.

Anna took the papers from the box and stuffed them behind the massive astrophysics tomes she had been cross-referencing and returned to the table where she'd left the magazine. She picked up the faded pages, but couldn't bring herself to look at the picture again.

The rushing water from the shower hummed softly in her ears. She tried to read the story about her mother and the celebration of time travel, but her eyes struggled with the words on the page as if they were in a different language.

The hum of the shower stopped with a shriek from protesting pipes. Anna hurriedly stuffed the magazine into the bookcase with the rest of the contents of the UPS box. A few minutes later she heard David rustling around the bedroom.

He emerged a few minutes later. He wore a tailored, light-green dress shirt and faded blue jeans. He smiled.

"Ready to go?" he asked.

Anna smiled, but her muscles tightened. She glanced toward the golf bag before answering. "Yep. All set."

David's eyes flickered after hers, pausing almost imperceptibly on the bag. "Is everything all right?"

"Yeah. It's just been a long day."

David approached her and held out his hands. "We don't have to go out. Anyone would be freaked out right now."

Anna flinched as he approached her.

He stopped. The look of concern on his face shifted to a blank, unreadable expression. "What's wrong, Anna?"

She turned her head to the side. "Nothing. I'm just tired."

"Anna. Talk to me."

She looked up. *Was there an edge to his voice?* She took a breath. "Did you know who my mom was before meeting me?"

"What?"

"David. Did you know my mom worked on time travel?"

"Of course not. Everything I know about your mom is from what you've told me."

"Stop it." She pulled away from him and went to the bookcase. She dug out the magazine and walked back to David. She shoved the magazine into his hands, the pages crumpling slightly. "Why are you photographed with my mom?"

He stared at the cover. "What are you talking about?"

"You're on the stage . . . with my mother!"

"Anna. This is fake." He shook the magazine as if emphasizing his point. "Did Walker give this to you?

"What difference does it make?"

"It's Photoshopped garbage." He shook the magazine in his hands. "Anna. Listen to yourself."

She placed a hand on the table and closed her eyes as the room spun. *This is crazy.* She tried to gather her thoughts.

"Anna. The box from Walker?" David didn't approach her, but the look of concern had reappeared on this face. "Was there anything else in it?"

Her vertigo dissipated with his words. "What do you mean?"

"The, uh, the box." He looked away from her and gestured toward the container. "It was big. What else was in it?" When he turned back toward her, his smile had reappeared.

"Why would you think there was something else in it?"

"I don't think that." His voice rose briefly before flattening out. "I mean . . . just . . . is that really all he sent?"

Anna stood, the image of a clean-shaven David behind her mother emblazoned in her mind. She'd never seen David in a suit. "Did my mom discover time travel?"

David walked to the table and put the magazine down. He reached for her hands, but she pulled them away. "Anna, listen to what you're saying. You've let Walker get into your head."

"I don't . . ." No words would come.

"Anna, please." He hesitated. "I'm trying to help."

"I think I need some time alone."

"What? No."

"Please, David. Just get out."

"I'm not leaving you."

"I'm all right. But if you really want to help me, then you'll just leave me alone for now. Just go."

"I'm not leaving."

"Then I'll leave."

"Fine." His words held a sharp edge that barely contained his frustration. "I'll go to Spumanti's and get takeout. I shouldn't be gone much more than an hour."

"Okay. Thank you."

"Are you sure?"

She nodded.

David grabbed his leather jacket off the coat rack, pausing in the doorway. "If you need anything, call. I'll be right back."

"I'll be fine."

He closed the door. Anna went to the window and watched as he hustled to his car. Her muscles didn't relax until the sedan was a black speck down the road.

161

She sat down on the couch and picked up Reginald. She sat the toy in her lap. "Am I going crazy?"

Reginald didn't respond, his torn ear hung limply near his shoulder. Anna pulled the damaged ear taut so both ears were symmetrical, as if the rabbit was listening. She sighed. Then, as if the memory arose from the back of her mind, she realized something was missing.

Taking the torn ear, she squeezed the fur until a small blob of white stuffing pushed out. *The stitches are gone.* Anna remembered sobbing when Reginald was first damaged, a vague memory of her mom, indistinct and unclear, mending the torn appendage. As she searched her memory, she realized that her mom didn't sew. Ever. The image crystalized. Five-year-old Anna sobbed as Adam Walker mended the maimed Reginald.

Anna gasped. She probed the torn fabric until her fingers struck something solid within the white fluff. Squeezing her finger and thumb, she pulled a crescent-shaped, circuit-inscribed metal object from the ear canal.

Anna stared at the small device. Her mind spun through her mom's research, but she had never found anything describing this object. She tried to remain calm as she fiddled with the circuit with her fingers. Eventually, she stood and walked to the grandfather clock. She pulled the front panel and snapped the crescent piece into the empty molding. The component popped in with a small "click." She followed Walker's instructions, turning the copper dial as he'd demonstrated. Nothing happened.

She noticed the second hand moving dutifully around the clock face. The minute hand snapped forward with a deliberate tick. She pushed the minute hand back an hour and repeated Walker's instructions. The copper dial clicked into place.

Nothing happened.

What did she expect? The room to spin and shake? Colors to appear and swirl around her? A DeLorean to screech to a halt in the driveway?

She banged her head softly on the side of the clock. She looked back toward the couch where Reginald, cast aside in her haste, lay on his side. "I am losing my mind."

The soft bang of a drawer closing echoed from the bedroom, followed by heavy footsteps. Anna glanced at the golf bag, but her legs wouldn't move.

David emerged from the bedroom a few moments later. He wore a tailored, light-green dress shirt and faded blue jeans.

"Ready to go?" he asked.

She opened her mouth to respond, but the clock chimed, the sonorous clang echoing throughout the room.

Miss Princott's
Time Travel Agency

Barbara Russell

Auckland, present day

THE DOOR OF THE TIME chamber opened with a hiss, and I staggered out, my head spinning.

Next to me, my client, Mr. Torvalds, exited and beamed. His eyes twinkled under bushy gray eyebrows. "That was something, wasn't it?"

Yeah, something awful. Who would enjoy running from peasants welding pitchforks on the streets of Paris during the Storming of the Bastille? Only a history professor.

He clapped my shoulder. "I have a lot of data to process. My research project on the French Revolution is going to be a success. Thanks, Priscilla. Your agency is the best."

Because it's the only time travel agency. "Th-thanks." I wiped my sweaty hands on my skirt and escorted Mr. Torvalds to the exit as he hummed *La Marsellaise*. I removed my voluminous wig and tossed it in a corner. Wearing my modern clothes again would be a relief. This bloody eighteenth-century gown with all those layers, skirts, and frilly laces weighed a ton.

"Goodbye." Mr. Torvalds waved. "See you soon for my next trip, the days of the Reign of Terror."

Horrible. "Lovely."

I groaned. Why couldn't I have a client who wanted to see the Beatles' first concert or Henry VIII's third wedding?

I shouldn't complain. Chronos, my agency, was doing great.

I straightened, stepped into the main room, and smiled. The twenty wooden desks were all busy with one or two clients each. My agents smiled, nodded, and listened to our customers with politeness and competence, exactly as I'd trained them to do. Wide floor-to-ceiling windows let the sunlight in, brightening the pink-salmon walls. Pots with yellow lilies and red tulips added a further touch of color.

My chest swelled with pride . . . as much as the stupid corset allowed. At barely thirty years old, I was one of the most successful entrepreneurs in Auckland, getting richer than Bill Gates.

The indigo carpet with silver stars muffled the sound of my heels as I strolled toward my office in a swish of silk. I grinned at a man who was buying a trip during the first North Pole crossing with Amundsen and shivered. Going back in time to experience that? No thanks. The sound of the phone ringing and emails pinging echoed in the wide room. Music to my ears.

I stopped in front of the shelves to straighten a brochure on Rome. *Watch the real gladiators fighting in the arena*, a bright red caption read. Not my thing. I adjusted a long blonde tendril that had escaped from my bun and opened the door to my office.

The front door bell chimed, and a man walked in. He gazed around, blinking at the crowd. Messy brown hair fell over his eyes and cheeks. Shabby clothes, worn leather bag tucked under his arm, moccasins with a hole on the tip—I knew the type. A scientist.

I swallowed hard, checking if any position was free. No luck. My agents were all busy. Now I almost regretted how full the agency was. Perhaps I could just steer him into the waiting area and let him stay there.

I cleared my throat and sauntered over. "Good morning. I'm Miss P-priscilla Prismott, I mean, Princott." Stammering. Great. But hey, scientists made me nervous. They were the only people who asked to witness Nobel's experiments with TNT, or to see Mount Vesuvius destroying Pompeii. All for research purposes, of course.

"Good morning!" The man held out a hand, his brown eyes shining with happiness as if I'd told him he'd won the lottery. "I'm Dr. Vance McAvoy."

I knew it. A scientist. I shook his hand. "I'm afraid we're a bit busy today. Would you like to take a seat and wait, please? You can help yourself to some hot drinks." I gestured toward the refreshment area where fresh pots of coffee, tea, and biscuits lay on a table.

There. Done. I pivoted on my heels.

"Actually . . ." Vance started. "I'm a bit in a hurry. I have to teach a class."

An academic, then, like Mr. Torvalds. Hopefully, not another historian. But a client is a client, that's my motto. I could talk to him and then leave the case to an agent. "How can I help?" I beckoned him to the sitting area as I sat in a creamy velvet armchair, collecting layers of petticoats. The aroma of coffee filled the air.

Vance tripped on his own feet. The bag fell from his arms, and when he scooped to pick it up, he hit his head against a table. "Ouch!"

I winced. Not a good start. A clumsy scientist could be a problem. How could we run from ancient tribes of head-hunters if he was a bumble-foot? "Are you all right?"

"Yes, yes." Smiling, he sat in front of me. "I'm a researcher."

I know. Please, not another paleontologist who wants to visit the Jurassic Era. I still had nightmares about that bloody T. rex chasing me. "What do you research?"

"British literature."

I blew out a long breath of relief that strained my bodice. "Fascinating."

He opened the bag and fished out a stack of papers. "I'm working on a project on Shakespeare."

Yes! "Oh, goodness." I fought the urge to bounce on my toes.

"Specifically, on one of his masterpieces, *Lorentio and Juliet*." He tapped a finger on the papers, where a picture of the famous battle scene in Verona gleamed.

Juliet looked terrific, pointing her sword at Lorentio whose arm lifted a shield. Capulets versus Montagues. The most exciting story ever told.

I smiled. "This story has a special meaning for me. I was in a theater, watching this very play, when I met Mr. Shidara, the investor who believed in me and in all this." I waved a hand to encompass the agency. "His company in Tokyo built all the time chambers."

"Great." He beamed and shifted his weight. "So, I was wondering how much a trip to Verona in 1527 would cost. I want to see every detail about the clothes, food, and language. The feud between the two families. If it's true that everyone died. You know, all the possible details."

I took out my phone and did a quick calculation. "Let's see . . . you know that, by law, you can't stay longer than ten hours, right?"

"What?"

I lifted a shoulder. "The longer you stay, the higher the probability of causing a time ripple. Or dying. We can't change history. Never. And of course, it's not allowed to go forward. No one should take advantage of knowledge of the future."

"Oh. That makes sense."

"And an agent must escort you and stay with you all the time."

He raised a brow.

"We need to keep an eye on our clients and be sure they travel safely." I punched a few numbers in the calculator. "Just a reminder, while we're in Verona, we can't interfere in any way with history. We're observers. We're watching a film. Okay?"

Vance nodded eagerly, his cheeks flushed.

"We do not engage the locals for any reason. We walk, listen, and come back here. Also, no gadgets from the future. They might shock the people. Last year, a theologist wanted to witness the Virgin Mary giving birth, and brought a camera. I can't tell you the mess it created. People thought *he* was the messiah." I shook my head, remembering those angry Roman centurions chasing us. "You want to take notes? You'll do it with pencil and paper. Clear?"

"Crystal."

"It's five thousand dollars for the trip to Verona, one thousand dollars for the installation of the microchip to understand the language, plus a few hundred dollars for the vaccinations. Yellow fever, tetanus vaccine, anti-black plague, insurance, clothes, induction course . . . the total is about . . ." I stomped a finger on the display. "Eighteen thousand dollars, and you'll have to sign a waiver in case, you know, you get stabbed, roasted, or eaten."

"Sheesh." Vance whistled.

"Will you manage to cover the cost? I can . . ." I sank my teeth into my bottom lip. Gosh, I wanted to go. Every client had to be escorted by an agent, and it could be me. Finally, a trip that didn't involve wild beasts, guns, or exploding volcanos. Just a family feud with lots of swords. I could handle that.

"I have plenty of funds." Vance smiled. "When can we go?"

"In a week or two? I need to study the era a bit, and I have to prepare a few documents."

"Perfect."

So here we were, Vance and I, in front of one of the time chambers. The three-foot thick, seven-foot tall metal door seemed like that of a Swiss vault, but the inside of the chamber with its dashboard, gauges, and the digital displays looked like *Star Trek's* Enterprise.

I beckoned Vance in. He was shaking.

"Are you nervous?"

"A bit."

"It's normal. You'll relax once we're there." I pushed a button on the wall, and the door closed with a thud. Blue and white lights shone from the dark ceiling. I opened two panels on the wall, revealing two dressing rooms.

"In you go. You'll be provided with clothes and money appropriate for the era, the shots, and the microchip."

Vance rushed inside. "I'm so excited."

On the display of Vance's room, I typed our destination and the year, and the door slid closed. I entered my dressing room and inserted the date. A panel opened, revealing a red and white gown with a golden sash. A fat leather pouch contained a few hundred dollars in golden florins.

I slid on the dress, a pair of slippers, and combed my hair into a long braid. I looked at my reflection in the mirror. The gown was fitted to the waist with a long skirt and wide sleeves. Perfect to conceal my Seeker, the device that would bring me back to modern Auckland. I fixed it on my wrist, closing the Velcro straps around it. With its rotund screen and blinking numbers, it could pass for a large watch.

When I left the dressing room, Vance was already out, wearing a green jacket with puffed sleeves and green tights encasing his thin legs. A leather satchel was strapped across his shoulder.

He rubbed his neck. "How do I look?"

The green brought out his hazel eyes. "Dashing. Is the micro-chip in all right?"

He nodded. "A bit painful."

Tell me about it. I had ten installed at the base of my neck. Could speak Latin, ancient Greek, and Sanskrit. "We're ready." I opened my bag and picked up a box of Snorinol, super powerful sleeping pills, and slipped the blue box with the glittering half-moon in my pocket.

"You said no modern stuff," Vance said.

"I know, but these pills, despite being for sleeping, help with the nausea. I always have it when I time travel. If you need them, let me know. Half of one, and I'm fine, just a bit sleepy." I inserted the coordinates for Verona and the year of destination, 1527, in the display. "You might experience mild discomfort and the sensation of being pulled down."

He paled. "I'm ready."

I pulled the time lever. The ground shook. Flashes darted in every direction. A hissing sound whistled in my ears. Vance cried out. The floor disappeared, and the feeling of being suspended in the void made me queasy. Then I was pushed down, and I staggered as my feet touched the ground again. "D-done." I gobbled half a pill to stop the wave of nausea.

"Oh, gosh." Vance staggered on the cobbled street, his eyes wide. "Please." He held up a hand.

I steadied him and handed him half a pill. "It'll go away in a moment."

We stood in a secluded alley. Vance sweated as he sidestepped the cracked stones and masonry.

"This spot," I stomped a foot on the ground, "is our starting point. We must come back here to return to Auckland. Otherwise, we might end up stuck in a wall of my agency."

Sunlight blinded me when we left the alley and reached Piazza delle Erbe, Square of the Herbs, in the center of

Verona. Horses pulled carts and carriages. People chatted, donkeys cried, a duck scurried across the road. Iron wheels clattered on the cobbles, and the stench of dung and unwashed human bodies hit my nostrils.

Vance leaned against the wall, his cheeks rosy again. "Wonderful."

"Where do we begin?"

"The open market."

I stretched out an arm. "Lead the way."

We strolled along narrow alleys, through piles of horse manure and rotting vegetables, women in large skirts, and men in tights.

"It's beautiful." Vance's eager gaze darted everywhere. "Lorentio and Juliet were real people, did you know that?"

"No." I moved aside to let a woman in a wide velvet skirt pass, a servant hurrying behind her.

"They could be around." He let out a small squeal.

I chuckled at his enthusiasm.

Hours later, my feet hurt, the stench of horse dung would probably remain in my nostrils forever, and an ache throbbed in my head. The half Snorinol I took didn't help with my energy level. "Are you ready to go back? We've been here for almost eight hours."

"Yes, I'm ready." With a heavy sigh, Vance nodded. "I'd like to return, as soon as I gather more funds." He folded his heavily written papers and stuck them into his satchel.

We were heading toward the starting point when a scream made me jolt. In a secluded alley, a young man was beating a young woman. Her slim body jerked every time the much larger boy punched her.

I gasped and clamped my hands over my mouth. "This is horrible." I looked around. Passers-by hurried along the street, ignoring the girl.

"We must do something." Fists clenched, Vance shot toward the girl.

"Wait. We can't interfere." I stretched out an arm, but too late. He sprinted off.

"Hey!" Vance shouted to the man. "Why don't you beat me, you swine?"

The boy stopped punching the girl and turned. Tendrils of blond hair covered his harsh face. He had to be around sixteen.

The boy spat on the ground, staring at Vance. "As you wish."

Oops. The boy stomped to Vance, rolling up the sleeves of his shirt and showing sturdy arms. The girl crouched in a corner, whimpering.

"Ah . . ." Vance staggered backward, fiddling with his hands. "Maybe we can discuss—"

The boy threw a punch at Vance's head and missed it by an inch. I gathered my skirt and strode to the thug. Vance tripped on a cobble and fell on his rear. The boy loomed over him with a fist lifted.

I grabbed a wooden stick lying on the side of the street and swung. The stick swished above Vance's head, and I hit the thug on the temple. His eyes crossed under golden eyebrows, then rolled backward, as if he wanted to look inside his skull. He swayed and dropped with a thud.

"Phew!" Vance wiped his sweaty forehead, standing up. "Thanks for that."

"Thanks?" I tossed the stick aside. "I just beat a man in Verona in 1527. We aren't supposed to interfere. That's rule number one!"

"Thank you." The girl's sweet voice made me jump.

I turned to her. She must've been around the same age of her assailant, with large lilac eyes and raven hair. A red spot marked the porcelain skin of her cheek.

"This Montague would've killed me if it weren't for you, my lady." She curtsied, and my heart melted.

I patted her trembling hand. "You're welcome, darling. Why don't you go home now?"

"I will. Thank you." She bobbed another curtsy.

I shook my head as the girl rushed away. "Poor thing." I pinned Vance with a glare. He had no idea what he'd done. No one could foresee the effect of a time ripple, even a small one. For all I knew, the ripple could cause the destruction of the entire city of Verona. I swallowed and smoothed my bodice. No panicking in front of a client. "Now we go home, and no more interfering."

He held up his palms. "Fine."

I walked briskly to the starting point, Vance in my wake. When we arrived at the spot, I lifted my sleeve and punched the security code into the Seeker. "Stay close to me."

I took his hand and . . . nothing happened. No ground shaking, no lights, no nausea. Nothing.

"Well?" Vance glanced at me.

I punched the code again. Nothing. *What the heck?* "Is it broken? This has never happened before."

"Oh, gosh." Vance touched his forehead. "The girl."

"What does she have to do with anything?"

He leaned closer. "What if she's Juliet? What if the man was Lorentio?"

Dread washed over me. Lorentio beat Juliet in a dark alley, and she swore to avenge herself. She learned how to spar. That was how the final battle between Capulets and Montagues started. "We rescued Juliet. She didn't defend herself, Shakespeare didn't write *Lorentio and Juliet*, and I never met Mr. Shidara. My agency doesn't exist."

"Crap."

"Crap?" My hands itched to grab Vance from the neck and shake him. A blip from the Seeker distracted me. On the display, the number seven blinked. "Crap, the countdown has started."

"Huh?"

I showed him the Seeker. "We caused a ripple, and we have seven hours to fix it, or the ripple will become permanent, and we'll stay here forever." Tears blurred my vision. Unless we did something, I was destined to remain in Verona, in 1527, for the rest of my life. I'd never see my agency again, my friends, and my family. I'd never eat Chinese food again. I'd never know how *Game of Thrones* was going to end . . . if it ended at all. A sob escaped me.

Vance touched my shoulder. "There, there. We'll find a solution."

We must. I squared my shoulders. "Let's go." I marched toward the alley.

"Where?"

"To find Lorentio and tell him . . . to attack Juliet again."

"But . . . that is awful."

I stopped and jabbed a finger at him. "Do you have a better idea? We must follow history."

We half-ran, half-walked through the crowd of the square until we arrived at the alley.

Lorentio sat on the cobbles, cradling his head. Another blond-haired young man, all spidery limbs, stood next to him, trying to pull him up.

Lorentio flinched, then picked himself up and glowered at me. "You won't take me by surprise again."

"Did this lady beat you?" the other boy asked. For a moment, the boy's sparkling green eyes distracted me.

"Shush, Roach." Lorentio wiped his mouth with the back of his hand. "You will pay for—"

"Lorentio Montague?" Vance asked.

"And?" Lorentio arched an eyebrow.

Roach shrank back. "Are you Capulets?"

"No." Vance smiled charmingly. "We just wish to apologize for having hit Lorentio."

I rolled my bottom lip between my teeth. We needed a plan. "In fact, we want you to beat Juliet again."

"What?" Lorentio and Roach chorused.

Roach shot a glare at Lorentio. "You were beating Juliet? A girl?"

Lorentio scoffed. "She's a Capulet."

"But—" Roach started.

Lorentio swatted Roach's chest. "Are you no longer a Montague, *Cousin*? Do you have any honor left?"

Roach flushed, his shoulders hunching.

I rummaged in my pouch and fished out a bunch of florins. "I'll give you more if you find Juliet."

"Why?" Roach crossed his arms above his chest. "What did Juliet do to you?"

My heart cracked. That poor girl hadn't done anything wrong, and here I was, plotting to attack her. Vance was right. It was horrible. We had to find another way. My shoulders stooped. "Let's forg—"

"Who cares why?" Lorentio's pale blue eyes widened as he snatched the money. "I'd beat Juliet for free, but it's better if I'm being paid."

Roach tugged at his arm. "Are you mad? Juliet is a lady. You can't hit a lady."

"I already did." Lorentio pocketed the money with a smirk.

My heart dipped to my stomach. I hated the idea of this brute attacking Juliet.

"Excuse us a moment." I dragged Vance a few yards away. "I'm not sure anymore. That poor girl."

Vance scratched his chin. "I know, but being attacked is the only way for her to become the defender of the Capulets and to trigger the story Shakespeare will write. And it's our only ticket home. After Lorentio attacked her, Juliet went to an old wife—a healer—and then she decided to stand up for herself. But since that storyline doesn't exist anymore, I'd say we go to Juliet's house and try to sneak inside. All we need to do is to provoke her. Lorentio doesn't have to hurt her, just scare her."

"Great." I clapped my hands. "Guys . . . ahem, gentlemen, we have a plan."

After three stinking hours spent discussing a strategy in an inn, buying supplies in the center, and convincing Lorentio that he just had to scare Juliet, we lurked in the shade in front of an imposing two-story house, the Capulets' mansion, ready to gate-crash a Renaissance party. The Seeker informed me that four hours were left to fix the darn ripple. A knot tightened in my throat. I wasn't even sure that Vance and I would exist after the deadline. We could disappear into thin air.

With its vine-covered thick walls and battlements, the house looked like a fortress. A double wooden door reinforced with brass bars took a good chunk of the portico.

"These are for the masquerade ball at the Capulets' tonight," Vance handed Lorentio and Roach a pair of masks. "We'll sneak inside, find Juliet, and Lorentio . . ." He swallowed. "You know what to do."

Lorentio's icy blue eyes glinted. "Yes, I do."

"No need to hurt her too much, remember?" I rubbed my goosebumped arms. This guy was a killer. Roach pressed his lips into a hard line and scowled at his cousin.

We gripped the vines and climbed over the wall. A jump, and we were in. Almost . . . Vance grunted as he swung his knee over the wall and plunged to the ground. He landed with a thud. "My back."

"Shush!" I helped him to his feet.

Lorentio and Roach seemed almost identical with their masks on, except for the smirk on Lorentio's face and Roach's thinner limbs. We skulked across a trimmed lawn bordered by tall oaks and arrived at a well-lit ballroom. Music, chatter, and songs mingled together.

Roach looked around with big eyes, ooh-ing and aah-ing every two seconds. I couldn't blame him. These Capulets knew how to throw a party: fire-eaters swallowing flaming torches, acrobats twirling up in the air, troubadours playing a catchy tune, and so much food being served to feed an army.

Lorentio grabbed a mug of mulled wine from the banquet table and polished it off with one tilt of his head. "Not bad. These Capulet pigs have good wine. Now, where's that wench?"

We strolled on the edge of the ballroom. I scrutinized the crowd. Women danced in flutters of brocade and velvet. Their flowery perfumes wafted in the air. With their masks on, it was hard to tell which one was Juliet.

"I think that's her." Vance elbowed me and nodded toward a corner of the room.

A petite brunette was sipping mead, half-hidden behind a pillar. The black velvet mask she was wearing didn't hide her lilac eyes or the red mark on her cheek.

I tugged at Lorentio's sleeve. "It's her. Juliet."

"All right." He snatched another mug from the tray of a passing waiter and sipped it in one go.

I shook Lorentio's arm. "Follow her. We don't have time." *Barely three hours, actually.*

"Fine." Lorentio rolled his eyes and strolled away.

"Don't kill her," I whispered.

He waved in reply.

Juliet left the room and headed toward the garden through an open floor-to-ceiling window.

I hid behind a curtain with Vance and Roach. *Here we are.* Lorentio strolled toward Juliet who was promenading under the trees. She pivoted and faced him. A flicker of fear passed across her face. Lorentio closed his fists.

I bit my knuckles, hoping the brute would follow our plan. Lorentio roared.

I whipped my head when Roach rushed past. "Roach!"

"Oh, no." Vance raked a hand though his hair.

Roach crossed the lawn with a few angry strides and tackled his much larger cousin. The noise of the music and the crowds covered Juliet's gasp. Lorentio shoved Roach away.

Roach landed on his back and gritted his teeth. "Go!" He sprang to his feet and gave Juliet a slight push.

Juliet scurried away as Lorentio punched Roach in the stomach.

"You idiot!" Lorentio hit Roach again.

I gathered my skirt and ran toward them, Vance following. "Stop this!"

Roach curled on the ground, arms protecting his head. Lorentio went to kick him, but I thrust him aside. "Enough!"

Panting, Lorentio threw his hands up. "Bah!"

I knelt next to Roach. "You all right?"

He staggered to his feet, staring at the ground. "I'm sorry, but Juliet is so beautiful and sweet. I couldn't let him hurt her."

Oh, boy. I exchanged a glance with Vance. "She'll be fine. It's very important that Lorentio scares Juliet one more time."

Roach glared at me, eyes burning. Shame made my cheeks warm. I took a peek at the Seeker. The countdown was still on, so Lorentio hadn't frightened Juliet sufficiently. We had to try again.

I kicked a pebble while walking in Juliet's garden. The stone arched in the air and landed with a thud on a tree trunk. Only a few people were around, drunk party-goers who staggered on.

The light of the torches cast dancing shadows on the ground. Vance shuffled his feet next to me while Lorentio and Roach trudged behind.

I checked the Seeker. Less than two hours left to doomsday. "What now?"

Vance huffed. "I don't know. I guess Juliet is in her chamber. Maybe we can see if she's awake."

"Let Lorentio sneak into her room?"

"Do we have another option?"

"Okay." I beckoned to Lorentio to come closer.

Lorentio scoffed, and Roach scowled, but they did as told.

"This is the plan," I whispered. "Lorentio climbs to Juliet's bedroom and—"

"Really?" Lorentio grinned.

"Don't overdo it. Just terrify her, and it'll be enough." I choked on the last words. If Juliet wasn't in her bed, we were done for. We'd stay here for the rest of our lives.

Smirking, Lorentio nodded. "It should be fun."

We crept into the shadows. Light spilled from a ground floor window, so we moved toward the trees.

"That's Juliet's room." Vance pointed at a marble balcony with vines reaching up to it like green fingers.

I clapped Lorentio's shoulder. "No need to hurt her."

Muttering something I didn't catch, Lorentio put a foot on the wall and grabbed the vines. With a pull, he lifted himself up. My heart beat in my throat. I wiped my sweaty palms on my skirt, sending a silent plea to Juliet that she would be really scared.

I waggled my eyebrow at Vance and tilted my head toward Roach. Vance nodded and grabbed Roach's arm. "Please stay h—"

Roach shunted Vance aside and sprang forward.

"Not again!" I chased him, but the darn skirt was all over the place, slowing me.

Vance tripped over his feet and sprawled on the grass. Roach leapt, grabbed Lorentio's shoulders, and dragged him down. Lorentio fell backward, landing on the rose bushes underneath him. Roach started to climb the wall toward Juliet's room.

"Crap!" I scurried forward.

Lorentio lay with his mouth open and eyes closed, tongue hanging out. Did he break his neck?

I froze. What the heck was I doing? I had turned into a murderer.

Vance checked Lorentio's neck. "Passed out."

"Phew!"

With trembling hands, Roach gripped the vines and yanked himself farther up. I arched an eyebrow. Actually, he wasn't bad. He was lithe and agile, climbing like a spider. He arrived at the balcony right when the window opened and Juliet stepped into view, frowning, probably wondering where the noise came from.

I chewed my bottom lip. If she screamed or pushed Roach down, the entire house would be on us. Then, we'd be trapped here and probably end up in jail. Not a place I was looking forward to visiting.

But Juliet didn't scream. She didn't move, either. She stood there, looking at Roach with huge eyes. Her white robe fluttered around her. Roach halted as well, his hands and feet in an awkward position that seemed painful.

"W-what are you doing here, my lord?" she asked, and I could barely hear it.

Roach swallowed. "Looking for you."

Another long silence stretched, and they did nothing but stare at each other. What the heck was going on here?

"Should we say something?" I whispered.

Vance shook his head. "He won't do what we say. Pretty obvious."

I checked the Seeker again. Barely twenty minutes left. My stomach churned.

"You're very brave. If Father sees you here, he'll have you killed." Juliet took another step toward Roach. "You stopped that man in the garden."

"Er . . ." Roach panted. "Do you mind if I climb to the balcony? This position is a bit uncomfortable."

"Of course." Juliet moved aside as Roach grabbed the banister and then swung a knee over it.

Fifteen minutes.

"You're a Montague, aren't you?" Juliet clenched her nightgown tighter.

"I am." Roach shuffled his blond hair. "I've noticed you at the church on Sunday. Your eyes are beautiful. I bet that when the fairest stars in heaven have some business to do, they ask your eyes to twinkle in their places until they return."

Juliet blushed.

I sighed. "That was beautiful."

Ten minutes.

Juliet cleared her throat. "You're very straightforward. What's your name?"

"Everyone calls me Roach."

Juliet giggled. "What's your real name?"

Roach straightened, looking taller and broader. "Romeo."

Eight minutes.

My stomach tightened in a knot.

They stared at each other.

Romeo inched forward. Juliet inched forward. He tilted his head. She tilted her head.

Four minutes.

"You're very kind." Juliet caressed Romeo's cheek.

I clutched Vance's arm. "I admit that they're cute together."

"They are." Sweat dripped down Vance's chin.

One minute.

I couldn't look. In one minute, my life would change forever.

Romeo closed the distance and kissed Juliet. She remained still on the spot.

The Seeker beeped, and I closed my eyes. Was the beep the signal that the countdown had been stopped? Or that I was done for?

I lifted the sleeve slowly. The countdown was gone.

"Well?" Vance leaned closer to the Seeker.

"I . . . I don't know. The countdown has disappeared, but I'm not sure what it means. At least, we're still here."

"Let's go to the starting point and see what happens."

"Okay." I lifted my gaze to the balcony.

Romeo and Juliet were whispering to each other, stealing kisses between words. Tears burned my eyes, but not out of desperation. Young love. Star-crossed lovers, considering that their families had butchered each other for decades. Those two seemed so sweet.

Vance and I trudged back to the starting point. My heart dunked deeper into my stomach at each step. Instead of a battle, we started a love story. The ripple couldn't be bigger.

We stopped on the starting point, which was right under a torch. I uncovered the Seeker and took a deep breath. "The moment of truth."

"Wait!" Romeo was running toward us, his boyish cheeks flushed. I hid the Seeker again. Once he reached us, he threw his arms around my neck. "Thank you. Without you, I would've never had the courage to talk to her."

I patted his shoulder. "It's all right, lad. Good luck."

"Good luck," Vance said. "Go back to your girl."

Romeo beamed and turned.

I lifted my sleeve. "Ready?"

"I am."

I punched the code and waited, holding my breath. The ground shook, flashes blinded me, and the familiar feeling of my stomach being pulled down assaulted me.

"Yes!" I lifted a fist as I landed on solid ground.

The flashes died down, and the dark walls of the time chamber appeared. I sagged against the door. "We did it."

"Phew." Vance bent forward and blew out a breath.

I fumbled with the levers, got the security code wrong twice before I opened the door and walked out. Vance followed, carrying his suitcase.

Yes! My agency is safe.

One of my employees, Laura, in a pink fluffy skirt and a pair of gossamer wings, brushed past us and stopped. "Welcome back."

"Thank you." I exhaled, eyeing her ridiculous outfit.

"What are you wearing?" She chuckled.

Funny, I was about to ask the same question. I lifted my skirt. "I was working."

"Hmm . . ." Laura's brow creased. "How was the date?"

"Huh? What date?"

"With the client." Laura drummed her pink-painted fingernails on the tablet she was carrying.

"I don't know what you mean."

Vance shrugged. "Me neither."

Laura frowned. "Okay." She hurried away, glancing at me.

What's wrong?

"Oh, gosh." Vance pointed at a poster on the wall.

Cupid, the first time travel dating agency.

What? I kept reading.

Worried about making a mistake with your date? Do you want to take back what you said to your girlfriend/boyfriend? Visit us at http://cupidfastdate.co.nz. There's always another chance for love. Remember to like us on Facebook.

I eyed the glossy pink leaflet. "Why did my travel agency turn into a dating agency?"

Vance scratched his head. "I think it has to do with this." He opened his suitcase and turned on his tablet. Then he fumbled with it and tapped a finger on the display. "Look."

It was a Wikipedia article on *Romeo and Juliet* by W. Shakespeare, the greatest love story of all the time. So good old Willy wrote a story about them after all. I grinned.

"Do they die in the end? Like in Lorentio and Juliet? Romeo and Juliet were star-crossed lovers."

"Let's see." Vance scrolled down the page and laughed. "No. They pretended to be dead after having ingested a sleeping potion they found in a blue box with a shiny half-moon."

Blue box with a half-moon. My Snorinol pills? I patted my pockets. The box was gone. I must've lost it in Juliet's garden. I chuckled. "And then what happened to them?"

"After that, their families believed they died for love and the feud between Capulets and Montagues ended. And they lived happily ever after."

A Peculiar Count in Time

Excerpt from: *The Curious Count of St. Germain*

M.K. Beutymhill

"He is the man who knows everything, and never dies."—
Voltaire

Lahore, India
May 1869
Isabella Cooper, age 15

I FIRST LEARNED OF THE mysterious Count of St. Germain
during a late spring afternoon, while I sat in the shade of the
courtyard fanning myself with a straw bonnet. I was fifteen,

and neglecting my Latin studies in favor of eavesdropping. The voices drifted from the terrace overhead, as the acoustics of the Mughal architecture tended to allow, yet there was a muted quality about them. I needed to be closer if I were to catch more than passing phrases.

Would I be considered less of a busybody if I insisted my interest was purely scholarly? I certainly wouldn't have looked anything else as I climbed the ivy-coated latticework, but this was the time in the afternoon in which I was often left unsupervised by my tutors. God bless the growing popularity of afternoon tea.

"Truly, Mary, I simply cannot fathom this obsession of his."

I'd suspected that my father was entertaining some visiting dignitary in the space he'd fashioned as a parlor, a pleasant lounge that had endured a peculiar transmutation as Victoria's England fused with relics from the Mughal Empire, and so I found myself initially disappointed to realize it was but a conversation between my parents. By now, I'd scaled high enough to peek through the banister and into the parlor, where my father—England's appointed commissioner—paced about with his long legs and his paunchy belly.

"I suppose he must be curious." My mother sat in her favorite chair, the only one in the room not swallowed by her voluminous skirts. "As are you, Henry, my dear. You must admit it's a curious notion, that the Count of St. Germain might have prophesied the rise of the Bonapartes amidst the collapse of the French monarchy. Could there be any truth to it?"

"Poppycock." My father waved his calabash pipe, as if to emphasize his utter dismissal. "The man would have to be damn well over a century upon this earth. Yet I've seen him myself and he can be no older than fifty. Logic be damned, Louis Napoleon ignores the obvious and bases his entire investigation out of the Hôtel de Ville, as if the people of France don't have better use of a municipality building. He is foolish to be drawn in by the occult."

I found the accusation ironic, considering my father was a Freemason. He'd never said as much, but he'd been involved in the recent construction of Lahore's Masonic temple, and I'd snooped his office enough times to figure out his association for myself. The man was a lifelong enigma, in and out of an endless stream of private meetings with renowned visitors who always seemed more intimate with my father than myself.

"Then we must only wonder who this man truly is," mused my mother, though I recognized the coy little smile upon her face. "Interesting that much the same was said of the original St. Germain."

My father nursed the long stem of his pipe before answering. "If that was even his true moniker," he said through a breath of smoke. "He was not of the Saint-Germains of France. If Louis Napoleon is to be believed, he was likely of the Transylvanian Rákóczis."

The turmoil of the Rákóczis was familiar to me, though it took me a moment to recall the decades of uprisings from my lessons. So consumed in thought was I that, for a moment, I disassociated myself almost entirely from how high I'd climbed. My fingers tightened their grip.

"Such a name was too dangerous to use after surrendering to the Austrians," my mother said. "It's no wonder he fashioned himself a new identity."

"One with which he claimed to be a scholar and alchemist," my father countered. "He'd convinced Louis XV well enough to fund his laboratory at Château de Chambord, as any charismatic charlatan may. It's a poor excuse to invent fantastical tales about one's life, yet such is how he became known as the Immortal Count."

I suppressed a chortle. *This* was what I'd climbed the terrace for—an old wives' tale?

"But even if there was any credibility to be had, Louis Napoleon chases ghosts; the Count of St. Germain—as history knows him—died in 1784."

My mother's expression was smug behind her teacup. "So they say."

My grip on the iron latticework had become sweaty as I listened, and as luck would have it, the toe of my foot slipped as I wiped a palm against my skirts. I secured my footing, but my squelched outcry had both of my parents wheeling their heads towards the balcony.

It was my mother who rushed to hoist me over the rail, though I had plenty of secure footholds and a choice angle from which to propel myself.

"My bricky girl, you'll break your neck someday!" she scolded through pursed lips. "Whatever is wrong with the stairs?"

Nothing, of course, except that one couldn't eavesdrop from there.

My father sat nonplussed in the armchair by the giant globe, his fingers tapping the top of the pipe bowl as the embers within reignited. He finally acknowledged me when I'd approached with a straightened blouse and dusted-off skirt.

"I'd hoped to raise a lady, not a thrill-seeking hooligan, Miss Isabella Cooper," he said. "Your assignments must be completed if you can afford the effort of such frivolous endeavors."

"I did not assume the Count of St. Germain to be a frivolous matter if you bothered to discuss him," I said. "Why do you criticize the use of the Hôtel de Ville? Important records are kept there. Where else should Louis Napoleon start his investigation?"

I expected my father to be displeased, but he gave a lighthearted chuckle as he puffed his pipe. "Perhaps Louis Napoleon ought to commission *you* to his investigation—if you attacked it with all the ardor you possess, those fopdoodles would eventually conclude that there is no support to this precarious 'Immortal Count' business. In the meantime, perhaps some additional lessons will help occupy that clever mind of yours."

I wanted to continue—at last, I'd shoehorned into adult discourse!—but my mother ushered me from the parlor with a stiff warning and a command to take my studies to the library until she fetched me at a later hour. I immediately obeyed.

As I waited, however, I consulted our books about the fates of the Rákóczi heirs, where I was most intrigued to discover that Louis XV's father had gifted the Rákóczis some estates, the rents of which went directly to the Hôtel de Ville in Paris. A generous gift, and a curious coincidence considering the friendship between St. Germain and Louis XV, though I was certain I did not yet fully understand its significance. I did wonder in passing, however, if Napoleon had known of this exchange before basing his investigative commission there.

Travels from Constantinople to London via express trains
September 1870 – January 1871
Isabella Cooper, age 17

I did not consider the Count of St. Germain much further until some years later, during my family's long journey from India to our native England. Our trip included an extended stay with kin in France, and though our arrival in Paris was uneventful, there was an unmistakable air of unrest about the streets.

We learned that during our travels, the Hôtel de Ville had been seized by protesters of the Franco-Prussian war, and since liberated again by soldiers through the underground tunnels. During our stay—safely outside of Paris at my cousins' chateau—the riots began, and the Hôtel de Ville was burned so thoroughly that the fire swallowed it from the inside, leaving nothing behind but a stone husk.

I cannot explain the reason, but the loss of France's extant records from the Revolution did not seem as important to me as the fate of Louis Napoleon's investigations about St. Germain. The name infected my memory, as did his association with Paris' municipality headquarters. I wondered what those investigations had found, if anything, or if they'd been lost forever.

My parents spoke no more of St. Germain these days, and my favorite cousin, Felicity, had never heard of him. She took to the intrigue, however, with all the fervor of a true gossip, and it was her recommendation that we explore the library at University of Paris. With such ample resources for theology and humanities available there, I could hardly refuse.

My father was less keen upon it, initially mistaking my request as interest in attending. The University of Paris had more artistic focus than he cared for, and now that Girton College's doors had opened to women, he'd expected me to carry on his legacy through Cambridge. The assurance of research placated him, though I was careful to keep mum regarding my true goal.

Felicity and I began with Voltaire's works, who I understood had been outspoken on the topic of St. Germain. When I returned to the elderly librarian for further reading, his bushy white mustache bristled at the mention of the count.

"You're not the first to inquire after such a particular subject in recent years, Mademoiselles," he said, beckoning us towards another wing in the archives. "Many have sought answers, but the Count of St. Germain remains a man of mystery. Here we are."

The spry gentleman paused his brisk stride to extend his arm and retrieve a book from the shelf before. He continued onward to another wing to collect a second and a third, and from these I learned St. Germain wasn't *just* an alchemist, but a savant who excelled at everything he did. He was a musician, composer, and a master painter. He was a great man of learning, believed to speak as many as ten languages, and an extensive traveler who recounted historical events throughout the ages as if he'd witnessed them.

His talents carried over to diplomacy, where his charisma aided his efforts to set Catherine II upon the Russian throne, as well as his attempt to thwart an assassination against Sweden's Gustavus III. The more references I found pertaining to such things, the more I realized just how well-connected the count truly was, having been sought amongst the highest of courts and social gatherings throughout Europe and beyond. Perhaps for that reason, Louis XV sanctioned him to commence peace talks on behalf of France during the Seven Years' War.

I also learned that the count was not without his enemies; amid accusations of charlatans and disgrace, contemporaries such as Voltaire made great sport of him. The Librarian was indeed correct about previous inquiries, but Louis Napoleon was not the first high-ranking official to possess such infatuation on the count's origins, nor was he the only one to fail in his investigation. Hard pursuit of St. Germain had a peculiar tendency to end in the disappearance of the evidence, or the count himself.

London, England
1882
Isabella Cooper, age 28

Despite my mother's warnings, I never did, in fact, break my neck climbing anyone's latticework. I *did* have a riding accident in '77 in which I tragically crushed my favorite topper, which was about as difficult to restore as my fractured hip.

Unable to walk for the better part of two years, I was afforded ample time to make additional studies into my burgeoning interest of theosophical studies, and much to my father's chagrin, St. Germain remained at the core of my obsession. By following a rabbit hole of tertiary accounts from various correspondences—letters, diaries, and other sources not often published in book collections—I'd uncovered his associations with a myriad of esoteric societies that had spawned the Immortal Count moniker. I wondered if he had discovered some great secret through his alchemy.

The more my father criticized, the more determined I was to prove that spiritualism and intellectualism were not required to be mutually exclusive. From my research, St. Germain was precisely the worldly, well-educated, mysterious type that my father would have met privately during his appointment as commissioner.

I was still coming to understand the philosophical angles of alchemy when I first met Alfred John Oakley, a man who shared my practical interest in fringe sciences, though he sought his degrees in mathematics and physics at Pembroke. He had particular theories regarding time travel, a topic he only introduced in conversation when he felt quite certain I wouldn't mock him. But why should I, when both our interests demanded a certain level of faith?

I crossed paths with him often in the Cambridge libraries, drawn to his warm disposition so that we began to meet more deliberately. John was a tall, lanky fellow that always seemed a bit disheveled, as if his studies possessed slightly more priority than strict adherence to presentation. Though my entry to the nearby Girton College was inevitable, it was also made exciting by our friendship. Felicity had long since grown bored with St. Germain, but John found threads in connection to his own interests and raised stimulating thoughts for my consideration.

"It was a Pythagorean who first posed that the brain was the seat of intelligence," he told me during one of our many conversations about the Immortal Count. "Hippocrates agreed; there's no discernable reason for humans to age once maturity is reached, and living indefinitely should not be long unknown from the scientific community, barring interference of injury or infection, of course. Perhaps your count discovered a universal medicine of sorts."

This was how we grew close. I could speak with John for hours about St. Germain, and he never once scoffed at even the more fantastical parts of the legends.

"I'm only rather jealous that he possesses your attention so thoroughly," he said to me once, after I'd spent the better part of the afternoon detailing the count's tendencies to disappear after having outlived a particular era.

The comment surprised me, and I looked up from my scattered papers expecting John to be staring at my flushing cheeks. Yet he'd turned away, one hand akimbo, with the other pressed thoughtfully against his jaw as he considered the charts he'd pinned to a board. His sleeves were rolled up and his shirttails had bunched out from between his pants and waistcoat. His hair—a bit long for what was deemed fashionable—was rather mussed from too many swipes of his hand, and the beginnings of a beard shadowed his cheeks. Unaware of my gaze, he leaned an ink-smudged arm against the board and scribbled a note upon one of his papers.

I daresay I'm going to marry him one of these days.

Milan, Italy
September 1884
Isabella Cooper-Oakley, age 30

John burst through the door to our apartment in London, breathless and sweaty, as if he'd sprinted the whole way to inform me, "Your St. Germain—he's in Milan!"

I rested my book into my lap and tilted my head. "How do you figure?"

"He was seen at a Freemasons' meeting there—reportedly the same man Louis Napoleon found in Paris years ago, though he answers to Francesco Giovanini."

My hand was shaking as I wrote him, introducing myself as a student of theosophy. His reply was swifter than I expected, with a much-welcomed invitation to visit. John and I boarded a train to Italy the following week.

The address given to us was in an affluent piazza near the Montanelli Public Gardens, where John and I strolled once we'd rested. With the completion of the new train tunnels, the city had become far more vibrant than I remembered as a girl.

Signore Giovanini matched every description I'd uncovered of St. Germain, from his dark hair and brown complexion, to the simple yet stylish manner of dress that implied old money. He was a man of medium height and build who appeared to be in his late forties, by the sprinkling of silver about his temples. There was nothing remarkable about his features other than a face full of genius brought about by the intelligence behind his gentle eyes. There were great secrets behind those eyes, I was certain of it.

He greeted John as if they had attended the same Masonic meetings all their lives; God, what I wouldn't have given for the bonds of fraternity. When he regarded me, however, my jealousy subsided, as if the entire universe behind those eyes shifted towards me. He granted me a warm smile, and there was a flicker there, as if I were a most pleasant surprise.

"I was so pleased to receive your letter, Mrs. Cooper-Oakley," he said in an accent that was molasses-thick and just as slow. "May we speak in Italian or French? Spanish, perhaps? Forgive me, but English has never been my strongest tongue."

"Good god, *Signore*," said John quite suddenly, still in English, as he stared at the room of antiquity beyond. "You have the makings of a museum in here!"

The fascination upon his face was understandable, but I gave him a deliberate nudge and whispered "*En français, mon amour*."

Giovanini seemed charmed as he stepped aside to allow us in and gestured towards a sitting area brimming with curios. "Do have a closer look, if it pleases you. These items rarely enjoy such admiration."

He excused himself then to fetch tea for us, and the instant he was gone, I let my eyes roam the space. There was so much to take in that it was difficult to focus upon any one thing.

Assorted cultural items lined the display cabinets like a parade of folklore through the ages: handscrolls and ceramics from the Orient, African headdresses and beaded necklaces, Celtic flagons, carved wooden figures from Polynesia, Islamic ivory, delicate painted fans, and European puzzle boxes. The texts sitting upon the floor-to-ceiling bookshelves did not appear contemporary, many without discernible labeling upon their spines, and some with rigid bindings and metallic latches. Portraits of nobles in courtly dress had been mounted between the shelving and cabinets upon the walls, so masterfully painted that the jewels looked authentic.

John was so eager for a closer look that he nearly knocked over a violin from its pedestal, and as I rushed to straighten the sheet music, I caught a glance into the space beyond the sitting room. A laboratory had been fashioned there, and shelving units stacked with an array of scientific devices ranging from astronomical to mathematical to chemical. Above the workstation was an old map of Nova Scotia's coastline, and blueprints to a complex series of underground tunnels. Just as I considered the romantic notion of buried treasure, I noticed the model of a steamship, though I couldn't make out the name from where I stood. My eyes were drawn farther back, where a massive star chart upon the far wall was marked with notations, and I marveled instead at the sizable telescope mounted at the windowsill.

Everything within these rooms was exactly what I thought *should* have been present when the Count of St. Germain's death had been officiated in 1784, not the Spartan husk that had been reported devoid of any personal keepsakes.

Giovanini returned with tea and regarded John—still nose-to-nose with his collection—with a pleased smile. John wasn't paying attention, having moved farther in towards the laboratory, and I was primed to summon him when Giovanini said, "It's quite all right," as he set a tray with a teapot and two cups upon a serving table. "There is no museum to which these items will ever belong, and they have precious few admirers. He will join us when he sees fit, I am certain."

I frowned at the two cups Giovanini filled with tea, which he set deliberately near the chairs intended for John and me; there was no third cup upon the service. "Will you not have any, Monsieur?"

"No, no, my dear, this is for you to enjoy. My needs are quite simple, and I prefer simple mineral water."

"Do you mean to say you don't drink tea? Whyever would you keep it, then?"

"Because, Mrs. Cooper-Oakley," Giovanini said. "I knew you were coming."

"Isabella, please," I insisted. I glanced once more at John, but his back was to us, focused upon some trinket from the shelves. I followed Giovanini's cue by taking my seat in a leather armchair, the cup and saucer resting in my lap.

"I was most pleased to receive your letter," Giovanini said to me. "You're a student of theosophy? Whatever attracted you to such a subject?"

"Alchemy."

Intrigue glittered behind his dark eyes. "How curious." Giovanini leaned back into his chair, his gaze thoughtful as his forefinger tapped against his clean shaven cheek. "Such a tricky subject, isn't it? Its very definition is so often confused, yet no matter where or when or how it's presented, the core of alchemy has remained consistent. Transmutation. Evolution, if you will. May it be spiritual or intellectual, it follows the same principles. Did you know, Isabella, that the term was used with so broad a stroke during eighteenth-century Europe that it referred to both medieval alchemy as well as emerging chemists?"

"It was quite a metamorphic time," I said with a nod. "Alchemy in particular was at an unusual crossroads between mysticism and reason." I paused before adding, "But I'm confident few would know as well as you."

Giovanini smiled, but I wasn't certain he'd take my bait. "Everything is connected," he agreed with a nod of his chin. "It's a chief principle of alchemy. Yes, I can understand your fascination, indeed. We succeed, we fail, we improve, and do it all again, don't we? We ourselves are the Holy Grail, and the Garden of Eden is still within us to rediscover. A new Atlantis, if you will."

"I beg your pardon?"

"The lost city of Atlantis," he clarified, and he sat up to drag a globe upon an iron filigree pedestal between us. He spun it slowly, his eyes searching. "There are those who believe it was the original site of Eden, but—ah, right here." He tapped at the Mediterranean Sea. "It was actually on the island of Santorini, just off the shores of Crete, though natural disasters have long since destroyed evidence of it. Pity."

I suppressed a laugh. "But Atlantis was merely an allegory." I hesitated. "Wasn't it?"

"No more than any other variant of heaven you'll find throughout the cultures of the world. What do you remember reading about Atlantis? Regarding the city itself, and not the cautionary aspects of the tale."

I took a moment to recall Plato's works. "I've only the impression that it was a city of great might and achievement."

"Your impression is correct. They were not the only ones, either. Worldwide, ancient civilizations possessed great power and higher learning. What the Greeks later recalled as gods were sophisticated beings who had mastered universal truths in mathematics and physics."

"If they were so advanced, how could they fail?"

"It is what we do, Isabella," Giovanini said, his hands open as he shrugged. "The aforementioned cycle we endure is constant, and sometimes quite long, but humanity has seen more enlightened days and will do so again. Would you dismiss it if I told you that the ancients had the ability to construct monolithic structures capable of withstanding earthquakes? Or that flying contraptions were conceived long before Sir Cayley or da Vinci? That medical treatments once achieved the sophistication to halt death?"

I was mid-sip of the last of my tea when Giovanini's words sparked a memory of something John had said to me once—a bit about St. Germain having found a type of universal medicine. I set the teacup back upon its saucer, afraid that the shaking in my hand might bring misfortune to the fine porcelain.

"Do you mean the philosopher's stone?"

My question came out almost as a whisper, one to which I half-expected to be laughed off, but Giovanini replied in all sincerity without a breath of hesitation.

"The secrets of the ancients may be scattered to the winds, but they are still there for those who seek them. In time, they will emerge."

At the mention of ancient secrets, my spine straightened and I leaned closer, searching the depths of those knowing eyes for some affirmation, some semblance of acknowledgement of my inkling. "Why not now?"

He gave a nonchalant shrug as he looked briefly away. "It is not always so simple, despite its fundamental simplicity. There are those who were shunned as heretics or burned as witches. You cannot force wisdom upon the unreceptive. The enlightened may influence those around them, disseminating ideas and nurturing them, but humanity must evolve on a grander scale before those ideas can be brought to fruition. But fear you not, my dear Isabella." His eyes returned to mine. "The teacher always comes when the student is ready."

"I say," said John, and his voice shattered my trance so thoroughly that I was surprised to see him standing aside the globe to which we had both leaned towards during our discourse. "This is all rather cozy, isn't it?" I had forgotten he was here at all, and he had a furrow about his brow that suggested he'd sensed as much.

"Oh, John! Here—" I got to my feet at once, reaching for his tea, though it had long gone cold. John wasn't interested in tea, however, and as I set it aside with some dejection, it occurred to me how threatening our deep conversation must have appeared to my husband. Sitting face-to-face with the man I'd researched for years put my obsession in an entirely different light.

Giovanini must have felt the misstep as well, as he also got to his feet. "Ah, Mr. Cooper-Oakley, I was hoping you'd join us. I understand you're a physicist?"

"And a mathematician," I added, ever grateful for Giovanini's silver tongue. "John, do tell him about your theories about space and time."

John cleared his throat; I'd embarrassed him a little, but Giovanini seemed pleased. There was a curious gleam in his eyes as he glanced from John to me and back again.

"Well of *course*, my good man. I should be enthralled to hear your theories. In fact, I have something that may be of interest to you."

Giovanini led my husband across the room to the laboratory beyond, and though John initially shot me a sour glare for mentioning time travel, it was surface deep. I lingered back and observed the pair chat about relativity and the perception of time. John's eyes were bright behind his spectacles as Giovanini showed him a particular device he'd brought down from the shelves of his laboratory.

I could not quite determine the purpose of it, aside from vague astronomical implications. It was fairly small, comprised of a base and a series of rotating brass cylinders and extended arms, all of which could have fit within the palm of my hand. Several gemstones had been fitted upon the extending arms to represent celestial bodies.

"My astrolabe timepiece," Giovanini offered, passing the device to John, who accepted it with both hands.

"You believe time travel is possible?" John asked, visibly stunned.

"It's quite possible, yes. The ambition to journey freely through time struck me some years ago, and so I fashioned this as a meager attempt. It doesn't work in practice, I'm afraid."

"But you truly believed enough to build it."

"I was driven by altruistic grandeur at the time. Alchemy is a miraculous transformation in all its forms, but it cannot be forced or cheated." Once again, Giovanini looked between the pair of us with a smile. "But my, what wondrous things one might discover."

John turned the device over in his hands, mulling over every centimeter of its construction. I knew him to have a handful of associates who enjoyed bantering the topic of time travel about, but this was the first practical attempt he'd seen for his own eyes, and he appeared changed to me during this conversation—quiet and distant and lost in his thoughts.

"Why do you suppose it doesn't work?" he asked at length.

Giovanini's mouth screwed up in consideration before he spoke. "Likely, the design is incomplete. Perhaps an astrarium is a more appropriate platform from which to start."

"Of course," John agreed, considering the device thoughtfully. "You need to establish fixed points in time—coordinates, if you will. The constellations must be supported with additional plotting points within a triangulated destination—but whatever are these gemstones for? And what kind of stone is this one here? I've never seen anything like it."

He pointed to a sizable gemstone in the center of the astrolabe, dark like ebony, but translucent and multidimensional. It reminded me of the northern lights in the far reaches of Norway, gleaming with gradients of every color, like oil seeping upon black water. Utterly beautiful, yet I had no name for it even as I drew closer.

"It looks like alexandrite," I offered, though my answer hardly satisfied. No stone had ever appeared so exquisite in any memory I could recall.

With an open palm, Giovanini gestured to the celestial map upon the wall, alongside several gem charts. "Gemstones have corresponded to particular celestial bodies since ancient days, as well as to points in time. They are the bridge needed between math and physics."

"Another alchemic combination?" I asked ironically, and Giovanini turned his gaze to me.

"Everything is connected," he reminded me with a knowing smile.

Rochester, New York, United States
April 1885
Isabella Cooper-Oakley, age 31

I had suspected, upon finally meeting Giovanini, that I would have left feeling somehow disappointed, but the more we interacted, the more he made peculiar allusions, the more his dark eyes twinkled at John and me, the more I grew convinced that he was indeed the elusive Count of St. Germain. He'd evaded all my hints at his identity throughout the evening, navigating the conversation with clever replies that neither answered nor ignored me. It was deliberate, and though always performed without offense, it tugged at me long after we'd departed Italy.

My irritation developed in the days, weeks even, after our meeting, when I considered all the secrets he carried that would benefit his fellow man if only he did not horde them away. It echoed of my childhood, when strangers occupied hours of my father's time for issues I was always excluded from, and I disliked St. Germain's secrecy all the more for it. I disagreed with Giovanini—in our day and age of technological advancement, humanity absolutely was ready for whatever he harbored, and it was cruel of him to withhold it. I wished that I'd had the opportunity to convince him as such, armed with his admission and indisputable proof.

I could not even be calmed by the gift Giovanini had seen me off with—in fact, the mysterious black stone from the astrolabe only added to my frustration, as he hadn't bothered to explain what I was intended to do with it aside from a simple assurance of "great things." I'd inspected, squeezed it, heated it, prayed to it, set it in water, even touched it to my tongue, and I could garner no reaction from it, let alone anything attributed to the philosopher's stone I suspected it to be.

The meeting affected John differently, galvanizing him to construct his own variation of a time machine. He'd built it from a longcase clock, inspired by a story he'd read in *The Sun* some months back sent by an American associate of his.

We moved from London to Budapest, where John was connected to fellow physicist and electrician Nikola Tesla—a somewhat disorganized personality, but a valuable contributor to the machine's functions—before the young Serbian left for Paris shortly thereafter.

At first, John attributed my general melancholy to the move across Europe, but in fact, my despair revolved more closely around St. Germain. I wanted Giovanini to admit who and what he was, not just to become his equal, but to see humanity restored to the utopia he'd implied. A return to the Garden of Eden. The thought of it made me sigh, which I did so many times that John couldn't ignore it despite his own distractions. I was hesitant to admit my mind still circled St. Germain after having made John so wary in Milan, but his response was considerate as he drew me into his embrace.

"When my time machine works, we'll find St. Germain and you'll have your proof."

He kissed my forehead and returned to his workstation, but I remained skeptical as I stood there watching him work.

"With what proof?" I asked him. "St. Germain of the past hasn't met us—Giovanini did."

John had a solution for that, too—photography. Current technology was too cumbersome and messy, of course, but the same friend who'd forwarded him the American newspaper also owned the Eastman Dry Plate and Film Company in Rochester, and John was certain if there was anyone working on a more portable solution, George Eastman would be our man.

We wrote to him at once, and though we made plans to travel together to New York, John became ill days before our departure and was advised to remain homebound for several weeks. I thus made the journey alone. At first, I was wary; America was an unfamiliar country, and Mr. Eastman was unmarried. John gave a good-natured chuckle when I expressed my hesitation and said, "No troubles there. I expect George is more likely to make advances at me than you."

Mr. Eastman, his mother, and his sister were kind enough to pick me up from the train depot in Rochester, and though he did seem rather fond of women, he had an unmistakable air of propriety about him. I was quite at ease in his company, even after we left my bags with his kin and separated from them for a visit to the Eastman factory.

Mr. Eastman was well-dressed, very polite and quite eager to talk about his passion for photography, and by the time we'd reached his office, I knew all about the formation of his company over the years, as well as recent developments. He selected a model from his workstation, a simplistic box camera small enough for the metal and wood framework to fit comfortably in my hands. It was preloaded, he explained, with a hundred-exposure roll that would capture any image at the push of the shutter button. I bent closer to inspect the single lens protruding from the front side, the two lines on the top face intended to aim the shot, and the rotating key that wound the film to the next frame.

"It's perfect," I breathed. "What will you call it?"

Mr. Eastman shrugged. "My mother suggested Kodak. I don't know how she came up with it, but I rather like the sound of it."

There was a knock at the door, and Mr. Eastman's secretary peeked his head in to announce the arrival of a visitor by the name of Mr. Cooper-Oakley.

"John?" Mr. Eastman turned a quizzical gaze toward me, but all I could offer was a shrug, for I was just as perplexed to see my husband stroll in. He had a disheveled bachelor's appearance, as though he'd not left the house much in my absence—he needed a shave, his clothes were quite rumpled, and his hair, always a bit longer than fashionable, had grown long enough to tie back behind his neck—but he was healthy and in good spirits.

He smelled faintly of perspiration as I embraced him. "It *works*!" he breathed into my ear, his arms clenching so tight about my ribcage that it stifled my breath for an instant. He broke away at once without elaboration, and greeted Mr. Eastman excitedly as he apologized for his delay and for the miscommunication.

I had to exercise great patience through the remainder of the evening as the two men caught up with each other, inwardly squirming for privacy and a thorough explanation. We brought John abreast of the phenomenal box camera Mr. Eastman intended to send us off with for field testing, and had dinner with his mother and sister. It wasn't until we'd retired for the evening that John revealed—nearly bursting with excitement—that he'd arrived by means of the time machine, which he'd left hidden in some trees upon the Eastman property.

"I was certain all the components were there for the machine to work," he said. "I completed it while you were gone, but it was your idea to add the stone Giovanini gave you. I didn't ask you before, but why didn't you tell me he'd given it to you? I could have had this puzzle solved months ago!"

"I didn't realize . . ." I began, my thoughts drifting back to countless hours spent mulling over the damned thing. I'd been so convinced it was a philosopher's stone that I'd failed to consider its usage outside of the traditional sense. Perhaps I'd been misguided by the fact that the stone had been given to me, and not John, or by the impression that it had been useless in Giovanini's own attempt at a time machine.

John did not appear truly upset however, still riding the high of his success, and I beamed at him. He had that boyish, nervous energy about him that had charmed me during those days at university when we'd met, and I caught his face between my hands so as to kiss him square on the mouth.

"This is incredible, John!" I declared, and he picked me up and whirled me once through the air. I held tightly to him even as he set me upon my feet again. "Let's return together, then!"

His face, boyishly pleased by my affections, suddenly turned aghast at the idea. "No!" he exclaimed, then having realized how much he'd raised his voice, forced his reply into a hush. "You'll have to return the long way, I'm afraid. I'll be returning to a Budapest three months from now, and you're already there. But," he added, with a good-natured shrug, "at least we have assurance that you'll return safely."

Budapest, Hungary
July 1885
Isabella Cooper-Oakley, age 31

The house was in nearly pristine condition when I returned several weeks later, not by John's efforts, but by his neglect. The cupboards were empty, and our rooms—the basement workshop notwithstanding—appeared unlived-in. John was

211

tinkering away in a disaster area of precision parts, maps, and measuring devices orbiting the husk of the longcase clock that would be his time machine.

I smiled at the sight of him; he hadn't heard me come in, and he bumped his head when I greeted him. Nonetheless, he greeted me warmly, the whiskers on his face scratching my cheek as he leaned in to kiss me.

He was all too eager to show me the intricate additions he'd made, not so unlike what we'd seen on Giovanini's astrolabe device. The clock's faceplate had been swapped with a multitude of settings, each which demonstrated the exact position of celestial bodies in any calculated point in time. Various dials and mechanical counters—the gemstones among them—allowed for the adjustment of physical coordinates.

"It looks quite nearly complete," I said.

"It is," he replied, though there was a tinge of dejection as he regarded the longcase clock. "Well, it *has* been, but I haven't quite gotten it up and running. Mechanically speaking, it functions, but it has yet to journey anywhere. I can't think of what it's missing."

I muttered to myself and dug around in my handbag. "Perhaps because you're missing Giovanini's philosopher's stone."

John's brow pinched. "That garish black thing? I don't even know what it is or how to find one, let alone how to utilize it. Oh my, is that it?" He adjusted his spectacles on the bridge of his nose as he took it from my hand. "It looks the same cut and everything—good gracious, Isabella, you didn't pilfer it, did you?"

I swatted his arm with my handbag. "I most certainly did not! Giovanini slipped it to me before we left, and he didn't say what for. Before my journey to America, I'd driven myself nearly mad trying to figure out how to use it, but it's rather obvious now, isn't it?"

After regaling John of his successful visit to Rochester, he consulted his charts and adjusted the dials accordingly.

"That's the tricky part with all this," he muttered. "If the coordinates are off just the slightest, the clock may very well end up in a wall or a lake. Wherever—or *whenever*—you decide to go, you need to be confident about where you're landing. Geographical changes don't just account for landmass. Cities have come and gone over the ages, haven't they?"

He placed the black stone upon the center faceplate, and a low humming fired up from the bowels of the longcase. It was quite subtle, only noticeable in our silence, mere white noise amidst conversation. But the air tingled now, electrified with significance.

"Go on, then," I said, squeezing his hand. "After all, we have assurance that you'll return safely."

It was only when John returned—and our celebrations thereafter—that we noticed the black stone did not appear quite as luminous as it once had. John removed it from its setting, and as the low hum ceased, he scrubbed the stone as if to clean it.

"I suspect there's a limit to its usage," he said, frowning. "If we're to chase after your St. Germain, we'll have to plan the journey carefully, coordinates aside. We should make the initial jump back to the earliest point in time your St. Germain can be traced, and move forward from there until we arrive again to the present."

I spent the next few days consulting my research—pages upon pages of notes taken from countless historical reports, books, and private correspondences—compiling all the speculated identities and cross-referencing them with sightings and associations throughout the eras. It was more difficult the further I went back in history, as recordkeeping muddied and there were far fewer threads to connect, but his patterns were the same, never failing to bear striking similarities to the Count of St. Germain's appearance, mannerisms, and habits.

From all this, I created his timeline for our itinerary, starting with Santorini Island—his supposed Atlantis. I traced him to Babylon, the library of Alexandria, house arrest in the Byzantine empire, a mathematics school in Muslim Spain, and several other points in time. He left his mark with the Knights Templar and the Rosicrucians, crossing paths with the likes of Nicholas Flamel, Vlad Dracul, and Shakespeare before eventually befriending Louis XV and Madame du Pompadour.

Panic flashed in John's eyes when he saw my proposed itinerary, a list of nothing short of a dozen places in time.

"We can't possibly risk this many stops!" he insisted, holding the diminished black stone between our noses. "We haven't a real idea how long its power may last! And, really, how many snapshots of the man do you need to prove your point?"

After a fair amount of arguing and compromising, we decided on a few limited locations, and while John carefully plotted our destinations, I begged the opera for the loan of some costumes. I stowed them within our travel packs and fashioned a leather carrying case for Mr. Eastman's Kodak.

With our preparations made, we stood before the clock, hand in hand. John reached forward to set the black stone, and as the time machine buzzed with life, the space within the longcase grew ethereal. I became dizzy the closer I drew to it, but followed John's lead as he stepped through.

Atlantis
1597 B.C.
Present-day Island of Santorini, in search of the inventor Talos

I experienced a sensation I can only describe as a dream-like freefall. It was dark at first, then light, then dark again, back and forth, as if day and night fought for advantage. I could not make much out beyond that, though I had the impression that objects came and went all around me. It was fuzzy about my periphery, as if I moved at light speed, and yet not at all. I stood upon solid ground, and yet none was there.

All that was true was John's hand upon mine, warm and solid and a bit clammy. He was there, my rock, my foundation, the only thing that made any sense in the chaos. It was he who dragged me from the neverspace, settling the earth and the sky and finally giving my eyes a fixed point to steady myself.

It was daylight—*bright* daylight; the sturdy construct of our rented house was gone, and we were surrounded instead by palm trees and beach grass. The afternoon sun hung languid in a deep blue sky, warm upon our skin. Mountains loomed on the nearby horizon, and all around us gusts of sea air rustled the sand dunes, carrying the caws of gulls and the scent of the ocean. There was no one around us, not a house nor a road nor any other sign of civilization. At first, I wondered where the time machine had gone, only to find it directly behind us, the belly of the longcase still open from where we'd stepped through.

John looked me over. "How are you feeling?"

"A bit like my insides are flipped."

"Right." Leaning towards the time machine, he removed the black stone from the main faceplate, and the queasiness faded. He shifted his spectacles as he stared at the stone within his palm, and I leaned closer to see the change in luster. "This trip certainly took more out of it."

I decided not to fret over the expenditure; the stone hadn't diminished so much as to be concerned about getting elsewhere, and I was so giddy with excitement that it was difficult to be a milksop over it. I regarded our conveyance as John tucked the gemstone safely away.

"It's a bit silly, isn't it?" I mused. "A longcase clock standing just so in the sand like this?"

We carried it towards a cluster of palm trees to conceal it, breaking quite a sweat in the process. The sand was unstable, and I stumbled over my skirt as often as John tripped over his own feet. With the time machine out of sight, and our packs in the husk of the clock, we debated how to approach the city. The ancients were not documented to have been a modest society, but we had little to guess at their actual attire, and so we decided to approach with caution and adapt our clothes as we came into contact with others.

Not far from our landing site, we crested a sand dune and found ourselves overlooking a sprawling metropolis flanking the oceanfront. My breath caught in my chest at the magnificent sight, a picturesque fusion of nature and civilization far apart from anything I'd seen anywhere in my travels. Unlike the tired, dingy edifices of most European cities, the city before us sparkled like a brand new thing, catching the sunlight as if built entirely from pale marble, silver, and glass. The sophistication of its architecture was difficult to comprehend, yet there it stood with spiraling towers and skyscrapers arching towards the clouds. Thousands of structures sprang from the sloping landscape as if grown from its very soil, and causeways stretched between them, buttressed by sweeping cantilevers.

Horseless carriages glided down the wide roadways, and conveyors swiftly scaled great heights without any rails or cables that I could see. On the far side of the cityscape, a sleek-bodied dirigible cruised the air with more dexterity I thought possible, and speeding upon the open water were scores of small ships that impressed me as recreational crafts and not merchant. Most lacked sails, but they didn't look like any steamship I'd seen. Nor did they perform as such, as one cut a path across the waves with remarkable speed.

It was marvelous and fantastical and entirely too awesome to be real.

"John . . . we did go *backwards* in time, yes?"

John's jaw hung open. He sputtered for a response, his head dipping down to consult the charts within his notebook. After a long moment of pages flipping back and forth, he gave an affirmative nod. Giovanini had not deceived us; great knowledge had indeed been lost.

"It looks like Heaven," John breathed.

"Or Mount Olympus," I said, nodding towards the mountain in the city's immediate backdrop. Perhaps it was sheer proximity that made it more imposing than those in the distance, or the fact that it loomed in the water, but I drew the Kodak from where it was nestled under my arm and snapped a photo. As I wound the key to the next frame, I said, "That's the volcano that destroys it all."

John consulted his maps again with a frown. "There's no mountain in the bay on any of these," he said. "It must have blown off its own topper and sunk into the water."

"Along with a quarter of the island," I said. "The eruption will be so intense that the ash from it will be found in Europe for centuries to come, blacking out the sun for weeks and prolonging winter by years."

I thought the information was fascinating, but John slid an annoyed side-eye at me—I hadn't mentioned any of this when we selected our destinations, and Atlantis had been a tough sell for him as it was. I pretended not to notice by raising my binoculars to my eyes, through which I observed how the pedestrians below were dressed. My bustled petticoats wouldn't do here, I quickly discerned, and I advised John to remove his waistcoat and unfasten the uppermost buttons of his shirt.

"You'd think a society that could engineer such marvels might choose a better place to settle than a hotbed of natural disasters," he said, pulling the shirttails from his waistband.

I lifted the hem of my limp skirt and stepped out from the pool of petticoats at my feet. "Perhaps not, if they were advanced enough to counter most of them. Giovanini said the ancients were far more sophisticated than surviving relics suggest."

"All the same, let's find St. Germain and be off." John paused with his hands at his suspenders, suddenly looking skeptical as he noticed me unhooking the front busk of my corset. "I say, are you sure we should be undressing this much?"

I passed him the binoculars. "Take a look for yourself," I said and tore the front of my chemise from hem to belly.

John flinched as I gathered the extra fabric and tied it just under my breasts. "That was nice underwear!"

"I do hope the Atlanteans agree." As I released my hair from its pins, John frowned at my exposed arms and stomach, and I sighed. "Did you not stress how important it was to blend in? Come on then, off with those suspenders. And tie your hair back."

He complied, albeit reluctantly. "How do these fellows keep their trousers up, anyway?" I caught amidst his low grumbles.

We found a path that led us down the slope and to the road below, where we encountered passerby along the wide walkways leading to the city. At once, John's discomfort seemed allayed as we not only passed without drawing much attention, but without being the most scandalous specimens about. Men and women alike strolled along with sun-kissed, bare limbs. The men were often shirtless and the women bared their midriffs and wore skirts ranging from the short and flouncy to the long and flowing. The textiles were light and gauzy, often brightly colored, so that our attire was drab and modest in comparison.

Immersed in the crowd, bits of conversations flittered to my ears, none of which I understood. Though I recognized the Cretan hieroglyphs upon scrolling marquis and painted signs, I knew little more of them other than the characteristics separating them from Egyptian, and the spoken variety was nothing like the Greek or Latin I was familiar with. A woman passed us seemingly talking to herself, until a secondary voice emitted from her handheld device, and I stared after her so intrigued that John had to tap my arm so that I'd face forward again.

We paused near an alley where an artist was suspended on a platform, painting frescoes similar to those that archaeologists found all over Crete.

I laughed. "It's but graffiti art to them," I said to John and snapped another photo. "What do you suppose they'd think if they knew *that's* what survived of them in our museums?"

John stepped closer and pushed the Kodak gently back under my arm. "I think," he said, "that we should be less conspicuous."

I disagreed, suspecting there was little reason to hide the Kodak; in this city full of technological wonders, John and I seemed almost primitive in comparison.

We pushed onwards towards the main plaza, where we were accosted by a young woman carrying pamphlets and wearing a brightly colored sash. John was so enthralled with the pamphlet—and the printing press that he surmised had produced it—that he hardly noticed a beaded trinket had been pinned to his shirt, or that a sash had been draped across my shoulders.

"Do you suppose we're supporting some political endeavor?" asked John as the woman moved on. "There's quite a few of these wranglers about the plaza."

I grabbed John by his shirt, inspecting the medallion more closely as it tickled a distant memory of something I had seen somewhere before, shrouded in age within a display case. "Giovanini had something like this among his collection," I said. "Talos is here, somewhere."

"Well, he's here in this pamphlet, surely," said John, and I snatched it from his hands.

I shouldn't have been surprised that the ancients possessed their own variant of photography, but upon finding the realistic portraits within the pamphlet, I lamented the Kodak's abilities; even Mr. Eastman's cutting edge techniques did not produce such refined results.

I zeroed in where John had pointed, and there was the Count of St. Germain—Giovanini—the man we'd spent an entire afternoon with in Milan. No span of time would ever blur his face from my mind. Looking up, my eyes searched the plaza for the woman who'd approached us, and when I'd spotted her, I waved for her attention despite John's protest.

"Where might we find him?" I asked the woman as we met halfway, not thinking at first of its impracticality. She didn't comprehend my English, of course, but my question was received all the same as I pointed fervently at St. Germain's portrait. She directed us to a large assembly hall at the corner of the plaza, and as John and I passed a series of columns and stepped into the cool shade, we found ourselves in what appeared to be a symposium of sorts. There was ample seating surrounding a center stage, upon which a demonstration was occurring before a panel of faces I recognized from the pamphlet. Among them was St. Germain.

I started to raise the Kodak, but then decided against it as a handful of people traversed the aisles between the seated areas, some departing, others finding more choice arrangements. "Let's get closer."

We found benches near the edge of the stage, off-center from St. Germain's focal point, and listened as the demonstration carried on. Sitting this close to him, watching

221

him interact with familiar mannerisms, I couldn't help but smile. He reached for a nearby chalice of clear liquid—his favored mineral water, I presumed—and our eyes met for the briefest instant. I raised the Kodak to my face, clumsy though it was, and pushed the shutter.

Alexandria, Egypt
48 B.C.
Roman Annexation, in search of the mathematician Carpus of Antioch

There was hardly a breath spared for motion sickness upon our next journey. Though John had set us successfully upon the roof of the Library of Alexandria, his calculations were flawed, and we arrived in the midst of a siege. Caesar's sacrificial ships burned in the harbor, destroying the Egyptian fleet and spreading to the city despite the blockades thrown up in the streets. John took one look at the billowing black smoke and chaos in the streets, and immediately set to work on the time machine. I stayed at the terrace and watched men flee from the library and dump armfuls of scrolls into waiting carts.

"St. Germain would want to preserve the knowledge," I said. "I'm going downstairs."

John dropped his notebooks and grabbed me as I reached for a cloak from our packs. "Are you mad? It's too dangerous."

"Very well, then," I said. "Recalculate."

John cast an uneasy glance at the black stone, now further spent, and shook his head. "I dare not risk it."

"Maslamah al-Majriti made the first recorded mention of conservation of mass," I said to John, keeping my voice low so as to not disturb those in study. "He used the concept to explore purifying gemstones, and later invented a process for producing mercury dioxide. His discoveries spread through Europe, and alchemy as we know it was born."

I nodded to the alchemical lab beyond the breezeway, where a figure paced amid the workstations within. I could not quite see his face, but my intuition prickled with certainty that it was St. Germain. I needed to get closer.

There were eyes upon us as we admired the star charts mounted upon the wall opposite the courtyard, and I looked over to see a dark-skinned beauty sitting at a desk surrounded by parchment and wells of ink. She was different from the others here, as she did not appear to be studying, but rather transcribing astronomical tables.

By my research, Maslamah was said to have a daughter, Fatima, but by all accounts St. Germain was quite celibate. Taking on a ward for the sake of learning sounded just like him, however, particularly during this golden age of Muslim intellectualism.

The quill was paused in Fatima's hand as she regarded us.

In truth, she looked right through me, bestowing all of her silent favor upon John. My husband was clueless—nose-to-the-wall without the aid of his spectacles, the long ends of his honey-brown hair curling from behind his ears and peeking out from his head covering.

"Don't be obvious about it," I whispered. "But you have an admirer."

Of *course* John was obvious about it, despite his efforts. was always clumsy about such things the instant he was

"Then stay here and set the next coordinates, while I try to salvage this opportunity."

"Absolutely not!" John cried, though I heard more fear in his voice than command. "Isabella, be reasonable—in all your studies, when have you found accounts of St. Germain in the seat of conflict? He most certainly would have received word of this and fled by now."

A nearby explosion startled us, and in the brief lapse of John's attention, I sprang into action, disappearing in the tower alcove. His distraught shouts did not follow me down the stairs, and with water from our cantina, I soaked my veil and wrapped the damp portion around my nose and mouth.

The library was massive, with a practical layout separating the various schools of learning. Shelves lined the walls, heaped with papyrus scrolls and surrounded by ladders and stairways by which to reach them, but as I coughed on smoke, I was reminded I had not the luxury of time to explore. I kept to the pillars as the men scoured the shelves, scouring for anything that might indicate a useful direction.

When a man rushed passed me carrying an overloaded basket, I recognized astronomical equipment and immediately traced his path. The hall took me to another set of stairs and opened to a prominent wing with a planetarium and several workstations. There were but two men left here collecting various apparatus, and an elderly scholar stacking texts and scrolls for the next runner, one of whom pushed me out of the way with an irritable bark.

I swore as much for the assault as I did for my general frustration. St. Germain wasn't here. Perhaps he was among those near the entrance, loading the carts. I turned heel and retraced my steps at a run as it occurred to me how much hotter it was than when I'd first passed through this hall.

The fire had engulfed much of the entrance and spread farther in along the draperies. As my eyes burned from the smoke, I realized someone called for me—or, rather, *at* me. The men remaining near the entrance, sweaty and smeared with soot, assisted escaping this way.

Crackling overhead gave everyone an increased sense of urgency, and a man turned to me, hand outstretched, as he spoke what I believed to be Greek. When I hesitated, he made a grab for me, withdrawing only to avoid to falling wreckage. It burst ablaze as it hit the floor, spitting flames and ash as the gap widened between us. Despite the close call, the man once again reached for me, but I was shoved aside as the runner from the planetarium caught his arm instead and hoisted himself over the blaze.

The heat was too intense now, and before another rescue attempt could be made, I fled in the opposite direction, back to the time machine and the safety of John's arms.

Córdoba, Spain
AD 1000
Al-Andalus, in search of the astronomer Maslamah al-Majriti

"I don't suppose you'll consider skipping this trek?" John asked, unsatisfied at his reflection in the longcase glass. We sat outside the city of Córdoba, hidden amongst trees just off the main road. "I don't look remotely Mediterranean. Your St. Germain has the right features to weave in and out of these cultures, but not me."

"Oh, but my dear John, you're quite in luck!" I declared as I fastened a sash over his tunic. He was tense under my hands. "Blonds are all the rage among the Berbers, and thanks to a thriving slave industry, you'll find plenty of folk boasting fair features."

Mentioning slavery was a poor choice; my jest not only fell flat, but it took lengthy persuasion to convince John to go through with the outing after that. He had not thoroughly forgiven me for my dash through the library, which I heard all about in a diatribe that was much like the first I'd received upon that burning rooftop. I held my peace as he criticized my reckless behavior, and only after he appeared to be losing steam did I promise endlessly that I'd never again endanger either one of us. As if to emphasize my vow, I fastened m veil across my mouth and pleaded with my eyes.

John looked away, still somewhat disgruntled, but I hopeful when he consulted his notebook. "Where will we your St. Germain this time?"

There was only one place to find him—teaching school of Astronomy and Mathematics he'd founded un name of Maslamah al-Majriti. Though my Urdu wa useless for conversing, the Arabic text was comprel and the school wasn't difficult to locate once we'd g town.

It was a modest structure, accommodating only of students; hardly the college I'd imagined, tho blessedly open to the public according to a notice entrance. The study rooms were open and bree tables stretching almost as far back as an archwa pleasant, yet modest, courtyard. Beyond that w area with more workspace and various scientif

"Then stay here and set the next coordinates, while I try to salvage this opportunity."

"Absolutely not!" John cried, though I heard more fear in his voice than command. "Isabella, be reasonable—in all your studies, when have you found accounts of St. Germain in the seat of conflict? He most certainly would have received word of this and fled by now."

A nearby explosion startled us, and in the brief lapse of John's attention, I sprang into action, disappearing in the tower alcove. His distraught shouts did not follow me down the stairs, and with water from our cantina, I soaked my veil and wrapped the damp portion around my nose and mouth.

The library was massive, with a practical layout separating the various schools of learning. Shelves lined the walls, heaped with papyrus scrolls and surrounded by ladders and stairways by which to reach them, but as I coughed on smoke, I was reminded I had not the luxury of time to explore. I kept to the pillars as the men scoured the shelves, scouring for anything that might indicate a useful direction.

When a man rushed passed me carrying an overloaded basket, I recognized astronomical equipment and immediately traced his path. The hall took me to another set of stairs and opened to a prominent wing with a planetarium and several workstations. There were but two men left here collecting various apparatus, and an elderly scholar stacking texts and scrolls for the next runner, one of whom pushed me out of the way with an irritable bark.

I swore as much for the assault as I did for my general frustration. St. Germain wasn't here. Perhaps he was among those near the entrance, loading the carts. I turned heel and retraced my steps at a run as it occurred to me how much hotter it was than when I'd first passed through this hall.

The fire had engulfed much of the entrance and spread farther in along the draperies. As my eyes burned from the smoke, I realized someone called for me—or, rather, *at* me. The men remaining near the entrance, sweaty and smeared with soot, assisted escaping this way.

Crackling overhead gave everyone an increased sense of urgency, and a man turned to me, hand outstretched, as he spoke what I believed to be Greek. When I hesitated, he made a grab for me, withdrawing only to avoid to falling wreckage. It burst ablaze as it hit the floor, spitting flames and ash as the gap widened between us. Despite the close call, the man once again reached for me, but I was shoved aside as the runner from the planetarium caught his arm instead and hoisted himself over the blaze.

The heat was too intense now, and before another rescue attempt could be made, I fled in the opposite direction, back to the time machine and the safety of John's arms.

Córdoba, Spain
AD 1000
Al-Andalus, in search of the astronomer Maslamah al-Majriti

"I don't suppose you'll consider skipping this trek?" John asked, unsatisfied at his reflection in the longcase glass. We sat outside the city of Córdoba, hidden amongst trees just off the main road. "I don't look remotely Mediterranean. Your St. Germain has the right features to weave in and out of these cultures, but not me."

"Oh, but my dear John, you're quite in luck!" I declared as I fastened a sash over his tunic. He was tense under my hands. "Blonds are all the rage among the Berbers, and thanks to a thriving slave industry, you'll find plenty of folk boasting fair features."

Mentioning slavery was a poor choice; my jest not only fell flat, but it took lengthy persuasion to convince John to go through with the outing after that. He had not thoroughly forgiven me for my dash through the library, which I heard all about in a diatribe that was much like the first I'd received upon that burning rooftop. I held my peace as he criticized my reckless behavior, and only after he appeared to be losing steam did I promise endlessly that I'd never again endanger either one of us. As if to emphasize my vow, I fastened my veil across my mouth and pleaded with my eyes.

John looked away, still somewhat disgruntled, but I was hopeful when he consulted his notebook. "Where will we find your St. Germain this time?"

There was only one place to find him—teaching at the school of Astronomy and Mathematics he'd founded under the name of Maslamah al-Majriti. Though my Urdu was nearly useless for conversing, the Arabic text was comprehensible, and the school wasn't difficult to locate once we'd gotten into town.

It was a modest structure, accommodating only a handful of students; hardly the college I'd imagined, though it was blessedly open to the public according to a notice posted at the entrance. The study rooms were open and breezy, with long tables stretching almost as far back as an archway leading to a pleasant, yet modest, courtyard. Beyond that was an adjoining area with more workspace and various scientific apparatus.

225

"Maslamah al-Majriti made the first recorded mention of conservation of mass," I said to John, keeping my voice low so as to not disturb those in study. "He used the concept to explore purifying gemstones, and later invented a process for producing mercury dioxide. His discoveries spread through Europe, and alchemy as we know it was born."

I nodded to the alchemical lab beyond the breezeway, where a figure paced amid the workstations within. I could not quite see his face, but my intuition prickled with certainty that it was St. Germain. I needed to get closer.

There were eyes upon us as we admired the star charts mounted upon the wall opposite the courtyard, and I looked over to see a dark-skinned beauty sitting at a desk surrounded by parchment and wells of ink. She was different from the others here, as she did not appear to be studying, but rather transcribing astronomical tables.

By my research, Maslamah was said to have a daughter, Fatima, but by all accounts St. Germain was quite celibate. Taking on a ward for the sake of learning sounded just like him, however, particularly during this golden age of Muslim intellectualism.

The quill was paused in Fatima's hand as she regarded us.

In truth, she looked right through me, bestowing all of her silent favor upon John. My husband was clueless—nose-to-the-wall without the aid of his spectacles, the long ends of his honey-brown hair curling from behind his ears and peeking out from his head covering.

"Don't be obvious about it," I whispered. "But you have an admirer."

Of *course* John was obvious about it, despite his efforts. He was always clumsy about such things the instant he was conscious of them. The woman smiled behind her veil and lowered her eyes to her work, though she was quick to hazard a second glance.

John cleared his throat and pretended to study the star charts further. "What do I do?"

"Stay here and distract her, so I can investigate the alchemical lab."

He blanched. "Distract her how? I can't speak a word of Arabic, and I don't want to walk out of here with *two* wives."

"Oh, for goodness' *sake*, John." I squeezed his hand to reassure him. "Just make eyes at her until I can sneak past."

I meandered about the room in my play to escape Fatima's notice, making a show of observing the various wall hangings, and suppressing jealousy every time she cast her sultry dark eyes towards John. I was about to make my move into the courtyard, but halted my steps at the last second and averted my face as St. Germain emerged from the alchemical lab.

He greeted Fatima, the timbre of his voice familiar and gentle as it always was, and regarded her work with a searching eye. I glanced over my shoulder towards John, who returned a nervous expression that implored me to make haste.

An idea occurred to me as I noticed a bench facing the archways to both the study hall and the laboratory. Feigning fatigue, I sought it for a short rest, and adjusted the Kodak at my side so the lens faced St. Germain and Fatima. When I was certain that the angle was proper, I pressed the shutter.

The gentle click of the box camera did not escape notice, and I held my breath and regarded the mosaic tile as if I hadn't noticed St. Germain pause. I chewed at my lip and refused to meet his eyes, though I felt the full weight of his scrutinizing gaze upon me and the exposed Kodak at my hip. He moved as if he intended to speak to me, but John appeared at the archway and said, "Let's go, Isabella."

I did not mind that he'd done so, for not only was I quite certain St. Germain could not yet speak any form of English, but the summoning provided a reasonable excuse to make a swift, albeit graceless, departure.

Loir-et-Cher, France
1742
Château de Chambord, in search of the alchemist Count of St. Germain

A return to the northern European climate was a relief, not only for the familiar trees and air, but because the black stone had lost so much of its luminescence that it was reminiscent of a black pearl.

"This is our last stop," I reassured John. "We'll be home in no time!"

Some of John's humor had returned, enough at least to permit a smile even if he laced me into a gown in silence. I was rather pleased how sharp he looked in his courtier's waistcoat and breeches, his longer hair for once in vogue. Though my praise pleased him, I was certain his disposition was bolstered far more by the forthcoming return to present day.

The chateau was not far, and its Renaissance-style towers and white bastions emerged from the summer trees ahead. There was little concern about security; though the chateau belonged to Louis XV, he used it primarily as a resort, and the staff was thus accustomed to a high turnover of visitors.

Keeping our chins up and our strides proud, we strolled to the chateau without disruption.

St. Germain was here on a semi-permanent residence, having set up his laboratory at the king's behest. He was easy to find, surrounded by so much company in one of the spacious sitting rooms that our arrival was hardly noticeable. Courtiers lounged upon low cushioned chairs arranged in no particular order, leaving but a chivalrous few standing. The arrangement was intended for easy conversation between several cliques, and though I did not have a perfect view of everyone, I had a reasonable view of most. There was little prattle to be heard, however; all faces were turned toward St. Germain, rapt with interest as he performed some captivating parlor trick, and the room went still with anticipation before bursting into gasps and delighted laughter.

John and I hung back near the doorway and observed; St. Germain was dressed in all black, somewhat unusual amongst all the bright silks, yet he did not appear sinister. His smile was endearing, gentle as it always was, and it almost surprised me that one elderly woman stared at him, horrified. Before she spoke, I realized who she was—the Countess von Georgy, the account of whom I had read several times during my years of research.

The countess could not take her eyes from him, which did not remain unnoticed. St. Germain nodded in her direction.

"How fare you, Countess? Would you prefer music instead?"

Countess von Georgy shook her head at once, and she made efforts to straighten her posture, as if waking from a trance.

"Will you have the kindness to tell me," she began, her old voice cracked with uncertainty. "Whether your father was in Venice about the year 1710?"

"No, Madame, it is very much longer since I lost my father," St. Germain replied. "But I myself was living in Venice at the end of the last and beginning of this century."

He spoke with such conviction that those around him hesitated to respond. While most laughed it off, the elderly countess replied with fortified resolution.

"Forgive me, but that is impossible! The Count of St. Germain I knew in those days was at least forty-five years old, and you—at the outside—are that age at present."

"Madame," said St. Germain, placing his hand at his breast. "I am indeed very old."

"But then you must be nearly a hundred years!"

"That is not impossible." His eyes momentarily unfocused. "I loved springtime the most, when we'd take the gondolas to the Pałaso Dogal for Carnivale. You were there of course, Madame—a favored ambassadress with impeccable tastes. Yellow was certainly your color, was it not? You were a great beauty in your time. Of course I could not forget you."

He cast a wink towards her; it appeared friendly to me, but the countess was the only person in the room not giggling at his antics. St. Germain clapped his hands together as if something had just occurred to him, and he reached for his violin.

"Your favorite melody, Madame!" he declared as he set the instrument under his chin. The bow slid against the strings to elicit a romantic tune I could not name, and I watched St. Germain play, the notes drawn easily, a bard wielding music like magic.

The Countess von Georgy waved her hands, visibly upset, and as St. Germain paused, his expression concerned, the audible protests of the countess became clearer.

"None of that, no! I am already convinced," she said, her voice trembling in her hysterics. "For all that, you are a most extraordinary man."

Nearby courtiers and attendants leaned towards the countess to comfort her, or to assure her that it was all in playful jest, but she ignored such gestures. Her eyes remained hateful upon St. Germain, as if she thought him pure evil—

"A devil!" she spat, before my own thought could be realized. The force with which she said it startled even me.

The tension in the room was perhaps too much for even St. Germain. I could see in his face that he realized he'd gone too far.

"For pity's sake," he said, returning his violin to its stand. "No such names."

He paused then, and I stepped backwards into John, shuffling the pair of us out of sight.

"Did he see us?" John whispered, and I beamed at him.

"No," I said, patting the Kodak under my arm. "But I got a shot of him playing."

His mouth spread into a relieved grin. "Brilliant!"

John took my elbow to lead me back to the time machine, but I resisted as a figure in black emerged quite swiftly from the room. I needn't glimpse his face to know it was St. Germain, who turned the opposite direction from us with a clipped pace. I touched John's arm, imploring him to let us follow.

"There's no need, Isabella. You've got your proof."

"But the laboratory!" I pleaded. "Don't you wish to see it?"

"We *did* see it! We spent hours there in Milan. Besides, you don't know that's where he's heading."

"But I do! His encounter with the countess is well documented—I've read it hundreds of times and, word-for-word, we witnessed it unfold. He retreats to his apartments and refuses all social invitations for the remainder of the evening."

"How do you expect to see the laboratory if St. Germain shuts himself in?"

"He'll go to his private room, I'm sure, but the laboratory still belongs to the king and would be expected to remain accessible. We've come all this way, John, please?"

John looked unhappy, but he sighed in that way that I knew meant he would offer no further protest. The chateau was no burning library, after all. In our hesitation to trail him, St. Germain had nearly cleared the hall and turned a corner. We hastened our pace, catching sight of him again as he disappeared through an open door at the far end of the next corridor.

As I expected, the entrance remained wide open, and St. Germain was nowhere in sight when I peered inside. John did not follow me in, urging me from the doorway to make haste with the Kodak. I meant to comply, but I found myself quite awestruck standing here among the count's things.

The laboratory was not the castle dungeon I had always imagined it to be, but a tidy workshop filled with light. The walls were white, gilded with gold embellishment, and the decor a cheery red. Tall windows looked out onto the chateau's green lawn.

I raised the Kodak and snapped several shots, particularly those of things I recognized. I noticed much of the equipment that had been present in Milan set upon long tables along the walls, but there were other familiar items as well—the stunning paintings, the star charts, the Templar relics, and the hardbound books with metallic latches. There was the map of Nova Scotia, accompanied by blueprints of the intricate, multi-leveled maze, and among the piles of parchment, I recognized drafts of the yet-unnamed steamship I had seen a model for in Milan. I found the unsuccessful astrolabe timepiece tucked among many other trinkets, along with an hourglass-shaped item bearing a prismatic black stone quite similar to the one we'd been given. As I leaned in for a closer look, the device appeared to be filtering mineral water into a small vial below the jewel, one tiny drop at a time.

"Forgive me, Madame, but I don't believe I've had the honor of an introduction."

St. Germain's voice startled me so much that when I turned and gave a curtsey, I replied in English instead of the French spoken to me. He'd emerged from a room against the opposite wall from where I stood, and as he closed the door behind him, it was evident by his weary expression he'd expected to find company less than I'd expected to be caught. His face brightened when his eyes met mine, however, and he approached with a kind, knowing smile.

"*Mon Dieu*! But you've traveled quite far to come here."

With my French returned to me, I said, "Oh, but England is not so far."

His smiled broadened at that, and before he could press me for a name, I flattered his collections, insisting I'd heard of his laboratory and had not meant to intrude.

"I will see myself out, Monsieur," I said with another bow as I made to depart.

"It is no intrusion, Madame . . . forgive me, but how should I call you?"

"Félicité," I blurted, as the name of my French cousin flew to the forefront of my mind. "Félicité du Chandler. Monsieur, I really must—"

"Félicité," St. Germain repeated thoughtfully, though it seemed more of a private consideration than a direct address. "Well! You've indeed come a long way to find my laboratory. Would it please you to see an alchemic demonstration? Come, Madame."

He beckoned for me to join him at one of his tables, and though I most certainly should have departed when his back was turned, my curiosity kept me drawn to him. The man I'd chased across time and space had just invited me to witness him perform the very thing my father insisted was bullocks.

"Madame du Pompadour is on her way to Chambord," St. Germain explained as he showed me a sizable diamond taken from his pocket. "And Louis wishes to give this to her."

It was a jewel worthy of a queen, except for a flaw buried in its center that I only noticed with the aid of a magnifying glass. I had read accounts of this diamond, of its value despite the imperfection, and Louis' request to purify it further for his beloved mistress.

"Shall we subject it to a bit of alchemy?" St. Germain asked me, to which I found myself nodding in earnest. He set the stone within an apparatus with a tight seal. "Do be so kind as to retrieve the protective eyewear from that drawer just by your skirts. Yes, that's the one."

Struggling to bend and control the Kodak at my side, I set the box camera at my feet and grabbed the eyewear, which he advised to place upon my forehead so that the tinted glass covered my eyes. As I did so, St. Germain took several moments to add chemicals and adjust the settings on the device. With a final warning to only observe through the filtered eyewear, he flipped a switch and the machine whirred to life. We both leaned in and watched. At first, nothing happened, but then the diamond twitched. Slowly, the defect within the jewel began to bubble towards the surface, and I cried out in astonishment.

St. Germain smiled, and while I stared, enraptured with the process, he returned his supplies to their shelves and drawers at our feet.

"It can take several tries to lift all the impurities," he said, still bent under the table. "I've spent the better part of a month working on it. With too prolonged an exposure, the diamond will melt, and I'd have great difficulty assuring Louis it to be the same one he's entrusted me with. Despite my laboratory, I am no jeweler."

Several minutes later, after the intense light had disappeared and St. Germain assured me we could remove our filtered eyewear, he opened the device and carefully inspected the newly solidified jewel.

"There we are," he said, tapping the diamond with a caliper. "That's better, isn't it? Somewhat smaller without the imperfection to bloat it, but all the more valuable. I do not think Louis will mind." He straightened and met my eyes again. "Is alchemy of interest to you, Madame du Chandler? I conduct discourse every month at Louis' behest, and I would invite you to attend."

My breath caught somewhere under my stays, and for an instant I considered it, except that I was certain John would refuse. If it weren't for the faint conversation where I'd left him—distracted interaction with another courtier, surely—I was certain he'd be in a panic over the invitation. A prolonged visit would reveal our fraudulence and risk the time machine being found. As it was, even I was beginning to feel nervous for how long I'd been here.

"My husband is a mathematician and a physicist," I said. "If he is also welcome, we may very well attend."

"But of course! I'm only sorry to have missed him presently."

"Then I should be delighted to tell him," I said, edging towards the door. "Thank you for the demonstration! Forgive me, Monsieur, but I must be on my way."

St. Germain gave a courteous nod. "Please, don't forget your bag."

At first I did not understand what he meant; I carried no bag. Then, as my eyes fell to place I'd been standing, my insides dropped. The Kodak still sat under the workstation where I'd set it! I rushed to retrieve it, but St. Germain had already bent to pick it up, and he passed it to me with a smile as his hand touched mine.

My departure could not have been better timed if I'd planned it, for just as I joined John in the corridor, Louis and his entourage passed us and filed into St. Germain's laboratory. We bent our heads and bowed low as the king passed, and with one final surge of ambition, I tilted the Kodak around the corner and pressed the shutter button.

Budapest, Hungary
July 1885
Isabella Cooper-Oakley, age 31

"Can you imagine?" I said to John, as we sat, finally returned within the familiar walls of our parlor in Budapest. Still reeling from our adventure, I wasn't sure if my shortness of breath was attributed to excitement or the lacing of my costume. I held the Kodak above our heads in triumph. "A photograph of St. Germain with the king of France! Let's see him deny this evidence!"

John laughed into the air as he squeezed my shoulders. "I cannot believe you dared that. Do you suppose they noticed?"

"It doesn't matter now," I said, hugging the box camera and winding the key to the next frame. "All that matters is my husband is a *genius*, and St. Germain most certainly must—"

I paused, realizing something was different as I wound the Kodak. There was less resistance than I recalled, and no sound of film rotating within. When I shook the box camera, it seemed somewhat lighter, and something loose shuffled around within. I was certain it had not been this way before.

"Is something wrong?" John asked.

Indeed! My stomach was twisted in all sorts of knots as I rushed to the basement workshop for John's tools. Ignoring Mr. Eastman's warnings not to open the camera, I pried away at its various safeguards until they released. John was beside me, bewildered and questioning and concerned, but he quieted once the hatch opened and we looked inside.

There was no film wound about the barren mechanisms or anywhere else within, just a loose piece of paper with writing scrawled upon it.

"*Veuillez m'excuser, Félicité.*"

A livid flame torched inside my chest as I recalled St. Germain's extended fussing under the worktable while I was distracted.

"That trickster!" I screeched, picking up my skirts as I took to the stairs. "I was afraid he was onto me. *Confound* it! I'm going back at once!"

John's futile attempts at reasoning with me were mere background noise until I noticed the philosopher's stone upon the faceplate, now deteriorated into a muted slate.

"But there must be something left," I insisted, reaching at once for John's notebook, despite having little practice at operating the machine's mechanics. I couldn't bear to face the reality of my fallacy, to admit that if I had listened to John for *once*, and left France when he'd asked, that the film would not have been taken. I gave a cry of despair as John took the notebook from me and set it aside. "Won't you even try?"

John regarded me with pity as he shook his head, and when he removed the stone from the faceplate, it shattered between his fingers.

I sniffed back stubborn tears and stood in quiet fury for a long moment as I reconsidered. "Very well," I decided. "I'm going to Milan."

Milan, Italy
August 1885
Isabella Cooper-Oakley, age 31

I did not write to Giovanini to announce my visit, for I did not wish for him to make himself scarce. Though John had tried to dissuade me from going at all, he accompanied me, managing the trip preparations and keeping his opinions mercifully quiet once we'd set out. He occupied himself with his reading while I stewed beside him, replaying what I might say to Giovanini again and again in my head.

John chose to wait in the street outside of Giovanini's address, and for all my plans, words escaped me as the door gave way to my insistent knocking.

"Back already, Isabella?" said Giovanini, and I could not discern if it was in reference to our previous visit, or because he was used to seeing me only once every few centuries. I held his apologetic note out to him, and after a cursory glance at it, he raised his eyes to mine. "Or is it Félicité?"

"Your list of aliases far outweighs mine," I spat back, though I regretted my tone at once.

Giovanini did not appear to take offense, however, instead granting me a conceding, not unkind smile as he stepped aside to let me in.

"I know you," I blurted, as he only just closed the door behind himself. "I know who you are—who you've been. Louis Napoleon knew as well, or he would not have kept a dossier on you. You carry the secrets of the ancients and have passed through the eras with them, waiting for the rest of us to match pace while humanity suffered around you. With your knowledge and skill, you could have rebuilt the great cities and led nations. You could have avoided centuries of war and famine and disease, but instead you lingered in obscurity and left us to our tragedies."

Giovanini listened with great patience until I'd finished airing my grievances. "Preventing humanity's atrocities would only postpone them," he finally said. "This is how we evolve—we succeed and fail, improve, and succeed again. It is necessary, my dear Isabella, a fundamental process of alchemy. Do you understand?"

A surge of emotion pressed against my eyes, and I tightened my mouth to suppress the sensation. "Whatever did you give me the philosopher's stone for, if not to discover your truths?"

"I gifted you the means to discover your own truths, which are of far more consequence than mine. Have you not stopped to consider all that you and your husband have accomplished? To appreciate what the human mind can be capable of? Does it not bring you any sense of hope or joy?"

Giovanini turned for his laboratory and picked up the model of the ship, the name of which I could finally read as we met in the sitting area—*Félicité*. He extended it to me.

"Frigates were originally acclaimed to be profoundly adroit, a suitable characteristic for one who could give such fearsome chase," he said, and for the first time I felt like I understood the twinkle in his dark eyes whenever he regarded me. "I might have reconsidered the name before its commission, but I would very much like for you to have this."

I accepted the ship, moved to tears I managed to smile through. "Is this as close to an admission to being the Count of St. Germain I am to expect from you?"

Giovanini's dark eyes were soft, as deep as the philosopher's stone in its truest form. "It is not impossible, is it? But St. Germain is a man of the past, and it is time for you to look forward, Isabella."

I happened to glance up as he spoke, through the parted curtains overlooking the street. John was in the distance, exchanging money with a street vendor for a cannoli. He consumed it so quickly that I scarce believe he could have tasted it, and I smiled as he stood, unassuming, with full cheeks. A twinge of guilt hit me as I realized we had not stopped to eat all day, yet John had kept quiet so that we could reach Giovanini's address at a reasonable hour.

Likewise, I had been so ecstatic about the notion of finding St. Germain that I'd never stopped to really admire what John had accomplished with the time machine. So much effort for my sake, chasing my dream of discovering the truth behind the many lives and times of the Count of St. Germain. In the end, St. Germain had remained as elusive as he had for everyone before me who'd tried to capture him, yet John was still here and always had been.

When I emerged from Giovanini's apartments some time later, John hastened to meet me at the doorstep. I flung my arms around him and rested my head against his chest, breathing in his familiar scent as his heart beat steady in my ear.

"You're the most wonderful man I know," I sighed.

"Truly?" he said, pleasantly surprised by the affection as his arms settled around me.

"You always believed in me."

We parted a moment later as we noticed Giovanini standing at his door, and he passed me the parcel in which he'd packed the *Félicité*.

"I do hope you'll keep in touch, Isabella," Giovanini said as I took John's arm. The invitation warmed me to smile.

"John and I are moving back to England," I told him. "I'll be sure to forward you our new address, along with a copy."

"Oh? A copy of what?"

"The book I'm going to write about you."

A PECULIAR COUNT IN TIME

San Francisco, California
July 1945
Elliott Bartley, age 42

Membership into the Bohemian Grove was no simple affair, but I'd earned my invitation through various credentials and valuable connections in the military. Under California's majestic redwoods, the world's finest leaders, businessmen, officials, and artists gathered to socialize during this annual retreat without the weight of responsibility upon their shoulders. Officially, no business was to be conducted during the event, a notion the society's motto enforced.

Weaving spiders come not here. The sign was posted upon an archway as we entered the grove. Still, certain matters, such as the Manhattan Project, naturally came up in private conversations. Considering the overwhelming support within current company, it was unusual to encounter someone in direct opposition.

I first saw him at dinner, a mysterious man out of time with a medium build, dark hair, and a Mediterranean complexion. His posture was regal and his suit princely, but he bore no crest to affiliate him. I couldn't place his deep accent either. He must have been European, or perhaps Jewish—he had that look about him.

"Tell me, old boy," I later said to one of my associates who'd been seated more closely to the stranger. "Who was that swanky fellow?"

Several inquiries confirmed his name to be Marcus S. Garmin, but no one could say with conviction where he'd come from. All that was certain was that Mr. Garmin possessed enough understanding of the higher sciences to debate more than the moral aspects involved with bombing Imperial Japan.

He was a pleasant fellow upon my introduction, setting aside his book—*The Comte de St. Germain*—when I invited him for a drink. It was only after I'd ordered myself an old fashioned that I realized Mr. Garmin intended to nurse at his hidden flask instead.

"It is but mineral water," he claimed, when I'd drawn attention to it. I didn't believe him, but I left it alone as inconsequential, though I did wonder what prestigious liquor he preferred that couldn't be acquired at the Bohemian Grove.

"I overheard some of your statements regarding the Manhattan Project," I said. "Did you share the same sentiments when they attacked Pearl Harbor?"

"But of course," Mr. Garmin said with great empathy. "These world wars have been tragic. This is not the first time in history we have tried to annihilate each other, but never once have we been the better for it."

"Everyone's tired of war, but the West wasn't won by taking threats to national security lightly, was it?"

"This is not untrue." Mr. Garmin tapped his forefingers together, and his dark eyes were distant for a brief moment. "However, the founding fathers of your great nation did not intend for their descendants to use tyranny against the rest of the world."

"Now, wait just a minute, Mr. Garmin! No one said anything about tyranny."

"Neither did they speak of it during the rise of such campaigns as the Crusades or the Inquisition or the Third Reich, and so forth."

I disliked that last comparison. I drained my old fashioned and slammed the empty glass upon the counter. Mr. Garmin did not appear affronted by my clipped silence, and, in fact, managed to summon the bartender on my behalf when I'd failed to catch his attention.

"It was terribly hot in Philadelphia that day," he said. "The First Continental Congress had gathered in Carpenters' Hall to review the final draft of the Declaration of Independence. As it was laid out, an apprehension filled the room. The men were afraid. To sign the document was to officially declare themselves against the most dominant power of the age. They were as David facing Goliath, and should they fail, they knew the fate of traitors awaited them. That day in July, your great nation very nearly was not."

I was aware of the clink against the counter as my drink arrived, but I only picked it up after staring hard at Mr. Garmin. Even then, I hesitated to drink. Perhaps it was his accent warping his word choice and inflection, but he spoke as if recalling a memory.

"You read about that in a book somewhere?"

I didn't feel mocked by the smile he gave me.

"Someone in the back of the room stood up and cried, 'Humanity has the freedom to be.' It galvanized the colonists and changed the course of that day, because at every corner of this earth, we seek the same thing: the freedom to be. As we engage in war across oceans, halfway across the globe, it is all the more important that we promote Atlanticism, not iron fists. Understanding the conditions under which our enemies arise is the only way to learn from our mistakes and transcend them."

"I read those fantasy books, too—*New Atlantis*, *Utopia* . . . Shakespeare, right?"

"Sir Francis Bacon and Thomas More, respectively," Mr. Garmin corrected. "But I have misspoken. Forgive me— English has never been my strongest language. It's not like French, you understand, particularly here in the United States. It's constantly changing."

I shook my head with a chuckle. "Your English sounds fine to me."

"The Atlanteans were a remarkable people, of course— another conversation for another time—but by Atlanticism, I meant bridging communication between the United States and Europe. The world will only grow larger, and its problems more complex, but we are all connected. Progressing together is the only way forward."

I was a military man and not one for fairy tales, but I didn't mind entertaining my amiable companion just a bit. "I suppose you have stories about Atlantis, too?"

Marcus Garmin just smiled.

Try Again

P.C. Keeler

WHAT HAVE I SEEN, YOU ask?

The world was a lonely place, once. My people were dead. The winter was sharp and cold, and the dry summer had left us little to store. I was youngest—youngest who could live on his own, at least. The ones older than me sacrificed themselves, one by one, so I might live. The ones younger than me were not given a choice, their lives taken to feed the rest. My last sight of another human was watching an older man drive himself onto a broken branch, that I might survive another day by eating the meat of his body.

As far as I knew, my people had been the last. I never saw any others. But then, when I was alone and sitting at a fire, thinking of nothing but the chewing agony in my empty stomach, the Different Ones came to me. I would have run and hid, but they did something I had no words for then, and I could not move. They did something to me that I had, and still have, not even a concept for and said only one thing.

"Try again." And then they were gone.

So I did. Whatever they did to me, I suddenly knew how to try again. I did not understand what I was doing, but I knew I could go back and see my people again. I went back as many summers as I could imagine—ten, as many as my fingers. So I had ten more years with my people, foraging and searching with them for food. They never questioned who I was; I spoke the people-tongue, so I was of the people. I saw myself, too, the me-of-ten-years-ago, younger but still me, still clinging to my mother and father. But what the Different Ones did had made him not-me at the same time. I knew because I never died when a cut foot turned red, then black, then blackness crept into his face, and . . .

My apologies. It is still a difficult memory, watching myself die like that. Even if it was a different version of me.

The sharp, cold winter came. I knew that none of us would survive, so I tried again. I went back to my people, and this time I tried to memorize where all the best foods were, so we would be strong and fat enough to survive the dry summer and bad winter.

It did not work. When we ate the best foods early, they were not there later. If we did not eat the best foods, other things would eat them instead. I did not know counting, then, so I have no idea how many times I tried again, but it was many. I remember a bush laden with berries that I wanted to save, and a deer that would strip it bare. I remembered the sharp tree branch that my elder had used to kill himself, in my first lifetime. I found a sharp length of wood and lay in wait.

Thus did I re-invent hunting.

Oh, certainly there had been hunting before that. But we were the ones that other things hunted. Wolf howls from amidst the trees meant to climb and hide, not fight. And when I killed that deer, it did not take long before wolves found the carcass and I was trapped in a tree while they waited for me to fall. I tried again and again, but my people had spent a long, long time living peacefully on what the woods offered. The wolves always survived the bad winter while we starved. I wanted to learn what they did.

I spent many tries there, learning to hunt. But no amount of foreknowledge is enough to let a single, naked man defeat an entire pack of ancient wolves. I felt their fangs in my body many times before I gave up that plan.

For the first time, I despaired. Even with the gift of the Different Ones, I could not save my tribe. Could not keep from being alone. So I tried again, and this time waited through the bad winter.

Once, the people had willingly given themselves to me that I would live. This time I did not ask their permission to claim the meat from their bones. I wanted to live through the bad winter so I could beg the Different Ones for more. But this time, they did not come. And I was alone once more.

So I tried again.

I spent a long time trying to summon them, but by now I am sure that they had ways to recognize that they had visited in an earlier try of their own, and stayed away. I invented ritual, then every gory and gruesome display my dark mood could concoct—which, in those days, was a poor and clumsy effort. It was a form of madness—killing everyone I knew to keep from being left alone again. Predators took me many times while I was drenched in the blood of my people, and then I would awaken once more from the time I'd last gone to.

Eventually, I gave up on commanding the Different Ones to return and make me powerful enough to save my tribe. My thoughts turned instead to a new idea—the time before I had lived at all. I tried again, and asked the elders of my people about others who had been old when they themselves were young. And then I went back to meet those people and ask them the same. I was, to my reckoning then, a very long way back, but there were many more people. They moved in several groups, not just one. I celebrated; surely I could never be left alone again.

I showed them how to use sticks and, later, sharp stones. We drove away the wolves, and I stayed with the people. I discovered many useful things in the time that followed— breaking bigger rocks to get new, sharp stones, and taking the pelts of the dead wolves to claim their warmth for our own. I saw whole generations be born and die, and it did not occur to any of us that it was odd for me to stay young and strong. The people were many and strong, as I was. I had children of my own.

And then there came a dry summer and a bad winter, and though we were strong, we were too many and almost all of the people died, and once more there was no one in the world but me. There could not be enough of us to destroy the wolves and deer without being too many for the land to support. We needed to be able to claim more land or have fewer people. So I tried again.

And again.

And again.

Slowly, bit by bit, I pieced things together. How to use sticks to hold rocks, and to throw sharp sticks from a distance. I invented what would eventually become farming—first by leaving some seeds to fall on their own, then by moving the seeds to a more convenient place, then by selecting seeds from only the best plants to keep. Step by step, I improved. I raised family after family.

And still the dry summer and bad winter kept killing us. I needed to have more people, so some would survive. I went back further, and further still. I went a long, long, long way back—if there were more people in the far-back time than there had been in mine, then there had to be lots and lots of people if I went far, far, far back, right?

Of course not. There were people there, but not my people. They did not speak the way I spoke, and these ones already knew sticks and sharp stones and hunting. They hunted me because I could not talk to them. So I tried again. It took a long time to learn their language, but I had all the time I wanted. I stayed with them, then, and saw how they lived.

They did not question my eternal youth any more than my own people had. I stayed with them while the world grew lush and rich; I learned war and fighting with them, the idea of having so many people that we had to fight with each other, not just fight with animals. I learned plague, too; a great sickness killed so very many of them. The survivors found a rich and bountiful land, and over many, many, many years, I watched them become the people I knew. With food plentiful and few predators, our peaceful land was happy and skills were lost. And then the wolves came, and the people once more diminished.

I hated the wolves. Always they were our death, they and the winter. They were fast and strong and clever. Too strong. I wanted their strength. So I tried again. I ate nothing but wolf meat the next time, wore their skins and bones. I would probably have given up on that effort had I not slain a she-wolf defending her newborn pups. They were too small to have strength for me to claim—so I decided to take them, raise them, and then devour their strength.

What I did not expect was to find them very different from the wild wolves. These learned to obey me; they came to my call and attended my mood, with heads low when I was angry and tails high when I was pleased. They hunted with me and waited for me to eat before they took their own share. So we grew great and strong, and now the wolves themselves were not a threat, but ours.

We lived that way for years. We survived the bad winter, though hungry. And then another bad winter came a few years later, and some of us survived that. And another, and another—as the Ice Age took hold.

So I tried again. And again. And again. And again. My original people could never have survived. We had gone weak in a brief time of plenty. It took a hardy and fierce people to survive those long, cold years. When I made such a people, we had migrated to what is now northern Africa. It was never covered in glaciers, but it was cold and the land was loath to feed us. More than once I led our people into wars simply to reduce the population and keep the rest from starving. I took no more families of my own; these new and hardy folk did not inspire me.

And so we progressed. Real farming began. I learned to nurture wild grasses until they were proper grains, just as the wolves became dogs and the humans stayed fierce.

I created history—real history, of all the people there were, not just my own life, because now there were enough people I could not meet all of them myself. I became very good at making other people invent for me, or lead on my behalf. I made myself a king, then *the* king, all others kneeling before me. I did what no one else has ever done—I conquered the world. All of it. We made much progress. Writing and mathematics were invented while I sat on my throne, surrounded by happy, peaceful subjects. I ruled unchallenged in peace and plenty. For thousands and thousands of years . . .

. . . we stagnated. I watched my people turning into, well, my original people. They became placid, soft. No major trouble ever befell us, because I averted any danger before it ever existed. I do not wish to explain how low my people had sunk before I tried again.

I did not rule after that. I made others rule, without the gift of the Different Ones. They made mistakes and died of them; kingdoms fought each other and were forgotten for all time by everyone but me. And that was how they grew strong. Conflict, everlasting warfare, was the heart of greatness.

So I still intervened, but more selectively. That which ended conflict would not be allowed.

My work, of necessity, followed the migration paths of mankind. Progress requires people. I thus began in the "cradle of civilization." My path through Mesopotamia is easy to spot, if you know what you're looking for. Ur, Eridu, Babylon, Baghdad, city after city, I gave them chances to found empires that would grow despite peace—and city after city, they failed, so I went back to destroy their dominions in their infancy. In the same region, much later, the Persians had promise—but if that had worked out, then I would not have guided their invasion fleets to sail into storms. Hundreds of others had their chances; some I allowed to develop for millennia before giving up on them. I have an excellent memory, but even so, many of those were so similar they run together like wax from the tablets they wrote upon.

Eventually, I gave Greece its turn. The Hellenes were a rare form of failure on my part; I simply could not get those quarrelsome philosophers to unite for long enough to conquer the world, where usually I found conquerors all too easily, followed by stagnation. I was intrigued by this difference and began to pay closer attention once more. I'd left Asia on a path to general stability, easy to manipulate later if I chose, and the Americas were too thinly populated, then, to be useful to me, so it was the West where my attention stayed. New histories began to unfurl. Memorable ones.

The Romans did well, and many times I chose another empire to shatter, leaving the Italians to consolidate their rule over Europe. But their martial spirit always gave way to complacency, and that I could not endure. So I drove their republic into corruption and manipulated their leadership until the endless and ruthlessly efficient Roman bureaucratic machine was never formed.

I spent some time in Moorish Spain, repeating years back and forth until I could ensure the victory or defeat of the Muslims. There were many things to admire about the Caliphate; invention and learning were prized, and a level of cosmopolitan tolerance I rarely see. But the Pyrenees made too much a natural defense against the rest of Europe, and they grew complacent in their peninsula; the Reconquista brought ambition and pride and provided a channel for the learning of the Islamic world into the culture of the Christians.

I decided to let events in Europe develop a while, so headed south to the African kingdom of Zimbabwe, where the arts of stonework and goldsmithing were flourishing. I was caught by surprise that first time when the Mongols swept through. I had not been paying much attention to Asia for many tries then, leaving them to form vast and stable empires, and had not noticed the Khanate's swift development of a great seafaring tradition. Their navy was unmatchable, and with their certainty in their own invincibility, they eventually conquered the world. I sat and watched that history unfold, and as always, stagnation followed in the wake of peace. So I returned to the younger days of the Mongols.

The Khan's conquests truly began when he saw the power and potential of naval assaults. With the speed that ships granted him, he could direct his forces throughout Asia, then Africa, before any response could be mustered. An assault on Kyushu a few years prior had ended in disaster, with his forces struck by a typhoon and driven into retreat. He was planning another, larger assault, with a hundred and forty thousand warriors. When I let events unfold naturally, Nippon became the Khan's newest province.

I left Zimbabwe to its own devices and became an astrologer at the Mongol court instead. I trod lightly upon history there, leaving few clues that I existed, but Kublai Khan listened to me at the moment I wanted him to. And so it was that he delayed his invasion just long enough for a particularly potent typhoon, the original "Divine Wind" that the word "Kamikaze" recalls, to sweep through his fleets when they met near Hakata Bay. The Mongol navy lost a hundred and forty thousand men that day and, moreover, lost the trust in the sea that had fuelled them around the globe. I let them make their mark in history—but they were not the *end* of history.

That timeline led to the Thousand-Year War. The world died as the Cult of the Jaguar-King chanted their rituals around nuclear launch sites, sacrificing all of humanity to their gods. I traced that conflict back to the first meetings between the Europeans and the Aztlan Empire. Wealthy and powerful, commanding both continents of the Americas, the Mexica and their allies drove off the efforts of the Europeans to colonize their lands, then invaded them in turn.

I tried arranging an Aztlan victory first—and the less said of the world that came of that, the better. The Cult of the Jaguar-King always rose no matter what I did, and brought practices I was glad to see destroyed. My long-ago rituals of gore and blood were as nothing next to the cruelty they exulted in, creating vast bureaucracies of torment and death— and once again, stagnation.

I went back two centuries before the Europeans had discovered the Americas, when the Aztlan had yet to expand beyond their heartland, and gave a man named Cristoforo Colombo the idea of sailing around the world. When that failed, I went back further and sailed with a Norseman named Leif Erikson, and left behind the seeds of a plague that would eventually spread across the Americas. The next time that Colombo sailed, he found a much-weakened population, and the invasion of the New World began.

Settled by religious exiles and the poor, that continent was naturally a hotbed of zealotry. The Massachusetts Bay Colony slaughtered their Quakers and invaded Rhode Island and spread their particularly violent, intolerant version of Christianity across the Atlantic coast. Conflict culls the weak and empowers the strong, so I let Inquisition after Inquisition roll by.

In the end, the Christian States of America rose to crucify the world on the altar of self-righteousness and ultimately doom everyone in atomic fire, no different in the end from the Cult of the Jaguar-King. I wonder, at times, if something about this troublesome continent encourages the urge to world-death. I had to introduce America's "original sin" of slavery, in order to concentrate men's minds on freedom and justice instead of gods and wrath. Between that and a few carefully-arranged adjustments to the survival rate of the Mayflower, and that theocratic dominance was deterred. The American Civil War made freedom their watchword instead of a strict and vengeful morality.

I prevented the Extermination. What was left was still horror—but consider a world where racism is considered "scientific" and the victorious Allies blamed Germany's Jews for years of nuclear warfare. Sadistic, merciless slaughter on a worldwide scale. I must not allow mankind to unite and grow weak, but neither do I desire a world of monsters. The wolves of my youth could be domesticated, but the beasts of the American Purity Institute and the German Schutzstaffel deserved nothing but eradication.

The Cuban Exchange was inevitably disastrous. Despite all my experience and skill, it was too easy for matters to get out of hand and humanity to be once again exterminated. In the paths where mankind survived, they drew instead the lesson that nuclear warfare was not suicidal, and then destroyed the world in fits and starts. It took much careful guidance to end that incident as a mere "missile crisis" without any launches. Most of the nuclear events I stopped were caused by accident, madness, or equipment failure; you have no idea how many Cold Wars ended in radioactive slag.

The end of the Soviet Union was no less troublesome. Communism inevitably fails any time I try to set it up, but the NATO World Order could only produce dull stagnation like so many other empires. Mitigating it with a drunken Russian leader followed by an unrepentant Soviet nationalist seems to work well. I have high hopes.

What's that? Oh, yes. This is a marvelous world by now, and I am going to let it run for a while and see what happens. Who knows? Sometimes an empire needs an incompetent in charge, to learn a lesson that scholars could never convey. Worldwide commerce may finally have overtaken the struggle for raw survival enough that I might not need to disrupt the current, comparatively peaceful world order. If we continue on this way, perhaps we'll go out and find the Different Ones somewhere in the galaxy.

And if not, I'll try again.

Reality Zero

Nikki Trionfo

NO, NO, NO, NO. THE blood. Put it back. I *can't* have shot him!

Cold sweat mists the bra under my thermal shirt. I come back to myself, returning from a mental state I've never experienced before. Blood? Gunshots?

With a shuddering breath, I glance furtively at my co-workers—the entirety of Utah's branch of the National Security Agency. What I'm looking at now is nothing like what I saw in my vision. No blood. No guns. Just men and women focused on the front of the classroom-style boardroom located at the center of our facility nestled in the Wasatch Mountains. The heat in the building has been out for six days. The heat in every building has been out. The county's main electric grid is down because of storms. Am I so cold I'm hallucinating?

I pull my coat close and turn my attention to my boss.

Standing at the head of the room, James Stricker opens a newspaper—a print copy typically seen only in surgical doctor's offices and swanky coffee shops.

"*New York Times*. February 28, 2023, Special Afternoon Issue," he reads from behind wire-rimmed glasses. He's black and wears a trench coat over his suit. His breath creates a fog that dissipates slowly.

The control room has a geeky, *Star Trek* feel. On either side of Stricker are desks manned by professionals with laptops and handhelds. Behind him, an array of flat screen televisions—powered by generators—mimic the giant windows of the USS Enterprise, only instead of the galaxy showing, it's news channels on mute. The other thirty or so of us sit stadium-style behind rows of desks that curve to form a semi-circle. We're like a sitcom audience hoping for a glimpse of Captain Picard.

I shift my shoulders against the fabric of my coat, calmed by the normalcy. Maybe I should talk to Hansen about blanking out like that—seeing things. Was what I saw a premonition? I hope not. Bullet holes in the flesh of a neck and jawline, the face unrecognizable, as if blocked by bad reception.

But a familiar face, all the same.

Stricker clears his throat and reads the headline. "TERRORISTS DESTROY STATUE OF LIBERTY; THOUSANDS DEAD."

Snapping the newspaper, he displays its image of human carnage over his head. He's nearly seven feet tall. Before his lengthy career in national security, he once played in the NBA. Literally, once. He came in, took one shot— which he made—and never played another minute. His scoring record was perfect.

He expects the NSA to have the same record. Perfect.

"Terrorism on American soil is the news of a now-defunct dimension. *Our* February twenty-eighth?" Stricker clicks a remote control, unmuting the televisions.

A female senator pounds her podium on every screen, shaking her blond hair and earrings as she demands a solution to climate change. She rattles off a list of western cities— among them our very own Salt Lake City. The mercury here hasn't crept above negative ten degrees Fahrenheit in six days. Record-breaking, she says. Mid-word, she goes mute. The screens go black.

Remote in hand, Stricker steps forward. His eyes sparkle. "Here in Dim Three, February twenty-eighth is so boring they're airing a senate session. And the man who planned the terrorist attack featured as front page news in Dim Two? Why, the CIA picked him up yesterday. With nothing more than the information here"—he raps the newspaper—"we've blocked an attack for the third time since launching Project Rewind."

Tucking the paper under his armpit, he claps. I exchange a worried glance with Hansen, seated next to me. He joins the applause, so I do too. The act places me firmly in the present. I need all of my faculties here, now. Three technicians in the audience keep their hands still, their faces defiant. Project Rewind has lost popularity recently with the handful of us on the planet who know of its existence.

To Stricker's left, CIA agent Marky "The Mark" stands. He has no last name that I'm aware of. He's short and balding with a crooked nose, a fast wink, and a great appreciation for well-timed wisecracks.

"Sir, it's time we talk about other data that may be contained in the newspaper—data that may prove critical to the survival of the human race."

The room's applause chokes and dies.

With a crinkle of the special edition, Stricker addresses him. "Marky, don't—"

"Oh, shut up. The details of the alternate, destroyed dimension are kept unknown for the purposes of corporate fairness and a moral sense of letting the universe be. Yada, yada. In other words, policy straight from the president says we can't read the newspaper. Well, when your precious newspaper got here two weeks ago, we called it a gift from a now-defunct dimension more troubled than ours. But now I've got my doubts. I've got plenty of doubts Dim Two was worse than freezing our nuts off here in Dim Three."

"Me, too," someone mutters.

"Check the newspaper," Marky demands. Many of us nod. I nod.

I'm not sure if I want to nod. I'm kind of a follower.

"If it mentions hundreds of thousands of cold-weather-related deaths in Western States, we're not exactly getting an unfair prediction, are we?" Marky continues. "What about a pan-area power-outage? A hopeless mess of an electric grid from Mexico to Canada? No heat for six days? But if there's no word about it in Dim Two's February twenty-eighth newspaper, then *we* caused this in *our* February twenty-eighth. *We* did this. We're messing stuff up."

"We're playing God," says Pastor Jason from the back row. His accent is South-Carolina thick. He wears a CrossFit shirt under his ski jacket and was appointed by the president himself to offer spiritual advice to the project. He used to be the president's life coach. Now he mostly appears to sit around. Oh, and work out. "God is reminding us how much bigger He is than us."

"Let someone read the newspaper!" Marky clutches his smart phone. The news he wants isn't there. Dim Two's news doesn't arrive digitally. Because the time machine alters electron-states, it can only properly transmit printed data. Like a physical copy of the *New York Times*, one of the only papers that still issues a daily.

Marky pounds his fist on the desk. "The matrix is unstable!"

Next to me, Hansen runs a hand over his hoody, which allows a glimpse of his brown hair. It's short, like a Mormon missionary's—one with two-year's experience gelling the front strands into a formidable wall above his forehead. Don't get too close, it says. He's picture-perfect and oh-so-off-limits.

In the front of the room, Stricker pinches his nose. "We are *not* violating a presidential directive by reading the newspaper. It's time to stop with wild speculation and listen to our theoretical physics report." He motions to Hansen.

Hansen glances at me. "Chloe?"

I stand. I'll follow his lead, no matter where it goes.

We go up front, passing drop-down blinds that slowly lower over the row of windows. Mount Timpanogos towers in the distance, separated from our facility by Utah County—a network of snow-white roads, carefully-sorted snow-white neighborhoods, and boxy, snow-white shopping centers.

At the press of a button, our first PowerPoint slide appears on the array of televisions. The upper right quadrant of the 3D matrix on display—a probability spread predicting matter stability—has no curve, only a series of nubs marked along the zero line.

One of the technicians stands, crying out, "*Completely* collapsed?"

"Impossible. When?"

"Two days!" the technician answers. "*Days*. Look at the y-axis. With deviations already happening now."

To protect Hansen from personal responsibility, I don't look at him, not even to figure out if he needs protecting.

"It's theoretical, we think." I repeat Hansen's words, verbatim. "The graph shows a situation where matter is unstable—a situation where matter is just as likely to transform into anti-matter as remain matter—but the matrix collapse shown here doesn't represent real matter, real objects. Hansen's early work at MIT proves the string theory is only a mathematical metaphor."

Marky comes to the front of the room to stare at the graph. His face reflects mint-green because that's the peppy color I chose for the slide. I was hoping to add, you know, *pep*. We need it, what with the potential end of the world and all.

He ticks off his fingers. "So what you're saying is that, one, my atoms and bones and cells might become anti-matter—along with everything else—two, the universe has never had that happen before, and three, we have no idea how that affects us. Solutions?"

Hansen faces him solemnly. "This isn't a single-entity event. These are phenomena that seem to indicate the nature of probability evolves in concert with the dimensions."

Stricker waves at me. "Ms. Dubois?"

"He means there's nothing to fix," I translate. "It's not a rogue wormhole. This is a negative-probability event, where probabilities are rolling like dice and ending in positions we've never seen. Like . . . imagine a die landing balanced on its edge on an ideally flat surface. Yeah, it's mathematically possible, but it's so rare, it's functionally equivalent to zero.

But it's happening. Dim Three is projected to soon have billions and trillions of dice landing on their edges—all of the dice on their edges. And soon, as was pointed out. The nonconformity will arrive in two days, with perimeter deviations already appearing—though we have less data on that than I'd like," I add.

"We can't get more data after last week," Hansen interrupts with a touch at my elbow.

The cold fades at his touch, replaced by hope. Comfort. Longing.

He looks at Stricker. "We ran a routine particle accelerator test on the gloves used while handling material sent through a wormhole. And Chloe's gloves came out three hours closer to collapse than our controls."

"A deviation until we run more experiments," I say. "So what if I handle more time-traveled material? In our years of tests, we've never found machine operators to be in danger of physical risk—"

"No." Hansen answers flatly. "Not you." Removing his hand from me, he looks at Stricker. "Besides, we can't run tests anyway, and she knows it. The generators aren't as powerful as the main grid. Until the electricity goes back on, our hands are tied."

I huff, defeated. "We *could* turn off the computer servers to save energy."

"Chloe," Hansen says, as dryly amused as if we were alone. A hint of a smile lifts his chapped lips. "We have to maintain appearances. We're *cyber data-collectors*." He makes quote signs. It's an oft-repeated joke around here.

"Right," I mutter. "So all the regular folk who think the NSA's primary job is spying will still think the NSA's primary job is spying." I frown so my resurging worry isn't visible. The matrix is collapsed. The weather is out of control. And my mental glitch, too—a vision of blood. What was that?

Marky the Mark rubs the back of his neck. "What happens during this collapse that you say will start soon? Don't say you don't know. Hazard a guess. We're blind here."

I hesitate. Co-workers shift in their seats.

Hansen speaks. "If wormholes don't behave according to normal probability theory . . . at best, we lose our stabilized traversable wormhole, and with it, the ability to time travel. At worst . . ." He drops his gaze.

I take a breath and voice a guess we've talked about at length. "At worst, our protons and electrons—as anti-matter— just . . . start doing new things . . . like collapsing into the positions they hold in other dimensions. That could lead to today's dimension combining with other probabilities. Like past or probable future events."

My own words jolt me. I whirl to face the nubs on the 3D matrix. The blood I saw. It's a past event. Or a probable future one. Or an event from another dimension.

Or . . . I'm not sleeping as much as I ought to.

Late nights take their toll, not just on me, but on everyone. Even on our spouses, or so I'm told. Late nights save me from falling asleep to a lingering violin-note of loneliness that represents my every moment now that I know Hansen will not break up with the girlfriend, who is now his wife of three weeks.

It's a bold move to think your co-worker is in love with you. The problem is, I still think he is. I can't shake the feeling that he's just too much of a rule-follower to ditch the girl who shares his childhood religion and fraternize with his one true love, atheist me. I could be wrong. It could be that he's simply too loyal to label Ms. Bipolar with her more fitting B title.

A violent chill rocks me, and I have to clench my jaw for a moment. I swear it's colder than ever.

The others are talking nonsense about how the frigid weather could be due to the matrix creating a zero-Kelvin black hole. That's as nonsensical as me wondering if my vision of blood was the manifestation of a mental state of a me in another dimension.

Hansen puts a stop to it. "Listen, everyone, your theories are all worst possible scenarios. We don't have any data that this is some kind of apocalypse. It's possible the collapsing matrix has nothing to do with the cold snap or blackout."

"Right. It could be coincidence." Striker is in front of the second quadrant of the graph. Therefore, his white hair is haloed by "dusty rose." Dusty rose is a special favorite of mine.

"Utah gets cold," Hansen adds with some degree of hope.

"True," I agree.

"Cold," Marky repeats with concise disdain, ignoring Hansen to stare down Stricker. They're five paces away from each other.

Sticker gives up first, turning to stare at the matrix. With his back turned, Marky moves into action. Fast action. CIA-field-experience action.

Marky the Mark dashes to snatch the newspaper out of Stricker's hand. Stricker notices him. He yelps and retreats, producing a cigarette lighter. Three uniformed FBI guys come out from the corners where they stand as sentinels. They rush to the room's center, weapons drawn. Stricker flicks on the lighter and holds it under the newspaper.

"I'm warning you, Marky!" Stricker yells.

"Put that lighter out!" Marky halts his pursuit, palms out. "Listen to reason. They're not reaching for their cuffs to apprehend me, because they agree."

Ten feet away, the FBI men hold their positions, casting tense glances at Stricker.

Unclenching my fists, I look at Hansen. Whose side are we on? Marky's, right?

"Guys?" Real-Time-Dimension Advisor Luanda Jorgenson stays seated, moving her concerned gaze over the screen of her laptop while typing. She's the only lesbian acquaintance I've encountered since moving to Utah, and she shaves her head weekly. I always smile in the hallways at her to show I'm not a bigot—which makes me somewhat of a bigot; I do see the irony—but she simply nods. "I'm getting reports of a lockdown from D.C. The whole government—"

With a wild audio blare, the televisions light up with seizure-inducing technicolor flashes. All the screens go black.

I stumble to the ground.

"Chloe!" Hansen yells over the general mayhem.

An icy grip seizes my very molecules. My mind blanks and comes back into focus.

Look! I point at Dad in the driver's side with his greedy forehead, gobbling up space that ought to be covered in hair. My sister Ava notices me and yells, *What are you looking at? You little un-showered, no-mannered, geeky, nose-in-a-book . . . !*

I cower before her.

"Chloe. Chloe!" The pupils of Hansen's brown eyes are dilated. He's shaking my shoulders. His hands are wrapped in the toilet paper we found in the trunk.

No, his hands are gloved.

Reeling back from him, I expand my lungs against the frozen air. The burning cold strips my throat like sandpaper, clearing my brain.

I press my head. "I . . . I don't think I'm mentally stable. Or something. I'm seeing memories."

"Are they real? Did they happen?"

"Yes."

Throughout the control room, coworkers race toward the exits. The FBI have Cody the maintenance guy, of all people, in cuffs, shouting as they muscle him toward the door. He ages before our eyes. His hair literally grows out of his head like a chia pet with iron-gray foliage.

I point at him. "But . . . that's no memory."

"The electron states aren't just theoretical," Hansen says, voice hollow. "It's the collapse. It's collapsing more than just the traversable worm—in your cereal." Hansen is gone and Mom has replaced him.

"I don't want to eat a worm." I wriggle away from her.

"We're being sucked to space-times we can't control," Mom yells. No, it's Hansen. "It's forcing you to collapse with other Chloe potentials—past Chloes, future Chloes—some of them not in our dimension."

I focus on Hansen's eyes, on my feelings for him, on digging into his forearms with a ferocious grip. "My . . . my reality will collapse back into the real me, though. Eventually."

He shakes his head, breath choppy. "Or you'll cease to exist, black-hole-style. We all will. We're collapsing within our own matrices, past and future; probability futures. It's happening to isolated entities now, but all of reality will be affected in mere days."

"Then we didn't create a new peace after all," I say. "This isn't the stable dimension. Reality Zero is the stable one."

"No! Don't you see? We stripped Reality Zero of its stability and created chaos. Chloe, these were *my* calculations. They're hurting you—*you*!"

"You'll fix it." I position my face in front of his. "Use the time machine. Send instructions to us in Reality Zero. Tell us to never time travel—no new dimensions."

"We can't get to it." His eyes won't focus. Our conversation has attracted the attention of the entire room.

"Fine, not Reality Zero," I shout at him in frustration, knowing that the other end of our dimensions' wormholes— the other end of Dim Three's wormholes—are in the second dimension. We can't access any prior dimension except the one directly preceding ours. I'm stumped. Rambling. "We can at least go back to Time Split Three, on the other side of the event—the Dim Two side. It's closer than we are now."

He snaps his gaze to me. "Recursion."

"Recursion! Yes! You've got it! We send an object to Dim Two, prevent Time Split Three, send the same object to Dim One, prevent *that* split, and go back to Reality Zero with instructions that *no one* splits dimensions."

"As long as we have an actual object to send back—a collapsing object—from here in Dim Three—"

Stricker and Marky both glance at me, a keen look in their eyes.

I remain focused on Hansen. "And transport it a few hours *before* the newspaper appears—"

"Possible only *if* the calculations are spot-on," he shouts. We race toward the super-computer. "The calculations to map the coordinates and get back to Dim Two are easy—a replication of the last split. But to get to Dim One—wait."

He stares at me.

"Chloe, we're getting ahead of ourselves. What communicates the problem? There's no time to write a report. Chloe?"

Like a slip through the ice over a tundra lake, I plunge into cold, my mental state wiped clean.

I return to mental clarity suddenly, like a reboot. I'm me, but I'm a different me. I'm a mentally stronger, more determined me. I fight with an FBI agent. He's cuffing me. Where there was no agent before, there is one now and he's real. I recognize him. He works here. We've never spoken before. I fall into the goals of the different me. The goal is escape. Escape! I pump my limbs, trying to get away.

"Chloe. Chloe, stop," he says. "You're hurting yourself. I can't do this without you. What will communicate the problem? Chloe, please! Come back to me! An object—no, that's it. *That's* what communicates the problem. Better than an object."

The FBI agent is now Hansen. He picks me up like a sack of potatoes. I get put in a box.

I gasp for air. The box is the time machine. When I realize I'm confined, I jolt, slamming my shoulders and scraping the back of my neck.

"Chloe, save Reality Zero. I trust you. I . . . I love you."

His voice disappears.

I'm on the cool tile of the kitchen taking a nap. No, I'm inside a time machine. The realization makes me jerk. I'm pressed on all sides by the walls of the machine. Far away, voices bark like a dog. Bark, bark! Jabs of pressure intrude on my numbness, along with a clattering alarm. The door of the box opens like a microwave oven.

". . . can't be. Ms. Dubois?" Stricker guides my head out of the time machine.

I'm retrieved exactly the way every newspaper is, lifted from the box as a gift from a future that will now never exist. I'm a message. A prophetess and executioner. Project Rewind started when we built the time machine in Reality Zero and waited. A year passed. A whole year of waiting and watching. Finally, we received a newspaper, sent by a future-us that planned to be made unstable—unreal. Government agencies used the info in the headline article to hunt down terrorists who were never given the chance to kill thousands. By so doing, we passed seamlessly from Reality Zero into Dim One. Simply lived. An effortless process. The only physical proof of the dimension change was the initial newspaper, which we burned by mandate after six months.

"Chloe?" Hansen's voice is hysterical. He must be the one supporting my legs. "Who would send a human? Chloe?" He nuzzles my face, leaning into me. His voice mingles with a memory.

I love you.

By coming back to Dim Two as a message, I've destroyed Dim Three.

I've destroyed that *I love you.*

271

Shaken, I lift my head. I'm in the control room, where more and more coworkers gather with gasps of shock.

"Hansen, I'm right here," a lady says, putting a hand on his shoulder. She steps back when she sees me in Hansen's arms and covers her mouth.

I stare at the lady. She's me. My mousy-blond hair is out of its pins, but it's not as bad-looking as I imagine. I'm a very small person with larger eyes than I realized. How I look to her, I can only guess. Worse, probably.

Hansen's confused gaze leaves mine to seek out the lady, almost in loyalty. She huddles toward him subtly. Jealousy and pleasure burst on me without even a matrix collapse to guide them.

"I'm future Chloe," I announce, leaving Hansen's arms and standing, though I'd rather stay. The alarm silences. "It's . . . what? It's October 2021, right? October in the second dimension. In a few hours or minutes or . . . I don't even know . . . this dimension will get the newspaper that creates Dim Two Prime. As soon as the CIA picks up the would-be attackers, boom, there will be a time-split and we'll all be in Dim Three. Here's the problem . . . Dim Three experiences a negative-probability event—a completely collapsed matrix."

Stricker stares like I've grown an arm out of my nose.

Hansen frowns. "We've tested for years and never seen negative probability."

Pastor Jason speaks up from among the crowd, many still arriving in the control room, called to it by the alarms. "It is not God's will to change destiny. The science never did that. *We* did that, kidnapping and secretly executing terrorists before they attacked—when they still had the chance to repent."

Hansen fingers his lower lip. "Repentance is an event that's also assigned negative probability."

I rip out a section of my hair with a minor yelp and hand it to Hansen. "Test this for matrix stability. You'll see. I'm about to collapse. Only you can fix this. Your ability to run the calculations quickly. You need to set things up so that at the moment of full collapse, the time machine re-forms my wormholes on Dim One's side of Time Split Two."

His gaze darts from my broken strands of hair to my eyes, lit with understanding. "Recursion."

"Exactl—"

Cold whirls through me from the inside—the inside of my very particles. Blood bursts from my hand, splitting the skin like a peeled can lid.

I scream and press my arm into my gut. Nearby, other-me staggers to the ground, fingering her forehead. Her hand is wrong. It's that of a child's, small and with supple skin.

"I've altered this dimension," I cry. "Every alteration speeds the matrix collapse."

Hansen kneels to care for other-me. She's a complete distraction to the mission.

I push Stricker aside and log in to the time machine controls. "I need to get to Dim One."

Stricker grabs my arm. "You have no authority to man those controls."

I shrug him off me, opening the program to run a schematic of Time Split Two to—

The next thing I know, I'm handcuffed by the FBI, removed from the control room, and left alone inside a secured cell. They say I'm a security threat. They say they need me to settle down and refrain from acting without their approval. I remember being handcuffed. I don't mean I remember it after it happens; I mean I remembered being handcuffed *before* it happened—I remembered it from Dim Three. I was handcuffed by the FBI in one of my visions. The vision was perfectly accurate. Not a missing detail.

While I'm in my cell, the lights overhead flicker. The temperature plummets and the heat kicks on, unable to keep up. Apparently, the black-hole collapse I herald is the temperatures-at-absolute-zero type, not the heat-of-supernova-blast type.

Shaking with cold, I scream for Hansen from inside the cramped space, fighting a wild obsession that seems to be part of a Chloe-potential I don't recognize. I'm wracked with guilt. I formulate scientific designs that are magnitudes of greatness beyond my skill-set. I flash back to the scene of murders, bodies on the floor. The blood I saw before. Bullet holes ripped into the skin of a neck and jaw. Visions that are perfectly accurate.

A face I can't quite focus on . . . .

I'm standing and rocking back and forth when Hansen, Stricker, and Marky come crashing in through the door of the cell.

"Chloe, you're right," Hansen declares. "Your matrix collapse is imminent. On the order of minutes."

I voicelessly whisper, "Return Rewind. Return Rewind," as I have been for minutes. I can't stop.

Hansen takes my face in his palms. "Chloe."

"Hansen." With the warmth of his fingers, I gulp air. I snap back to his reality. "Matrix collapse. Order of minutes. My favorite color is dusty rose."

His brown eyes soften and crinkle at the corners. He nudges my cheek softly with his thumb.

Stricker himself scoops me into his arms. "We've got to get her to the time machine."

Marky races along the hall ahead of him, shouting for bystanders to move.

Hansen coaches me as we run. "You need to arrive in Dim One without triggering a timeline disruption—understand? *We* . . ." he gestures at himself, Marky, and Stricker, ". . . can't find you in the time machine. That's a statistically significant deviation from Dim One, creating an immediate Dim One Prime. You'd have so little time you wouldn't be able to convince me—Dim-One-me—to help you. Since you will be cramped for space in the box, I'm going to put in a hard drive and keyboard only. Use key stroke commands."

"Wait," I ask. "You mean manually enter the launch codes?"

"Yes. To open the time machine," Hansen says. "You can't be found inside of it, as you were when you arrived in our Dim."

We get to the control room. Stricker rattles off a string of letters, numbers, and symbols. I repeat them, going back and forth with him until I've got the sequence.

"Hansen, even if I make it to Reality Zero, how do I convince everyone not to use the time machine?" I ask. "And what about the alarm in Dim One that goes off when something arrives in the box? I must disable it, or I'll be found immediately."

"Terminate the time machine," Hansen says.

"A gun?" Marky asks, handing over his. It's colder and heavier than I expect.

Hansen scoffs. "That won't terminate the time machine."

Marky rolls his eyes. "No, the alarm."

"Good idea. Worry first about the alarm," Hansen says. "Then disable Project Rewind."

"You want stealth." Marky screws a long piece of metal to the end of the gun barrel. "I'm attaching the silencer."

I try to comment and can't. I'm gone somewhere.

Resolve that is not my own runs up the back of my neck, its coldness swirling violently with memories I have of warm brown eyes. With the memories comes an obsession—a mania, a fixation. I'll create scientific greatness. I'll stop at nothing.

A man with the very same brown eyes talks to me. "Point the gun toward the box's base. That's where the internal monitoring is. The alarm has a slight delay to cut down on aberrations."

"Hurry! Her weight is fluctuating," says a tall man. I don't know why he's holding me or why the pores of my skin are frozen. My hairs are on end.

Mr. Brown Eyes gets in my face, speaking urgently. "There's a failsafe on the time machine. Like cyanide in the tooth of a Nazi. We want time-travel technology, but won't let it be stolen. The same codes that operate the launch also destroy the machine and all of the schematics."

The tall man shakes his head at Mr. Brown Eyes and cracks a cynical joke. "Unless it destroys *you*, we'd just build it again."

Bone-cold, I shift to stare at the tall man's narrow face. "Build it again," I whisper. My emotions coil, dangerously ready to strike. I have no idea why or at what.

I start repeating, "Project Return Rewind." I don't understand what I mean. Or the part of me that's me doesn't understand. I'm collapsing with another dimension's Chloe.

The tall man frowns and sets me down.

Mr. Brown Eyes straightens and takes my cheeks in his hands. I gasp. It's Hansen.

Heated to the core, I hiccup with sobs. "I can't do this. I don't have the knowledge-base to program the launch from Dim One to Reality Zero. Only you can do that. And you won't help me, not when I need you to. Why would you help *before* you see a collapse?"

He takes my hands. "I'd do it for *you*. I'd do anything for you."

I don't breathe.

With a wild cry, I lift onto my toes and press my lips to his. He embraces me, one arm cradling the small of my back, the other tangled in my hair.

With a moan, he lifts his head. "Get in the time machine. Hurry!"

The others help position me inside the box, tucking in my elbows and knees.

Hansen never leaves my side, coaching me. "When you arrive in Dim One, you'll have more time than you had here in Dim Two, since you won't be triggering a timeline disruption by merely arriving. Also, you'll be further from the collapse of your dimension. You'll have much more than minutes; perhaps several hours."

He squeezes my hand one last time. "Time enough to save Reality Zero."

I wake with a start. Alone. Stuffed inside the dark of the time machine box.

When am I?

Marky's gun rests awkwardly in my cramped hands. No alarm has yet sounded.

I wedge the barrel between my thighs and shoot at the base of the time machine. The sound startles me, despite the silencer. I expect pain and injury from ricocheting metal but remain unharmed, save for the kickback which sends the gun deep into my gut, making me gag. Repeating the process, I expend every round.

The alarm never sounds.

Finished with the gun, I locate the sleek hard drive near my knees. It turns on with a whirl of the processor. I awkwardly finger the keyboard. Log in. Boot the code-entry program. Enter the sequence.

The door to the time machine pops open horizontally. I manage to fall to the floor, thinking about the kiss, the brown eyes, the alternate-thoughts I had of a Chloe-potential with desperate thoughts. I yearn despairingly for a dimension— somewhere, somehow—where Hansen and I can be together.

I stand.

I'm alone.

I'm also being recorded by security cameras, but act naturally, hoping to escape notice. After all, I'm a familiar face in the control room. Unless the guards were especially focused during my moment of arrival, they'll have no reason to think I didn't enter through normal channels. I make my way to the particle accelerator lab, slipping inside easily and checking the time. It's past 9:00 a.m. on July 23, 2020. The newspaper will arrive in less than an hour. Cursing my short-sightedness regarding my use of bullets, I hide in plain sight while technicians go in and out. I grab what I need and wait in the hall. Thirty minutes later, other-me arrives. Dim One me. As luck would have it, she stops at a bathroom. I follow her inside.

To have any hope of survival, Reality Zero—humanity—needs Hansen's brain power. Hansen's feelings for other-me is the ticket to Hansen.

My replacement of other-me in Hansen's mind is the ticket to bringing Hansen into the fold of fighting for survival.

"Hello?" I say.

"Yeah?" Other-me turns around, a mild crease in her forehead.

When she sees me, she gasps.

I jump forward and flick a wire-splicing knife across her neck. I'm too timid and shallow. Her arms convulse forward as she arches away from me. I panic and shove the knife into her trachea, crushing it with a crunch and bruising my knuckles in a painful collision with her chin. We fall to the floor, blood spreading like a sewage leak.

I drop the knife and clean my shaking hands in the sink. The mirror shows blood on my shirt and pale face, above feral eyes.

When I finish cleaning, I tuck the empty gun in my pants and find Hansen in the hall. The lower front half of my shirt drips with water and hangs funny from being hastily wrung out. It's clean at least. The moment Hansen sees me, he leans into me in worry.

"Are you okay? What's wrong?"

I had to look myself in the eye when I killed myself. Sympathy is a weakness I have no time to master. Other-me could have shown up while I spoke with Hansen. Two Chloes. The last time there were two Chloes, the timeline was disrupted in such a significant way I nearly collapsed before finishing the mission.

"Come here." I lead him to the control room. Outside the door, I stop. "Oh, Hansen, I . . ."

I pause. I put shaking fingers on his arm. Hansen—the last Hansen; the Dim Two Hansen—told me I'd have power over him by virtue of his feelings for me. But was he right? Isn't early romance as much a probability event as wormholes?

I swallow and ignore the memory of my own blood spurting onto my cheek.

"I can't . . . take it anymore. I . . . I love you."

He glances sideways and laughs. "You . . ." His face goes red.

"I mean, I like you. Like I have a crush on you. Hello, dramatic." I laugh off my panic. I forgot this was before our late nights together, analyzing telltale hints of collapsed matrixes. Before he opened up about his many problems with the manically-depressed girlfriend he will not decide to leave.

At least not in Dim Three.

An alarm blares—not the normal one that signals a newspaper arrival, but a security alarm. The guards know I came out of the box. Or they know the box alarm is damaged. Something.

Hansen glances quizzically at the control-room doors. "Security?"

A chill rocks me. My hand sprouts lifeless flesh—the mixing of me with dead other-me.

I grab Hansen's shoulder with a weakened grip. "I'm from Dim Three, two time splits from now. The negative probability event we discounted is happening—a collapsed matrix."

"*What*? Chloe?" He tries to break my grip.

"God, okay? We're playing God and now He's playing God . . . *more*. You have to help me. Future-you is dead. Only *this* you." I splay my fingers on his chest. "*You*-you can get me through the collapse and back to Reality Zero."

"Recursion," he says.

"Your idea."

Stricker and Marky come down the hall at a run and I scream at them, "Come inside the control room! All of you! Lock us in!"

I either command their respect or their curiosity, because they all obey. Once we're inside the control room, Stricker empowers the computers to bar the windowless doors.

I relate my story to them.

"Hansen is key," I say in conclusion. "Every time I time travel, I need precise calculations to get me from the dimension I'm in to the previous one. Every time, Hansen resists, wanting proof that I'm collapsing. Hansen, you can't resist this time. Giving you proof I'm collapsing makes me collapse faster. I don't even have time for this conversation. I tried to avoid a timeline alteration, but it's not possible. I can't alter time without altering time and then I collapse." My voice rises in pitch with each subsequent sentence.

Hansen refuses to look at me, glancing instead at Stricker. "She's panicking."

"Well, *I* think she's cracked." From his sock, Marky produces a clip loaded with bullets. "But that's my gun she's showing us. The scratches on the butt will line up with this."

Frowning, he tosses me the clip. He shakes his head with a deep frown. "Makes no sense."

I load the weapon and I shoot him in the chest.

Stricker radios for the FBI as I shoot him, too.

"Chloe!" Hansen dives to the floor, covering his head. Men in the hall pound the doors.

I lower the gun, shaking. "I don't have time for you to run tests. I tried to cause no change here, but it's not possible. I collapse soon. Maybe in minutes. All of humanity needs you. Map the coordinates that'll take me to Reality Zero. Save the world!"

Wincing, Hansen crawls toward me with a look of determination that can only mean one thing.

"If you won't map the coordinates, *I* will," I warn. I'm lying. What I really mean is that I'll run the schematics to *try* to map the coordinates, but the probability that I succeed in programming the time machine correctly is slim. Hansen is the powerhouse around here.

He gives a wild cry as he scrambles toward me with amazing speed. He will bring me down. He will stop me from any sort of time jump, let alone the correct one. Of all the things in all the dimensions that could pull my attention away from the only chance the world has—getting back to Reality Zero—Hansen is the biggest distraction of all.

I run my finger over the trigger.

I won't.

I can't.

I close my eyes and squeeze four times.

Silence.

He moans in pain.

Crying out in horror, I run to him and crush his throat with the NSA's required steel-toed work boots.

More and more of my body is combining with dead Dim One Chloe's body. Tears run from my cheeks, splashing to the dead flesh on my elbows. My feet are numb. I think my toes may no longer be attached to the rest of me. How long before my Dim Three mind is gone and with it the knowledge of the matrix collapse?

"The coordinates," I whisper as I log in to the main system.

I'm denied access.

I slam my fists onto the keyboard. I turn a circle.

The time machine computer is separate from the main system.

Running to it, I shake my head. "No good. No good." With all the recursion involved, only a supercomputer could map the coordinates I need—even with Hansen at the helm.

I slam my fists onto that keyboard as well. I failed. I failed. I failed. I—

"Wait!" I cry. "Faith!"

Wincing with effort, I load the gun. Once, while bending down, I convulse with the horror and surprise of being shot. But I haven't been shot. I know I haven't been shot, but I also know I have been. I'm slipping into Chloe-potentials that won't save the world.

I punch in my faith—my guess at the coordinates needed to reach Reality Zero—and climb into the box, shutting myself in. The air is frigid.

"God," I whisper urgently. I feel low on oxygen already. "Um, I mean, God, sir. I'm gathering Hansen was right about you existing. I entered a probability event into the time machine that's likely negative. Assuming You're selecting events to prove You're in charge, You can choose the negative event. You can make this work. I'll fix the whole humans-in-control-of-destiny thing. As long as Hansen and I end up togeth—"

A great volume of noise rages as frozen blood fills my nasal passages and ears. Cramped inside the box, I choke, vomit, and cry out as an involuntary spasm rams my head into the top.

I breathe in. Breathe out. The blood in my nasal passage is gone, as is the cold.

I'm somewhere in time. Somewhere stable. Somewhere other than Dim One it seems.

Could it be?

Shooting only one bullet this time, I prevent the alarm from sounding. I use the launch code and release myself from the box. I fall. The inflexibility of the tile lends reality to Reality Zero.

Reality Zero.

I've made it. I've prevented the end of the world.

For now.

Wiping drool from my mouth, I train the loaded gun on the door to the control room. The clock ticks forward. The time is half past noon. That means I'm—I have to gather my thoughts for a moment—fifteen, no, seventeen, minutes ahead of the newspaper.

Miraculously, no one rushes into the room at my appearance.

I decide to hide the hard drive and keyboard, setting them inside the garbage.

Nothing to do now but wait.

At 12:45:52 March 2, 2019, the blackness inside the box stirs and produces a sight as magnificent and terrible as a living god. The Alpha Newspaper. The first aberration in time. The beginning of time's undoing.

Snatching up the paper, I stuff it into my jeans. I've shot the alarm system that would otherwise have gone off when the newspaper arrived. I can only hope the guards watching on camera fail to notice the details of my actions.

I slam the box door shut and race to destroy the paper—

Before I reach the door, Stricker comes bounding into the room.

"Mr. Stricker." I say in a too-innocent voice. I'm out of breath. "Sir."

He stops fiddling with his smart watch and focuses on me in confusion. "What?"

"Nothing."

He gives me a funny look and heads to the front of the room. "Whatever. When you and Hansen present, don't try to make sense of the science. We don't have time for that. Just wave your hands and say it's technical."

"Oh, that's right. I remember. We have two visitors today from the pentagon." I'd forgotten about that—how we were about to meet before the Alpha Newspaper arrived, changing not just our plans for the day, but the very dimension.

Stricker gives me another funny look, like I'm acting weird.

That means . . . that means I've done it! I've allowed Reality Zero to continue as it would have had the time machine never been invented!

Marky and Hansen arrive.

"A year of waiting and no newspaper," Hansen is saying.

"Maybe the pastor is right," Marky answers, dejected. "Maybe no paper will *ever* come."

"They want to cut our funding," Stricker calls, coming to meet them. He's the most upset of anyone. "Not one terrorist event that would warrant a timeline alteration, after all the mass shootings of the recent decades."

"And that's good. No violence," Hansen concedes. Then he sighs.

Marky rolled his eyes. "Maybe the authorizing of Project Rewind caused the terrorists to become saints."

Stricker shakes his head, disgusted. "All we need is one attack to prevent."

Only I am unaffected by the dark cloud of frustration—of intense itching to prove a technology by using it.

I approach the group stiffly so I won't crinkle the newspaper inside my clothes. "What if we *have* been given a signal from the future? What if the message is that remaining in this dimension brings us closer to our objective than creating a new one?"

Hansen notices me. "Chloe?" He looks over his shoulder in confusion. "How did you get here all the way from the south campus?"

"I . . . left earlier than you thought." Wanting to feel less vulnerable, I lean toward him instinctively. At the brush of my elbow against his, he looks down at me, eyes surprised. The corners of his lips curve up. I remember he's not married and break into a smile. He's not even serious yet with She Whom the Cosmos Must Obey. Instead, *I'm* here, with my feelings fully-formed, ready to change the course of our relationship.

I want to float away, bliss-style, but instead crash to reality. Other-me is in the south campus, bound to show up soon. As soon as my co-workers see me alongside a separate Chloe, I'll have ushered in a statistically significant deviation from Reality Zero. I'll have created a Dim One, Subset Prime. I can't allow that.

Do I throw myself in a river somewhere and hope I don't float? And what about the *next* newspaper from Reality Zero Prime? It's bound to show up because of the *next* terrorist event on the horizon. How do I stop a time-split brought on by news of the future, without revealing news from that future about its matrix-collapse, thereby bringing on the time split that collapses it?

Marky sniffs. "You know, the trigger-attack doesn't have to be on American soil. Violence is violence. I bet the Pentagon guys agree with me."

Stricker perks up. "The vice-president has been receptive to a more aggressive use of Project Rewind. Maybe that's why we're getting visitors."

"Libya is at it again," Hansen offers hopefully.

My hand glitches.

No, no. No, I shouldn't be glitching. I'm in Reality Zero, the stable dimension. But obviously not actually stable. How can Hansen forever not know if his theories are correct? How can Stricker forever long to tinker with reality and choose not to? Anyway, there are two Chloes—an inherently unstable situation.

Marky exits to hit the bathroom, leaving only three of us. I know Hansen is unarmed and have always suspected Stricker keeps FBI guys around for a reason. I'm a foreign object from a doomed dimension with the potential to spread my collapse like the plague.

I make my decision.

I go to the garbage can and retrieve the computer I brought with me from Dim One. I enter the failsafe code.

Black smoke pours up from the time machine.

With a wild cry, Stricker runs toward me. "What are you doing?"

"Chloe, no!" Hansen shouts.

I melt under his panicked brown eyes. "I love you." Without the schematics and machine I just destroyed, Hansen is the only human on earth who can make time travel possible. I therefore choose the only option available to me. Maybe in destroying so much, I'm altering the timeline significantly. Maybe not. I'll never know.

I shoot him three times. Stricker is quicker than I anticipate, giving me time only to aim at my head and squeeze.

No, no, no, no! The blood. Put it back. I *can't* have shot him!

Cold sweat mists the skin under my bra as I come to myself, back from a mental state I've slipped into several times in the past days, always chilled to the bone afterward.

Ever since a terrorist destroyed a key section of Utah's NSA building and killed Hansen on March 2, 2019, I haven't been mentally stable. I'm plagued by invented memories of the shooting, as if I were the one holding the gun. But I'm no terrorist—I'm just a theoretical physicist who wonders if time-travel really would make dimension-alteration possible. My fellow scientists and I abhor Reality Zero and its terrorism. Dim One and beyond—where every danger is averted before it strikes—seems a dream of impossible peace. Especially now that Hansen and his time-machine have been destroyed by the hand of the exact violence he aimed to prevent.

If only we'd been able to usher in the Alpha Newspaper we longed to see arrive.

The opportunity is gone now that the time machine is destroyed. Reality Zero is all we'll ever have.

Reality Zero without Hansen.

Life is colorless. It takes me weeks to return to work. The media follows along the snowy road at the base of the mountain, asking if I was friends with the victim.

Stricker waits in the newly-refurbished control room. The door behind him is open. His tie is loose. The heat is on and aggressive.

He speaks pompously, though we're alone. "Ms. Dubois, you've known this is coming. I'm appointing you head of theoretical studies for Project Return Rewind."

"Sir, I can't accept. I'm not Hansen. No one is Hansen."

"No one knows his science better than you. And the science works. It works."

"What do you mean it works?"

"It works."

"You mean . . . are you saying the machine—?"

"I'm not saying anything. I'm only saying time travel *works*."

He gets a strange gleam in his eyes—a reckless determination. He was the only person with Hansen when he died. He managed to escape. He alone knows how. He alone knows what happened there, and what was left when the shots stopped firing. A dead Hansen and a dead terrorist—no details released on the nationality or even gender of the terrorist. Did Stricker use the machine to try to stop the terrorist? Did the terrorist have something on his or her person that clarified the reality of time travel one way or the other? Why is Stricker so confident?

While I swim in wild theories, he continues. "May I say? You and Hansen had more than a professional connection. That fire, that drive, is the link we will build on."

We did have a connection, I realize. I really did love him.

Didn't I?

Confusion runs up the back of my neck, mingling with the memories I have of warm brown eyes. The images are poignant and real—like I've spent time in Hansen's arms and listened to him reveal how desperately he cares about me. These moments I'm mentally reliving never happened. But . . . but they're so real. *So real*—like they happened, just not here. Not in this reality.

Okay, that's impossible. Hansen's theories allow for the combining of dimension-realities, but it's a zero-probability event. Dice landing on their edges. Anyway, Hansen didn't survive to see other dimensions, though he died trying. Died for a better future. A future I'm now contemplating, professionally, to decline pursuing.

What could be better than dedicating my soul to Hansen's work?

"Sir." My resolve firms. I draw on memories and compulsions I barely recognize as my own. The idea feels comfortable, true. I even see flashes of time travel schematics that are iterations beyond what I'm capable of creating—like Hansen's future work is stored in the recesses of my mind. Impossible, but real. "I will make Project Return Rewind succeed."

The whining heat of the nearest vent gives way to a blast of frigid air. The door slams behind us.

Neighbor

Jacqueline Masumian

IT IS 1986. 1986, THE year I lose my Cassie, and I can't find my way out. My mind has propelled me, as it has time and time again, back to those days. I find myself cornered there with one of my greatest regrets, a minor thing, but one that looms in front of me and won't let me pass.

In those days I am fit and can move pretty well, but one fall day, I am not quick enough. Before I can dash indoors to hide, my neighbor Branford Wilson ambles up my driveway with that stiff-legged walk of his and snares me.

I picture myself turning my back on him, walking up the driveway and into my house, Bran open-mouthed at my rudeness. Instead, I cannot move. I am forced to stand still, forced to listen to my neighbor once again.

"Hi!" he calls, laughing with a hint of apology. "Wow, what a day!"

I am trapped like an animal in my very own yard. At least a half-hour of useless discourse lies ahead with no chance for escape. Those icy blue eyes and lantern jaw lined with crooked, yellow teeth will now commandeer my attention for the rest of the afternoon, robbing me of the time I have set aside to cut back my peonies and pull out the garden stakes from the phlox and *Baptisia*. I need to finish these fall garden chores, the ones my husband used to help me with before he walked out, but my neighbor's visit will surely prevent that.

"Well, hi, there, how are *you*?" I say, trying to sound welcoming. It is the custom on our little lane to be tolerant and patient with our neighbors. And being a woman alone, I never know when I might need someone's help. So being polite is necessary. "Yes, it's a lovely day. How's Nell?" His wife rarely accompanies him on these jaunts down the lane; she's probably delighted to have time to herself at home.

"Oh, she's just fine! Say, I was watching a red-tailed hawk just now flying over our property. They're amazing, don't you agree? You know, when we lived down in Brazil, there were a lot of terrific birds of prey, but not the red-tail. Oh, Brazil was a fabulous place. We had more fun down there. My gosh, we went to so many parties! Mixed with all the right people, you know, bankers, Navy officers, really great guys. And they were good golfers, too. We must have played golf two or three times a week, and after a round we'd all have drinks. Martinis in those days . . ." and on and on he talks.

Hostage to yet another recounting of Bran and Nell's sojourn in Brazil thirty-five years ago, I smile and nod as he rambles, feeling it would be rude to bend over and continue my gardening as he speaks. Passing my pruning shears from hand to hand, I take in his angular features and close-cropped silver hair beneath a weathered commodore's cap.

As he continues his monologue, my dog Cassie, tennis ball in mouth, dashes over to play, her wavy golden fur absorbing the afternoon sunlight. "Good girl! Now, go fetch!" I toss the ball across the lawn, sending her tearing after it.

My neighbor continues, "You know, Chippy had a great time down in Brazil, too. He had all his friends over every day . . ."

Already I'm getting annoyed. I wonder how he could be so insensitive, so self-absorbed, denying me the sanctuary of my garden. Can't he see all the work I have to do?

"I remember when he was about five, how Chippy . . ." Speaking of his only child, he interrupts himself, "Say, did I tell you? Chippy's come up with a new design for our pool deck! Wow, what a creative guy, don't you agree?" My neighbor blathers on, oblivious to my nervous glances around the untended garden.

"I wish I could have had Chip's creative genius when I was his age. But I had an important job with the Merchant Marine. Of course that was some time after I left the Navy . . ."

Our mutual neighbor Eliza once informed me in hushed tones about Bran's injury as a World War II pilot and how he suffered shell shock, a possible explanation for his incessant banter. But he is old. I figure he just needs to talk. My ex, Larry, if he were still around, would just tell Bran to go on home.

And that might be the best thing. If I told Bran to go on home and never return, all the rest could be avoided. But instead, I am tethered to what happened. He stays.

Cassie has returned with her tennis ball and drops it, panting through a huge smile on her face. Nudging my hand with her damp nose, she urges me to play. I bend down to stroke her and rough up her shoulders. "Okay, good girl, go fetch!"

My back begins to ache as I shift my weight from side to side, half-listening to Bran's nonstop narrative. Across the driveway and past the loose hedge between our properties, I spot Eliza calmly snipping at her rose bushes, unfettered by a self-absorbed neighbor's ramblings. How she escapes his visits I can't guess.

"How *is* Chip?" I ask, the words escaping my lips unbidden. "What's he been up to?" Having no children of my own, I have little patience with stories of other people's glorious offspring, but Chip is different.

Chip has been living at home with his parents for about six months. A single man in his forties, he's arrived from somewhere down south and moved in with them, apparently to stay. I've come to know him only slightly; he sometimes stops by to admire my garden, and we exchange plants from time to time. Perennially tan, Chip elicits a vaguely effeminate air, which I would have dismissed if he didn't occasionally share with me tales of his vivid social life in New York.

"Oh, that son of mine!" Bran answers. "Wait till you see his design for the pool deck! What a talented guy." I have no idea what Chip's profession is or was, but he is now clearly unemployed and apparently content to stay that way.

Performing odd jobs for his elderly parents provides some rationale for his living at home, I suppose.

"Bran, you're so lucky to have him around to help you with the house and garden," I say.

"Are you kidding? He's great at coming up with *ideas* for projects, but he expects *me* to do the work!" he says, laughing his crooked laugh.

I pretend to chuckle along with him. A gust of wind comes up just then, and the sun recedes behind a dark cloud. It is a crucial moment in which I can escape, tell him I really have no interest in his son, dismiss him, and create a total break in our relationship. But instead I only drop a hint. "It really feels like fall, doesn't it?" I say. "Just hope I can get all these perennials cut back before winter." I gesture around my large flower and shrub gardens nagging for maintenance. Cassie, also impatient, jumps up and barks.

"Oh, you probably want to get back to work. I have to head home and rake some leaves myself. Can you believe it? I've been raking those leaves for thirty years. That's a lot of leaves!" Taking in the surrounding scenery, tall trees lining a communal algae-ridden pond, he continues, "You know, where we live on this lane is the best place in Connecticut, don't you agree?" He is standing his ground, awaiting my reply.

At this point I can be rude and refuse to answer his question. That would put an end to it. But I am unable to. The past will not be undone.

Instead I say, "Yep, it's the greatest. Gee, you know, I've got to get back to this gardening, or I'll be in big trouble if the weather turns."

"Okay, okay. My rake is calling me." He laughs. "Bye, now!" he calls over his shoulder and staggers away home.

The thing that irritates me about Bran is he never asks about *me*. He knows that Larry walked out on me and I am having to manage on my own. He might surmise that I am struggling to get by on a part-time job at the garden center. He should realize that taking care of my gardens and mowing my own lawn is a horrible chore. And yet he never asks how I am doing or if I need help. Never once. Of course, he knows how private and independent I am, but occasionally he could *ask*.

Is my resentment about this the reason I do what I do?

Later that month Chip stops by bearing a gift, a tiny pot of rosemary. Though I am unaccustomed to company, I invite him in and pour us both a glass of wine while he launches into one of his great stories. Chip has his father's penchant for talk, but I find his tidbits about the gay scene in Greenwich Village intriguing. For some reason, perhaps because I once mentioned my early career in the theater, he feels comfortable sharing details of his lifestyle with me. He often mentions his friend, David, who I assume is his boyfriend or lover or whatever they call it. It's always "David this" and "David that," making it easy to imagine the two of them arm in arm, gadding about New York City.

As he continues on one of his tales, I notice an edge to his voice, just a hint of hysteria in his laugh. He leans back and hoots, "So, there David and I were, ripping apart our hostess, when . . ." He halts. His eyes narrow. His visage crumbles. He places his wine glass on the table.

"David's sick," he says. I wince at the code word. "I'm spending a lot of time in New York playing nursemaid to him these days. I don't know what else to do." Chip stares at the carpet. He suddenly seems an old man. "He's been hiding his illness pretty well," he continues. "But he's lost so much weight. Every day he seems weaker, and now he's got those miserable sores in his mouth." He leans forward and holds his head in his hands. Being "sick" for a gay man is a death sentence; there is no treatment, no cure.

Unsettled by this intimate disclosure, I can find no words; after all, he and I are just neighbors who exchange plants and stories. I sit, mute, unsure how far I want to be drawn into this conversation. His shoulders tremble, the heels of his hands press into his eye sockets. At last I say, "Chip, I'm sure you'll take good care of him. But shouldn't you be worried about your own health?"

"No, I'll be fine. Listen," he wipes his hand across his cheek, "I don't want my father to know about this. He's not exactly tuned in to my lifestyle." That is putting it mildly; if Bran knew Chip was gay and had a boyfriend who was sick, he would be destroyed.

Just then Cassie, who'd been sleeping at my feet, rises up, stretches, and eases her head beneath my hand for petting. I fondle her ears and stroke her sleek forehead.

"Don't worry," I promise, "your dad won't hear it from me."

I wish I could unlearn what I just learned, unhear this entire conversation, but I am compelled to relive it instead.

Eventually winter arrives and pounds us with a series of blizzards, keeping all the lane neighbors indoors, and I see very little of either Bran or Chip. But in spring, we are all out in our gardens again, full of anticipation of the season. And so comes the inevitable annoying visit from my neighbor.

"Hi! What a glorious day!" Bran calls. "We must have a thousand daffodils blooming at our place!" Cassie bounds up to him, offering her tennis ball. He ignores her and goes on, "You know, this is the greatest place in Connecticut, don't you agree?"

I affirm his familiar question and catch a glint of something uncertain in his glance. As I pause in my work, he starts in on his customary monologue about the old days in Brazil. Then, on his own, he switches topics.

"Say, Chip wants you to stop by sometime and identify some of the plants coming up in that new garden of his," he says. "He plants these exotic things he can't remember the names of. Who knows what they are, or if they'll even survive."

"I'm happy to take a look," I say, always eager to offer gardening advice. "When's a good time?"

"Well . . . actually," he says, his normally steady gaze flashing to the trees, "Chip's been feeling not so great lately. He's got constant chills and fever, and he's exhausted all the time and losing weight. He tells me the doctors can't figure out what's wrong. These doctors today, they don't know a goddamn thing!" Nearly choking on the words, he points his chin toward the sky in defiance. "Anyway, I'll have him give you a call when he's feeling better, okay?"

"Of course," I say. "Tell him . . ." I hold back from expressing undue concern. "I'm sure he'll be fine. Give him and Nell my best."

He moves to leave, but turns. "We live in the most beautiful place in Connecticut, don't you agree?" His eyes insist. I agree.

I am trapped. I have been carried away on a rushing river. Dread lives on my shoulder.

I don't hear from my neighbor for some time after that and never receive any further invitation to visit Chip's garden. My own chores consume me through spring and summer. Cassie, chasing her tennis balls and wagging her golden tail, keeps me company as I plant, prune, and stake. I revel in our quiet time together without my neighbor's intrusion.

One day in early fall, though, my beautiful girl suddenly loses interest in her tennis ball. As many times as I toss it, she simply lies on the lawn staring at me. Then I start to notice other things. Her elegant gait develops into a stumbling one, her lithe body becomes bloated, and her kibble sits untouched. A visit to the vet reveals a malignancy, along with no cure, no hope. My brain stalls at the idea of losing my sweet companion. At home I sit on the floor, her head in my lap, stroking her golden coat for hours. One murky morning, Cassie's sad eyes find mine, and we are forced to say good-bye.

For weeks afterward I sit alone in my kitchen staring out at the weedy garden, unable to stir myself without my dog at my side. Wads of damp tissues clutter the kitchen table as the unwelcome days slog on. The emptiness and the silence floating about the house suck all my energy until I am nothing more than an empty sack of sorrow.

One afternoon a knock on the kitchen door rouses me from my chair. I glance out to see Bran. The last person in the world I want to see. Eliza must have told him Cassie has died. I go to the screen door to accept his condolences.

"How are you?" he asks, his gnarly smile absent.

"Not very good, really. I just can't get over losing her. I miss her so much." The hollow place in my stomach aches.

"I know," he says through the screen. "Eliza told me. I'm so sorry to hear." He pauses and gazes about the yard awkwardly. He wants to be invited in. But I can't bring myself to unlatch the door. And that one act of un-neighborliness is what has put me in this place.

He clears his throat. "I just came over to tell you—"

"She was my baby," I interrupt, "my sweet companion." A flood of tears takes over.

"I know. I know." He pauses and stares down at his worn topsiders as though they are nailed to the ground.

I've never seen him so distressed. But I simply cannot let him in.

"Well . . . I'll be going. Hope you feel better." He turns slowly, glances back at me once, his blue eyes cloudy, then hobbles down the driveway.

A few minutes later, Eliza calls me. "I just saw Bran leaving your house," she says in her muted tones. "Did he tell you?"

"No. Tell me what?"

"Chip, Bran's son, Chip." She sounds baffled. "He died on Tuesday. He *died*. I didn't even know he was sick," she says, "did you?"

The dread has grabbed me by the throat. My stupidity at not connecting the dots, my blindness to the obvious, my inability to help a neighbor through a terrible time, all because I'm too wrapped up in my own loneliness and grief. Or maybe I just don't want to see what is happening. Maybe, like most people, I don't want to know anything about young men's sickness and death, don't want to be anywhere near it.

In the future, will there be new neighbors on the lane who will listen to me, help me when I need it, when I am an old lady? Or will they be standoffish, keep to themselves? If I become ill and need people's sympathy and understanding, will I receive it? Will my neighbors be there for me?

Certainly they will. They will. I'm sure that's true. But until that happens, I am sunk in the past. Deeply embedded in what I do the year I lose my Cassie.

A Winter's Day

Edward Ahern

PETER STOOD IN THE COLD next to his converted garage. The serviceman from Sub-Zero Cooling walked over to him.

"That'll be twenty-four fifty for the overhaul. Just set your finger here for the transfer."

Peter winced. "So much? Last time it was only around fourteen thousand dollars."

The Sub-Zero rep shrugged. "Last update was ten years ago, and you admitted you hadn't run the refrigeration unit since then. Things get clogged and rusty."

It wasn't his money, but Peter hated spending that much for four days of use. "You've checked the insulation in the garage? No leakage? And it'll handle an outside temperature up to eighty Celsius?"

"No problem, Mr. Kessler. The original install was forty years ago, but we've replaced just about everything except the framing. Couldn't help noticing that the interior had also been updated. Responsive art work, interactive internet, voice-activated hospital bed, height adjusting solvent toilet. Nice."

"Thanks."

Peter paid by finger and hustled back inside the house. The outside temperature had sagged into minus five Celsius, and his hands were already numb. Alison met him at their back door.

"Unit up and running?"

"Yeah, now we just agonize until Rob's arrival."

"Nobody else is coming. Sarah holoed. Says she's committed to a seminar in California, but I think she just dreads meeting her brother. Roberto is still in the nursing home. So even his brother and sister aren't coming. What also hurts is that Eunice and Preston aren't coming, either, so even our kids will be missing at Christmas."

"What excuses did they offer?"

"Does it matter, Peter? Rob's a nightmare for the grandkids. I know we rely on what he pays us, and I know he's your cousin, but I just can't warm to an ethanol popsicle."

Peter stared at the refrigerator calendar so he wouldn't see Alison's expression. December twenty-second. Rob arrived Christmas Eve early. Then he worked up a crooked smile. "We've talked this to death. What he pays me to administer his affairs keeps us afloat. And we only put up with him once a decade."

"It's been forty years' worth of decades, Peter. He's still thirty-three, and you're already seventy-four. God forbid you should die between now and eighty-four. What would I do? I couldn't handle things."

Peter admitted to himself that she was right. "Okay. Once he's out of the cryonics facility and been shipped over here, once he's had a chance to acclimate, I'll ask him to switch to institutional resurrection. The kids are long gone, we can hopefully get by on what we have."

Alison stepped over and hugged him. "Thank you. It's like having Lazarus as a roommate and wondering when the miracle's going to wear off."

The cryonics facility called the next morning. "Mr. Kessler?"

"Yes."

"This is Teresa Richardson at the Ever-Young Preservation Facility. Your cousin, Rob Tomassio, has been successfully revived. He is being acclimated with internal and external solvents so that his body can handle up to minus ten Celsius. Is your accommodation ready?"

"Yes."

"Our representative will be at your house at eleven a.m., as scheduled, to inspect your system and maintain it during the visit. Is it running?"

"Yes, and the plastic tunnel is set to be hooked up to your delivery vehicle."

"Excellent. And I'm required to remind you that despite the low temperatures, his internal solvents are highly flammable, so no open flames or equipment that might spark."

"Yes, yes. How does he look?"

"Ah, I haven't actually seen him, Mr. Kessler, but his records indicate full consciousness and only minute dermal flaking."

"And his nutrition?"

"Mixed and ready to be injected into his permanent IVs. Our technician will be bringing them with her."

"Thank you, I'll be waiting." Peter hung up, still bemused about alcohol-based life. If the sun burns out, he thought, Rob will be able to go outside for a walk.

Carolyn the technician hovered in the next morning. After three hours she closed her checklist. "Serviceable," she pronounced. "We can proceed."

As Carolyn left, Peter felt a tinge of regret. If she'd flunked his juiced-up garage, there would be no visit.

The Porta-Patient flew in three minutes early on Christmas Eve morning. Peter had been waiting outside in his thermal suit, scarfed, hooded, and gloved. Alison waited alongside him.

"Mr. Kessler?"

"Yes?"

"I'm Eliza. Mr. Tomassio's had his breakfast injection and shouldn't need to be fed again until one p.m. If you could please show me your power grid, I'll set up the data display and monitors."

"Is he cheerful?"

"We don't interact with our transports, Mr. Kessler, so I can't tell you about his emotional state."

"Of course. I just meant . . . never mind."

Once the passage had been hooked up, Rob stepped out of the container and through the passage to the garage. The plastic was translucent, and Peter got flicker views of a distorted biped moving toward its lair. Five minutes after the container left, Eliza let him in through the double doors of the temperature adjustment chamber.

"Hello, Rob."

"Peter." The voice was slushy, like Rob's lungs were full of ice crystals.

They shook hands, Peter's thick glove almost hiding Rob's bare hand. Over time, Rob's skin had turned clear. Peter could see blue blood vessels and stringy muscles.

Eliza keyed the intercom. "Mr. Tomassio. If you need something, just buzz me. I sleep from eleven p.m. to six a.m. but if you need me during that time, just ring and I'll be suited up and ready in ten minutes."

"Thank you, Eliza."

Peter chimed in. "Everything's set up for you, Rob. The computer has the condensed world and national histories for the last ten years. The usual interactive internet. The holo projector is set up, but cable television finally died a few years ago, so just feed programming from your devices onto the big screen." Peter realized he sounded nervous and stopped talking.

"Is everyone already here?"

"It's just Alison and me again this decade."

Rob looked down. "What happened?"

"Well, Roberto is in a nursing home now, heavily sedated because of his manic attacks. Sarah says she has to stay in California because of a teaching seminar. And our kids need to spend the holidays with their kids. I've arranged a holoconference the day after Christmas."

"So nobody. Sorry, nobody except you and Alison."

"She'll conference with us when I feed you this evening. Do you need to rest up?"

Rob smiled, his lips tinged gray-brown rather than pink. "I think I've had plenty of that. You know that when I'm dormant there's no breathing, no heartbeat. But I dream. Not happily. Ten years of bad dreams. It's like files rasping my skin until it's ground off."

Peter wanted to sit down, but knew the cold would seep through his insulated pants. "I've provided a copy of your living estate account in a folder labeled "Revenues and Expenditures 2060-2070."

"Thanks, my auditors provided a summary before I left the center. You've been a faithful steward. How's your health, Peter?"

Peter hesitated, then guessed that Rob would have had that audited as well. "Pretty good, except for a heart attack. They had to put in a couple self-monitoring stents. I'm okay now."

Just then the refrigeration fan shut down. They waited in uncomfortable silence for several seconds and then the backup generator kicked in and the fan started whirring again. The intercom clicked and Eliza's voice came in. "Gentlemen, the refrigeration motor has shut down, I don't know why yet. The solar back-up generator will keep your unit refrigerated to a safe level, but there's not enough power available to use your exterior comm devices. I've shut them as a precaution. Please bear with me while I investigate the problem."

They stared at each other. Being locked in made Peter feel colder, much colder. Because of sparking dangers, he had no battery-operated heating elements, and unlike Rob, he was going to progressively lose warmth.

Peter let out a nervous laugh. "I knew I should have put a chess set in here."

"That's all right, Peter, I have both too much time and too little. Tell me about Roberto."

"Not much to tell that you haven't already viewed. Your brother's fantasy trilogies sold quite well for some years, but a few years ago he developed clinical euphoria and had to be moved to a facility. He's not taking our calls, but the hospital sends reports from him. It's on your menu."

"And he's seventy-six, no, no, wait, seventy-seven. And Sarah, what's she doing?

"Well, you were still active when she married the ex-priest. She buried him six years ago. She's still working, teaching half days at a Japanese school. We exchange Christmas selfies, not much more contact than that."

Rob reached over and touched Peter's shoulder. "Peter, you're my hold-fast while I'm awake, my only source of unfiltered truth. Please tell me what's really happening with the family."

Peter hesitated. The truth was brutal. But it burst out.

"They've avoiding you. Their big brother morphed into something they didn't know. You look and act differently now. You have memories and they have lives. They're afraid of you. They loved who you were and not what you are."

"Alison, I know, feels the same. What about you?"

"We've always been grateful for your support, couldn't have put the kids through school without it—"

"That's not what I asked."

Peter's breath exhaust formed a transient bridge between the two men. "We were close before your change, Rob. Your care has supported us and I'm grateful. But I can't get over a sense of unease. You're different now, Rob, a new species, and maybe you need friends like yourself. There, I've said it."

Rob slowly nodded. "Thank you for being honest. I so wanted to see Sarah. She and I were closest. But even twenty years ago she was afraid of me. Have I become a ghoul, Peter?"

"No, of course not."

Rob stared at his right hand. "They barely mentioned that I'd lose all sense of touch. Taste and smell as well, of course, but I really miss the tingle of touching another's skin. Interesting that you and Alison haven't divorced."

"Pardon?"

"Thirty years ago I thought you two were barely civilized to each other. I made contingency plans for institutional care."

Peter remembered. They'd fought over Rob's impact on their children. "No, we got over that. But I'm old and getting older. Have you thought about transferring the awakenings to an institution? Or maybe, better still, just sleeping until they find a cure for mucosal melanoma?"

Rob's smile tightened, his teeth visible under the translucent skin. "Well, cousin mine, I had to choose between being frozen stiff for up to a century or two, or coming back every decade for ersatz living. But once reanimated I couldn't shift to long-term cryonics—the body chemistry has been altered—so I have an eternity of ten-year look-ins."

"I know. But I still think you need to switch to institutional care. Alison and I won't be able-bodied the next time you come back."

Peter smelled alcohol. Flammable tears were meandering down Rob's cheeks.

"I'd assumed, Peter, that each generation would want to meet with me, to meet the frozen old/young man. Morbid curiosity, if nothing else. They wouldn't know me enough to love me, but they'd be interested and sympathetic. Hasn't happened. It's just you and Alison, and I pay you both to be here. If I turn myself over to Ever-Young, it'll be worse, I'd be with a bunch of high-octane mummies."

The intercom clicked. "Mr. Tomassio, Mr. Kessler, the solar cooling generator's not handling the load well, so I'm going to have to raise the temperature to minus ten and shut off the lighting."

Peter felt a surge of worry. "Eliza, what about the primary cooling system? Is it fixable?"

"Not good news, sir. It's fried. There were years of wasp nests built inside the compressor, where they wouldn't be seen in routine maintenance. The fire took out the wiring and the microchips. We're having a new unit droned in, but it'll be at least two or three more hours. It would have taken even longer to arrange a conveyance vehicle for Mr. Tomassio. Your wife is here and wants to talk with you before I key off the speakers."

"Peter, are you all right in that cold?"

"Cold as hell, but otherwise all right." The lie didn't hurt nearly as much as the plumbing in and around his heart, which had started aching as his body strained to maintain its heat. Nothing to be done, so no point mentioning it.

Alison's voice became agitated. "Rob, you can hear me okay?"

"Yes, Alison. Hello. How are you?"

"Rob, you have to let us go."

"Alison!" Peter yelled.

"No, don't stop me. I can be a little braver talking into a mic rather than face to face. Rob, we've known each other a long time. But that's just it, we're old, we won't be able to handle your requirements next time. We'd be a danger to you. You have to move on, to be with your own kind."

Peter interrupted, "Alison, please stop. She's just concerned about me, Rob, but she's right. Our clocks are running down."

Rob cleared his throat, a sound like crackling ice. "Thank you, Alison. I appreciate your candor. Peter and I will sort this out."

"Mr. Tomassio, I'm going to have to dial down lights and comms now."

"Okay, Eliza. Don't worry, Alison, I'll take care of Peter."

"Powering down in three, two, one." The lights went out, leaving Rob and Peter in complete darkness. The fan blades slowed, and the cold seemed a little less bitter to Peter.

The two men remained silent for two or three minutes. Peter sat down, hoping it would be easier on his heart.

"She didn't—"

"Never mind, Peter. Funny. In the dark, it's like my ten-year naps, except I can control my thinking. What are the doctors telling you about your life expectancy, Peter, given your heart issues?"

"They aren't willing to give me an end date, but the insurance actuarial tables say I've got maybe fifteen more years."

"Did you ever think of going cryonic?"

Peter laughed. It hurt his chest. "Don't have the money and I don't want to leave Alison alone."

"Yeah, it was different for me."

They sat again in total dark and almost silence, listening to the muffled noise of the cooling unit and their chesty rasps. Peter hadn't thought to bring his nitroglycerine tablets and hoped he wouldn't need them.

"Peter, do you lock up your house at night?"

"Out here? No, almost never, unless we're going away on a trip. Why do you ask?"

"Just wanted to get a taste of how you live. Tell me about what you do every day."

They spent what Peter guessed was two more hours talking about Peter's daily life-errands, the layout of the house, neighborhood spats, conversations with his children. Toward the end, as Peter was shivering uncontrollably, they heard the screech of heavy equipment being dragged over concrete, which made the waiting worse, like the moment between when the doorbell rings and when it's opened to reveal the police.

Relays clicked, the lights came on, and Eliza's voice came through the speaker. "The new unit's installed. Give me a few minutes to run checks and I can let you out, Peter. You must be frozen."

"De-de-damned near."

As the fans revved up and the lights came on, Peter could feel the temperature drop. "Rob, you're overdue for your feeding. Now that I can see to work, I can give you the injection."

Rob let out a breaking glass laugh. "You're hypothermic. I'll get Eliza to do it. Another fifteen minutes won't matter. Go take a hot bath and get human. One of us should."

Ten minutes later, Alison helped Peter across the lawn and into the house. His legs were so wobbly he opted for the downstairs bathroom. As Alison ran the hot water, he chucked his thermal clothes and underwear and stepped into the bath. The hot water shocked his nerve endings so badly he dropped into the water, splashing Alison. "God, I hurt so much, but it's delicious."

Alison stayed with him while he soaked. "Do we have to go back and give him his ethylene injection?"

"No, I think he knows I'm shot until tomorrow."

"Ouch."

"Best I could do while still frozen. Once I've thawed, just feed me something and we can go to bed. Maybe a couple sleeping pills to drown out the sound of the compressor."

"You're on."

The alarm went off at five a.m., and Peter, still groggy from the pill, knocked the alarm off the table before retrieving it and shutting it off. Alison stirred but dropped back to sleep. As Peter got up to go to the bathroom, he smelled something sweetly alcoholic, like anisette or strega, and something harsher. He postponed the pee and sniffed his way downstairs, following the smells. They came from the first floor bathroom.

The tub was full to almost overflowing, and the water was tinted green-brown. A skin sack lay at the bottom of the tub, filled with what Peter knew were bones. "Jesus Christ," Peter blurted out. "Jesus Christ."

He ran out of the house in his underwear, ignoring the cold, and banged on the door of the service cubicle. "Eliza! Eliza!"

"What is it?"

"Rob's killed himself!"

Eliza opened the door and stepped out, wrapped in a frumpy gray robe that looked warm. "There hasn't been an alarm."

"Check your visual monitors. Is he in there?"

She stepped inside the trailer and ran back out. "He's gone. Where is he?"

"In my tub, I think."

314

Eliza called her center and the local police, and followed Peter back into the house and the downstairs bath.

"Holy shit!" she said. "Another one. Can't tell if it's him."

"Who the hell else would it be?"

Within a half hour, the yard swarmed with police and technicians from Ever-Young. By late afternoon, Rob and Alison were summoned into the garage, now equalized with the outside temperature of minus three Celsius.

A police sergeant seemed to be in charge. "Mr. and Mrs. Kessler, here's what we've established so far. The DNA of the remains in your bathtub matches that of Robert Tomassio. Someone, perhaps Mr. Tomassio himself, jiggered the sensor alarms so his departure wouldn't be noted by the technician. And he left us a hologram selfie. Please sit down and watch it."

Rob appeared in front of them, the image quality good enough that his teeth showed through his lips.

He smiled at the recorder. "This selfie is done for the police, Ever-Young, Peter and Alison, and my immediate family. Neither Eliza, Ever-Young, or Peter and Alison are responsible for my demise, which will have been self-inflicted. The death is assured, but before then, I plan on a few seconds of feeling human. Arrangements for my estate can be found on a separate file. I love you with the same intensity that I had a dozen conscious days ago. But I understand that after forty years, your memory of me has worn away and distorted. I want a few persons to mourn me rather than continue on without context."

Peter glanced around at the faces in his converted garage. The cops and Ever-Young technicians had their game faces on. Alison was crying.

315

Rob concluded, "For my ransomed time to be meaningful, it needs positive experience. But I sentenced myself to loops of troubled sleep and conscious moments without sensations, but full of pain. I'm going to feel myself once more. Goodbye."

As they filed out of the garage, Peter took Eliza aside. "Back when I brought you into the bathroom, you said, 'Another one.' What did you mean?"

Eliza glanced around. "Okay, you deserve to know. Few people who sign up for decade revival last fifty years. They get too lonely, too alienated. They usually just go for a walk outside until they thaw and sublimate. I have to leave."

Peter watched her lift off. Time, he thought, to clean the bathtub.

Turns of Fate

Teresa Richards

CRESSIDA STOOD IN LINE AT her summer job, waiting to be scanned in. Her right hand circled her left wrist, flipping the standard-issue damper cuff around and around and around. She stared at the sign that greeted her to work every day:

Turning strictly prohibited
Dampers must be worn at all times
No exceptions

This summer she was serving hot dogs and fried dough at Good Ol' Daze, the retro-themed fun park where she worked. It promised twenty-first century fun for anyone who cared to take a step back in time. Most of the patrons were school groups going through for history class, but there were a decent number of bored middle-agers, too.

She'd rather be spending her summer swimming at the quarry with her friends like she had last year, but the day she'd turned sixteen, she'd gotten a job. There was her little sister to think about. And since her Da couldn't stop using . . . well, a job was the only answer.

Cressida pushed her already frizzy hair out of her face. It was still early in the day, but the air was sticky and stale. She'd worn the lightest-weight shirt she could find—navy blue to satisfy the stupid dress code, but super breathable and, honestly, not a whole lot thicker than tissue paper. But it wasn't helping much; she was already sweaty. Standing over the deep fryer for the next six hours was definitely not going to help.

When she reached the front of the line, she held out her arm to have her damper cuff scanned. "It's been acting funny," she told the guy operating the cuff scanner. "This morning when it woke me up, the tone sequence sounded strange."

The guy eyed her. "Strange, how?"

"I don't know, all high and whiney—like the power source was dying."

He grunted. "How would you even know what that sounded like? You're on broadcast power, right?"

She nodded. "So, what should I do about it?"

The guy shrugged. "Trumped if I know."

"Can I still work?" She needed the coin. Her Da had used all his credits again, instead of selling them like he was supposed to.

Scanner Guy shrugged. "It's still working, right?"

"I think so. The Turning office isn't open this early, so I couldn't have it checked before I came in."

"Well, didn't you test it?"

Cressida's face flushed. She looked down at her arm resting on the scanner. "I presold my Turning credits. I'm out for the month." She didn't mention she was also out for the following five months. Six months in advance was as far out as the STC would let you go.

The guy avoided her gaze—he was embarrassed for her, she realized. Well she was embarrassed for her, too. So at least they agreed on that.

He waved her into the park. "Don't do anything stupid."

Stupid, like going into Time Turning debt for a measly twenty-second re-wind? No, she wouldn't do anything like that. Other than the high, twenty seconds back in time wasn't good for much. Not to mention, she'd get fired for Turning on the job.

There were stories about what it was like in the old days when the time travel gene was first developed. Back then, it had just been for the wealthy; they'd paid to have it genetically engineered into their offspring. Those who possessed it could travel back any number of years—millennia even—completely at will. It was as easy as flexing a muscle. They returned unharmed every time, on a high scientists later found was like shooting up your brain with a dozen feel-good chemicals all at the same time.

The rich began treating anytime pre-twenty-first century as a vacation destination. They'd go on holidays and gawk at the natives with their bulky metal cars and awkward handheld devices that were so clumsy and breakable. Everything anyone needed was implanted now. Shatter-free and theft-free.

And some people used to go back further still, to see the colonists discover a new land, or experience the height of the Roman Empire, or witness the birth of a Jewish king.

Within a few centuries, though, the trait had spread until almost everyone had it. And then people found they couldn't go back as far. A thousand years became the limit. Then a hundred. Then one.

And now it was down to twenty seconds.

Apparently, the space-time continuum was being depleted, right along with the ozone layer, and now there was a government agency—the STC—whose single purpose was to conserve the space-time continuum. Because, they said, depleting it entirely could cause the collapse of the universe.

No biggie.

The easy answer was to quit Turning. But nobody wanted to do that—the highs were just too good. So every citizen had an allotted amount of Turns they could make each month, and they wore damper cuffs to keep them on track. The cuffs inhibited the brain's ability to flex the muscle required for time travel and could only be unlocked by the wearer's fingerprint.

To incentivize people not to use all their Turns, the government offered monetary credits for unused Turns. For most people, the money was too good to pass up. So the space-time continuum was rebuilding itself and, once again, Turning was just for the rich.

Or the addicted.

Cressida hadn't Turned in over a decade. She could barely remember what it felt like.

When the fun park opened to the public, Cressida had the hot dogs ready—rolling in those metal rollers to keep them warm—the deep fryer bubbling, and the cotton candy spinning. And she was dripping with sweat. The *pop, pop, pop* of a toy gun sounded as the first customer at the stand across the way shot at a row of rubber ducks.

Everything in this theme park was supposed to be *vintage* and *retro*. That's how it was marketed, anyway. But a lot of it was just old. Basically garbage. She understood why society had moved on.

She pushed her bangs off her forehead just as her coworker, Trace, sauntered in, late as usual. As if working at a glorified carnival stand wasn't bad enough, Cressida had to endure six hours of Trace.

The first thing out of her mouth that morning was, "I love what you've done with your hair. It almost makes your face look thin."

Cressida pressed her lips together. "Nice to see you, too," she said. But really she was just thinking, *Wait, do I have a fat face?* She'd never even thought to wonder whether her face was fat or not. But maybe it was. Maybe she'd just never noticed.

How had she never noticed her fat face?

And why hadn't she responded with something more clever, like, "*It's a new look. Desert Blossom Chic. Only those of us with extra bouncy hair can pull it off,*" or something like that?

"Thanks for getting everything ready," Trace said, not seeming to realize that she'd just given Cressida a face complex.

Or maybe just not caring.

"My hover update hasn't been approved," Trace continued. "Mom didn't want me operating my old one. She read some story about a kid whose hover implants glitched and it blew him and everyone in a five-hundred-yard radius to bits. She made me take the rover."

Trace rolled her eyes, like riding the outdated hovercraft was the worst torture ever. Sure, the new hover slabs that communicated with implants in your feet to take you anywhere you wanted to go were sleeker. But either method got you from one place to the next, so Cressida didn't see what the big deal was.

Trace said, "You're lucky your dad is so laid back."

Translation: *You're lucky your dad doesn't give a trump about you.* Cressida's own hover implants hadn't been updated in five years. There were probably a million bugs in her software, but nobody at home cared about that, and the update was expensive.

Trace stood with a hand on her hip, waiting for a reply.

Target practice continued on the row of rubber ducks across the way.

Pop, pop, pop.

"Right." It was all Cressida could think to say. She was really just wishing for a mirror, so she could examine her face for evidence that she'd gained weight since yesterday.

Trace twisted her damper cuff around so that the indicator lights were on the inside of her wrist and not easily visible to passerby—couldn't have the green lights clashing with her outfit.

Cressida tightened her hands into fists, fighting the urge to adjust her own cuff to match Trace's. She didn't like the neon green lights either. Nobody did.

"Hey!" Trace said, grabbing Cressida's hand and examining her cuff. "How'd you get them purple?" she demanded.

Cressida blinked.

"The lights, Cres. Yours are purple, not green. How'd you do that? Purple lights would totally go with my outfit today. Did they put out a new update that lets you change your light color to match what you're wearing?"

Trace touched the chip implanted on her pinky finger and started scrolling through a holo of her notifications, searching, no doubt, for an update she'd missed. "I've been saying they should do that for ages. You've heard me say it, right? Is that what they did? Wait . . . are you beta testing it? Where did you sign up for that? Do you think they still have room for more testers?"

Cressida finally found her voice. "Stop! I'm not beta testing anything. I don't know why my lights are purple. My cuff was making a funny sound this morning—I told the scanner guy it was doing something weird but he told me not to worry abo—"

Cressida's throat closed up as she felt a yawning sensation in her head. Like something in her brain was stretching after a long nap. It was a feeling she hadn't felt in a very, very long time.

"Oh, no," Cressida said.

Trace's eyes went wide. "What?"

Cressida held out her arm, trying to swallow. "My cuff. It's not working."

Trace's shoulders slumped. "Is that all?"

"Trace, I'll get fired. No Turning on the job, remember?" Cressida fought the urge down. She was dangerously close to going into unauthorized Turning debt, too, but she wasn't about to admit that to Trace.

"So don't Turn," Trace said, tossing bits of dough into the deep fryer and watching the oil hiss angrily.

Not Turning was easier said than done. That's why everyone had damper cuffs. When the brain wanted a fix, it demanded one—kind of like a yawn. And Cressida was way out of practice at controlling it.

"Stop wasting the dough," Cressida said.

Trace tossed another glob of dough into the hot oil. "Turning at work is only a problem if you get caught. They don't actually check the logs, you know. Ever since that one girl quit, the logs have just been stacking up on Mr. Wahl's desk. Just don't let anyone see you."

The only way to catch someone Turning, other than to see a record of it on the Turning log generated by their cuff, was to see it. When someone Turned, there was a shift in the air around them—like a water mirage in the desert, only up close.

But Cressida's real concern was going into Turning debt and, unlike her employer, the government absolutely did check the Turning logs. If they found out she'd used more than the six months of credits she'd pre-sold, she'd be sent to labor camp. It was three months minimum for a first-time offender.

Cressida took a deep breath, trying to get herself under control. She just had to make it through the next six hours. As soon as she got off work, she could comm the Turning office for a cuff repair.

Or . . . maybe she should just comm them now. You weren't supposed to send comms while on the job, but surely a malfunctioning cuff warranted a little rule breaking?

"Are you open yet?" asked a smooth voice.

Cressida darted behind an ancient ICEE machine, out of view of the customer. She fought to stifle the Turning urge, swallow it down where it wouldn't get her into trouble. Trace had gone back to scrolling through her notifications and was paying zero attention.

"Trace," Cressida hissed. "There's a customer."

"It's all you, girl," Trace said without looking up. "I took first customer yesterday."

"Hello?" the customer called.

Argh. She'd have to comm the Turning office later.

Cressida took a deep breath. Calmed herself. Came out from behind the ICEE machine and locked eyes with the customer.

Heat crawled up her neck.

It was Grayzon, the boy she may or may not have been crushing on for the past three years. He wore a zip-up hoodie and an old-fashioned red hat, like the kind baseball players used to wear, and he stood there with all the confidence in the world—like the hat was some trendy vintage classic and not just a ratty old piece of junk.

Grayzon had won the title of "Best Hacker" in their school's hack-off in the seventh grade, and Cressida had been a fan ever since. He was a programming genius and didn't care what anyone thought of him.

He was also a daredevil on the hover ramps, which only made his nerdy side sexier. They'd worked on a project in science together a few weeks ago—the first time they'd ever actually spoken—but they hadn't really talked since.

Her Turning urge twitched again. She clenched her hands into fists and tried to keep her voice light. "Yep, we're open."

Grayzon smiled. "Hey, Cressida. I didn't know you worked here."

Well, he still remembered her name, at least. That was something.

"Don't you tutor on the weekends?" he added.

Wait, how did he know about that?

Oh, maybe he'd seen that public awareness infogram thing she'd done to get more volunteers for the elem school. Was that airing on the school feeds already?

Or had he hacked into the system to study up on her?

She found her voice. "Yeah, um. I tutor every other weekend. But only on Saturdays. I get to spend Sundays here." Cressida's arms swept out to the side, indicating the theme park. She smiled sweetly, like sweltering over a vat of hot oil at Good Ol' Daze was the best thing ever. She hoped he could read the sarcasm in her expression.

A raised eyebrow and lopsided grin said he had. "Lucky you." Grayzon's gaze stayed glued to hers.

She felt her face flush. And it wasn't because of the oil or the outside temps. It was because Grayzon was looking at her like . . . like . . .

Well, like she'd always hoped he would.

Her Turning muscle twitched again. She had to say something. "Um, what would you like?"

Grayzon blinked. "Oh. A hot dog, please."

Trace picked that moment to butt in. "You want a hot dog at nine in the morning? You're not planning to stuff yourself silly and then ride the Scrambler, are you? Because that's just gross."

"Umm. No, I'm just hungry." Grayzon said, his mouth twitching up into a tiny smile. He glanced at Trace, then back to Cressida, like he was sharing some private joke.

Wait, was he trying to point out to her how ridiculous her co-worker was? Finally, *finally,* someone other than her saw it.

Okay, he was definitely the absolute love of her life, no doubt about it.

Sold! To the boy in the red cap.

Trace glanced from Grayzon's face to Cressida's. "Whatever," she said, retreating to a stool and pulling up a holo of her social feed.

"This job comes with all kinds of perks, huh?" Grayzon said, nodding in Trace's direction.

"Oh, yeah." Cressida slid on some plastic gloves, wishing they hadn't banned the laser sanitizers on account of them not being retro enough, then got Grayzon's hot dog. "Sassy co-workers are just the beginning. You should see the amazing breakroom. There's a fan. And, umm," Cressida racked her brain. What else was there that she could make fun of? "A cat poster."

Ugh. Lame.

"A cat poster?" Grayzon grinned. "How exciting. Is it one that makes you contemplate the meaning of life, or one reminding you to hang in a little longer until life stops to suck?"

Cressida laughed. "It's actually more like, *'Look at me, I'm totes adorbs. Aren't you happier just knowing I'm alive?'* "

"Wow. That is quite the perk. How sad that I don't work here."

"It totally is. I'm going to cry, I'm so sad for you."

Grayzon took the hot dog and waved his cuff under the scanner to pay. The pay scanners were the only non-retro thing left in the park, and that was only because paper money was so retro it was obsolete.

On her stool in the corner, Trace huffed.

Oops, had she heard them making fun of her?

Cressida glanced over, but Trace was frowning at something on her feed, not paying any attention to her and Grayzon.

The toy guns at the stand across from hers went *pop, pop, pop* as two kids battled it out to see who could knock down the most ducks.

"Ketchup, mustard, napkins—all that stuff is on the cart." Cressida pointed to a little stand, which was placed just far enough away to keep the hot dog line moving.

Not that the line ever got backed up.

"Thanks," Grayzon said. He hesitated, like he wasn't sure what to do next. Or like he wanted to say something more.

But then he just smiled and headed for the condiments.

Cressida grabbed a rag and wiped down the already clean counter, watching Grayzon in her side vision as he pumped mustard onto his hot dog.

The condiment stand was ancient, just like everything else in this park. It was stainless steel, with sharp corners and rickety doors that hid several giant condiment bottles beneath the surface. The only thing showing from above were the pumps the customer used.

Trace closed her holo and walked over to where Cressida stood. "My boyfriend uses this hip new body spray and it makes him smell super sexy all the time."

Okaaaay. What did *that* mean?

"I'll comm you a link so you can get some."

Cressida stared at her. "Are you saying I smell?"

Trace laughed. "No, silly. It's for your friend." Her gaze darted to Grayzon, who'd moved on to the ketchup. "Sometimes boys smell, you know? It's like they can't help it."

Right. Of course that's what she'd meant.

But Grayzon did *not* smell.

Trace wrinkled her nose. "Ugh, he's coming back. I'll just be over here—out of smelling range."

Wait, what? Cressida whipped her head around.

Grayzon was indeed coming back.

Her heart knocked against the sides of her chest like a bull in a pen. The urge to Turn pressed at her mind stronger, more insistent than ever.

Cressida fumbled with her cuff. The lights had gone pale blue—like an oxygen-starved corpse.

Her mind flexed, tugging at her. Pulling. Telling her to let go and just Turn already. It would feel so good. And she deserved a fix. She'd been depriving herself for so long, all because her Da couldn't.

"I think you're out of ketchup," Grayzon said.

Cressida pressed her fingernails into her palms. *No losing control in front of the hot guy!*

"Sorry about that." Cressida said, hearing the nervous tremor in her voice and hating herself for it. "I'll just, um, get some more."

She knelt and pawed through the shelves until she found the ketchup refill bottles.

She took a deep breath.

And another.

Her Turning muscle relaxed. She could not afford to lose control.

She gripped the ketchup bottle, pressing her thumbs into the plastic and feeling it give slightly. For whatever reason, Grayzon seemed to like her. And he didn't smell. And she would not risk being sent to labor camp right when her three-year crush suddenly decided to pay attention to her.

She calmed her mind and stood, holding up the ketchup. "Found it."

She smiled at Grayzon, then let herself out through the flimsy metal door at the back of the food stand. "I'll just replace it for you."

She walked over to the condiment cart and knelt to remove the old bottle. She peeled the freshness seal off the new bottle and snapped it in place, then stood, closing the door of the cart and making sure the latch clicked.

"Voila!" Cressida held an arm out, like an artist presenting her newest creation.

Pop, pop, pop, went the toy guns.

And the rubber ducks fell one by one.

Grayzon smiled. "So, you're handy in a tutoring dilemma or a ketchup crisis. Good to know."

"What can I say, I'm a girl of many talents . . . Oh, wait, let me just . . ." She pumped the ketchup a few times to get it flowing.

Nothing happened.

She peered closer. Pumped again. "Actually, I think the tube is blocked." She pumped it harder.

Suddenly, ketchup spurted out.

No, exploded was more accurate.

Cressida shrieked as the ketchup splattered all over her. She jumped back, and something yanked at her shirt. She heard a rip, lost her balance, and landed hard on her butt.

She looked down. And heat raced up her face.

Her super-light t-shirt had super ripped open—right up the center. The hem must have gotten caught in the cart door when she'd closed it, and now—oh, trump—now she was sitting on the ground, her shirt completely open, exposing her stomach, her bra—everything.

Shame turned to mortification when she saw the bra she'd put on that morning.

Why, oh why had she picked the one with extra support? This one wasn't even remotely cute. Even worse than the ugly bra were her rolls of extra-white tummy flesh now out in the open for all to see. Her skin was so pasty it was almost translucent. She looked like a fleshy grandma.

She told herself not to look at Grayzon.

Too late.

His mouth was hanging open in shock. Or horror.

Of course it was horror—she was a giant, albino, grandma-bra-wearing whale!

Trace emerged from the hot dog stand, laughing. She pressed a finger to her pinky, and a holo popped up. Cressida heard the tell-tale click of a camera.

Cressida's body shook. Her face burned. The Turning muscle flexed inside her, promising a fix. Promising to make it all better.

And suddenly, she didn't care if she got caught or fired or even sent to labor camp. All she wanted was to undo it. A rewind. To erase the humiliation of the past twenty seconds. If there'd ever been a time to use her Turning gene, it was now.

Cressida closed her eyes and let herself go.

There were fireworks. And a rush.

Then calm beyond compare.

"I think you're out of ketchup," Grayzon said.

And Cressida smiled. It had worked. Nobody would ever see Trace's picture, and Grayzon would never know she wore grandma bras. Cressida felt lighter, happier, like she wanted to skip or jump or sing.

What had she been so afraid of? That had been the easiest fix ever. People probably did that all the time, even if they were out of Turning credits. They probably had some sort of warning system for first-time offenders and she'd just get a slap on the wrist. Everything was going to be fine.

"I'm on it," she said to Grayzon, getting the ketchup refill and peeling the seal off the top. She joined him outside, then replaced the bottle. She made sure not to get her shirt caught in the cabinet door when she closed it. "Voila! Ketchup for you."

Pop, pop, pop, went the toy guns.

And the rubber ducks fell one by one.

Grayzon smiled. "So, you're handy in a tutoring dilemma or a ketchup crisis. Good to know."

"What can I say, I'm a girl of many talents . . . Oh, wait . . ."

Trump, she'd forgotten to clear the blockage out of the ketchup pump. Oh well, at least her shirt wouldn't rip this time.

She unscrewed the top of the pump. "Let me just make sure the ketchup doesn't make you look like a Jackson Pollock when it comes out."

Grayzon eyed her.

"Oh, sorry, Jackson Pollock is that painter guy who got famous by splattering paint all over his canvases."

"I know who Jackson Pollock is," Grayzon said.

"Really?"

"Well, I'm not an art guy or anything, but there's this line of vintage skateboards called J-Polls that are a nod to his work. He did some wild stuff."

"Yeah, he did." Cressida cleared the clump of dried ketchup out of the tube, screwed it back in place and stepped aside.

Right into some guy who was walking past.

No, running past.

The guy slammed into Cressida's shoulder and the empty ketchup bottle flew out of her hands, flipped in the air, and splattered the last bits of ketchup onto her shirt. "Watch where you're going!" he said, barely slowing down.

Cressida felt something yank at her shirt.

Oh, no. *You have got to be kidding me.*

There was a bottle opener dangling from a keychain on the guy's backpack. It had snagged her shirt when he'd bumped into her.

She heard a rip. And watched her tissue-light t-shirt tear open. Again.

She lost her balance and fell backward, landing hard on her butt. And once again, her stomach and granny bra went on very public display.

All the blood rushed to her head, scalding on its way up.

There was Grayzon's horrified face. And Trace's laugh. And the camera snap.

Cressida would already be in trouble for Turning. What was once more?

She closed her eyes. Flexed her mind.

And then there was bliss.

"I think you're out of ketchup," Grayzon said.

Cressida's mind whirled. Okay, this time, she was not leaving the stand. No matter what.

"Trace, can you switch out the ketchups?"

Trace gawked at her. "But I just did my nails."

Now it was Cressida's turn to gawk. "You just did your nails, as in *just now*? While you're supposed to be working?"

"Yeah, there's this new nail art app. The designs stay on for weeks, and it's super easy to change them out anyti—"

"Will you just do your trumping job for once?" Cressida's blood had reached a boiling point. She rocked back on her heels to keep it from spilling over.

Something in her tone must have struck a nerve because Trace got up. "Fine, calm down. I need some air anyway."

Cressida turned back to Grayzon and forced a smile. "It'll be just a moment."

"Okay, no problem."

Cressida unclenched her hands—how long had they been in fists? She took a deep breath. "Who'd you come with today, anyway?"

"Just some friends from the ramps. There's a hover competition later."

"Oh." Had she known about that? She didn't remember them announcing it at the morning meeting, which they should have done if they were expecting larger than normal crowds.

Pop, pop, pop, went the toy guns.

And the rubber ducks fell one by one.

Trace bounded back into the stand. "The ketchup is now flowing." She tossed the empty ketchup bottle into the garbage.

Only, it missed by an inch and hit the edge of the counter instead. And did a flip in the air. And splattered ketchup all over Cressida's shirt.

"Trace, seriously?" Cressida said. Only she was really thinking, *Oh no, not again.*

Trace's eyes went wide. "I'm sorry. Really." And she actually seemed to mean it. "I know you don't have very many clothes, and ketchup is so hard to get out. Here, let me help you clean it."

Trace grabbed a wet rag and rushed forward.

Cressida jumped back. "No, thanks, I can do it myself." For all she knew, Trace would have on a belt or bracelet or something that would snag her shirt and rip it open. Again.

"Seriously, I'm really sorry," Trace said. "I know you can't afford another—let me help you clean it." She grabbed the edge of Cressida's shirt and started scrubbing. "I'm so, so sorry."

Trace was smearing ketchup everywhere.

Cressida stepped back, moving slowly so nothing could rip her shirt.

But her foot came down on something—the empty ketchup bottle, she realized. It slid out from under her, tipping her backwards.

Her shirt was still clenched in Trace's fist.

Cressida went down hard on her butt.

And her shirt ripped, right up the middle, leaving a fistful of super-breathable fabric in Trace's hand.

"Oh, my trump," Trace said, her mouth dropping open in horror. "I will totally buy you a new shirt. I'll just take a pic so I can find something similar."

She pointed her holo at Cressida, who was sprawled on the floor like she was posing for some granny pinup calendar.

Snap.

Cressida dropped her chin to her chest.

For the third time, she let her mind yawn.

This time, the fireworks seemed less colorful. And the bliss had lost its edge.

Why hadn't she been able to change anything? What good was a twenty-second rewind if you couldn't actually get a do-over?

Maybe she was doing it wrong.

Or maybe this was just her life. No matter what she did, no matter which changes she made, maybe she was just a horrible screw-up.

Her face burned. She couldn't look Grayzon in the eye.

"I think you're out of ketchup," he said.

Cressida ducked her head. "Yeah, we are. I'll get right on that." She got a new bottle, removed the seal, and went out to the cart.

"Hey, what are you doing later?" Grayzon asked.

Cressida worked the blockage out of the ketchup pump. "I'm working all day."

He smiled. "But what about after that?"

"Then I'm just going home." She still needed to get her cuff fixed. If they didn't come arrest her first. But she wasn't about to say any of that to Grayzon.

Pop, pop, pop, went the toy guns.

And the rubber ducks fell one by one.

"Well, do you want to hang out later?"

Any other time and Cressida would have been jumping for joy. Grayzon was actually asking her out. But Cressida knew what was about to happen.

Grayzon waited for an answer.

"If you still want to, sure." Cressida stepped out of the way of a guy running toward her. The bottle-opener guy.

Grayzon's brow furrowed. "If I still want to, when?"

Cressida looked around. Where was it going to come from this time? Her shirt wasn't caught in the door, the guy with the backpack weapon had already passed, and her co-worker was safely inside the hot dog stand.

"Just . . . in ten minutes, if you still want to hang out with me, then sure. I'd love to."

Grayzon's lips turned up in an adorable grin. "Okay. Cool." He pumped ketchup onto his hot dog, then fell silent.

Cressida fiddled with the empty ketchup container. "Aren't you going to eat your hot dog?"

Grayzon stared at it. "I'm actually not that hungry."

Suddenly, the sound of a gunshot.

Much louder than a pop gun.

And a white-hot pain exploded inside her.

Cressida looked down. Red blossomed on her shirt, darkening the navy to almost-black. And it wasn't ketchup this time.

Her hand flew to her throat.

That had been the sound of a gun. An actual, real gun.

Had she been shot?

The pain in her chest was searing. Like a burning knife.

She gasped for air.

"Son, what you did was illegal," Cressida heard a gruff voice say.

"I know, sir, but it was a gunshot." She recognized Grayzon's voice. "I couldn't not Turn."

Cressida's head throbbed. And her eyelids felt sticky. Heavy. She opened them anyway.

"I understand," said the man—a Turning officer. He walked to the door and eased it closed.

Cressida was lying on a bed in the employee breakroom, wearing the zip-up hoodie Grayzon had been wearing all morning. Beneath the hoodie, her shirt felt wet—she couldn't tell with what—and it was ripped open in the front. She pulled the zipper up to her neck so she was fully covered.

"What happened?" she said. Her brain felt hazy.

Grayzon glanced down at her. His eyes went wide. "Shhh."

Her gaze wandered to the wall, where a fuzzy kitten sat in a tin bucket with a wide-eyed look of innocence.

"Close your eyes. Pretend you're still asleep," Grayzon muttered. Then, to the authority, he said, "When can we go?"

"Well, your story checks out. We caught a man with a loaded weapon not far from where you were. Had some stolen goods on him."

"So I helped stop a crime," Grayzon said.

The authority remained silent. Then, as if he didn't want to admit it, "Yes. You did. But you still went over your Turning limit."

"To save a life!" Grayzon shot back. "Obviously I wouldn't have sold all my credits this month if I'd known someone might die unless I Turned."

Wait, *what* was he talking about? She remembered that she'd Turned, what, two, three times? There'd been several ketchup incidents. And lots of shirt-ripping. But had something worse happened? Had Grayzon Turned in order to keep her from getting *shot*?

Cressida's eyes flew open before she remembered she was supposed to be asleep. Her head pounded.

The authority pulled up a holo of something and studied it. He sighed.

Cressida snapped her eyes shut.

"Alright, son. This is your first offense and you don't appear to have any Turning debt. I'll let you off with a warning. Don't do it again."

"But what if—"

The authority cut him off, "Even if someone is dying—that's what we're here for. It's our job to keep the peace and protect people. We use Turning whenever necessary. But you have to have prior authorization to go into Turning debt."

"I understand, sir," Grayzon said.

"Is the girl okay?" the authority said.

"Oh, yeah. She just fainted. She'll be fine."

Wait, she'd *fainted?* If Cressida wasn't already embarrassed beyond belief, now it was a hundred times worse.

"Keep that cuff on for the rest of the month, kid." Footsteps headed for the door. It opened and clicked shut.

Cressida's eyelids fluttered. "Is he gone?"

"Yeah, we're in the clear." Grayzon helped her sit up.

She pressed a hand to her head and the throbbing eased. "Did I really faint?"

"Not exactly." He didn't elaborate.

"And what about the gunshot?" Cressida looked down and saw a stained red corner of her white shirt poking out. "Is that blood? Did I seriously get shot?"

"Yes, you got shot. But that's just ketchup—I Turned in order to fix it, so you're fine—you just don't remember that part." Grayzon paused. "I saw you, you know."

Cressida's cheeks flushed as she remembered the way her shirt had ripped open over and over and over again. Yes, he had seen her. Way too much of her.

"Turning time," he clarified.

Oh, that.

"Before you got shot. I saw you come out of a Turn. So when it happened again, I didn't think. I just moved. I figured you'd already Turned once to try and stop it. But I didn't tell the authorities; I don't think they know you Turned."

Cressida bit her lip. She'd Turned a whole lot more than once, and it hadn't been because she'd gotten shot. The authorities would find that out when they checked her logs. But maybe she wouldn't lose her job, at least. "You didn't have to do that for me."

"I wanted to." He glanced at her sideways. "You don't remember what happened next, do you?"

Cressida's brow furrowed. Technically, she should have been able to remember, since no-one had Turned since then. But her brain seemed to be off-duty.

"Okay, I'll tell you." Grayzon said. "I just have to say, though, that I'm really sorry."

"Seriously, just tell me. It can't be worse than getting shot."

"Well, when I Turned, things moved so fast. I was frantic to get you out of the way before the crazy guy with the gun appeared, and I had to reactivate my cuff so I wouldn't Turn again. I ended up dumping my hot dog on you—ketchup got all over—and then my cuff caught on the hem of your shirt and . . . well . . ." His ears went pink.

Cressida knew what happened next, even though she didn't remember it happening that particular time. "My shirt ripped open, didn't it?"

Grayzon grimaced. "Yes. I'm so sorry! It's better than getting shot and having an EMT rip it open, though, right?"

"Is that what happened the first time?" Or . . . Cressida thought back . . . the fourth time, maybe? Grayzon wouldn't remember all her other attempts to avoid the ketchup-and-shirt-ripping fiasco.

"Yes," Grayzon said.

"And you Turned in order to save me?"

Grayzon nodded. "But then, after I attacked you with my hot dog and accidentally ripped your shirt open, well, then I saw a guy who looked like he was pulling a gun, so I tackled you to get you out of the crossfire. You hit your head. And it wasn't even him." Grayzon's shoulders slouched, like he was the worst person on the planet.

So that's why her head had hurt when she woke up. She put a hand on his arm. "Thank you for saving me. That was really brave. And, hey, I'm sorry you had to see . . ." She waved a hand vaguely over her torso. "All this." She folded her arms across her chest.

Cressida couldn't look at him. Embarrassment didn't even begin to describe how it felt knowing he'd seen her so exposed. She wanted to crawl under a boulder and never come out. She wanted to join a nunnery. She'd have to switch schools so she never saw Grayzon again.

Grayzon placed a finger under her chin and tilted her head up so she had to look at him. "Cressida." He held her gaze with his. "You're beautiful."

Her thoughts stuttered to a halt. Heat crawled across her skin. She wasn't sure if it was because she was still embarrassed or because his hands were so warm or because he was looking at her like he could see straight into her soul and that he liked what he saw there.

Okay, maybe she could skip the nunnery.

"I have cuter bras," she said.

"I'm sure you do." Grayzon grinned. "Want to know a secret?"

Cressida didn't trust her voice. She nodded.

"I didn't really want a hot dog this morning," Grayzon said. "I just wanted to ask you out."

Cressida melted into a puddle right there in the employee breakroom.

"I got you off work for the rest of the day," Grayzon said.

Cressida grinned. "That might be the best news I've ever had."

"What should we do n—"

He was cut off by the door banging open. Authorities swarmed in. "Put your hands where we can see them!"

Cressida gasped. This was it. They'd figured out what she'd done and now they were here for her.

The same guy Grayzon had been talking to earlier said, "Sorry, kid. I got overruled. Quotas and all. You understand." He grabbed Grayzon and forced him to his feet, knocking over the chair he'd been sitting in. It clattered to the floor.

The guy pulled Grayzon's hands behind his back and slapped a pair of lasercuffs around his wrists. "Unapproved Turning debt is a crime; you're coming with us."

"Wait, no!" Cressida screamed. "Where are you taking him?" She jumped up, her head swimming.

"Labor camp," the authority barked. "Standard three months."

Cressida's voice was shrill. "But he didn't do anything wrong. It should be me instead." She felt her body sway.

Grayzon said, "No, Cressida, don't. It's only three months." He stumbled as they dragged him out of the break room.

Cressida grabbed one of the authorities' arms. "Take me instead."

"Not allowed." The man shook her off and followed the rest of his squad.

"But I Turned first—it was my fault. And I'm in debt."

The man whirled on her. Grabbed her wrist. The rest of the authorities filed out the door, taking Grayzon with them. "You're lying."

"I'm not. Check the logs."

The authority eyed her. He sighed, but pulled back and scanned her cuff. He scrolled through the holo that popped up. Then his jaw went slack and he looked at her with new interest. "You've been in Turning debt for over a decade."

Cressida squared her shoulders. "I've never gone over the pre-sale limit and my debt has all been pre-approved."

"Until today, I see," the authority said, studying her logs.

"Yes," Cressida said. "It was all my fault. Let Grayzon go."

The authority shook his head. "Can't." He slapped a pair of cuffs on Cressida's wrists. "But I'll take you, too."

Two Weeks Later

Cressida's fingers curled around the metal of the chain-link fence separating the boys' camp from the girls'. Her polyester jumpsuit itched, but she barely noticed as she watched and waited. Her trial had been non-existent. Unlike Grayzon, she hadn't had a good reason for the unapproved Turning debt and she'd been sent to the juvenile labor camp immediately.

She'd been issued a shovel, gardening gloves, and a sun hat. Apparently, growing things helped build back the space-time continuum, and giving back to the environment was how people worked off their Turning debt. Also, picking up garbage and painting over graffiti and cleaning up the parks. Which didn't help the space-time shortage, exactly, but whatever. She was free labor. The end.

But maybe they'd let Grayzon go. Maybe they'd realize he didn't belong here. She hoped for it. That she wouldn't see him for the next three months until she got out.

But each day when the boys and girls were let out to their respective courtyards to run laps, she couldn't help but wonder if he'd be among the crowd. And what she would say to him if he was. And how she could ever make this right.

The answer was that she couldn't. There was nothing she could do that would ever make this right.

She straightened up as the boys started coming out. She scanned their faces as they spilled from the building and began running around the perimeter of their courtyard. One by one, she ticked them off.

Not Grayzon. Not Grayzon. Not Grayzon. Not . . .

"Grayzon?" she said, her voice a mixture of surprise and dread. She gripped the chain-link fence harder. "Grayzon!"

Grayzon's head whipped around, searching for the person who'd called his name. He saw her standing by the fence. Smiled. Jogged over.

His hair was shorter. They must have made him cut it.

"Hi," she said. It was all she could come up with.

"Hi, back," he said, squinting into the afternoon sun.

Her fingers went white at the knuckles. "I'm so sorry you're here."

Grayzon shrugged. "Illegal Turning to save a girl's life. Worth it." He winked. "What about you, what are you in for?"

Cressida gawked at him. How could he be so nonchalant about losing his freedom?

He continued to grin at her until it became impossible not to smile back.

"Fine, I'll play. Illegal Turning to make sure a boy got enough ketchup on his hot dog."

"Wow. You must have really cared about that hot dog."

"Or I must have really cared about the boy." Cressida caught his gaze. Held it. "I really am sorry," she whispered.

"I'm not." Grayzon's fingers found hers through the chain links. His hand was warm, shocking compared to the cold fence. "And, anyway, we won't be here long."

True, it was only three months.

But it was three whole months! Summer would be over when they got out. School would have just begun.

And her sister would have had to spend her Turning credits on keeping Da out of trouble.

Grayzon was looking at her, a mischievous glint in his eyes. "Your release orders should come in tomorrow."

Cressida frowned. Her brow furrowed.

"Best Hacker, remember?" Grayzon grinned. "I took care of it during my trial."

Cressida gripped the fence tighter as she realized what he was saying. Her voice dropped to a whisper. "Seriously? You hacked the STC?"

"Yep."

Cressida stared at him. "You seriously did? You got us out?"

"Yep."

"How?"

Grayzon laughed. His fingers tightened around hers, weaving around the metal links. "It's a little hard to explain. But maybe I'll show you someday." He held her gaze, his eyes boring into hers.

And their connection was electric, like a jolt of lightening. Cressida felt it sparking through her bones. And she knew he felt it, too.

And then a sharp voice barked, "Hey, you two. No loitering by the fence. Get on with your laps."

Grayzon pulled back, slowly, keeping one hand on hers as long as he could. "I guess I'll see you on the other side."

"I guess so." Cressida squeezed his fingers one last time.

Then they turned and went their separate ways—for now—wearing matching Cheshire grins and polyester jumpsuits the color of the setting sun.

Blue Sandman

Eddie Cantrell

Since I can't write you a song, I wrote you a story.
For Sia, Maria, and Marcel.

STEVIE ROLLED THE CAB ONTO a dark street. Dilapidated factories, warehouses, and weed-riddled parking lots hoarded the pavement. *Why is it always the last customer of the night that has to be El Weirdo?* He glanced at the GPS mounted to the windscreen.

"Um, Mr.—"

"Harrison. Name's Jack Harrison," the old man said from the passenger seat. Three things struck Stevie about Harrison.

Firstly, the old timer sat in the passenger seat. Most folks crept into the back seat, mumbled a "hi" and an address, and that was that. Also, he didn't just introduce himself to Stevie (which folks simply never did, not to a cab driver) but he announced it—like, "Hey, everyone, drop what you're doing. Jack Harrison has entered the building." But the thing about Harrison that delivered a good, generous shot of sadness and guilt right into the pit of his gut was the old man's smell—an "old yet clean clothing" smell mixed with a dash of cologne and whiff of spearmint gum. The exact smell Stevie's father had. His father's words whispered in his ear—"Well, how do you like that, cap'?"

"Oh. Yeah, right. Well, Mr. Harrison, you sure we got the right address?" Stevie waved a hand at the less-than-cheery surroundings. "I mean, unless you're visiting Frankenstein or something."

Jack Harrison gave a gruff, "Ha! Frankenstein? That ol' creep-show moved up to Washington into a big ol' house with white walls and suit-wearing gorillas with hearing aids, kid." He gestured ahead. "Keep drivin'. Almost there."

Despite the day's fatigue, Stevie smiled.

The old man was a character, alright. Dressed like some honky-tonk gangster in a cool-cat, cream blazer, a checkered shirt, and slick black trousers. As they drove, Jack Harrison hummed a ditty Stevie heard only fragments of—"*You showed me this place, where we once sang the blues . . .*"

Stevie glanced down at Harrison's hands. His leathery, knobbly fingers tapped away on his knees in a jittery—*tap-tap. Tap-tap-tap.*

A niggling concern lingered in the back of Stevie's mind. Giving the shadowy industrial area an uneasy look, Stevie thought maybe there was something about where they were headed that bothered Jack Harrison. This place was a long way from the quaint neighborhood of Green Hills where Stevie had picked Harrison up.

He ignored the churning in his chest and guided the cab through seedy pools of streetlight and the patches of darkness between.

"Over there on the right, kid. See the sign?"

Stevie slowed down. A wonky sign hung from a street pole. "Yeah. Says 'Parking.' One with the arrow?"

"You got it, kid."

Stevie pulled up to the solid, barbed-wire-topped gates that were locked with a thick, rusty chain and padlock. The narrow driveway crept its way between two factory buildings for a hundred meters before vanishing into darkness black as a dead crow's ass, as Stevie's father would've said.

Harrison exited, stepped round the hood, and limped into the headlights. When he fumbled with the keys to the gate, his hands trembled so much that the keys rattled.

Stevie felt a tingle of guilt. Watching Harrison tremble like that, the penny dropped. The old man wasn't some weirdo druggie or honky-tonk gangster. At least, not likely. Maybe he was sick. *Parkinson's disease.* That bitch of an illness. Yeah, a bitch Stevie knew all too well. Had seen it work its tragic magic on his father, who went from being a tough cop to a weak, trembling recluse in a mere six months. His condition had deteriorated to such an extent that Stevie, the prodigal son, had slowly started visiting his father less and less. *That's all he wanted in the end. His son by his side.* That had been Stevie's waking thought in the mornings and his final thought in the evenings for the last year and half. *That's all he wanted in the end* . . . some prodigal son.

Stevie reached for the door handle, ready to assist when the gates screeched open. Chest heaving, Harrison waved him through, but Stevie hesitated. All he needed now was to be caught in the middle of some weird old timer trouble. Jack Harrison knocked on the hood with his fist. "Go on, kid. I ain't got all night." Stevie shot the dashboard clock a look— 23:19—let out a groan, and drove past the old man. *Probably going to have to call dispatch up and tell 'em I'm running late.* His shift was ending in ten minutes and the cab needed to back at the terminal. Or Ms. Gomez would start getting edgy. And you didn't want that warhorse edgy.

The headlights swept over a dreary single story covered in a labyrinth of cracks, weeds, and water stains. "Hope honky-tonk gangsters are peaceful," Stevie whispered as he stopped the cab in front of a long, tattered awning that jutted out from over a bright blue door.

A faded red carpet, frayed and dirty, ran from the door to the end of the awning. He gazed up over the row of black windows. A flashy, neon sign leapt across the building's face with jazzy musical notes trailing behind it. "The Blue Sandman," he said. Must've been decades since that sign lit the night and ladies in frilly, glitzy gowns and gents in tuxedos queued under the awning.

Stevie rolled the window down as Jack approached the cab. The old man tilted his head at the building. "You got the V.I.P spot, kid. Cut the engine and come on inside. I wanna show you something."

Stevie glanced at his watch again—23:21. "Mr. Harrison, I don't know—" The last thing he needed was his fortune read backwards to him by Ms. Gomez.

The old man raised his hand. "Of course, leave the meter running, kid. Ain't stiffing no working man his money."

"Listen, I got to get going. My shift is about to end and I got to get the car back, Mr. Harrison. But I can get Joey to come and get you in an hour. He's a good guy, so—"

"You got someone, kid?"

Christ! The old man wants to know about my love life. This is getting weirder by the second.

"A wife? A wife and kid? A boyfriend? What?"

Oh Jesus. Should I say I'm single?

The old man stared at Stevie, his dark eyes black as onyxes. "Well, do you?"

Stevie quickly lowered the sun visor. Next to a hand-written note that read, "Remember, there are more stars beyond the few we can see," a photo was tucked behind a plastic sleeve. Two happy faces, a blonde woman and a young girl, sunny smiles, a sunny beach. A sunny memory. "My girlfriend and my little girl." Stevie slapped the visor back and turned to Harrison. "What's it to you, Mr. Harrison?"

Shadows seeped into Harrison's face, made him look frailer, gaunter. Sicker. When he spoke he sounded out of breath and tired. "All these New Age, Facebook gurus, they talk about the meaning of life. Every day a new theory or wonderful quote. A new way to tap into life's secret meaning. As if it's a big mystery."

"Isn't it?"

"C'mon, kid. Whatever happened to Jimmy Hoffa is a mystery. Or which Bermuda Triangle swallowed up Bush's weapons of mass destruction. Papa bear mystery, that one," Harrison huffed. He looked at the visor and back at Stevie. "The meaning of life is right there in that picture, on the faces of those two girls. When you fill your days up with as many of those moments then you don't give a shit about the meaning of life because you're living it. You get me, kid?"

Stevie nodded. "Think I do. What does that have to do with whatever's in there?"

The old man kept his trembling hand on the door but turned toward the building. "This hunk o' bricks houses my most special moments. Where all my dreams came true. Met my girl there. Jo-Lee. Proposed to her there." He gave a gruff laugh. "Seven times. She gave in. Finally. My friends and I wined and dined in there till the early hours. All my dreams are in there, kid." He sighed. "And it's getting torn down next week."

Stevie had an urge to say something but only came up with a quiet, "Shit."

Harrison shrugged and said, "Dunno 'bout you, but I believe in God. Believe the big Man up in the sky is a pro in his big, ol' heavenly kitchen, too." Harrison turned back to Stevie. "He fixed me up with a mean club sandwich, you know. Slapped on a few slices of diabetes and Parkinson's with some chunky arthritis sauce, all between a crispy cancer bun. And a few hemorrhoids on the side."

Stevie muttered another, "Shit," but when he heard Jack guffaw, he couldn't help but smile. The smile faded though when an image of his ailing father came to mind.

The laughter died and Harrison leveled Stevie with a sober look. "Now I believe in God, like I said. I know He's there. I know it because the docs told me I was going to die and I'm still standing here. But I got a feelin' that won't be the situation much longer." Harrison said this without a trace of fear or pity. "And I want to say a big, hearty 'Howdy' one last time."

"To who?"

"To them. They'll all be here till this place gets demoted to a parkin' lot next week." Harrison nodded over his shoulder.

Stevie paused, looked at the building, and back at Harrison.

Harrison seemed to shrink as he lowered his head. "And I don' wanna, you know, do it alone."

"Why?" Stevie asked with a whisper. "Are you afraid?"

The old man looked up and gave him a tired smile. "No. And I could tell you a long, soppy story about dead friends and faraway kids, but—" he waved his hand in a dismissive gesture. "But it comes down to this—I'm old enough that I've outlived anyone who's cared a tinker's damn about me."

The image of Stevie's father hit Stevie like a shot. Shortly before his passing, father and son spoke on the phone. His father had had a rare lucid moment. He took the moment to ask his son to come by the hospital. Because he missed him. Stevie said he would. He promised.

That was the last time they spoke. And his father died alone in a hospital room downtown. No one by his side. Not even his prodigal son who had made a promise he couldn't keep.

Stevie killed the engine and nodded. "Let's go, Mr. Harrison."

Harrison smiled. "Call me Jack, kid." He turned and walked to the edge of the red carpet. "Before we go inside,"

Jack said, as Stevie caught up to him. "I got a little, what could one call it? A show of gratitude." He reached in to his cool-cat jacket and, like a magician, pulled out a gold hip-flask and unscrewed the lid. He took a small swig, smacked his lips in delight, and passed it to Stevie.

"Mr.—I mean, Jack—I'm driving. I can't—"

Jack waved him away. "One nip, kid." A wry smile uncurled across his face. "I bet you've never tasted anything like this." He peered at Stevie, eyes bright.

Stevie grabbed the flask and took a small sip. A grimace contorted his face as the spirit burned a highway of fire down his throat. "Holy mother of Satan."

Jack laughed cheerfully and whisked the hip-flask back into his blazer.

"What was that note about, the one in your cab, next to the pretty photograph?"

Stevie rubbed his chest and shrugged. "Just a note to remind me to keep believing."

"And are you? Still believin', kid?"

"No. Not really."

"Fair enough. Let's get this show on the road."

Stevie watched the old man stroll toward the blue door. The moment didn't feel like God was around. Stevie didn't believe in God. But when he stepped onto that faded red carpet, something gave an electric buzz. Stevie froze. He looked up. That sign—The Blue Sandman—buzzed to life for a few staggered seconds and blinked out. Stevie stared. He shrugged and stepped forward.

When Jack opened the red door, a whisper of music trickled out from the darkness inside—a jazzy splash of drums, a bluesy twang of a guitar.

Then silence.

Jack glanced over his shoulder and gave Stevie a smile that brightened the twinkle in his eyes. "Comin', kid?"

A light tingle of excitement and curiosity rushed across the surface of Stevie's skin and dove into his gut. Although that sign was dead as a lamp in a haunted house, there was a sudden electricity in the air. It was undeniable. Stevie stood on the tattered carpet and looked around for a clue to something he wasn't quite sure of. A moment later, he reached the door and stepped into the darkness.

Jack led the way through a shadowy foyer that smelled of dust and wood shavings. And cigar smoke? In the bad light, Stevie barely made out a counter to his right and a long rod with a row of wire coat hangers to his left. Stillness swirled in the small foyer.

"Did you just hear music, Jack? Like a few seconds ago?" Stevie asked but, in the quiet, his voice filled the room nonetheless.

"Kid, I always hear music."

Somehow that wasn't the answer Stevie had hoped for.

Jack moved toward the end of the foyer and opened a set of double doors. More darkness leaked from the new opening as well as a rich, somehow nostalgic scent of floor wax and cigars. Stevie kept his hands in front of him and widened his eyes but the gloom persisted.

"Wait here, kid. Don't want you bumping into anything and hurtin' yourself. I'll get the lights." Jack's footsteps echoed as he drifted from sight.

"What the hell is going on?" Stevie mumbled.

At what sounded like the other end of the room, the old man slowly climbed four steps.

Jack mumbled something Stevie couldn't make out. There was a loud clank and a scatter of quieter noises.

A warm spot of light faded up in the middle of a small, elevated stage. The soft light spilled into a semi-circular room scattered with round tables surrounded by wooden chairs. A small dance floor lay directly in front of the stage. Right in the middle of the spotlight, a gleaming red electric guitar leaned against a large Marshall amplifier. Stevie wasn't a musician, but when he was a boy, he spent Sunday afternoons with his father, who was a guru when it came to music trivia, listening to old Johnny Cash, Elvis, or Chet Atkins records. Stevie could tell that the electric wasn't one of those demonic things metal bands played, but a classy instrument probably out of the forties or fifties. A wooden stool stood next to the guitar.

Jack ambled up to the edge of the spotlight and turned in the direction of Stevie. He raised his hand to cut the glare. His hand no longer trembled but shook uncontrollably. "Ah, there you are. Grab a seat over here." Jack gestured at a table up front.

Stevie weaved through the labyrinth of tables to the edge of the dance floor. He slid onto a chair.

"Best seat in the house, kid." Jack lingered in the shadows. Dust motes swam in the bright light.

When Jack stepped into the spotlight and took a seat, the motes converged around him as if he floated in a spell. A trembling hand reached for the guitar and placed it on his thigh. He leaned over, flicked a switch on the amplifier. A soft electric hum shaved the stillness. "Okey-dokey, kid. Ready to go?"

Stevie leaned forward, elbows on the table, and shrugged. "Sure, Jack."

Jack's trembling hand glided to his lips. With his shaking fingers, the mere action of clasping the triangular pick became gargantuan and Stevie gave a heavy-hearted sigh.

Jack lowered his hand toward the guitar strings. His face, wrinkled and tense, contorted in concentration. The plectrum stopped just above the bottom string and hovered there, caught in uncontrollable shaking.

"Ah, shit, man," Stevie mouthed into his clasped hands. *Old man's going to mess this up. Ah, Christ. What am I doing here?* As if in a cruel confirmation of Stevie's thought, Jack struck the strings and—

GWAAAANNNGG—a dreadful mutation of reverb and out-of-tune noise spawned through the room. Stevie sunk his head behind his hands and closed his eyes. "Jesus." He looked up without raising his head and peered at Jack, eyes peeping through fingers.

The old man glared at his traitorous hand.

Stevie shifted in his seat and sighed. "Okay, Jack. Listen, why don't we come on back tomo—" Stevie froze, ". . . tomorrow." He lowered his hands, raised his head—"We can come back—" and stared at the stage.

Jack's hand floated above the strings with the stillness of a held breath. Only the illuminated dust motes danced around him .

His right hand pounced on the string. *DWANG.* He looked up for a moment and his face brightened. In a flash, Jack's fingers galloped up and down the guitar's neck in a blur of motion. Stevie immediately recognized the tune as "Guitar Blues." *Pops loved this one!* Suddenly, the complex but jovial ditty flitted though the room. And the stillness was gone.

A bewildered smile lit Stevie's face. *What the hell.* Not only could he not believe what he saw, but the melody and the perfection in which it was being played shot through Stevie's chest and hit him right in the ticker. Gone were Jack's shakes and debilitating trembles. In less than three seconds, Jack became a magician casting spells with a red guitar. His fingers charged across the instrument's neck from left to right, right to left, up and down, down and up—notes bulleted out, one after the next.

Stevie sat dumbfounded.

Jack drove one song out after the next, each one more impressive than the first. Bam, bam, bam. "Jam Man," "Cannonball Rag," "Alabama Jubilee." Instead of tiring, Jack became more invigorated. On a highway of sound, Jack Harrison was an outlaw drag-racer.

Stevie's breath caught. Were the wrinkles on Jack's face disappearing? His thinning grey hair thickening? His murky eyes crystal clear?

The long, draped curtains to the left of the stage fluttered, caught by a sudden gust of wind. The same happened to the right. A large man in a ten gallon hat walked on from stage left, a bass guitar under his arm.

Stevie sat bolt upright. *Where the hell did he come from?* No drug dealer he had ever seen looked like this fella. This place had been a graveyard of tables and stools.

A massive grin illuminated Jack's face when the man stepped next to him. The Hat-Man bopped to the rhythm for a moment and, without missing a beat, slid his hand down his guitar's neck—*DUUUUUUUMMMM*—and suddenly broke into a galloping bass line.

"Holy shit," Stevie whispered as goosebumps broke across his arms and chest.

The two musicians played off each other, riding a wave of sound. The thumping bass formed a rollicking, driving ride that Jack's jovial and intricate finger-picking style rode with synchronized perfection. Their boots tapping, their heads bopping.

Stevie said, "Holy shit," because two more men entered stage right. The one was a tall cat in a white suit and slicked-back, black hair. He carried a stool in one hand and, in the other, a simple drum-rig comprised of two toms and a snare. The second man, with a beard big enough to scare-off a stray cat, wore a banjo on his back. The two sauntered up to the others.

Both Jack and the bassist guffawed as the drummer and banjo player took places to form a semi-circle quartet.

"Hit it, Bones," Jack roared, and the drummer slammed into a machine-gunning roll before thumping out a swinging groove. The floorboards rattled as Jack and the bassist rode on the back of the building drum roll. Just as Bones was about to break into a crescendo, the music suddenly stopped. The four musicians shared glances between one another, each member's face plastered with mock surprise. Jack gave a cock-sure grin and said, "Someone stole the music, boys. Who's gonna call the cops?"

Hat-Man said in his deep baritone, "Not me."

"I sure ain't," Strings said with a shrug.

But Bones craned his neck to face the ceiling and howled out a long, police-siren—"Weeeeeeeewaaaaaaa."

The windows rattled and the floors vibrated as all four members broke into a raucous version of Merle's "Boogie

Woogie." The song, played with such raw and organic energy, stirred something deep inside Stevie and he had to smile because, if he didn't, he just might've been moved to tears. For the first time in his life he truly understood his father's love for music.

A loud "whoooop" bellowed out behind Stevie and he swivelled around. His mouth fell open.

The Blue Sandman had awoken. The room filled with guests. Some sat nodding to the groove, others tapped their hands on the tables that were decked with bowls of snacks, glasses of wine, whiskey, and beer. Trails of cigar smoke twirled up from the ashtrays, filling the room with a rich and luxurious smell.

"No way!" Stevie mouthed.

The Blue Sandman had gone from a depressing and silent shell to a thumping, raucous temple of jazzy blues filled with glitzy music worshippers.

A man in a suave black suit and a woman in a floral purple number slid out from their table, grabbed each other's hands, and hit the dance floor, breaking into a jive. Within seconds, more guests were up and out of their seats and descended on the floor with joyful cheers, swings, and twirls.

Stevie shut his eyes tight. What he was seeing wasn't possible, didn't make sense, didn't fit into his idea of how the world was supposed to work. Seriously, was he seeing some sort of meta-psycho-physical representation of all Jack Harrison's memories? His dream or wishes? Shit, was there something in that whiskey?

Someone tapped Stevie on the shoulder. He opened his eyes.

Her beauty bowled him over. She looked to be in her forties. Her silky skin glowed and her blue eyes teased him with youthful secrets. One hand on her hip, she jigged from side to side. She leaned over and whispered into Stevie's ear, "Hi, there, stranger."

"Hi, I'm Stevie."

"You wanna give an ol' gal a dance around, Stevie, or just sit there like a wet rooster?"

Before Stevie could think of something to say, she grabbed his hands and pulled him onto the dance floor. Stevie had never learned to dance, in fact didn't like it much, but now here he was doing the boogie as if he had been doing it his entire life. Yet it wasn't just that he suddenly knew steps to dances he'd never dare try, certainly not sober, but that he swivelled and turned around the floor with a sense of unbound joy he had never felt before. And this woman with her enchanting smile was a goddess of dance.

"There you go, kid. Like a cat on a hot tin roof," Jack shouted from the stage. The woman blew Jack a kiss. Out of breath, heart pounding, Stevie stepped back and looked at the woman. The warm light bathed her fair skin and Stevie watched her mouth at Jack—"I love you."

Jack called back, "Right back at ya, Jo-Lee."

She took Stevie's hand and placed a small, dried daisy in it. She closed his hand with hers and leaned in closer to him. "Give this to your gal, Stevie. Tell her you love her, say it so she knows it's true. Understand?"

Stevie nodded with a smile.

"And take her to a fancy place and dance till the sun sneaks up on the night." The woman swung on her heel and disappeared into the crowd.

Stevie walked back to his table. A large, barrel-chested man with straight posture sat in the chair next to his. He raised a glass of beer as Stevie took his seat.

The quartet eased into a slower blues tune and the crowd cheered as Jo-Lee the dancing queen walked up the steps onto the stage.

"Time to let the most beautiful gal this side of the *Ol' Man River* sing us a ditty she wrote herself," Jack said.

Jo-Lee stepped up behind Jack and placed a hand on his shoulder. She cocked an eyebrow as the crowd moved closer to the stage. Silence beset the room. With a slight raise of her chin, she eased into a quiet solo.

"*Yoooou . . . once showed me the place, where we once sang the bluuuueees. Now that we've kissed . . .*" She glanced down at Jack, who looked up at her. The two shared their own little smile before she continued. "*Honey, what is there left to dooooo . . . but go on back and sing the bluuueees.*"

She let the last word linger until the silence in the room swelled. Her pitch-perfect, smoky voice and sensual charisma transfixed everyone in the room, including Stevie. Every gaze on the dance floor basked in the hypnotic allure Jo-Lee exuded.

If a glass of expensive red wine could sing, Stevie thought, it would sound like Jo-Lee.

She gave Stevie a wink when the silence shattered, as the band let loose with a rowdy version of "Mr. Sandman" Stevie knew would've made his father nod his head in approval. The guests didn't wait for an invitation, and the dance floor came to life once more with claps and cheers.

"You know that man's a legend. Invented his own style of guitar playing. A pioneer of the Nashville sound, he is," the man next to Stevie said.

"Is that right?" Stevie gazed at Jack's dexterous fingers pluck out another arrangement.

The haze of smoke and gloomy light shadowed the guest's features but there was something very familiar about the way the man spoke, his placid way of speaking, the authority in his voice underpinned by gentleness.

"I had a feeling there was more to him than meets the eye," Stevie said. But he looked down at the table and shook his head. "Man, what the hell is going on here?"

"What do you mean?" the man asked.

Stevie rubbed his eyes. "I'm not sure. I'm sitting here watching a bunch of ghosts and an old legend the world has forgotten."

"Well," the man said. "No one said they're ghosts. And if the music is playing, they'll never be forgotten."

Stevie frowned and looked at the band. "If all these people aren't ghosts, then what's going on here?"

"Remember, captain," the man said. "There are more stars beyond the few that we see."

Clarity washed over Stevie and his body went cold. There was only one person Stevie knew who had ever said that to him. He turned his head. "Pops?"

But his father was gone.

Stevie blinked.

Gone.

So was the music. So were the guests, the dancing. So was the band.

All that remained was Jack. He sat on the stage, surrounded by dust motes, the guitar on his lap. The old man reached forward, his hand trembled, but only lightly, and switched off the amp cutting the electric hum. He leaned the guitar on the amp and stood up. His joints popped as he walked to the side of the stage. One slow, careful step at a time, Jack left the stage and walked past Stevie. "Let's get out of here, kid."

Stevie remained seated. He still heard his father's last words in his mind. His father always said that when things were tough. It was a way of saying, "It's all good, kiddo. Don't sweat it." And for the first time since his father's passing, Stevie felt—well, maybe not *all* good. Maybe just good. And that was a start.

When they got to the foyer door, Stevie paused. "Ah, Jack, you forgot the lights."

"Lights are out, kid."

Stevie walked across the room to the exit door but glanced over his shoulder. An outside street lamp cast a beam through a dirty window and over a bare stage. No spotlight, no amp, stool, or red guitar. Stevie turned and followed Jack outside before climbing into the cab and starting the engine. He glanced at the clock in the dash board—23:25. Only five minutes had passed since arriving at The Blue Sandman.

After a long, quiet drive, where neither man spoke about what had just happened, Stevie turned the cab onto Maple Street, where he had picked Jack up what felt like a lifetime time ago. "What was all that, Jack? A dream?" Stevie asked as he stopped outside Jack's home.

The old man looked at him, eyes tired. "You would need some strong shit to dream up something like that, kid. And if so, tell me where I can get some." He clapped Stevie on the shoulder and gave him a wink. "That's the problem with these New Age gurus. Always looking for explanations. And that's fine and dandy. But some things don't have answers just coz you're askin' for 'em. Some things you either choose to believe or you don't. Sometimes you should just listen to the song and not ask why it makes you happy, you know?"

Stevie took a deep breath. "My father came and spoke to me."

Jack nodded. "Did he sound alright, was he happy?"

Stevie ran his hand through his hair—"I think so."

Jack smiled. "Hold on to that, then. The rest ain't worth fretting."

A heaviness in Stevie's chest, that had been there so long, slowly lifted. And it felt good.

"Here you go, kid." Jack placed a wad of notes in Stevie's hand.

Stevie looked at the money. "This is too much—"

"It ain't nearly enough. Thanks, kid."

Stevie shook his head. "Thank you, Jack." The two sat in the cab a moment longer not saying anything. A deep thumping of electronic drum and bass came from a party down the road. Boy, how times change, Stevie thought.

Jack opened the door and climbed out. He bent over and leaned in the window. "If you're in the neighborhood again, kid, feel free to pop on by."

Stevie was struck by a memory of his last conversation with his father. "I just might do that," he said.

He meant it.

Jack gave him a relaxed salute and walked to his front door. Without turning around, he unlocked the door and disappeared in the gloom beyond.

Undressing in the quiet darkness of his bedroom that night, the soothing inhale of his girlfriend's slumber brought a relaxing melody of its own. He lifted his hand to his shirt pocket and pulled out a small, dried daisy.

No, it wasn't a dream.

He wandered over to her side of the bed and placed the flower on the bedside table. In the gloom, he made out her lips, slightly parted, her face serene.

Maybe, he thought as he lightly brushed a strand of hair from Lena's face, maybe once you closed your eyes for the last time, you go to a place like The Blue Sandman and there you sip whiskey, listen to the blues, and jive the night away.

Maybe, just maybe.

Acknowledgements

A collection of such marvelous stories like this is never the work of one person, and so I would like to take a moment to extend a hearty thank you to a number of people who made this book possible.

First of all, thank you to the editors of the Fairfield Scribes, who worked tirelessly reading contest entries and editing the stories in this collection. Namely: Edward Ahern, P.C. Keeler, P.M. Ray, Teresa Richards, E.J. Shoko, Leslie Burton-López and Robert Tomaino. Special thanks also go out to Roberto Calas, original founder of the Fairfield Scribes who helped conceive of the theme of this anthology, and without whom the Fairfield Scribes would not exist.

And a hearty thank you to all the entrants to our inaugural Feature Story Contest—we very much enjoyed reading your stories, and we were humbled by the breadth and scope of the great fiction we received. Thank you for sending us your words, and we wished we could have published every quality story we received.

And a final thank you to the inventor of pizza, which is the staple food for the editors of the Fairfield Scribes. Without you, we would have fainted away with hunger long ago.

This book would not exist without all of you.

About the Authors

Cynthia C. Scott

Cynthia C. Scott has been a writer ever since she was a teenager and doesn't recall a time when she didn't want to write. Her work has appeared in *Glint Literary Journal, Copperfield Review, Flyleaf Journal, Graze Magazine, Strange Horizons*, and others. She has a Creative Writing degree from San Francisco State University. She still lives in her hometown of Richmond, CA. with six cats and books. Currently she is a book reviewer for the website Bookbrowse.com. For more info, please visit her website at: https://mstie68.wordpress.com.

Edward Ahern

Edward Ahern sometimes detours into literary fiction and poetry, but he's best known as an innovative genre writer. He's tucked away several awards and honorable mentions for over two hundred short stories and three books. The stories have appeared in ten countries and, counting reprints, over three hundred publications. His stories can be listened to through Audible and the New York Public Library. And he started writing fiction at sixty-seven.

His editorial skills are based on a degree in journalism from the University of Illinois and extensive experience at the

Providence Journal. Ed's been honing the skills for several years at *Bewildering Stories*, where he serves on the review board and as review editor with a staff of five. (*Bewildering Stories* is widely known for the author-friendly quality of its critiques.)

Ed also serves as the newsletter editor for the Connecticut River Salmon Association. He's a member of several writing groups, including the Fairfield Scribes, where he's known for his tough-love comments.

He has his original wife, but advises that after fifty years together they are both out of warranty. Two children and five grandchildren serve as affection focus and money drain.

His work career after university has been an enjoyably demented hopscotch game. U.S. Navy officer (diver and bomb disarmer); reporter for the *Providence Journal*; intelligence officer living in Germany and Japan; international sales and marketing executive at a Canadian paper company (twenty-three years, seventy four countries visited, MBA from NYU); same job for the company that also owns the New England Patriots; and retirement into writing like hell to make up for lost time.

M.K. Beutymhill

As a shy, awkward kid, M.K. Beutymhill found sharing her stories intimidating, especially when her interests were such a departure from what pop culture insisted was acceptable. She never outgrew her adoration of Victorian lifestyle, fairy tales, or RPGs, and no matter what contact sports or activities she distracted herself with, she always returned to writing.

A childhood spent in dance and orchestra eventually led to a career in professional theater, where she often found herself inspired by the thrill of the arena. She watched the empty black box transform into a total immersion experience, all brought to life by words upon a page. Her own words itched for a spotlight, and now, as a shy, awkward adult, sharing these stories is no longer a closet hobby—it is a necessity.

When not writing—or daydreaming about writing—M.K. Beutymhill is likely adventuring across the Pacific Northwest, navigating conventions and faires, or getting her waltz fix at local dance events. After all, now that her closet space is freed up, there's a lot more room for bustles and parasols. She still loves contact sports, which save her trips to the chiropractor by realigning her spine after hours of writing in poor posture. She's known to host afternoon tea parties for her friends, and will rage hard on a Saturday night with a good jigsaw puzzle. She's an author with the Fairfield Scribes, as well as a proud member of the Avenger's Initiative, a cosplay community outreach organization. To learn more about M.K. Beutymhill and her shenanigans, please find her online at www.mkbeutymhill.com.

Leslie Burton-López

Leslie Burton-López is your typical angsty, tortured soul, whose only escapes are the words her fists pound out on the keyboard and curses thrown at the demons driving her on this mortal coil.

Just kidding. She is just a normal, boring nerd-pie who loves contact sports and Bud Light. Most of what she writes does not involve demons, as such, but some of it is semi-autobiographical, semi-funny and only semi-good.

A recent transplant from California to Connecticut, Leslie's literary career is as dry as the state she hails from. During her college days, she was an Editor for *Watershed*, a collection of short stories and poems, with a total readership base of about eight people. After graduating, she co-authored the Spanish textbook *¡Chevere!* which enjoyed the spotlight at several universities for a few years. Then she started a marketing company, Every Page Marketing, which focuses on scintillatingly dull and horrifyingly banal writing for business proposals, grants and other must-read works. And she actually enjoys it (see earlier reference to "nerd-pie").

Leslie has lived in three different countries, three different states—and if her Amazon shipping list is any indication—at about thirty different homes. She gets around! While she sojourns in Connecticut, she plans to build a tiny house so she can further her wanderings.

Eddie Cantrell

Eddie Cantrell loves music as much as he loves writing. When his patient wife goes to bed and the lights go out, he retreats to his small but cozy man-cave, turns on something by Alice In

Chains, Soundgarden or Royal Blood, and the writing begins, often slowly but sometimes in a fever. His short stories "Teeth," "A Grave Tale," "Please Keep This Toilet Clean" and "Driftwood" were published in *Dark Alley Press* and *The Reader's Abode*. In an effort to keep improving his writing, he is an active member of Scribophile and hopes to publish more works.

Elizabeth Chatsworth

Elizabeth Chatsworth is a British author and actor (SAG-AFTRA) based in Connecticut. She creates voice-overs for commercials, videos, and computer games. If there's an elf, a witch, or an aristocrat in a video game, it might be her!

Writing is Elizabeth's passion. Her award-winning alternate history novel *The Brass Queen* became a 2018 RWA® *Golden Heart®* finalist in the Mainstream Fiction category. Elizabeth is represented by Natalie Grazian of Martin Literary Management. A Pitch Wars alumna, she's a member of the RWA (PRO), the Women's National Book Association, and the Authors Guild.

Elizabeth's hobbies include archery, kung fu, horseback riding, cosplay, video games, and baking. She possesses the world's best scone recipe. Contact her, and she may just send it to you!

For more information, and to be the first to receive exclusive news and giveaways, please visit www.elizabethchatsworth.com.

Gabi Coatsworth

Gabi Coatsworth is an award-winning British-born writer and blogger, who has spent half her life living in the United States. Her essays, short fiction and poetry have been published in the anthology, *Tangerine Tango: Women Writers Share Slices of Life*, E-chook's literary memoir app, and literary journals, both in print and online. You can find her blog for writers, and her personal blog, online at www.gabicoatsworth.com. Her memoir, *A Handprint on My Heart*, is currently with editors and due out in 2019. She has never wanted to travel back in time to change the past.

P.C. Keeler

Born in the far-off days of the Second Millennium, P.C. Keeler spends his days writing detailed instructions for very dim but precise silicon brains to follow and finds it a relaxing change of pace to write more conversationally for charming, handsome, intellectual readers like you. He enjoys past, present, and future, preferably all at once. Steampunk and Ren Faires work well for this.

Currently residing in the wilds of Fairfield County, Connecticut, he grew up in New Hampshire and as such has never quite gotten used to sales tax. His first published work was a short poem printed by a local newspaper at the tender age of six. Him, that is. The newspaper was considerably more well-established. He has continued writing since, as a member of the Fairfield Scribes. His works have appeared in multiple locales, such as *Diabolical Plots* with "Do Not Question The

University," and in the anthologies *When You're Strange* and *Z Tales*. He can also be found on Twitter @PCKeeler.

When not writing code at the day job, writing fiction after hours, or visiting Ren Faires in a vacuum-tube-bedecked top hat, P.C. can be found trying frantically to catch up on sleep. He is pondering a trip into Mad Science simply so as to be able to build a device to slow the rotation of the planet and create the 26-hour day for this purpose. Donations welcome.

B.T. Lowry

B.T. Lowry is a writer and filmmaker who roams between Canada, Britain and India. He's the founder of *Storypaths*, a loose confederation of writers, artists, musicians, and other riffraff. Fate started him in Canada where the plains meet the Rockies, with an engineer father and English teacher spiritualist mother, then moved him on to study multimedia art in college. Not satisfied with this, fate kicked him into India to live as monk for about a decade, and now he's inspired to channel all these influences into storytelling. He likes ecological and spiritual themes—think *Bhagavad Gita, Rumi*, and oatmeal recipes.

Non-European fantasy invades his dreams with endless possibilities.

You can see more of his work on storypaths.net/stories, and support him on https://www.patreon.com/user?u=967085.

Jacqueline Masumian

Jacqueline Masumian is the author of *Nobody Home: A Memoir*. She grew up in the suburbs of Cleveland, Ohio, and has enjoyed careers as actress, performing arts manager, and landscape designer. Her stories have appeared in *Brilliant Flash Fiction*, *Indiana Voice Journal,* and *Gravel,* among others. Visit her at jacquelinemasumian.com.

Alison McBain

Diversity is one of Alison McBain's passions. With dual Canadian-U.S. citizenship, a Japanese-American mother and a B.A. in African history and classical literature, she has an eclectic background and a wide range of experience. She grew up in California and moved to the East Coast in her mid-twenties. Currently, she lives in Connecticut, where she is raising three girls and her husband.

She started her writing career at age four with a "self-published" horror story about the monster in the closet. The story was highly lauded by her closest family members. Since then, she's received a number of writing awards and accolades from people not even vaguely related to her, but she still has a soft spot for that first short story.

Her interest in diversity also extends to fiction. With over seventy publications to her name, her stories and poems range in tone from serious to silly. They cover nearly every genre, including literary, romance, horror, science fiction, fantasy, history and adventure.

When not writing fiction, she follows her own personal mantra of, "Do something creative every day." She serves as the Book Reviews Editor at the magazine *Bewildering Stories*. She also blogs about local events, showcases her art and conducts author interviews on her website, http://www.alisonmcbain.com/. When life gets a little too hectic, she does origami meditation or draws all over the walls of her house with the enthusiastic help of her kids.

P.M. Ray

When he was eleven, P.M. Ray picked up *The Hobbit* and *Tess of the d'Urbervilles* and became an avid reader of speculative fiction. After twenty years writing business specifications and other software documentation, he decided to write fiction as well as reading it. To pursue his passion for writing, he joined the Fairfield Scribes nine years ago, and he—and they—haven't been the same since.

P.M. has provided developmental critiques for eight novels, ranging in subject from apocalypse horror to epic fantasy to YA. He's also been the lead editor of an anthology of fantasy and horror short stories about zombies. All eight books have gone on to be published and are currently in print.

An avid medievalist, he has spent over three decades immersing himself in all things feudal. He's jousted with lance and shield in full armor on horseback, which isn't as easy as it sounds. He's also been knocked on his ass while on horseback in full armor. He is notorious on the battlefields of medieval reenactment in New York and earned the sobriquet, "The Butcher of Acre."

When not on horseback, he's sparred with all sorts of medieval weaponry, including broadsword and shield, polearm, two-handed spear, and bastard sword. When the armor comes off, he brews mead and performs medieval dance to educate the public about the Middle Ages in Western Europe and Outremer. He married his dance partner and lives with her, one horse, one dog, three goats, and three cats in Western Connecticut.

Teresa Richards

Teresa Richards lives and breathes young adult fiction, either because she spends most of her time with teens (who call her Mom or master of the universe, depending on the day), or because she never actually grew up.

Her debut YA novel, *Emerald Bound*, was released by Evernight Teen in 2015. *Emerald Bound* is an editor's pick, and was nominated for a Whitney Award in 2016. It also won LASR's book of the month award. *Topaz Reign*, the sequel to *Emerald Bound*, was released by Evernight Teen in 2017. It received 5 stars from LASR and was named Best Book, in addition to being book of the month for December—a distinction reserved for only a few select novels. Her novella, *You, Me, and Comic Con*, was released as part of a YA romance collection by Teenacity Books in 2017, and her most recent book, *The Windfall App*, was published in July 2018.

She also has several short stories published in ezines and anthologies.

Teresa is a member of SCBWI, and was accepted into the LDStorymakers guild in 2016.

In recent years, Teresa had manuscripts accepted into both Pitch Madness and Query Kombat, which are contests that focus on honing pitches, query letters, and first chapters. In 2017, she was invited to be a Query Kombat judge. In this capacity, she critiqued pitches and first pages in order to help the authors make them better.

Teresa has attended several writing conferences, where she's gained valuable insights into the publishing process, met agents and editors, and studied craft from veterans such as James Dashner, Ally Condie, and J Scott Savage. Her educational background at Brigham Young University included training in technical writing. In the past year, she's been a panelist at both the Northern and Southern Kentucky BookFests, and has taught writing workshops to elementary and middle school kids. She also started a Read Local program for her region, and loves connecting with young writers.

When Teresa's not writing, she can be found chasing after one of her five kids, dancing in her car with the music up too loud, or hiding somewhere in her house with a treat she's not planning to share.

Barbara Russell

Barbara Russell is an entomologist and a soil biologist, which is a fancy way to say that she digs in the dirt, looking for bugs. Nature, brains, and books have always been her passion.

Her debut novel, *A Knight In Distress*, will be published in August 2018 by Champagne Book.

She was a kid when she read *Ivanhoe* by Sir W. Scott and fell in love with medieval novels. Then she discovered medieval fantasy and fell in love again. In fact, she took it too seriously and believed that her elderly, bearded neighbor was Merlin and his black cat was Morgan le Fey. When she read *Harry Potter* and learned about Animagi, she knew she was right. Then she grew up and . . . nah, it's a joke. She didn't grow up. Don't grow up, folks! It's a trap.

For more info, please visit her website at: https://barbararussell.blogspot.co.nz.

Abhishek Sengupta

Abhishek Sengupta is imaginary. Mostly, people would want to believe that he writes fiction & poetry which borders on Surrealism and Magical Realism, and is stuck inside a window in Kolkata, India, but he knows none of it is true. He doesn't exist. Only his imaginary writing does, and have appeared or are forthcoming in *FLAPPERHOUSE, Bete Noire, Aurealis, Outlook Springs,* and others. According to a rumor doing its rounds, he is also 2018 SFPA Rhysling Nominee, but it may

When he breaks awa
Robert writes fiction,
occasional poem may
well. Robert is also a
officiated three weddi
spends time regaling h
youth, before pumpin
them back to their par

Nikki Trionfo

Nikki Trionfo lives in
husband who writes
background music. He
place in the League
Alongside Heather C
YouTube at #50First
serves as director
Conference, the larg
notable stuff include
Future and several sto
anthologies. This all
her, she gets down.

*For more information about the authors
and editors, including their forthcoming
publications, interviews, and how to get in
contact with them, please visit the
Fairfield Scribes' website at
www.fairfieldscribes.com.*

43155406R00236

Made in the USA
Middletown, DE
20 April 2019